image comics presents

CHEW

KT-433-693

CHICKEN TENDERS

created by John Layman & Rob Guillory

written & lettered by
John Layman

drawn & colored by
Rob Guillory

Color Assists by Taylor Wells

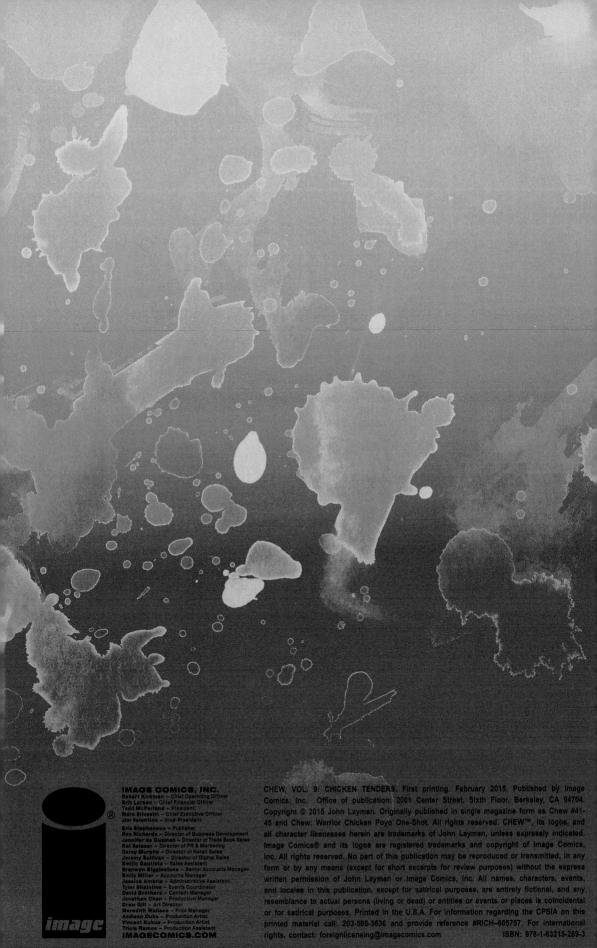

IMAGE COMICS, INC.
Robert Kirkman – Chief Operating Officer
Erik Larsen – Chief Financial Officer
Todd McFarlane – President
Marc Silvestri – Chief Executive Officer
Jim Valentino – Vice-President

Eric Stephenson – Publisher
Ron Richards – Director of Business Development
Jennifer de Guzman – Director of Trade Book Sales
Kat Salazar – Director of PR & Marketing
Corey Murphy – Director of Retail Sales
Jeremy Sullivan – Director of Digital Sales
Emilio Bautista – Sales Assistant
Branwyn Bigglestone – Senior Accounts Manager
Emily Miller – Accounts Manager
Jessica Ambriz – Administrative Assistant
Tyler Shainline – Events Coordinator
David Brothers – Content Manager
Jonathan Chan – Production Manager
Drew Gill – Art Director
Meredith Wallace – Print Manager
Addison Duke – Production Artist
Vincent Kukua – Production Artist
Tricia Ramos – Production Assistant
IMAGECOMICS.COM

CHEW, VOL. 9: CHICKEN TENDERS. First printing. February 2015. Published by Image Comics, Inc. Office of publication: 2001 Center Street, Sixth Floor, Berkeley, CA 94704. Copyright © 2015 John Layman. Originally published in single magazine form as Chew #41-45 and Chew: Warrior Chicken Poyo One-Shot. All rights reserved. CHEW™, its logos, and all character likenesses herein are trademarks of John Layman, unless expressly indicated. Image Comics® and its logos are registered trademarks and copyright of Image Comics, Inc. All rights reserved. No part of this publication may be reproduced or transmitted, in any form or by any means (except for short excerpts for review purposes) without the express written permission of John Layman or Image Comics, Inc. All names, characters, events, and locales in this publication, except for satirical purposes, are entirely fictional, and any resemblance to actual persons (living or dead) or entities or events or places is coincidental or for satirical purposes. Printed in the U.S.A. For information regarding the CPSIA on this printed material call: 203-595-3636 and provide reference #RICH–605757. For international rights, contact: foreignlicensing@imagecomics.com
ISBN: 978-1-63215-289-3

Dedications:

JOHN: To all the readers who write us (letters@chewcomic.com), tweet to us, or visit with us at conventions. It's appreciated.

ROB: For Dave Hedgecock, the first person crazy enough to pay me for this. And for my Grandfather, a former cockfighter who my mother tells me used to put tiny boxing gloves on his roosters. This is not a joke.

Thanks:
Taylor Wells, for the coloring assists.
Tom B. Long, for the logo.
Comicbookfonts.com, for the fonts.

And More Thanks:
David Baron, Jeremy Bastian, David Brothers, Ryan Browne, Chris Burnham, C.B. Cebulski, Kody Chamberlain, Brian Duffield, Ray Fawkes, Otis Frampton, Drew Gill, Dan Goldman, Paul Hanley, Sina Grace, Jonathan Hickman, Daniel Warren Johnson, Robert Kirkman, Hansel Moreno, Nick Pitarra, Shaun Steven Struble, Ross Thibodeaux, Irene Strychalski and Sweet Josh-Josh Williamson.

Chapter 1

CHEW
LOSE $2.99 INSTANTLY!
BEETS
3 × = $ YOU GETS PAID!!!
3 × = YUCKY YUCKY BEETS!!
3 × = DEATH BY CHICKEN!!
WARNING: GAMBLING MAY LEAD TO BEING FILTHY FILTHY RICH.
DISCLAIMER: MAY ALSO LEAD TO CRYING..
ROB!
THEY LIE.

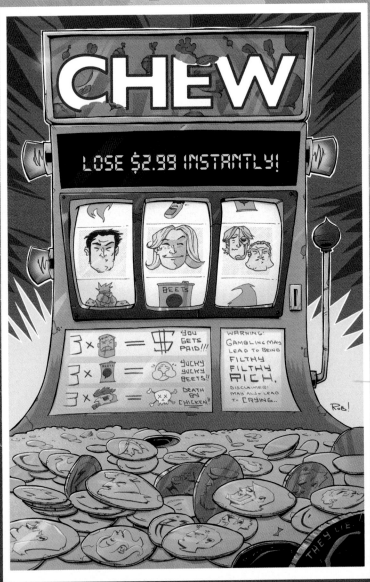

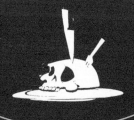

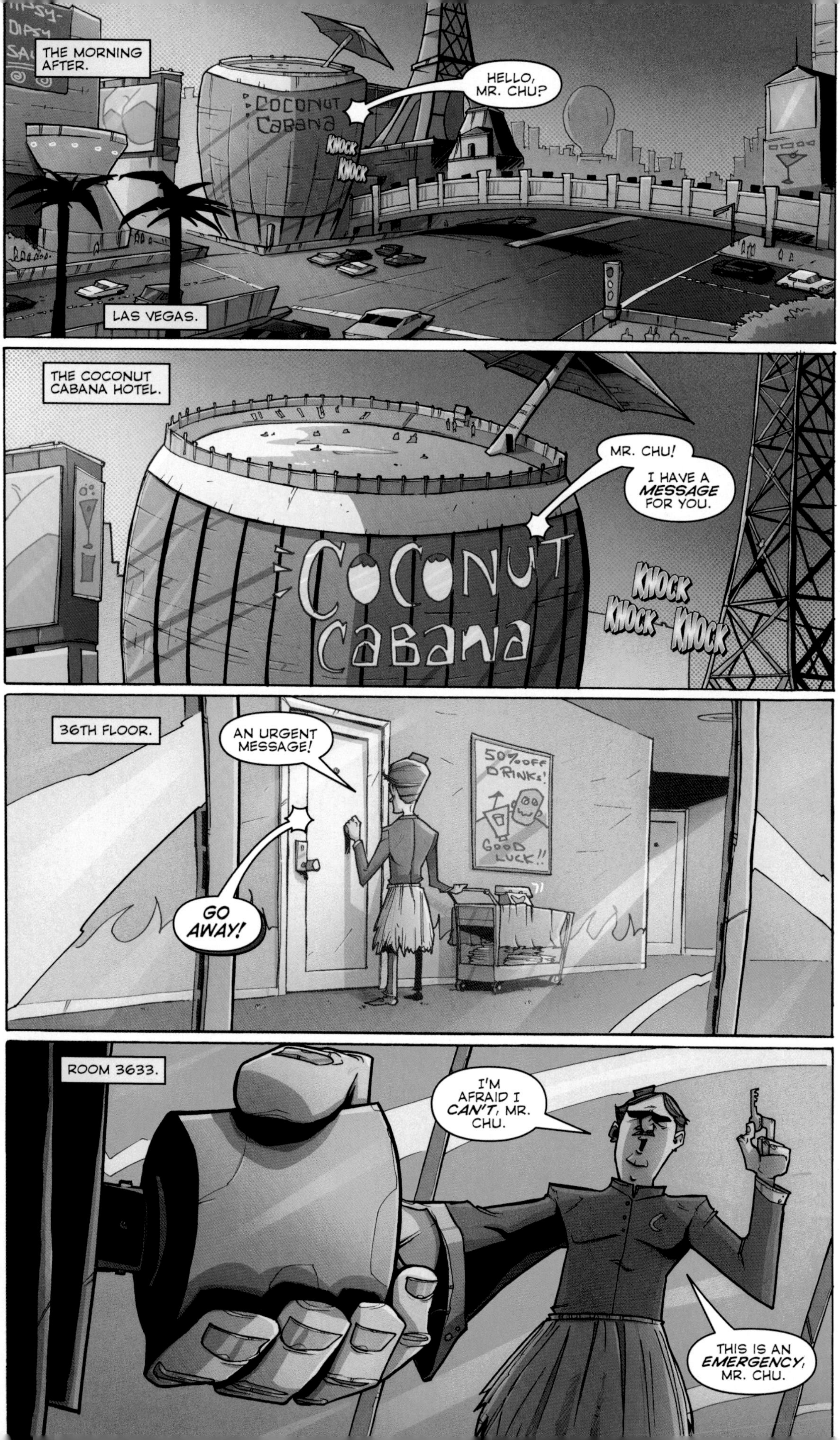
THE MORNING AFTER.
COCONUT CABANA
HELLO, MR. CHU?
KNOCK KNOCK
LAS VEGAS.
THE COCONUT CABANA HOTEL.
MR. CHU!
I HAVE A *MESSAGE* FOR YOU.
COCONUT CABANA
KNOCK KNOCK KNOCK
36TH FLOOR.
AN URGENT MESSAGE!
50% OFF DRINKS!
GOOD LUCK!!
GO *AWAY!*
ROOM 3633.
I'M AFRAID I *CAN'T*, MR. CHU.
THIS IS AN *EMERGENCY*, MR. CHU.

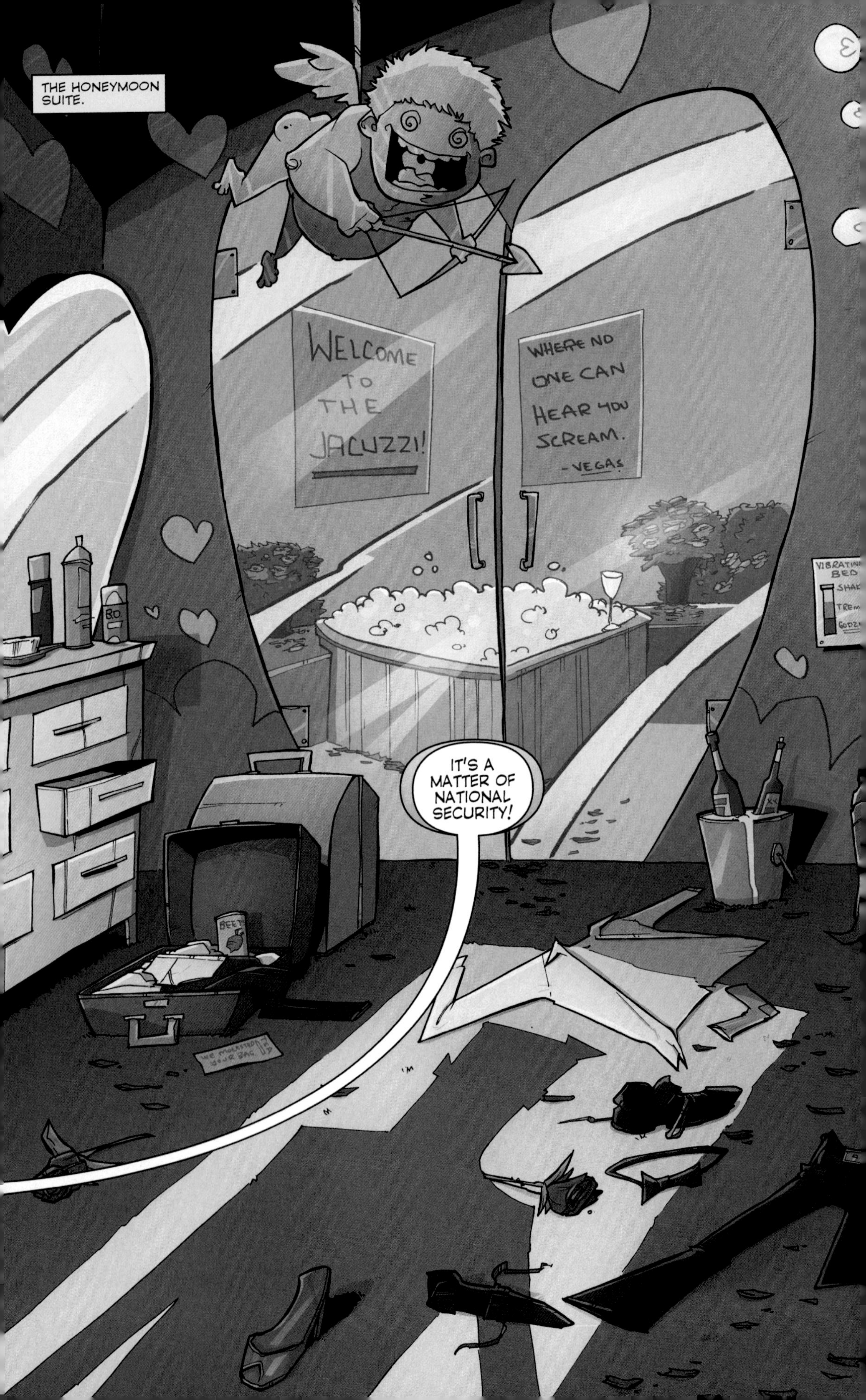
THE HONEYMOON SUITE.
WELCOME TO THE JACUZZI!
WHERE NO ONE CAN HEAR YOU SCREAM. -VEGAS
IT'S A MATTER OF NATIONAL SECURITY!

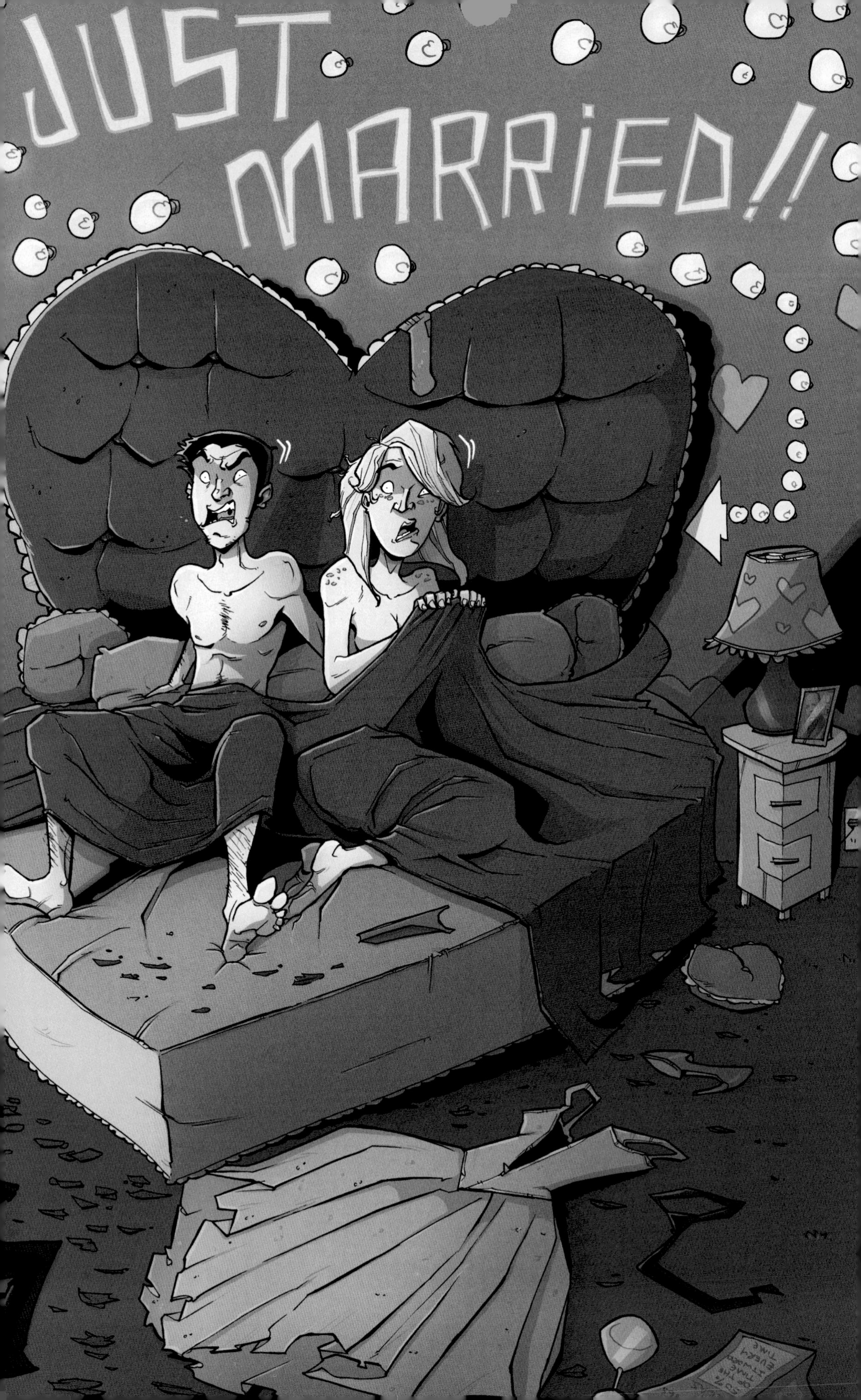
JUST MARRIED!!

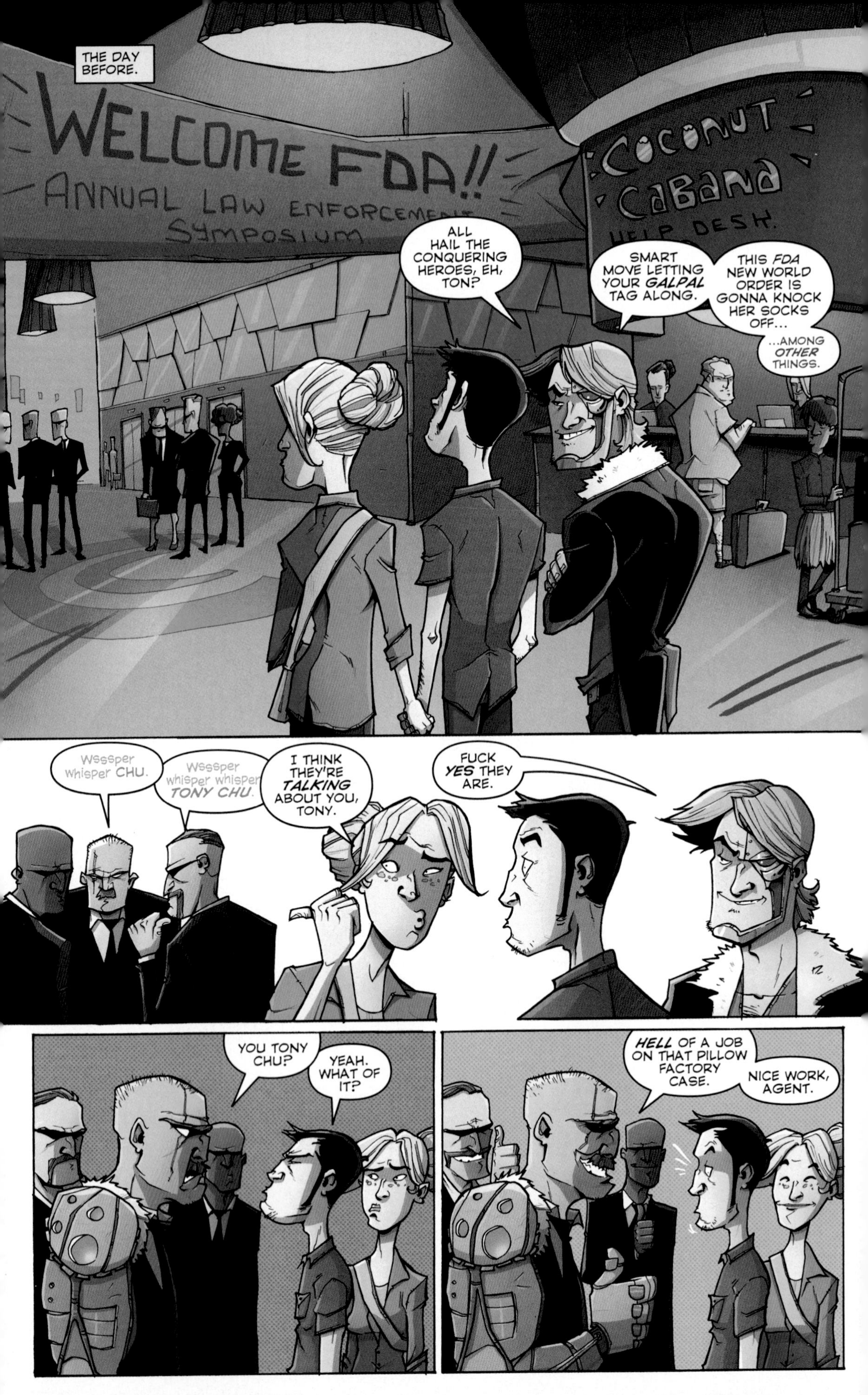
THE DAY BEFORE.
WELCOME FDA!!
ANNUAL LAW ENFORCEMENT SYMPOSIUM
COCONUT CABANA
HELP DESK
ALL HAIL THE CONQUERING HEROES, EH, TON?
SMART MOVE LETTING YOUR GALPAL TAG ALONG.
THIS FDA NEW WORLD ORDER IS GONNA KNOCK HER SOCKS OFF...
...AMONG OTHER THINGS.
Wsssper whisper CHU.
Wsssper whisper whisper TONY CHU.
I THINK THEY'RE TALKING ABOUT YOU, TONY.
FUCK YES THEY ARE.
YOU TONY CHU?
YEAH. WHAT OF IT?
HELL OF A JOB ON THAT PILLOW FACTORY CASE.
NICE WORK, AGENT.

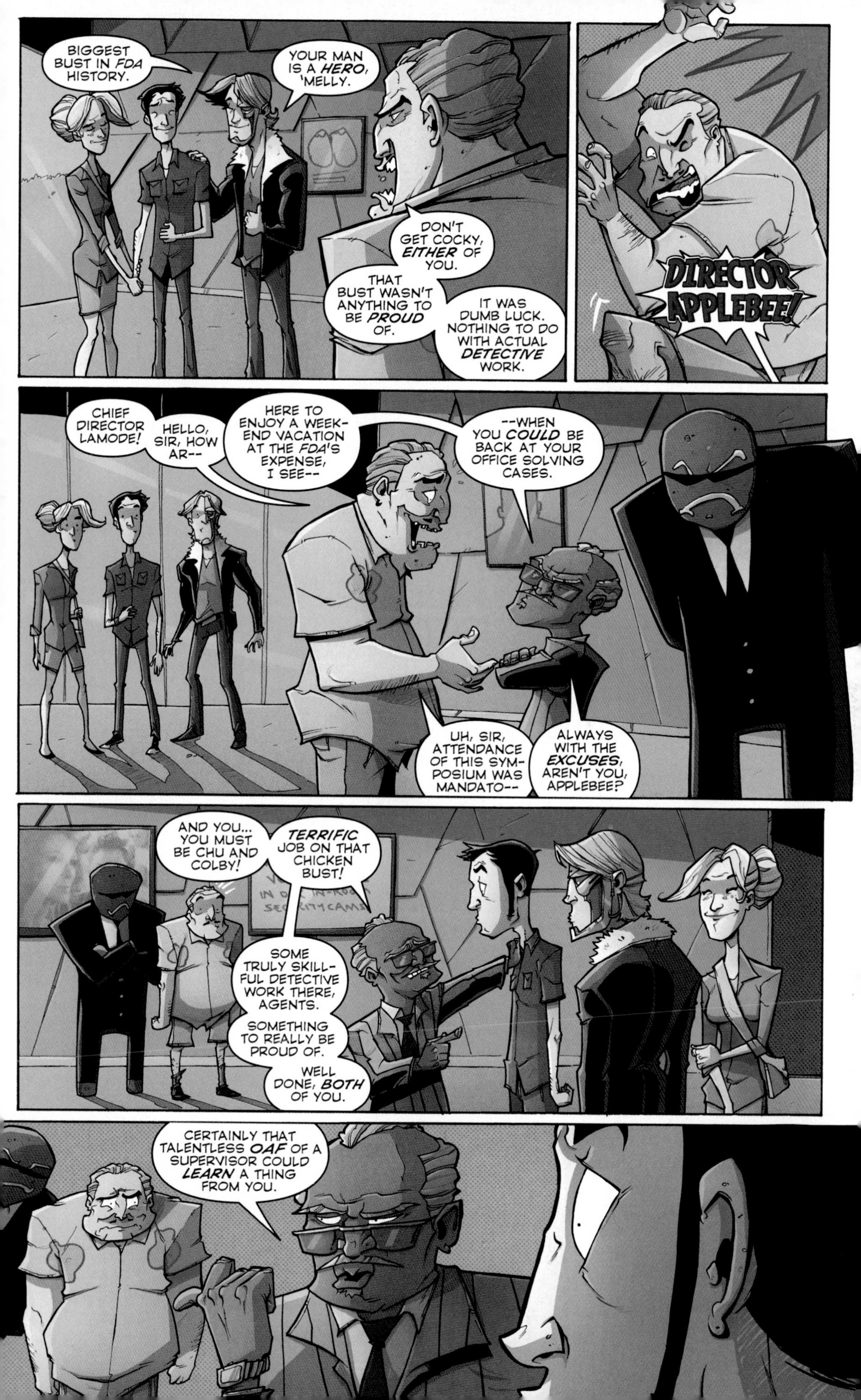
BIGGEST BUST IN FDA HISTORY.
YOUR MAN IS A HERO, 'MELLY.
DON'T GET COCKY, EITHER OF YOU.
THAT BUST WASN'T ANYTHING TO BE PROUD OF.
IT WAS DUMB LUCK. NOTHING TO DO WITH ACTUAL DETECTIVE WORK.
DIRECTOR APPLEBEE!
CHIEF DIRECTOR LAMODE!
HELLO, SIR, HOW AR--
HERE TO ENJOY A WEEK-END VACATION AT THE FDA'S EXPENSE, I SEE--
--WHEN YOU COULD BE BACK AT YOUR OFFICE SOLVING CASES.
UH, SIR, ATTENDANCE OF THIS SYM-POSIUM WAS MANDATO--
ALWAYS WITH THE EXCUSES, AREN'T YOU, APPLEBEE?
AND YOU... YOU MUST BE CHU AND COLBY!
TERRIFIC JOB ON THAT CHICKEN BUST!
SOME TRULY SKILL-FUL DETECTIVE WORK THERE, AGENTS.
SOMETHING TO REALLY BE PROUD OF.
WELL DONE, BOTH OF YOU.
CERTAINLY THAT TALENTLESS OAF OF A SUPERVISOR COULD LEARN A THING FROM YOU.

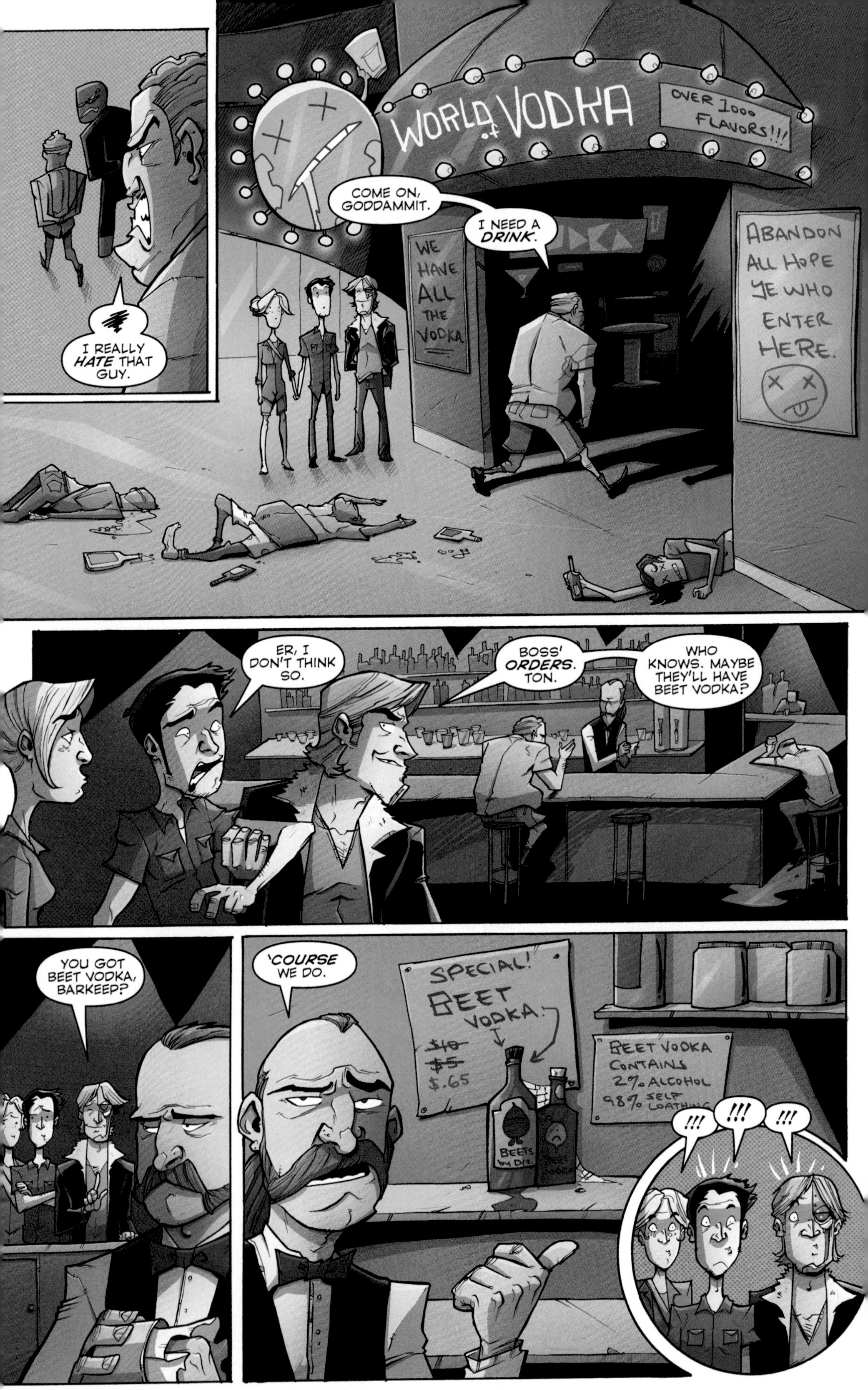
I REALLY HATE THAT GUY.
WORLD of VODKA
OVER 1000 FLAVORS!!!
COME ON, GODDAMMIT.
I NEED A DRINK.
WE HAVE ALL THE VODKA
ABANDON ALL HOPE YE WHO ENTER HERE.
ER, I DON'T THINK SO.
BOSS' ORDERS. TON.
WHO KNOWS. MAYBE THEY'LL HAVE BEET VODKA?
YOU GOT BEET VODKA, BARKEEP?
'COURSE WE DO.
SPECIAL! BEET VODKA
$10
$5
$.65
BEET VODKA CONTAINS 2% ALCOHOL 98% SELF LOATHING
BEETS
!!!
!!!
!!!

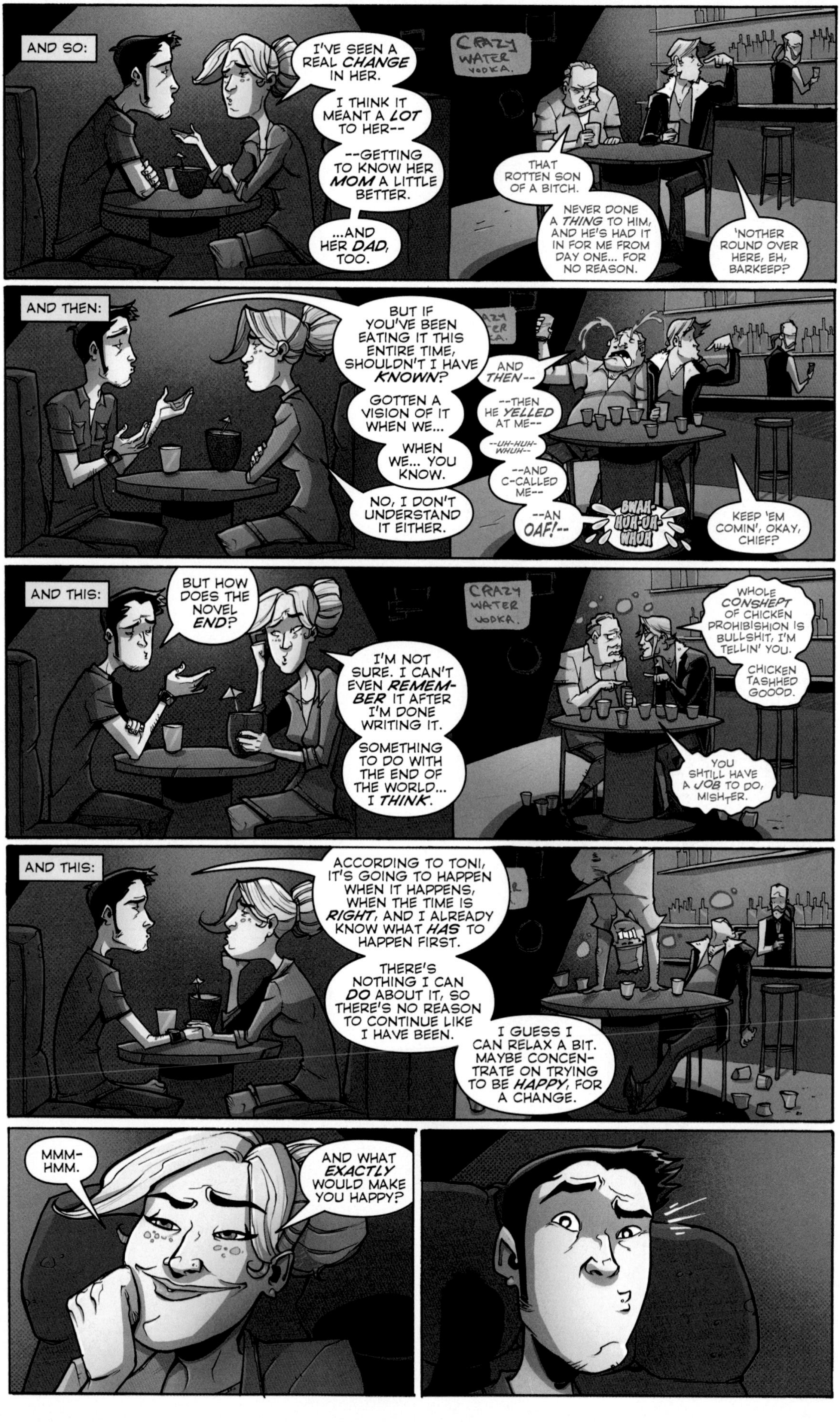
AND SO:
I'VE SEEN A REAL CHANGE IN HER.
I THINK IT MEANT A LOT TO HER--
--GETTING TO KNOW HER MOM A LITTLE BETTER.
...AND HER DAD, TOO.
CRAZY WATER VODKA
THAT ROTTEN SON OF A BITCH.
NEVER DONE A THING TO HIM, AND HE'S HAD IT IN FOR ME FROM DAY ONE... FOR NO REASON.
'NOTHER ROUND OVER HERE, EH, BARKEEP?
AND THEN:
BUT IF YOU'VE BEEN EATING IT THIS ENTIRE TIME, SHOULDN'T I HAVE KNOWN?
GOTTEN A VISION OF IT WHEN WE...
WHEN WE... YOU KNOW.
NO, I DON'T UNDERSTAND IT EITHER.
AND THEN--
--THEN HE YELLED AT ME--
--UH-HUH-WHUH--
--AND C-CALLED ME--
--AN OAF!--
BWAH-HUH-UH-WHUH
KEEP 'EM COMIN', OKAY, CHIEF?
AND THIS:
BUT HOW DOES THE NOVEL END?
I'M NOT SURE. I CAN'T EVEN REMEMBER IT AFTER I'M DONE WRITING IT.
SOMETHING TO DO WITH THE END OF THE WORLD... I THINK.
CRAZY WATER VODKA
WHOLE CONSHEPT OF CHICKEN PROHIBISHION IS BULLSHIT, I'M TELLIN' YOU.
CHICKEN TASHHED GOOOD.
YOU SHTILL HAVE A JOB TO DO, MISHTER.
AND THIS:
ACCORDING TO TONI, IT'S GOING TO HAPPEN WHEN IT HAPPENS, WHEN THE TIME IS RIGHT, AND I ALREADY KNOW WHAT HAS TO HAPPEN FIRST.
THERE'S NOTHING I CAN DO ABOUT IT, SO THERE'S NO REASON TO CONTINUE LIKE I HAVE BEEN.
I GUESS I CAN RELAX A BIT. MAYBE CONCENTRATE ON TRYING TO BE HAPPY, FOR A CHANGE.
MMM-HMM.
AND WHAT EXACTLY WOULD MAKE YOU HAPPY?

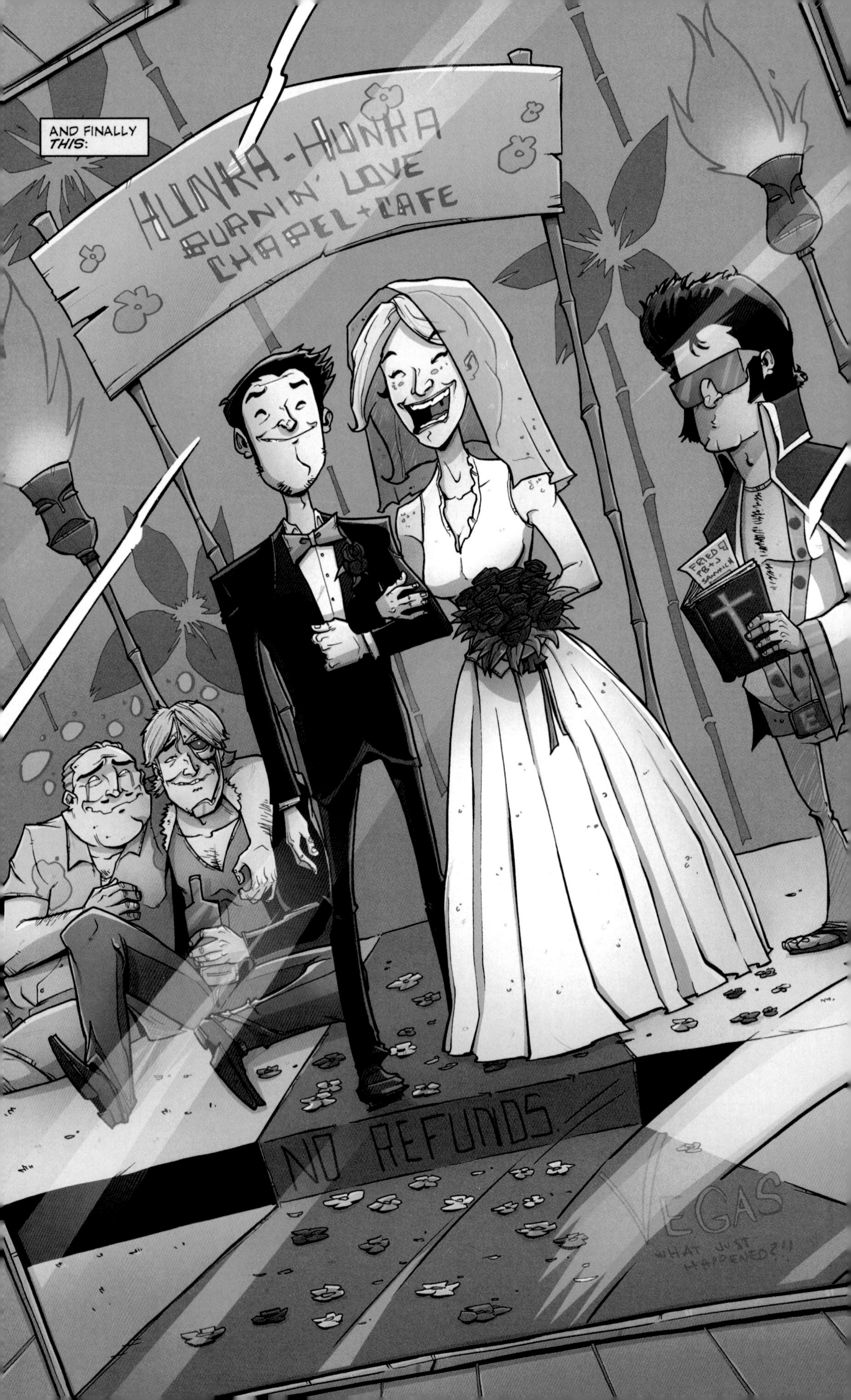
AND FINALLY *THIS*:
HUNKA-HUNKA BURNIN' LOVE CHAPEL+CAFE
FRIED PB+J SAMMICH
NO REFUNDS
VEGAS
WHAT JUST HAPPENED?!

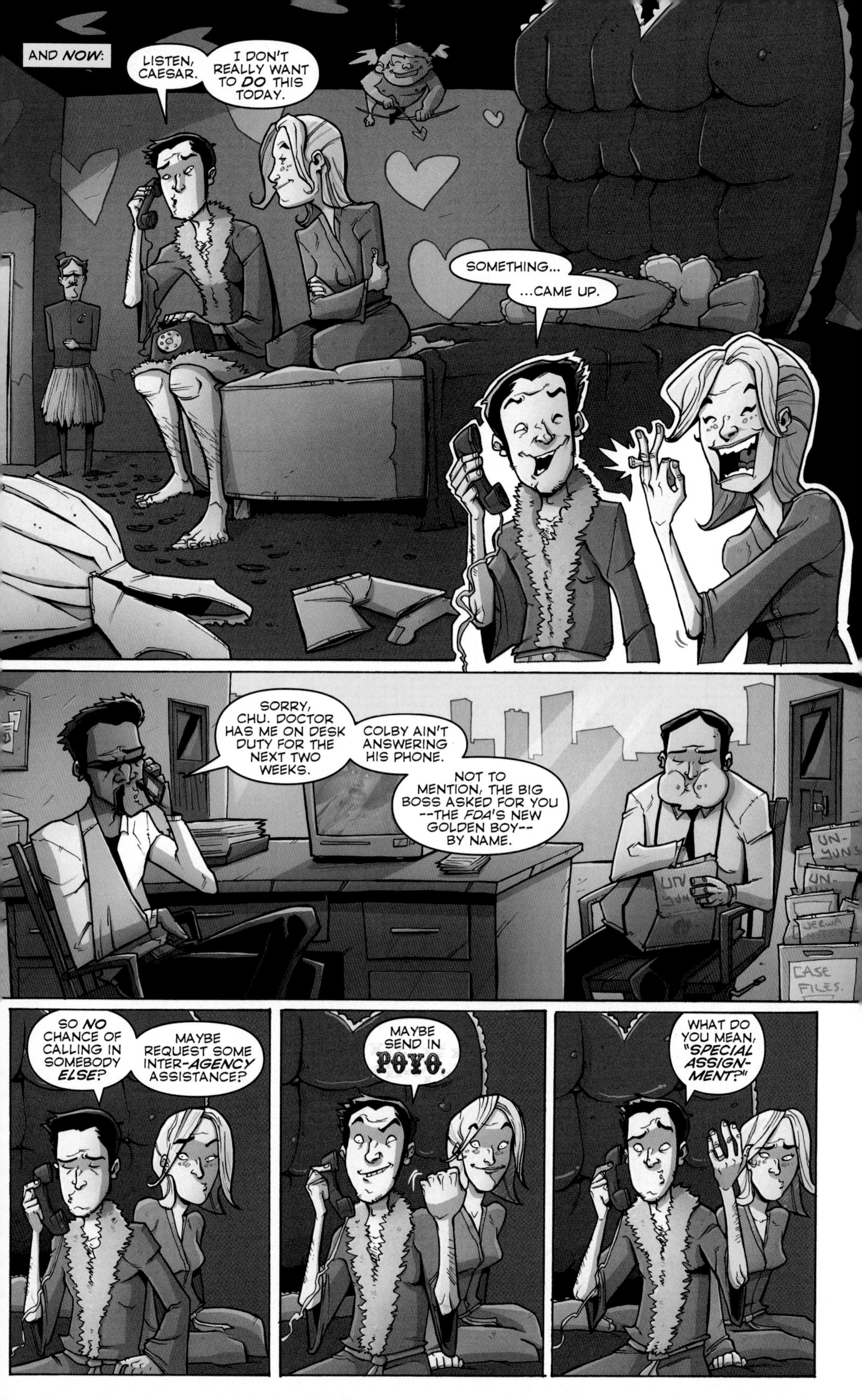
AND NOW:
LISTEN, CAESAR.
I DON'T REALLY WANT TO DO THIS TODAY.
SOMETHING...
...CAME UP.
SORRY, CHU. DOCTOR HAS ME ON DESK DUTY FOR THE NEXT TWO WEEKS.
COLBY AIN'T ANSWERING HIS PHONE.
NOT TO MENTION, THE BIG BOSS ASKED FOR YOU --THE FDA'S NEW GOLDEN BOY-- BY NAME.
CASE FILES.
SO NO CHANCE OF CALLING IN SOMEBODY ELSE?
MAYBE REQUEST SOME INTER-AGENCY ASSISTANCE?
MAYBE SEND IN POYO.
WHAT DO YOU MEAN, "SPECIAL ASSIGNMENT?"

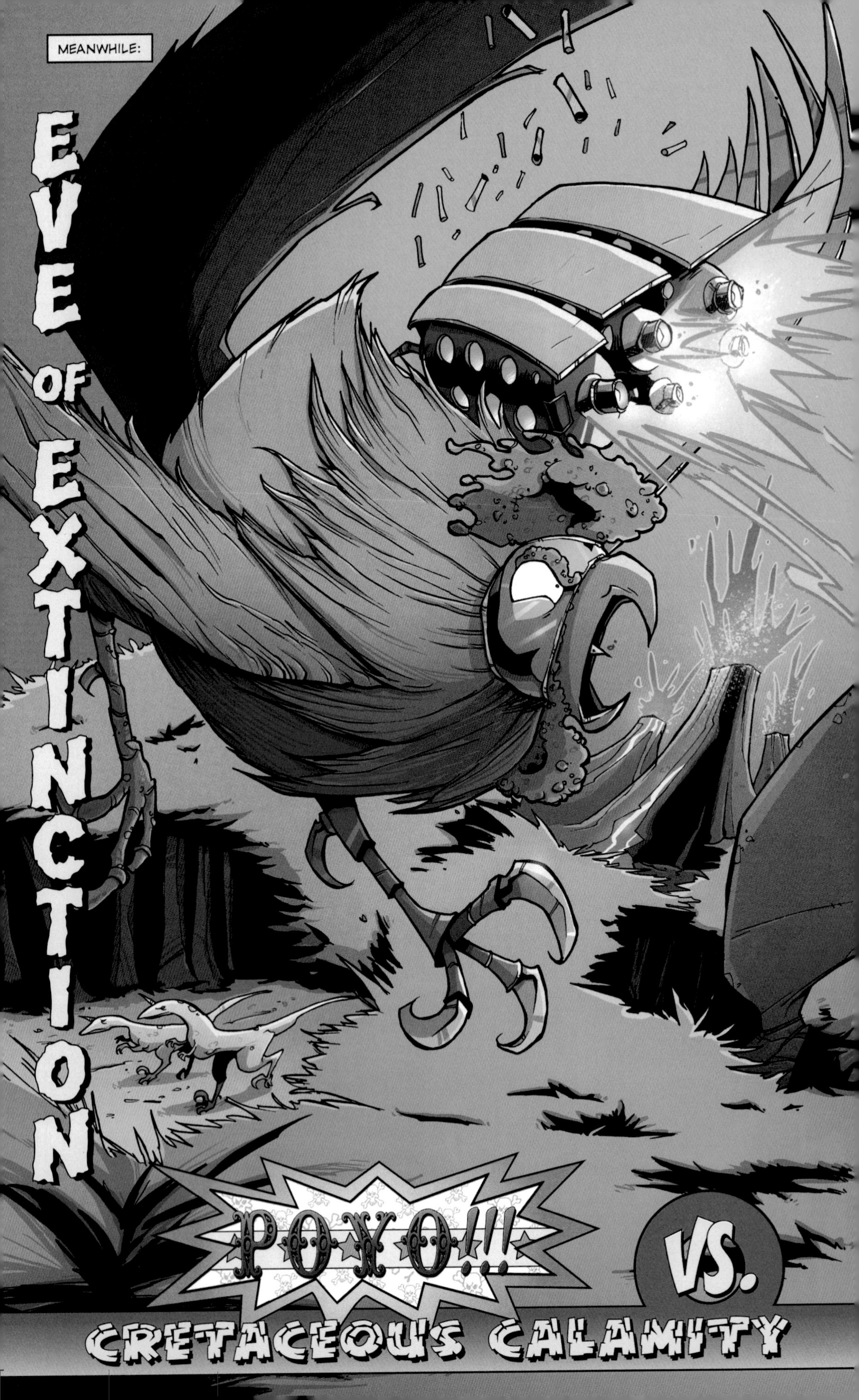
MEANWHILE:
EVE OF EXTINCTION
POXO!!!
VS.
CRETACEOUS CALAMITY

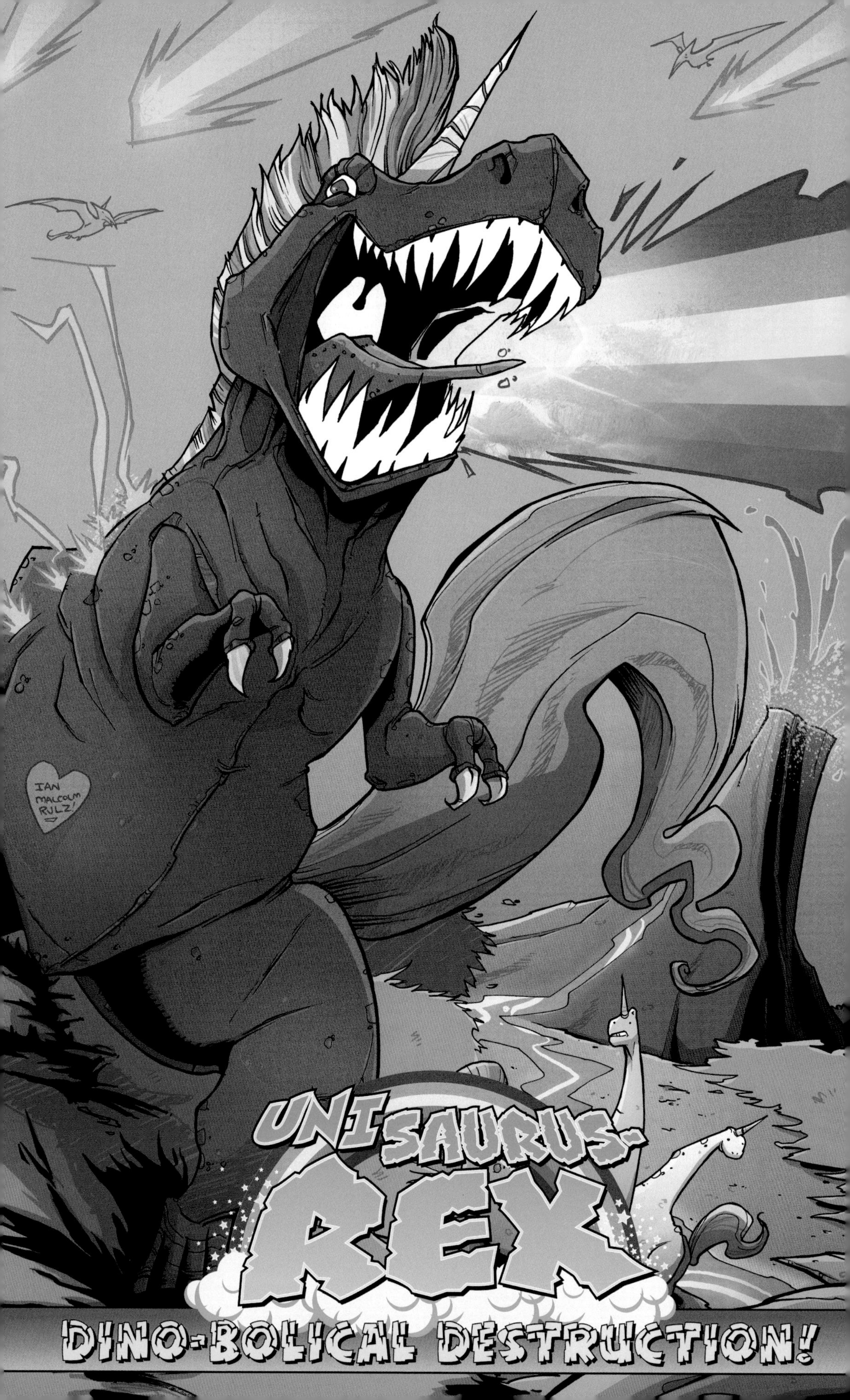
IAN MALCOLM RULZ!
UNISAURUS-REX
DINO-BOLICAL DESTRUCTION!

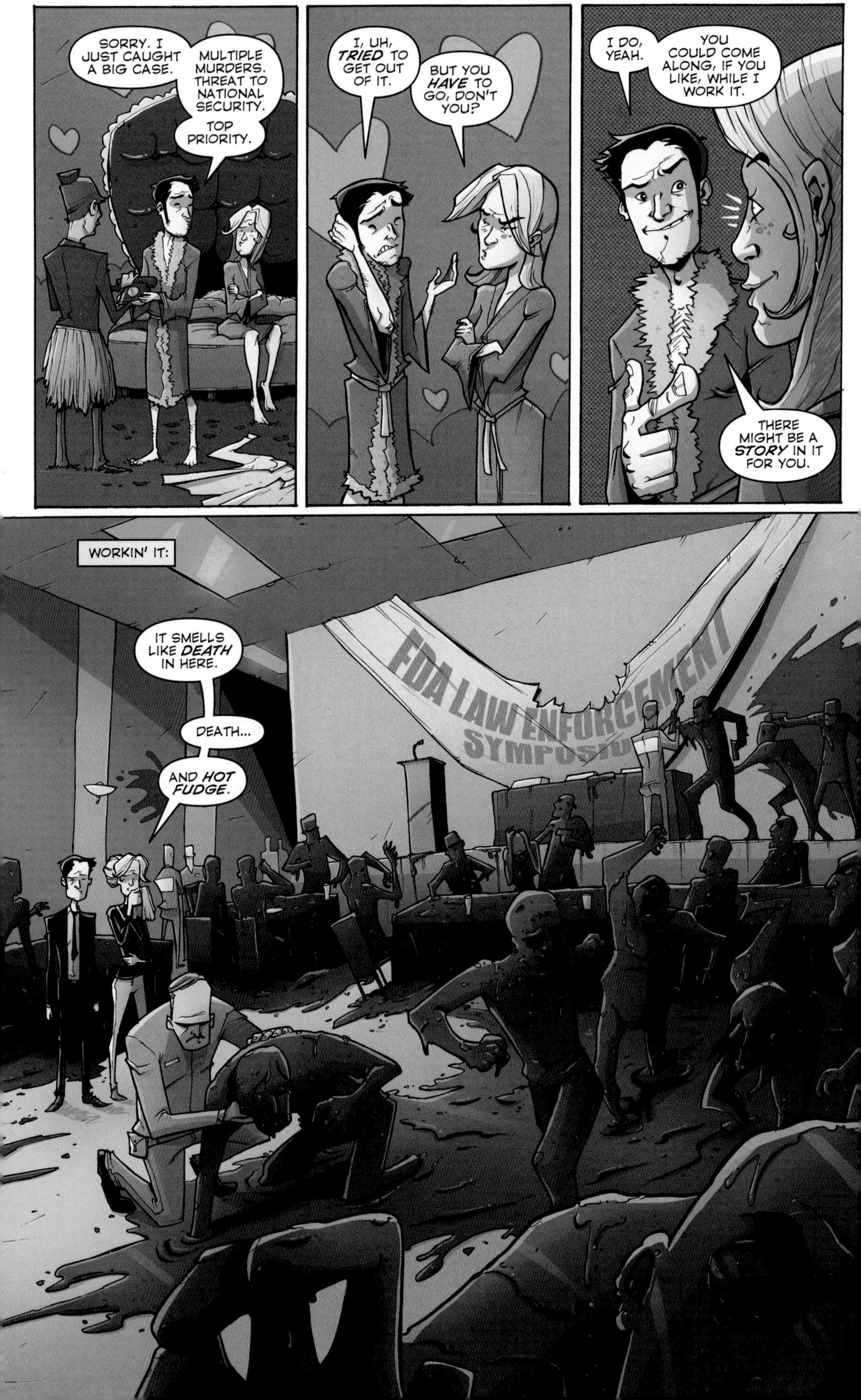
SORRY. I JUST CAUGHT A BIG CASE.
MULTIPLE MURDERS. THREAT TO NATIONAL SECURITY.
TOP PRIORITY.
I, UH, TRIED TO GET OUT OF IT.
BUT YOU HAVE TO GO, DON'T YOU?
I DO, YEAH.
YOU COULD COME ALONG, IF YOU LIKE, WHILE I WORK IT.
THERE MIGHT BE A STORY IN IT FOR YOU.
WORKIN' IT:
IT SMELLS LIKE DEATH IN HERE.
DEATH...
AND HOT FUDGE.
FDA LAW ENFORCEMENT SYMPOSI

HEY! WE GOT A LIVE ONE OVER HERE!

AGENT CHU! AGENT CHU!

THANKS FOR COMING SO QUICKLY, AGENT.

I FIGURE IF *ANYBODY* CAN GET TO THE BOTTOM OF THIS, *YOU* CAN.

THEY MADE A REAL *MESS* OF THINGS, DIDN'T THEY?

WHO DID?

THEY *L-LIED* TO US.

T-THEN THEY KILLED E-E-EVERY-ONE.

CHIEF DIRECTOR, I'M SORRY TO INTERRUPT.

WE'VE JUST DONE A FULL ACCOUNTING OF THE VICTIMS--

--AND I'M AFRAID WE *FOUND* PRO-FESSOR LIMA.

WHO?

VEGA BUFFE WE HA CRAB

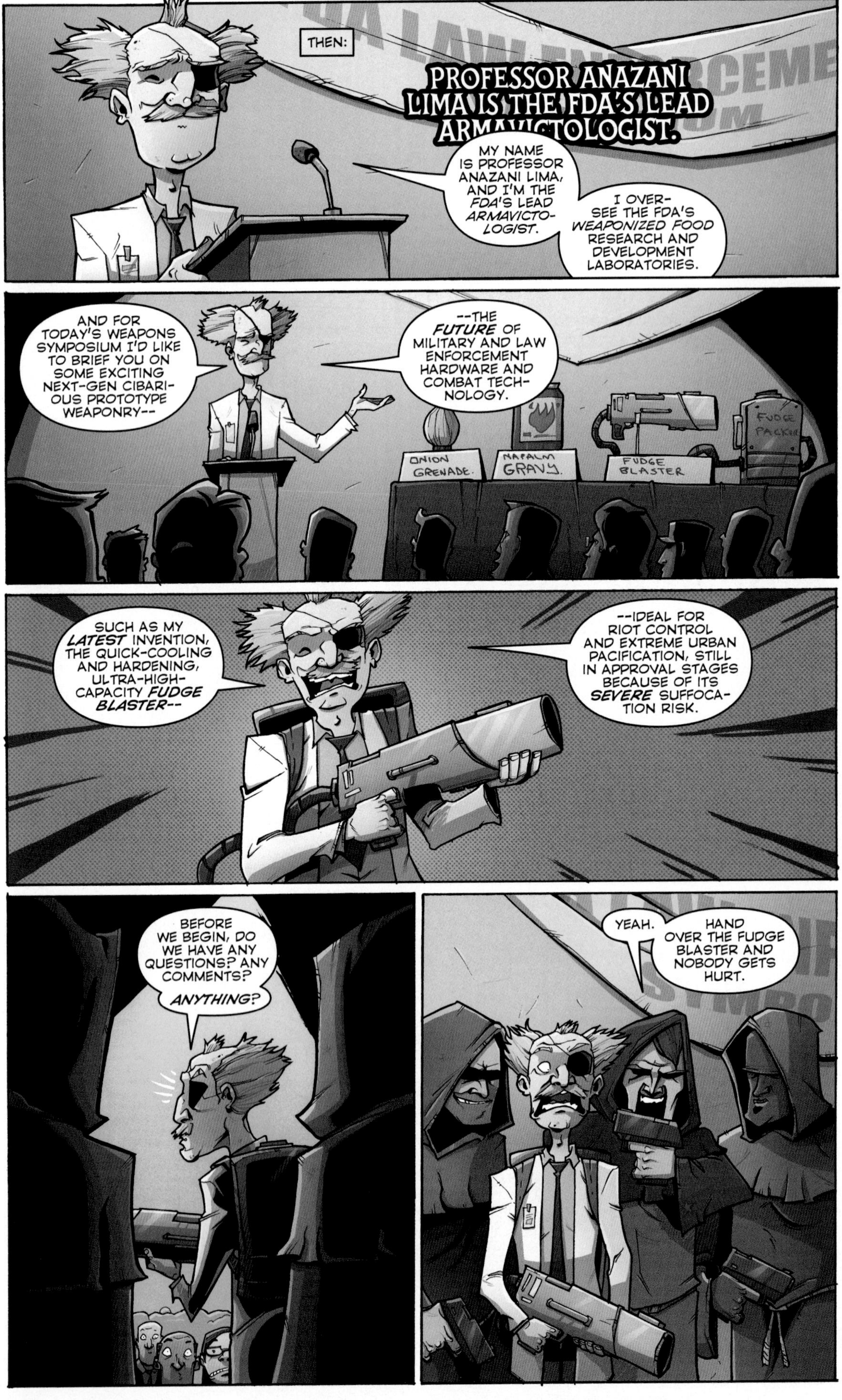
THEN:
PROFESSOR ANAZANI LIMA IS THE FDA'S LEAD ARMAVICTOLOGIST.
MY NAME IS PROFESSOR ANAZANI LIMA, AND I'M THE FDA'S LEAD ARMAVICTO-LOGIST.
I OVER-SEE THE FDA'S WEAPONIZED FOOD RESEARCH AND DEVELOPMENT LABORATORIES.
AND FOR TODAY'S WEAPONS SYMPOSIUM I'D LIKE TO BRIEF YOU ON SOME EXCITING NEXT-GEN CIBARI-OUS PROTOTYPE WEAPONRY--
--THE FUTURE OF MILITARY AND LAW ENFORCEMENT HARDWARE AND COMBAT TECH-NOLOGY.
ONION GRENADE.
NAPALM GRAVY.
FUDGE BLASTER
FUDGE PACKER
SUCH AS MY LATEST INVENTION, THE QUICK-COOLING AND HARDENING, ULTRA-HIGH-CAPACITY FUDGE BLASTER--
--IDEAL FOR RIOT CONTROL AND EXTREME URBAN PACIFICATION, STILL IN APPROVAL STAGES BECAUSE OF ITS SEVERE SUFFOCA-TION RISK.
BEFORE WE BEGIN, DO WE HAVE ANY QUESTIONS? ANY COMMENTS? ANYTHING?
YEAH.
HAND OVER THE FUDGE BLASTER AND NOBODY GETS HURT.

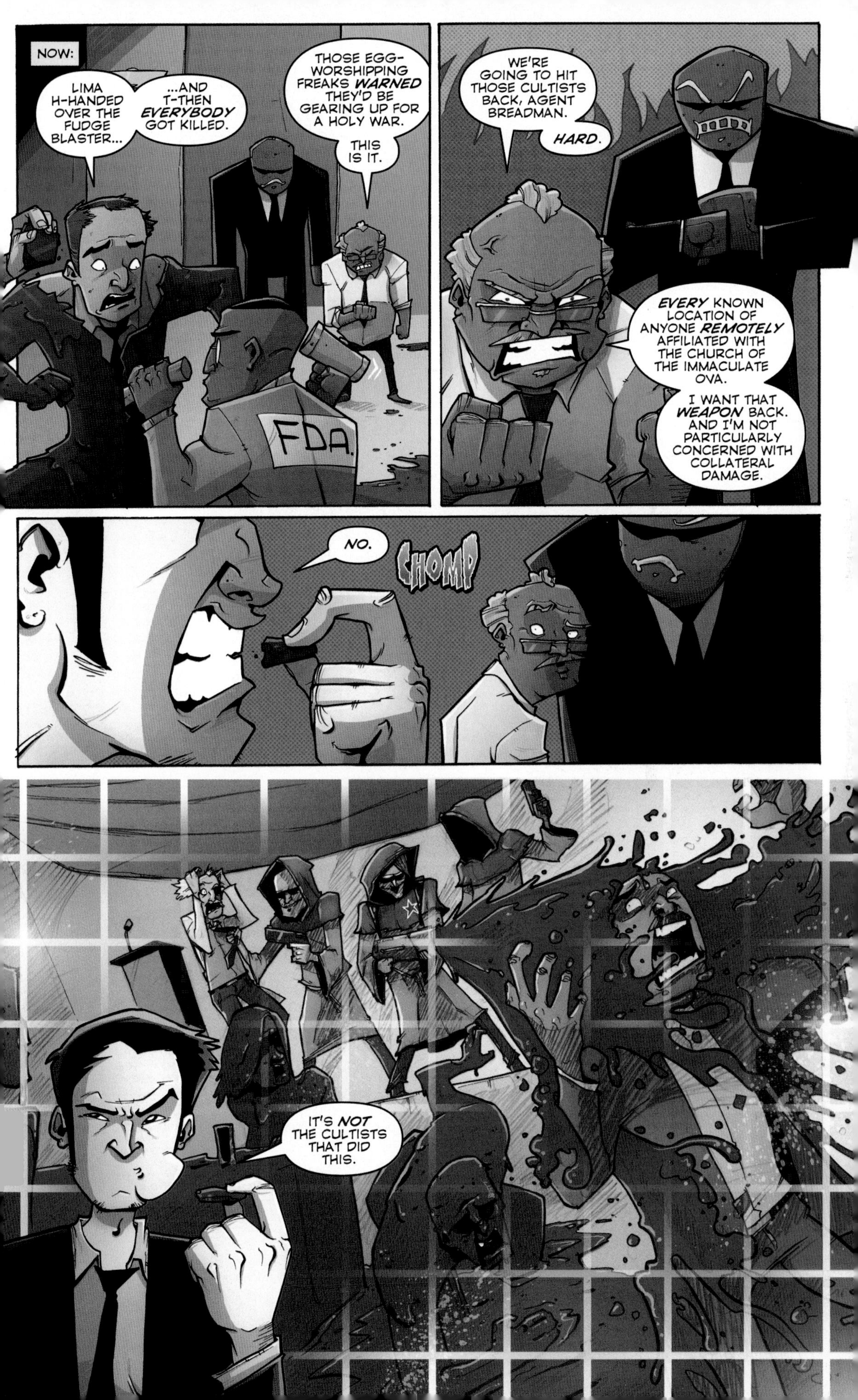
NOW:
LIMA H-HANDED OVER THE FUDGE BLASTER...
...AND T-THEN *EVERYBODY* GOT KILLED.
THOSE EGG-WORSHIPPING FREAKS *WARNED* THEY'D BE GEARING UP FOR A HOLY WAR.
THIS IS IT.
FDA
WE'RE GOING TO HIT THOSE CULTISTS BACK, AGENT BREADMAN.
HARD.
EVERY KNOWN LOCATION OF ANYONE *REMOTELY* AFFILIATED WITH THE CHURCH OF THE IMMACULATE OVA.
I WANT THAT *WEAPON* BACK. AND I'M NOT PARTICULARLY CONCERNED WITH COLLATERAL DAMAGE.
NO.
CHOMP
IT'S *NOT* THE CULTISTS THAT DID THIS.

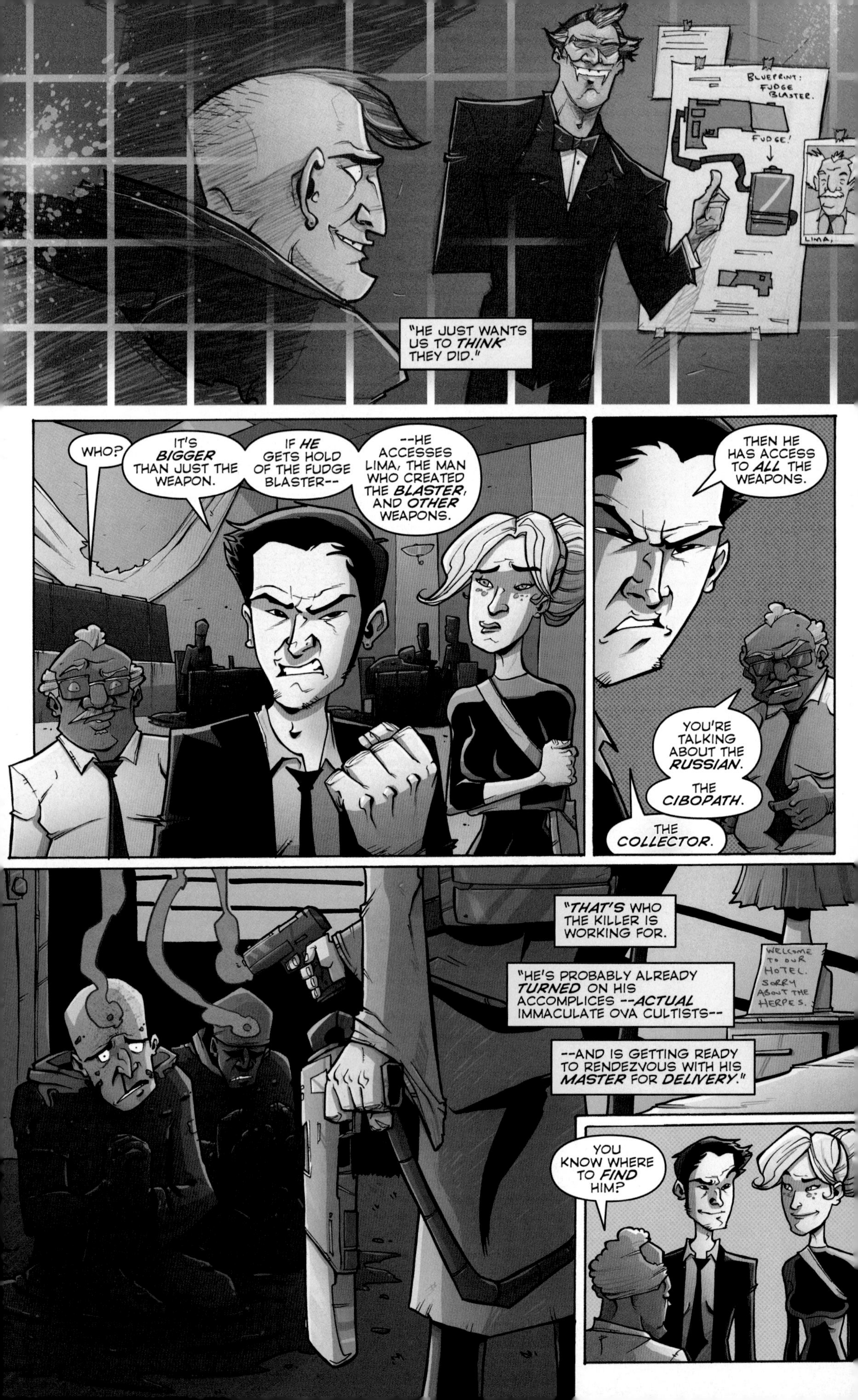
BLUEPRINT: FUDGE BLASTER.
FUDGE!
LIMA,
"HE JUST WANTS US TO *THINK* THEY DID."
WHO?
IT'S *BIGGER* THAN JUST THE WEAPON.
IF *HE* GETS HOLD OF THE FUDGE BLASTER--
--HE ACCESSES LIMA, THE MAN WHO CREATED THE *BLASTER*, AND *OTHER* WEAPONS.
THEN HE HAS ACCESS TO *ALL* THE WEAPONS.
YOU'RE TALKING ABOUT THE *RUSSIAN*.
THE *CIBOPATH*.
THE *COLLECTOR*.
"*THAT'S* WHO THE KILLER IS WORKING FOR.
"HE'S PROBABLY ALREADY *TURNED* ON HIS ACCOMPLICES --*ACTUAL* IMMACULATE OVA CULTISTS--
WELCOME TO OUR HOTEL. SORRY ABOUT THE HERPES.
--AND IS GETTING READY TO RENDEZVOUS WITH HIS *MASTER* FOR *DELIVERY*."
YOU KNOW WHERE TO *FIND* HIM?

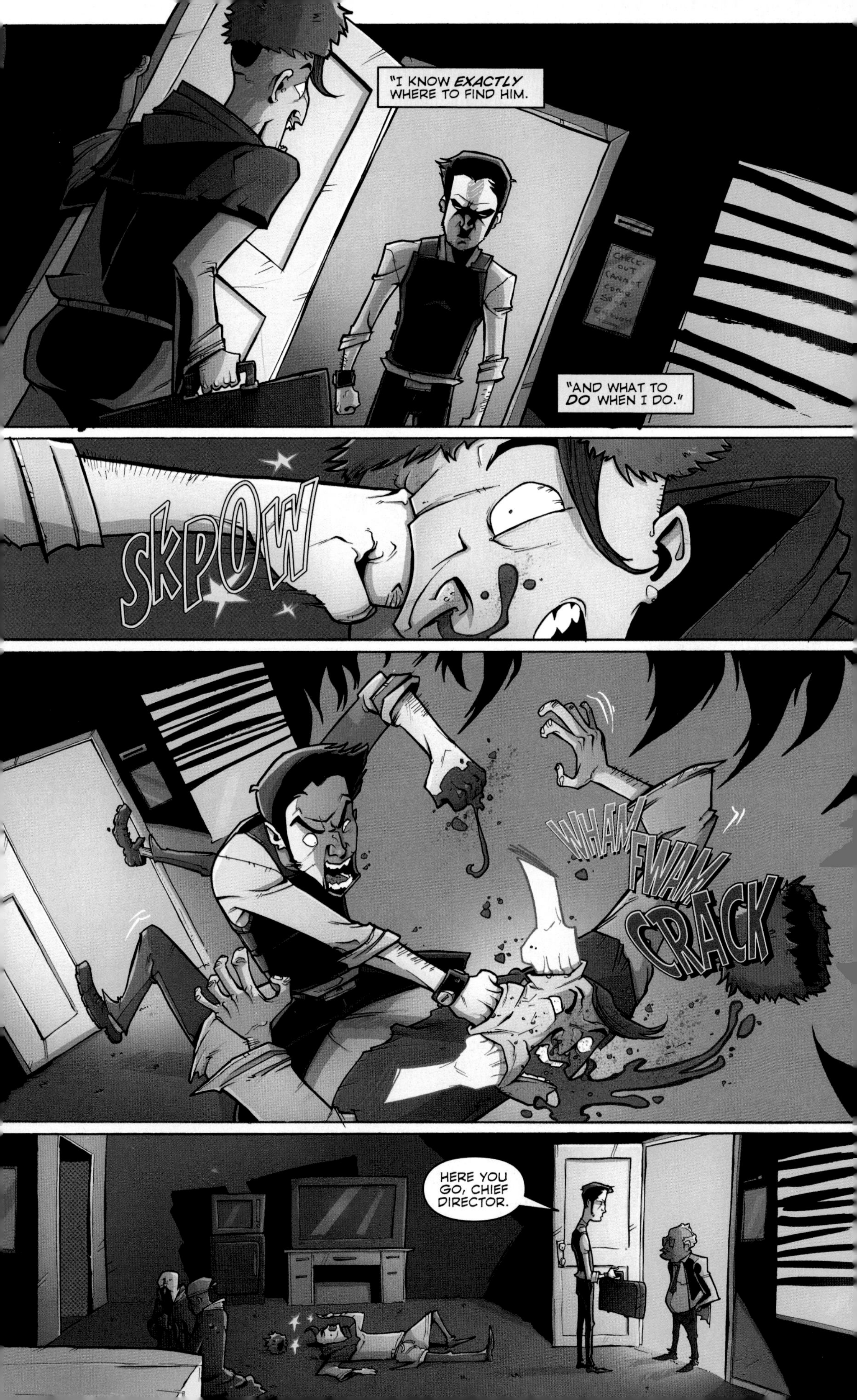
"I KNOW *EXACTLY* WHERE TO FIND HIM.
"AND WHAT TO *DO* WHEN I DO."
SKPOW
WHAM
FWAM
CRACK
HERE YOU GO, CHIEF DIRECTOR.

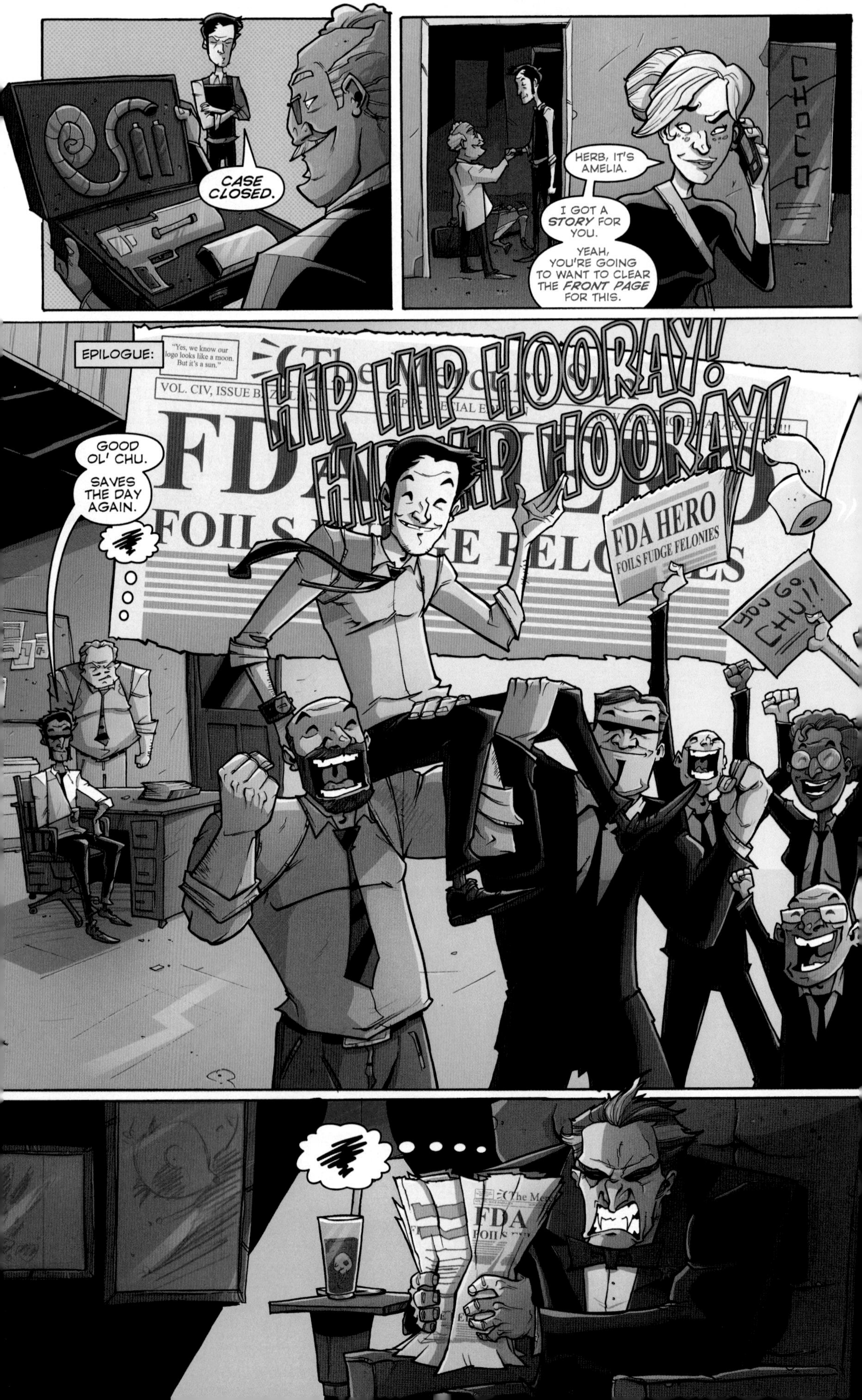
CASE CLOSED.
CHOCO
HERB, IT'S AMELIA.
I GOT A STORY FOR YOU.
YEAH, YOU'RE GOING TO WANT TO CLEAR THE FRONT PAGE FOR THIS.
EPILOGUE:
"Yes, we know our logo looks like a moon. But it's a sun."
VOL. CIV, ISSUE
HIP HIP HOORAY!
HIP HIP HOORAY!
GOOD OL' CHU.
SAVES THE DAY AGAIN.
FDA HERO
FOILS FUDGE FELONIES
you go CHU!!
FDA

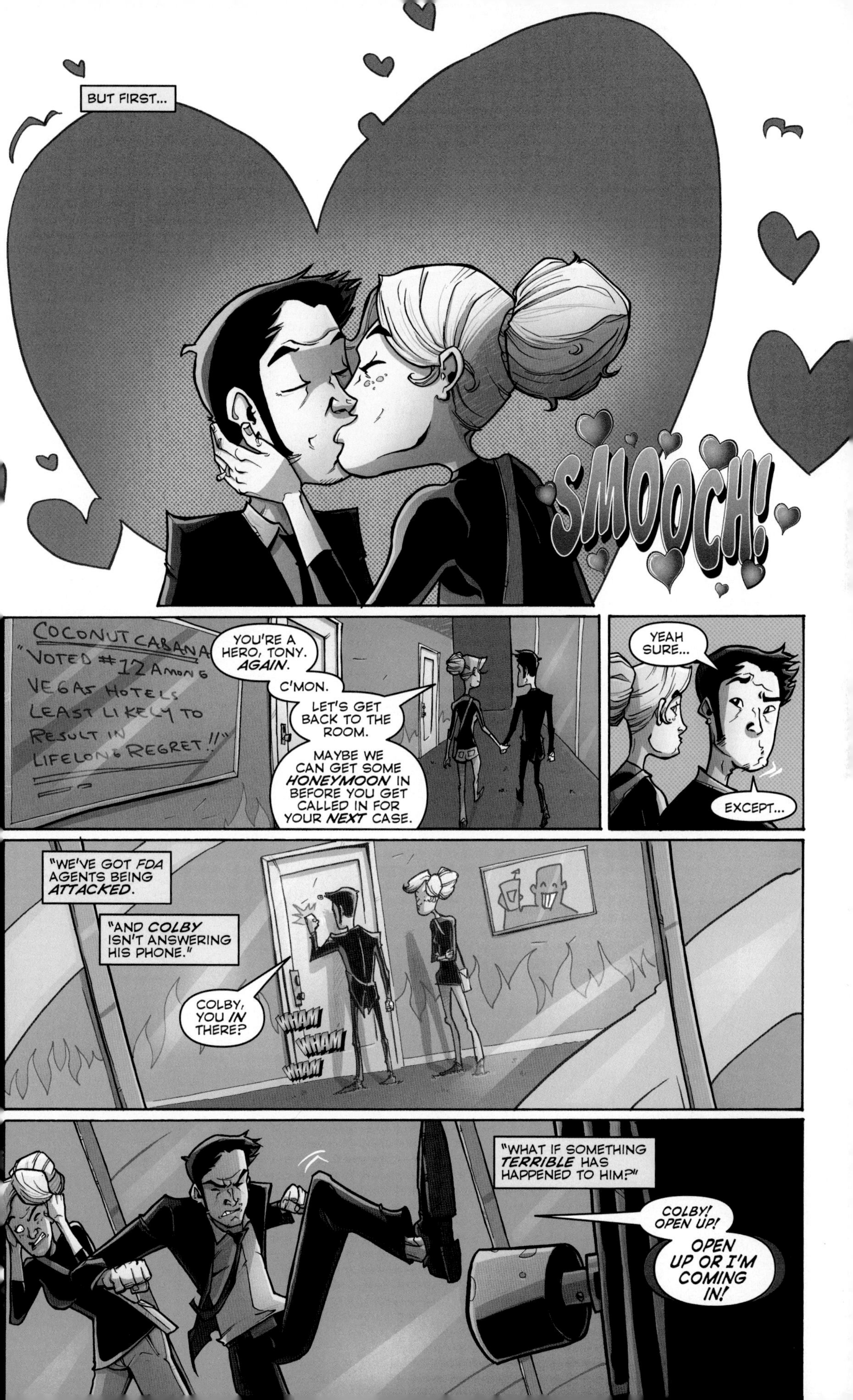
BUT FIRST...
SMOOCH!
COCONUT CABANA "VOTED #12 AMONG VEGAS HOTELS LEAST LIKELY TO RESULT IN LIFELONG REGRET!!"
YOU'RE A HERO, TONY. AGAIN.
C'MON.
LET'S GET BACK TO THE ROOM.
MAYBE WE CAN GET SOME HONEYMOON IN BEFORE YOU GET CALLED IN FOR YOUR NEXT CASE.
YEAH SURE...
EXCEPT...
"WE'VE GOT FDA AGENTS BEING ATTACKED.
"AND COLBY ISN'T ANSWERING HIS PHONE."
COLBY, YOU IN THERE?
WHAM
WHAM
WHAM
"WHAT IF SOMETHING TERRIBLE HAS HAPPENED TO HIM?"
COLBY! OPEN UP!
OPEN UP OR I'M COMING IN!

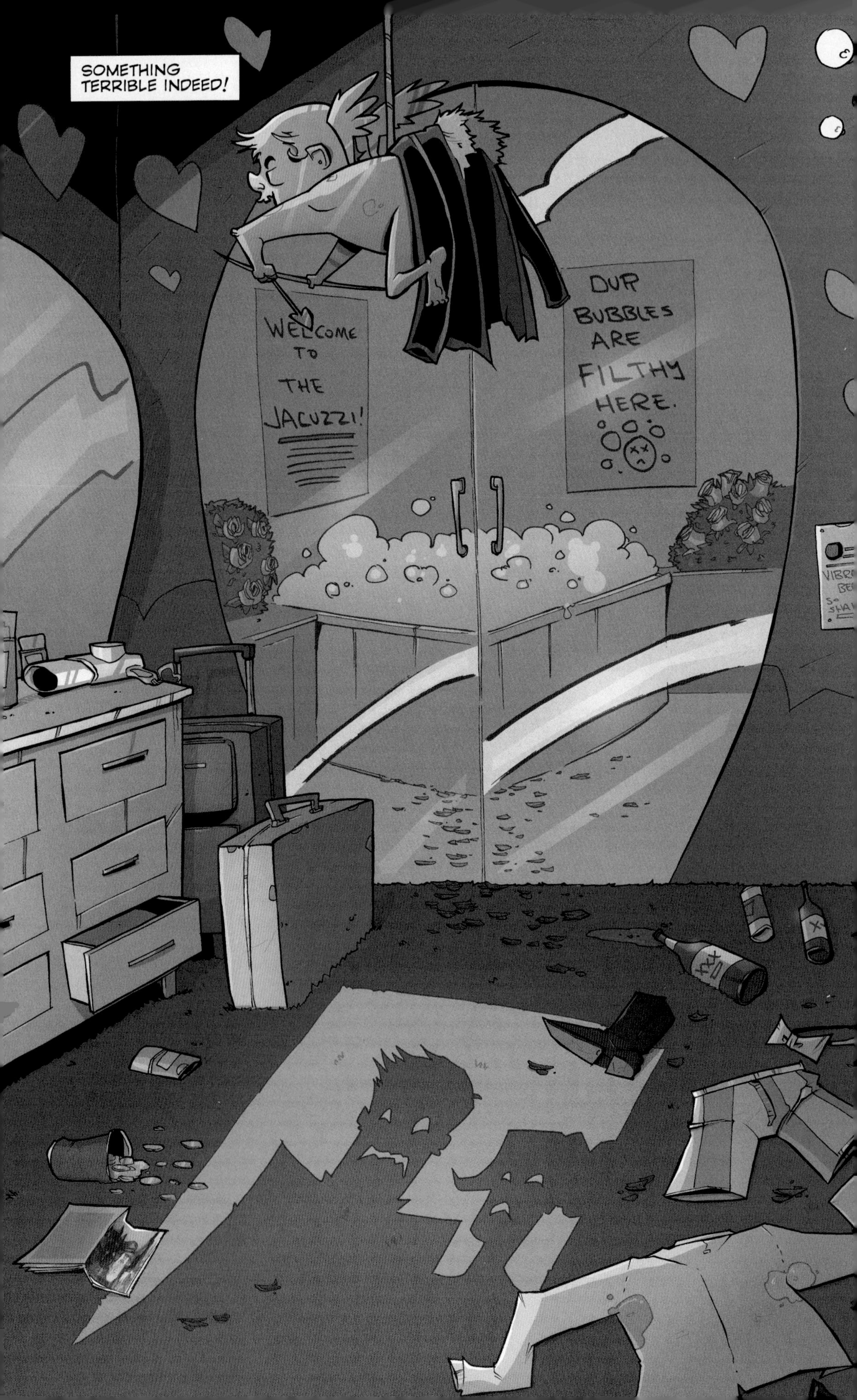
SOMETHING TERRIBLE INDEED!
WELCOME TO THE JACUZZI!
OUR BUBBLES ARE FILTHY HERE.

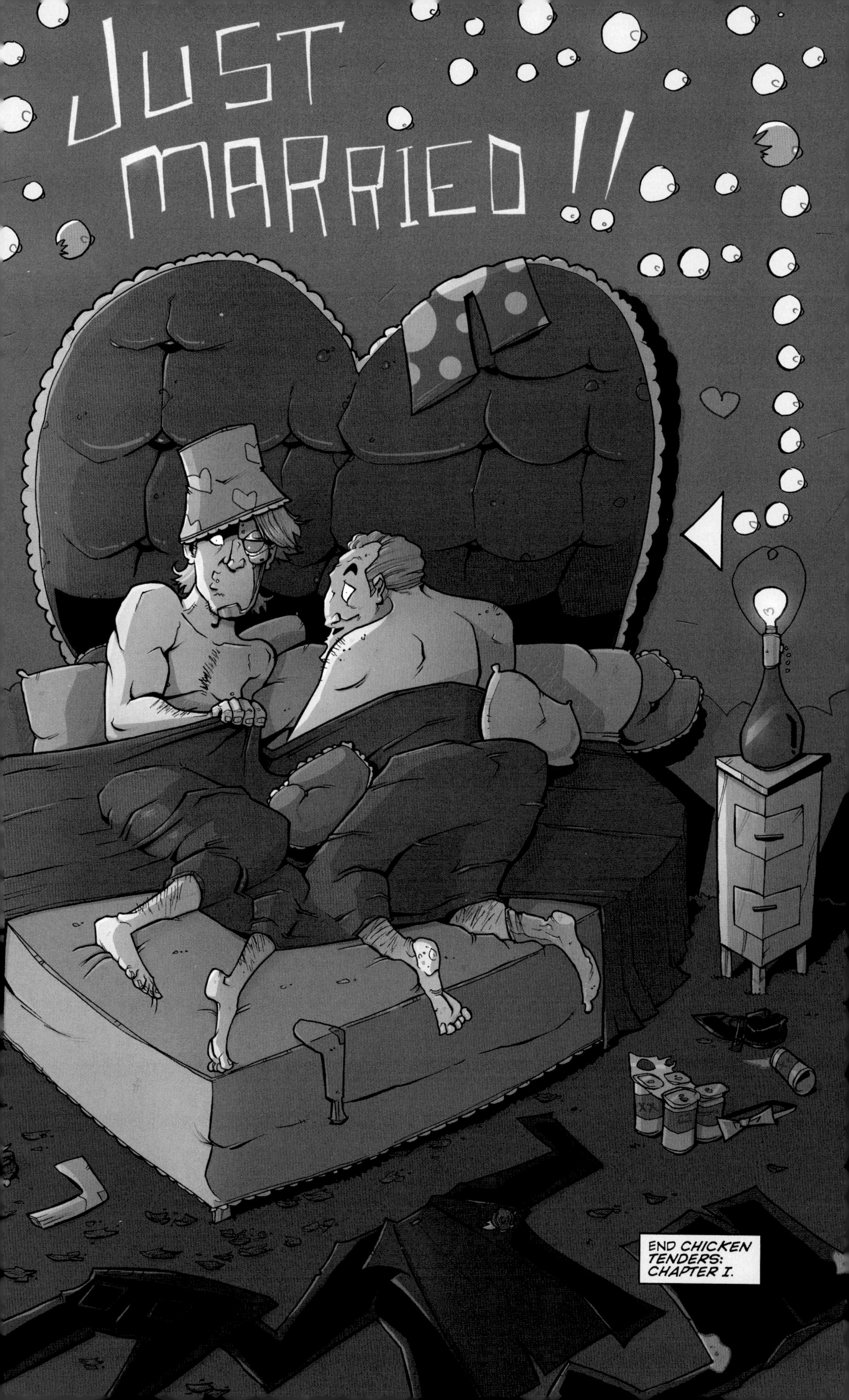
JUST MARRIED!!
END CHICKEN TENDERS: CHAPTER I.

Chapter 2

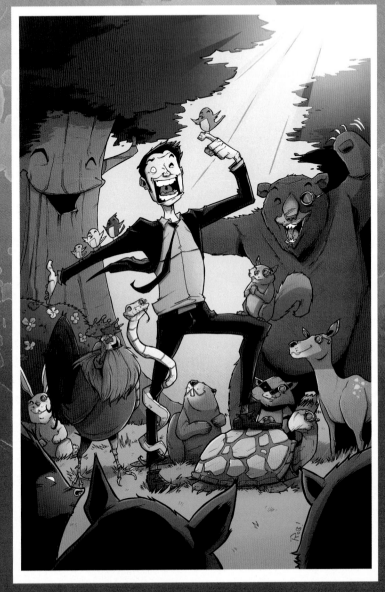

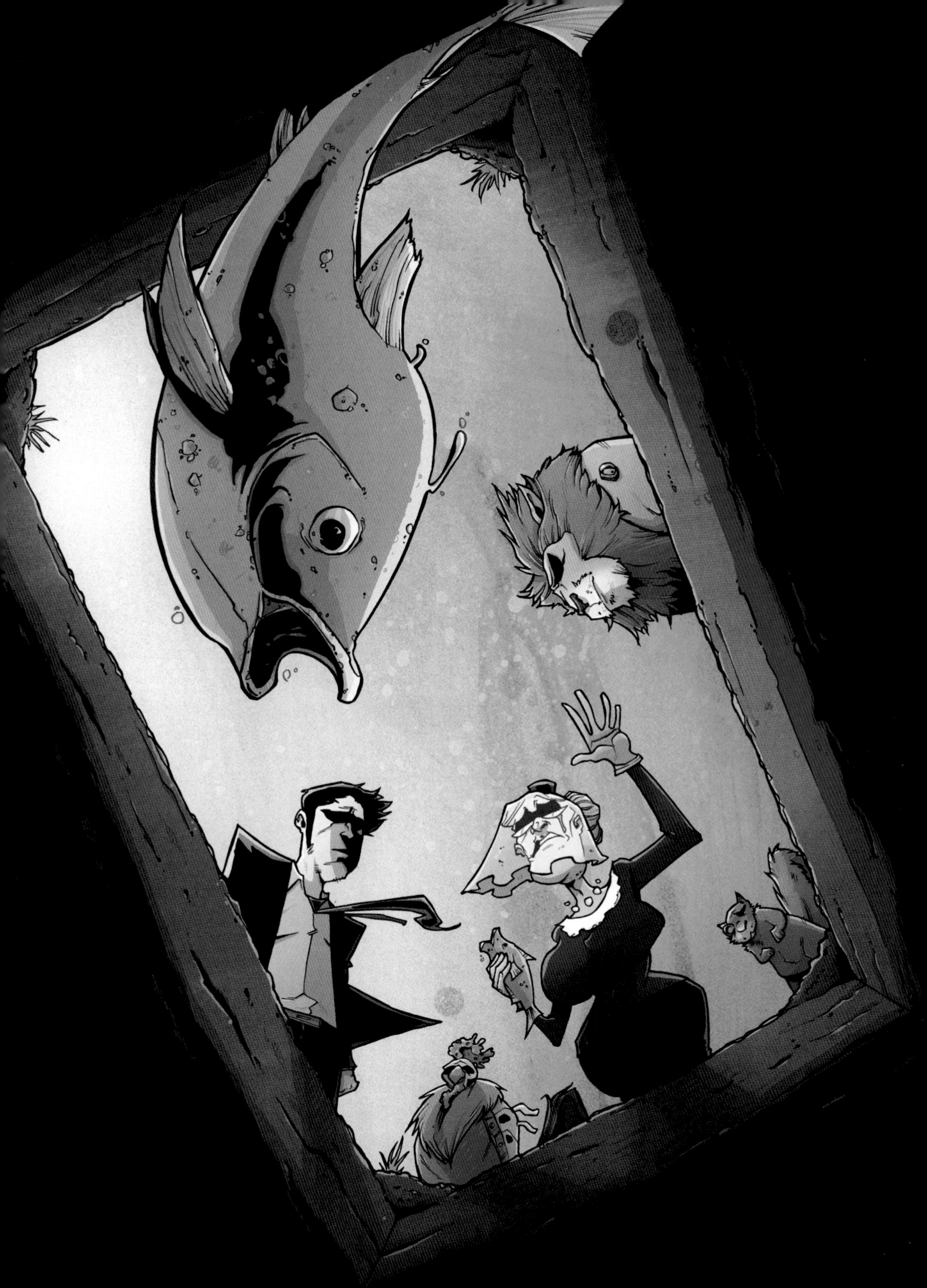

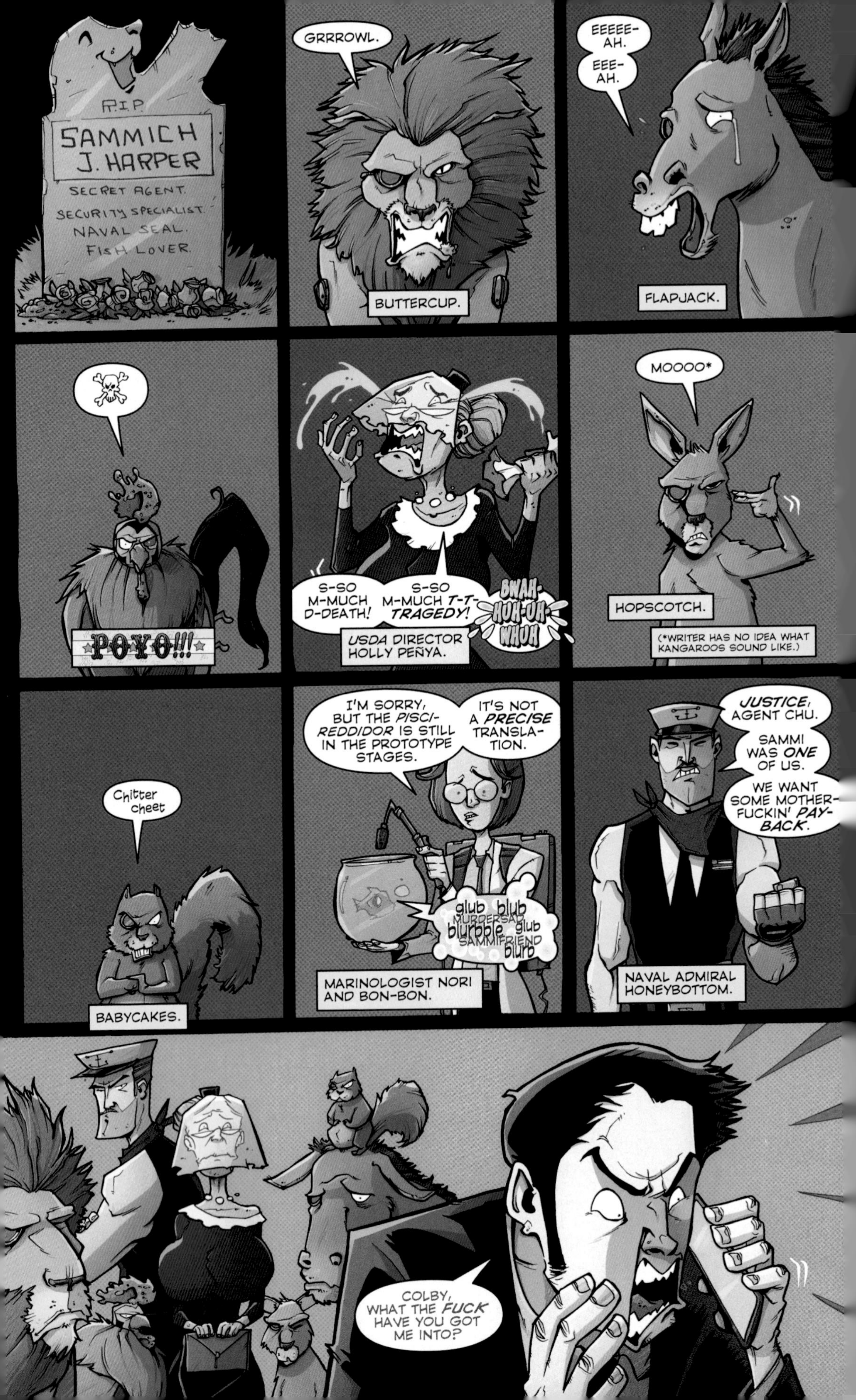
R.I.P.
SAMMICH J. HARPER
SECRET AGENT.
SECURITY SPECIALIST.
NAVAL SEAL.
FISH LOVER.
GRRROWL.
BUTTERCUP.
EEEEE-AH. EEE-AH.
FLAPJACK.
POYO!!!
S-SO M-MUCH D-DEATH!
S-SO M-MUCH T-T-TRAGEDY!
BWAH-HUH-UH WHUH
USDA DIRECTOR HOLLY PEÑYA.
MOOOO*
HOPSCOTCH.
(*WRITER HAS NO IDEA WHAT KANGAROOS SOUND LIKE.)
Chitter cheet
BABYCAKES.
I'M SORRY, BUT THE PISCI-REDDIDOR IS STILL IN THE PROTOTYPE STAGES.
IT'S NOT A PRECISE TRANSLA-TION.
glub blub MURDERSAD glub blurbble SAMMIFRIEND blurb
MARINOLOGIST NORI AND BON-BON.
JUSTICE, AGENT CHU.
SAMMI WAS ONE OF US.
WE WANT SOME MOTHER-FUCKIN' PAY-BACK.
NAVAL ADMIRAL HONEYBOTTOM.
COLBY, WHAT THE FUCK HAVE YOU GOT ME INTO?

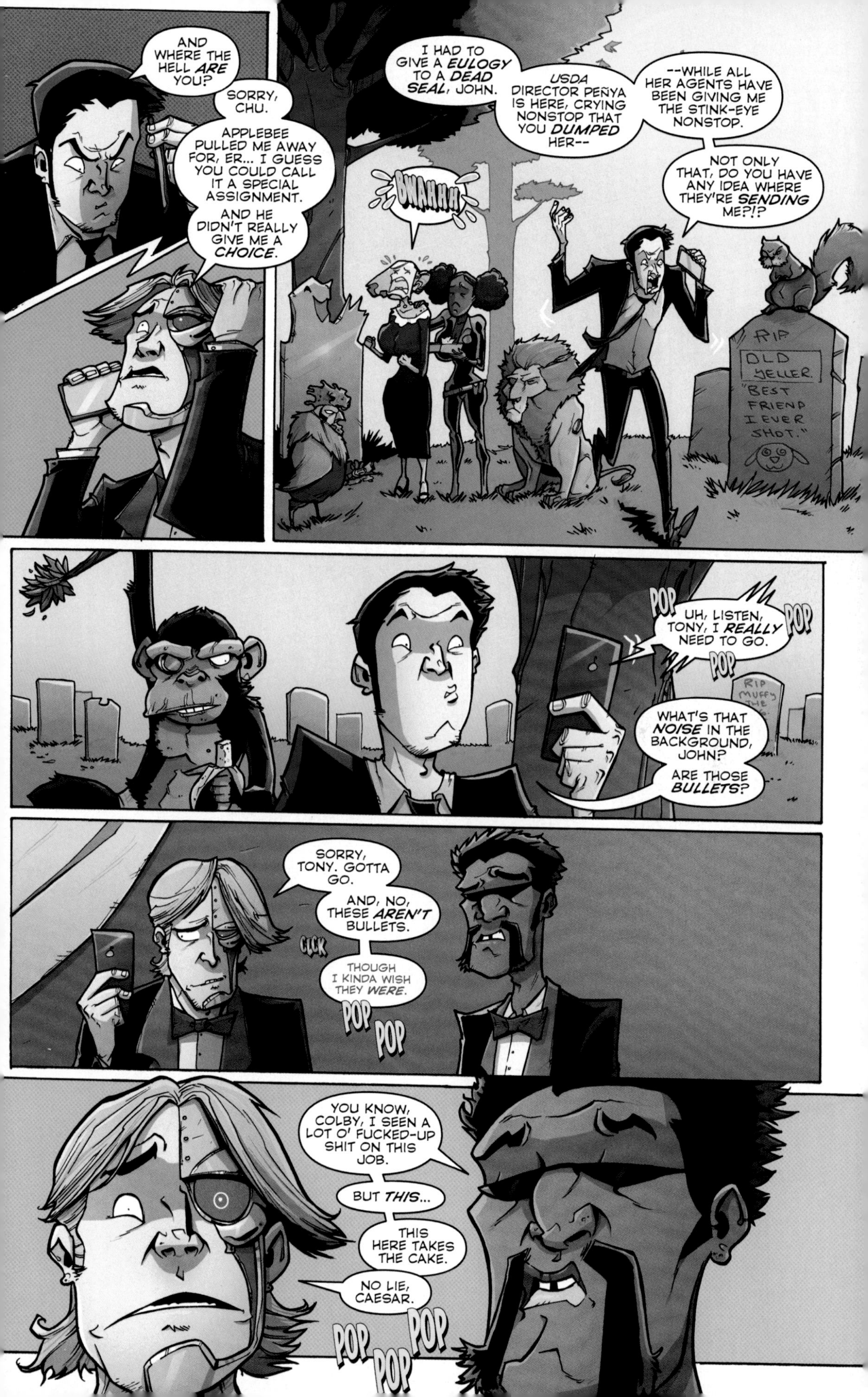
AND WHERE THE HELL ARE YOU?
SORRY, CHU.
APPLEBEE PULLED ME AWAY FOR, ER... I GUESS YOU COULD CALL IT A SPECIAL ASSIGNMENT.
AND HE DIDN'T REALLY GIVE ME A CHOICE.
I HAD TO GIVE A EULOGY TO A DEAD SEAL, JOHN.
USDA DIRECTOR PEÑYA IS HERE, CRYING NONSTOP THAT YOU DUMPED HER--
--WHILE ALL HER AGENTS HAVE BEEN GIVING ME THE STINK-EYE NONSTOP.
BWAHHH
NOT ONLY THAT, DO YOU HAVE ANY IDEA WHERE THEY'RE SENDING ME?!?
RIP
OLD YELLER
"BEST FRIEND I EVER SHOT."
POP
UH, LISTEN, TONY, I REALLY NEED TO GO.
POP
POP
RIP MUFFY THE
WHAT'S THAT NOISE IN THE BACKGROUND, JOHN?
ARE THOSE BULLETS?
SORRY, TONY. GOTTA GO.
AND, NO, THESE AREN'T BULLETS.
CLICK
THOUGH I KINDA WISH THEY WERE.
POP
POP
YOU KNOW, COLBY, I SEEN A LOT O' FUCKED-UP SHIT ON THIS JOB.
BUT THIS...
THIS HERE TAKES THE CAKE.
NO LIE, CAESAR.
POP
POP
POP

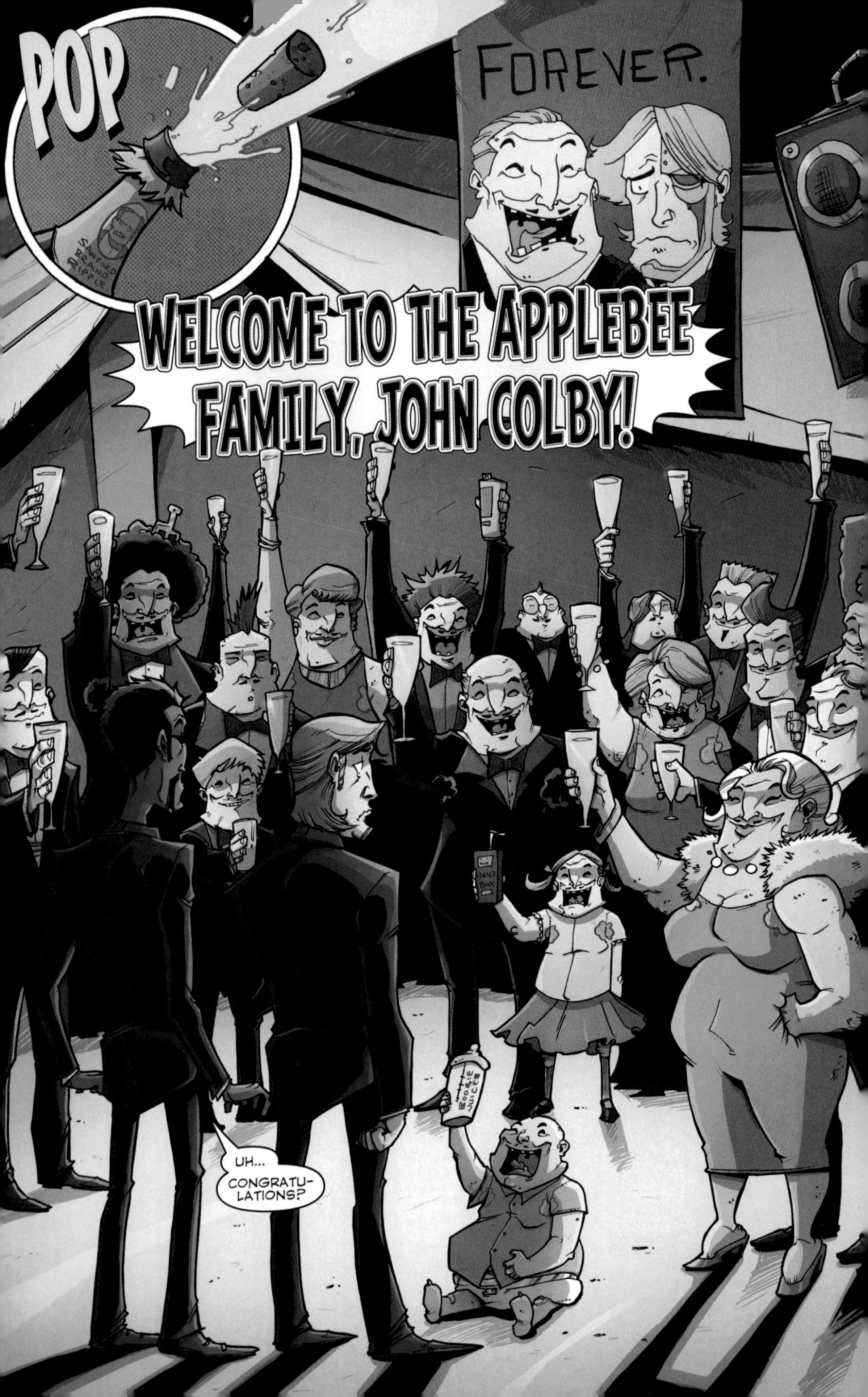
POP
SANFORD BRAND RIPPLE
FOREVER.
WELCOME TO THE APPLEBEE FAMILY, JOHN COLBY!
JUICE BOX
BOOGIE JUICE
UH... CONGRATULATIONS?

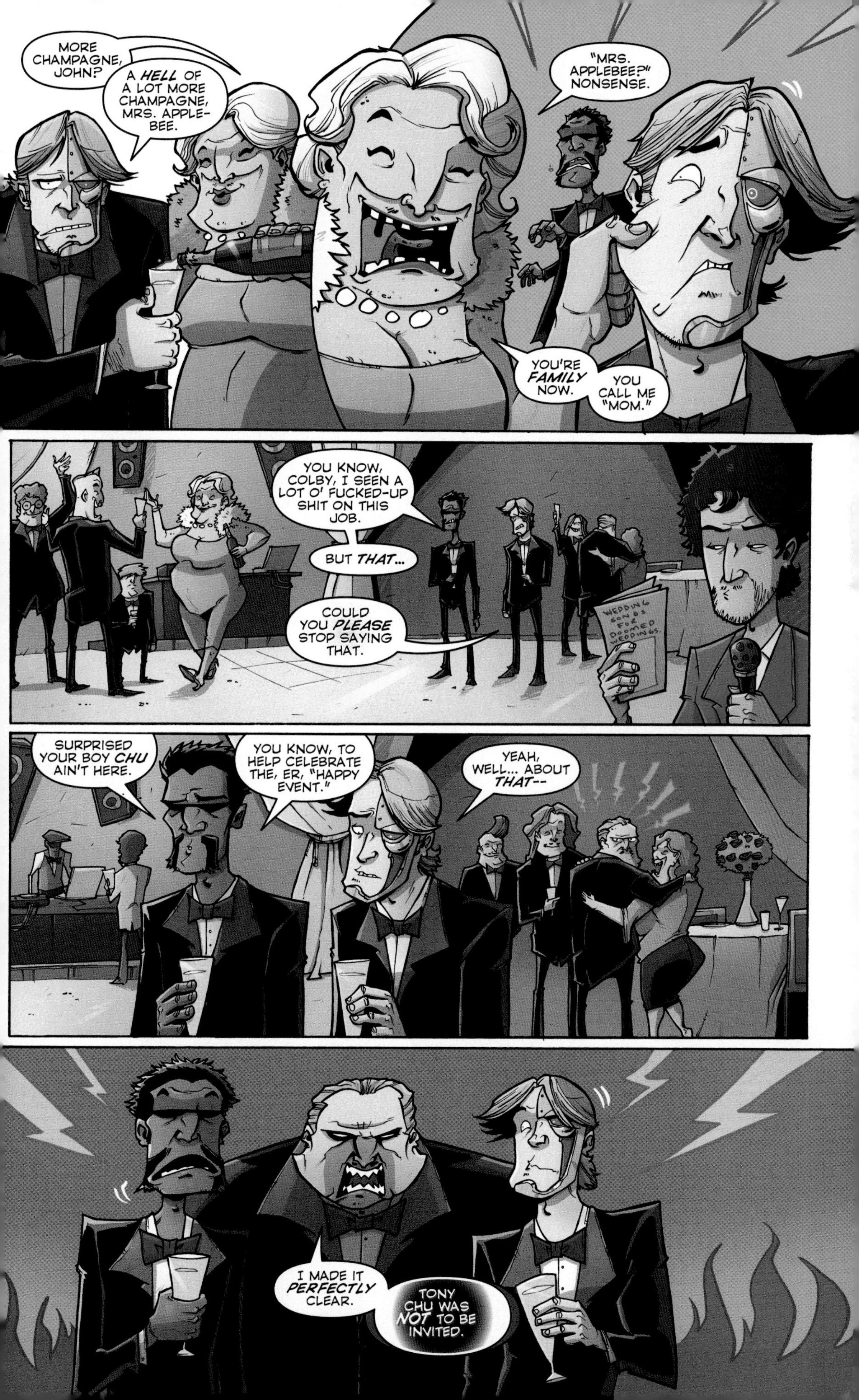

MORE CHAMPAGNE, JOHN?
A HELL OF A LOT MORE CHAMPAGNE, MRS. APPLE-BEE.
"MRS. APPLEBEE?" NONSENSE.
YOU'RE FAMILY NOW.
YOU CALL ME "MOM."
YOU KNOW, COLBY, I SEEN A LOT O' FUCKED-UP SHIT ON THIS JOB.
BUT THAT...
COULD YOU PLEASE STOP SAYING THAT.
WEDDING SONGS FOR DOOMED WEDDINGS
SURPRISED YOUR BOY CHU AIN'T HERE.
YOU KNOW, TO HELP CELEBRATE THE, ER, "HAPPY EVENT."
YEAH, WELL... ABOUT THAT--
I MADE IT PERFECTLY CLEAR.
TONY CHU WAS NOT TO BE INVITED.

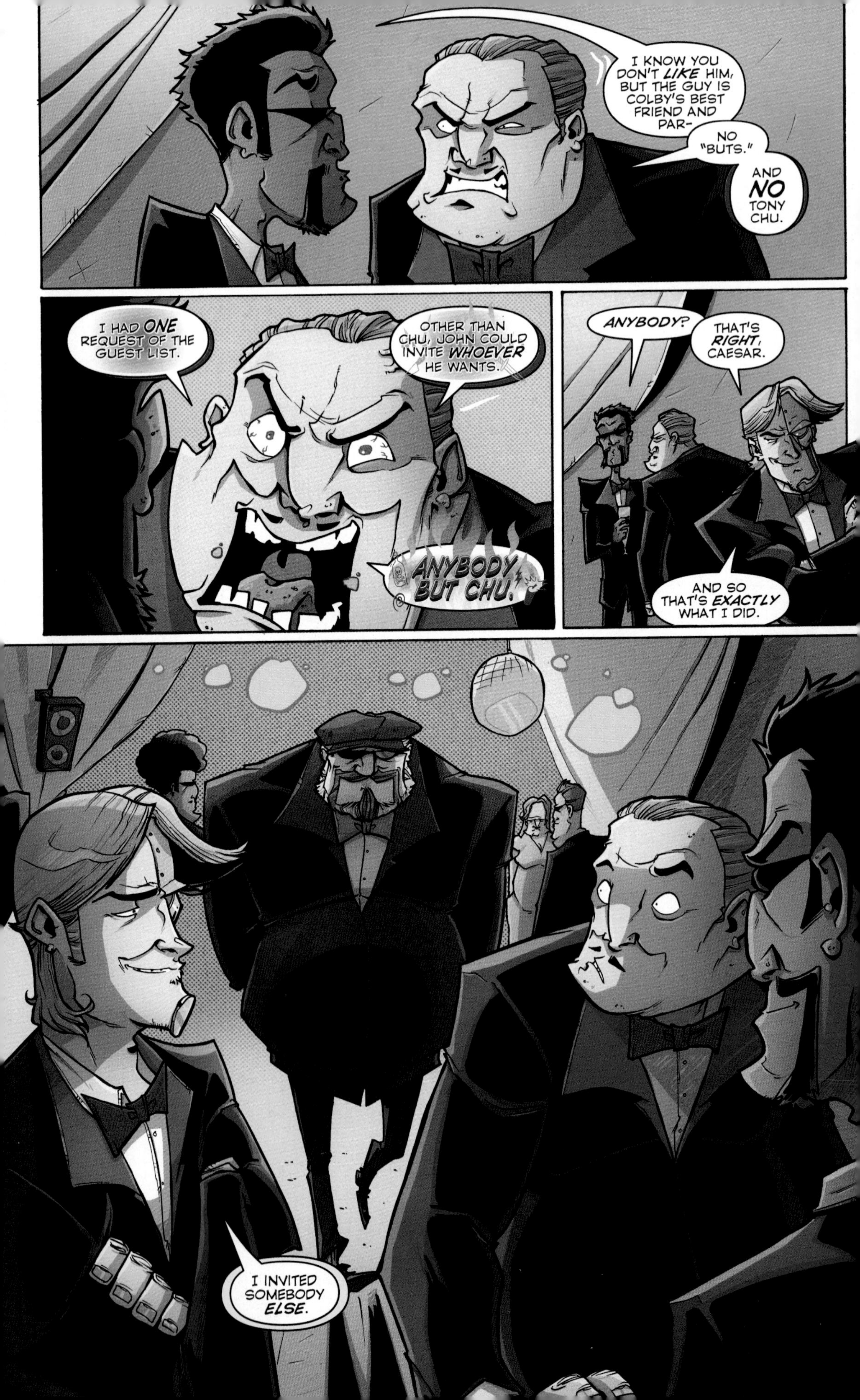
I KNOW YOU DON'T *LIKE* HIM, BUT THE GUY IS COLBY'S BEST FRIEND AND PAR-
NO "BUTS."
AND **NO** TONY CHU.
I HAD *ONE* REQUEST OF THE GUEST LIST.
OTHER THAN CHU, JOHN COULD INVITE *WHOEVER* HE WANTS.
ANYBODY BUT CHU.
ANYBODY?
THAT'S *RIGHT*, CAESAR.
AND SO THAT'S *EXACTLY* WHAT I DID.
I INVITED SOMEBODY *ELSE*.

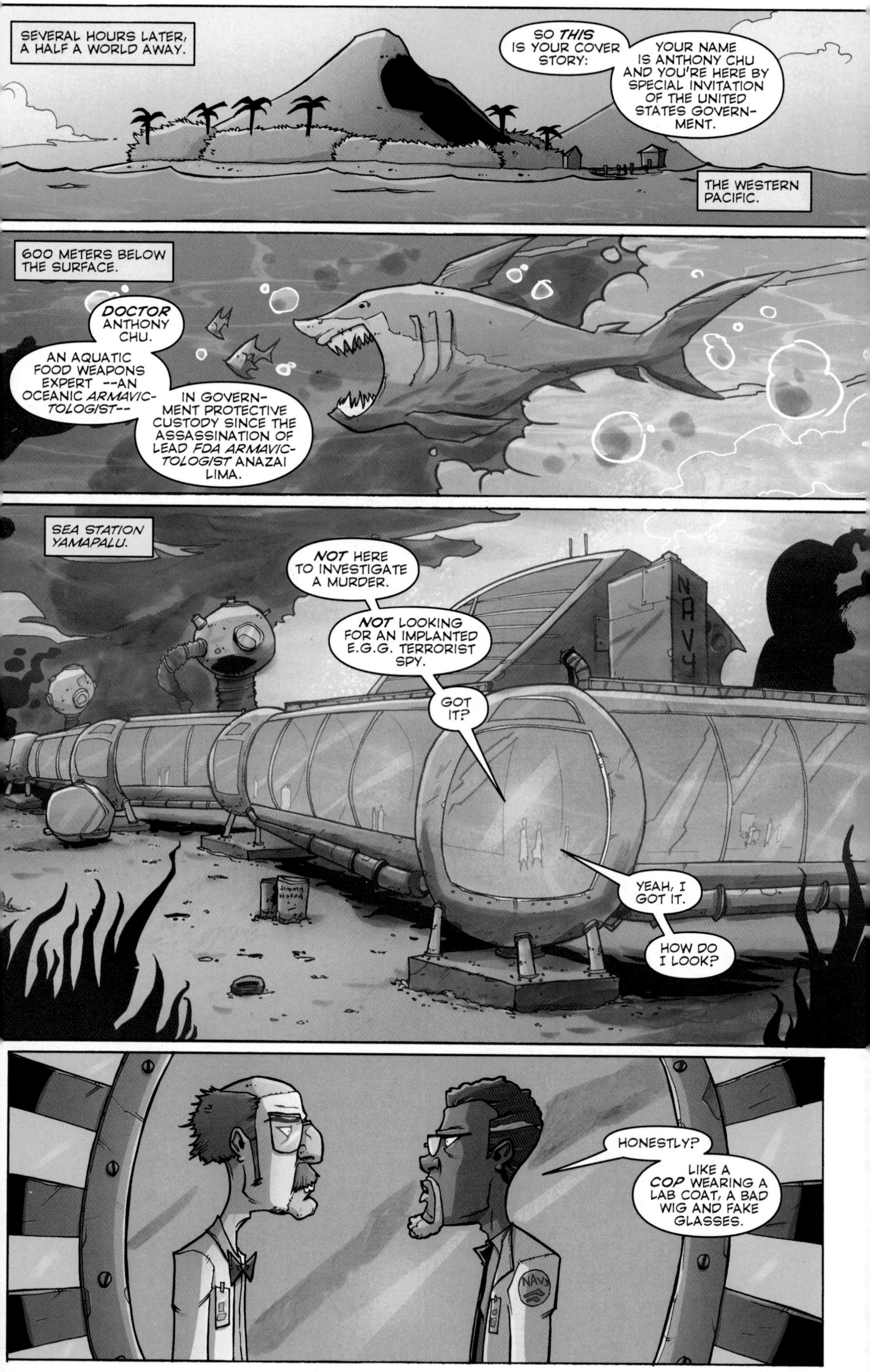
SEVERAL HOURS LATER, A HALF A WORLD AWAY.
SO THIS IS YOUR COVER STORY:
YOUR NAME IS ANTHONY CHU AND YOU'RE HERE BY SPECIAL INVITATION OF THE UNITED STATES GOVERNMENT.
THE WESTERN PACIFIC.
600 METERS BELOW THE SURFACE.
DOCTOR ANTHONY CHU.
AN AQUATIC FOOD WEAPONS EXPERT --AN OCEANIC ARMAVICTOLOGIST--
IN GOVERNMENT PROTECTIVE CUSTODY SINCE THE ASSASSINATION OF LEAD FDA ARMAVICTOLOGIST ANAZAI LIMA.
SEA STATION YAMAPALU.
NAVY
NOT HERE TO INVESTIGATE A MURDER.
NOT LOOKING FOR AN IMPLANTED E.G.G. TERRORIST SPY.
GOT IT?
JIMMY HOFFA
YEAH, I GOT IT.
HOW DO I LOOK?
HONESTLY?
LIKE A COP WEARING A LAB COAT, A BAD WIG AND FAKE GLASSES.
NAVY

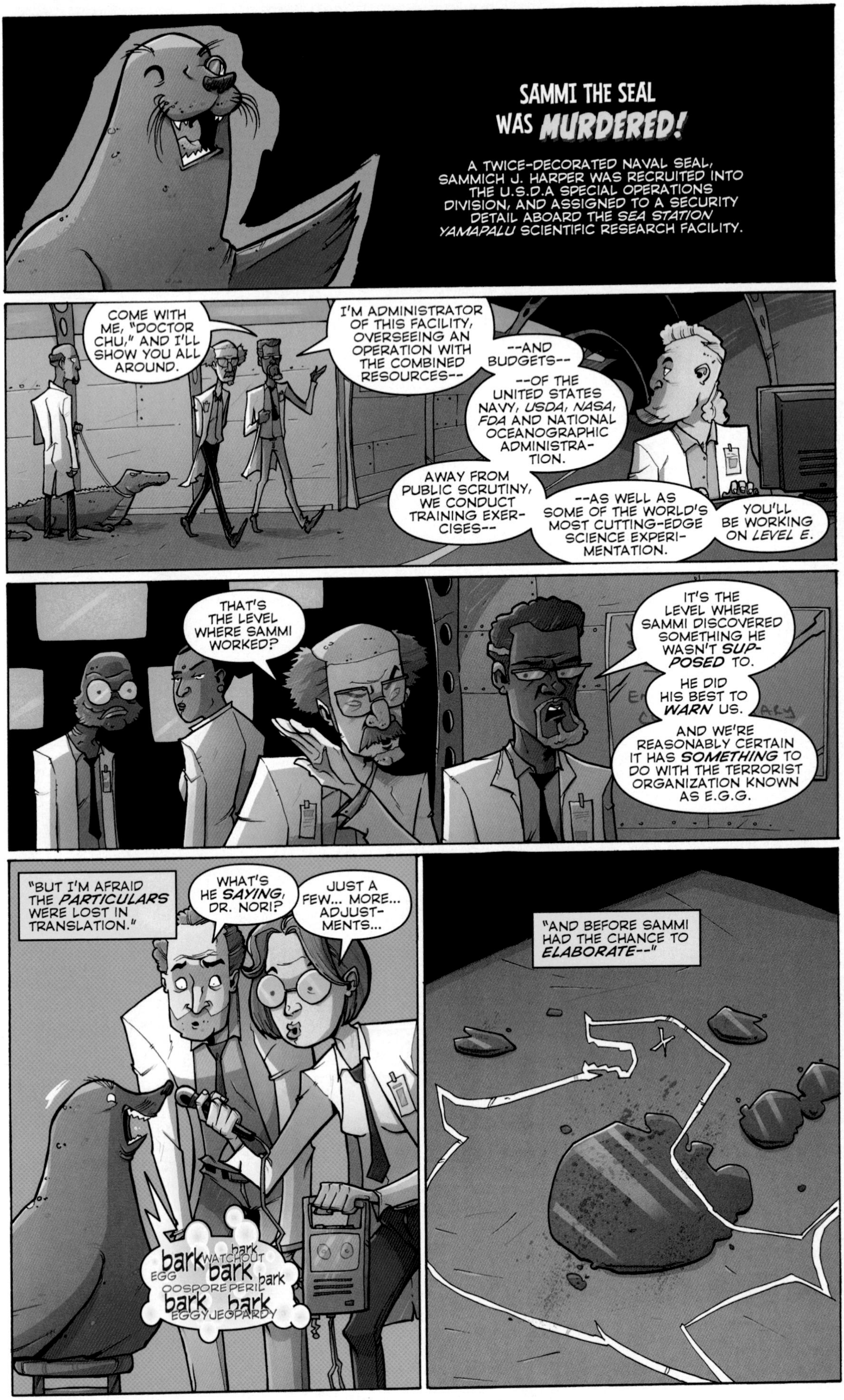
SAMMI THE SEAL WAS MURDERED!
A TWICE-DECORATED NAVAL SEAL, SAMMICH J. HARPER WAS RECRUITED INTO THE U.S.D.A SPECIAL OPERATIONS DIVISION, AND ASSIGNED TO A SECURITY DETAIL ABOARD THE SEA STATION YAMAPALU SCIENTIFIC RESEARCH FACILITY.
COME WITH ME, "DOCTOR CHU," AND I'LL SHOW YOU ALL AROUND.
I'M ADMINISTRATOR OF THIS FACILITY, OVERSEEING AN OPERATION WITH THE COMBINED RESOURCES--
--AND BUDGETS--
--OF THE UNITED STATES NAVY, USDA, NASA, FDA AND NATIONAL OCEANOGRAPHIC ADMINISTRATION.
AWAY FROM PUBLIC SCRUTINY, WE CONDUCT TRAINING EXERCISES--
--AS WELL AS SOME OF THE WORLD'S MOST CUTTING-EDGE SCIENCE EXPERIMENTATION.
YOU'LL BE WORKING ON LEVEL E.
THAT'S THE LEVEL WHERE SAMMI WORKED?
IT'S THE LEVEL WHERE SAMMI DISCOVERED SOMETHING HE WASN'T SUPPOSED TO.
HE DID HIS BEST TO WARN US.
AND WE'RE REASONABLY CERTAIN IT HAS SOMETHING TO DO WITH THE TERRORIST ORGANIZATION KNOWN AS E.G.G.
"BUT I'M AFRAID THE PARTICULARS WERE LOST IN TRANSLATION."
WHAT'S HE SAYING, DR. NORI?
JUST A FEW... MORE... ADJUSTMENTS...
bark bark WATCHOUT EGG bark bark OOSPORE PERIL bark bark EGGY JEOPARDY
"AND BEFORE SAMMI HAD THE CHANCE TO ELABORATE--"

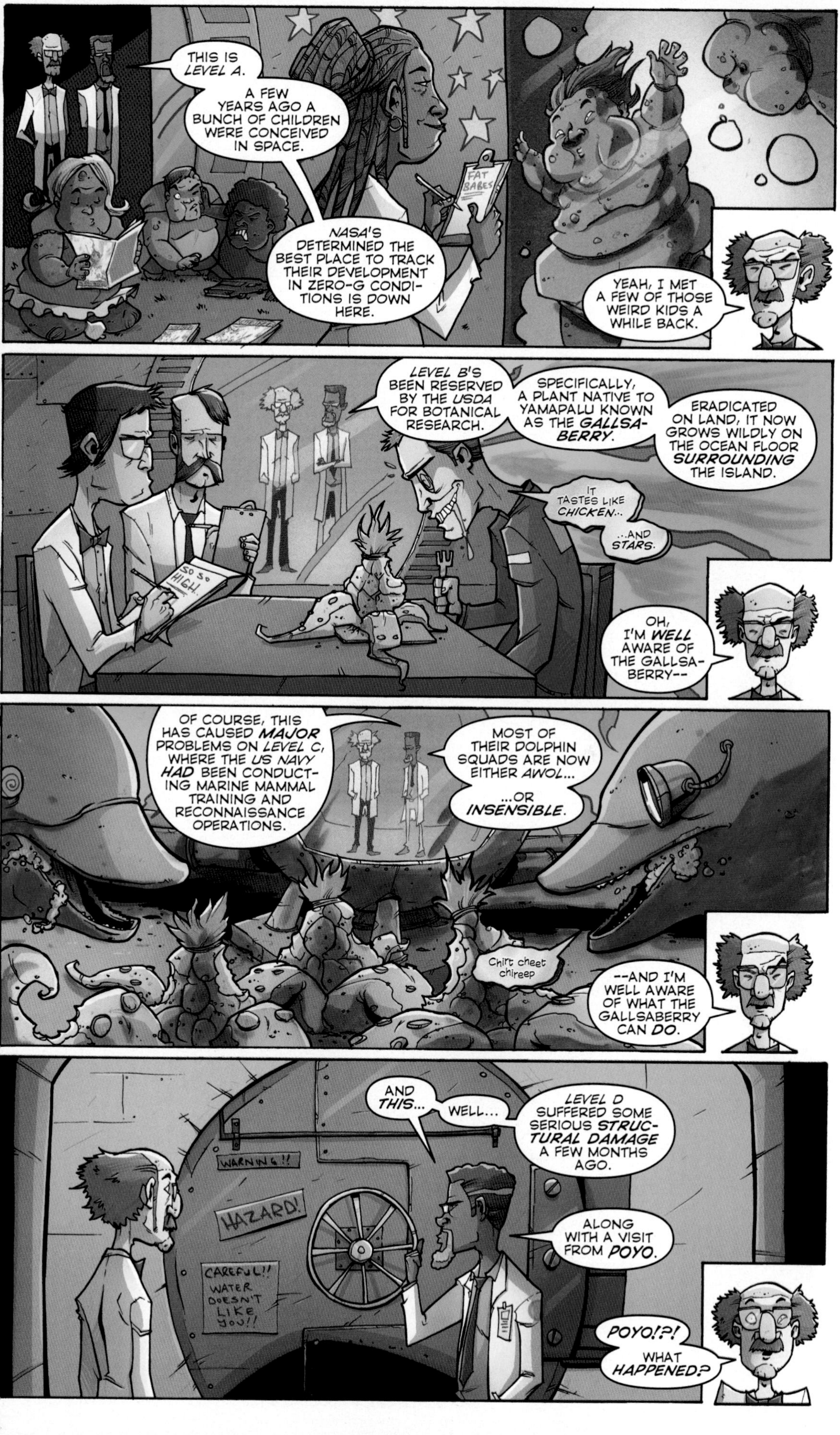
THIS IS LEVEL A.
A FEW YEARS AGO A BUNCH OF CHILDREN WERE CONCEIVED IN SPACE.
FAT BABES
NASA'S DETERMINED THE BEST PLACE TO TRACK THEIR DEVELOPMENT IN ZERO-G CONDITIONS IS DOWN HERE.
YEAH, I MET A FEW OF THOSE WEIRD KIDS A WHILE BACK.
LEVEL B'S BEEN RESERVED BY THE USDA FOR BOTANICAL RESEARCH.
SPECIFICALLY, A PLANT NATIVE TO YAMAPALU KNOWN AS THE GALLSABERRY.
ERADICATED ON LAND, IT NOW GROWS WILDLY ON THE OCEAN FLOOR SURROUNDING THE ISLAND.
SO SO HIGH.
IT TASTES LIKE CHICKEN...
...AND STARS.
OH, I'M WELL AWARE OF THE GALLSABERRY--
OF COURSE, THIS HAS CAUSED MAJOR PROBLEMS ON LEVEL C, WHERE THE US NAVY HAD BEEN CONDUCTING MARINE MAMMAL TRAINING AND RECONNAISSANCE OPERATIONS.
MOST OF THEIR DOLPHIN SQUADS ARE NOW EITHER AWOL...
...OR INSENSIBLE.
Chirt cheet chireep
--AND I'M WELL AWARE OF WHAT THE GALLSABERRY CAN DO.
AND THIS... WELL...
LEVEL D SUFFERED SOME SERIOUS STRUCTURAL DAMAGE A FEW MONTHS AGO.
WARNING!!
HAZARD!
CAREFUL!! WATER DOESN'T LIKE YOU!!
ALONG WITH A VISIT FROM POYO.
POYO!?! WHAT HAPPENED?

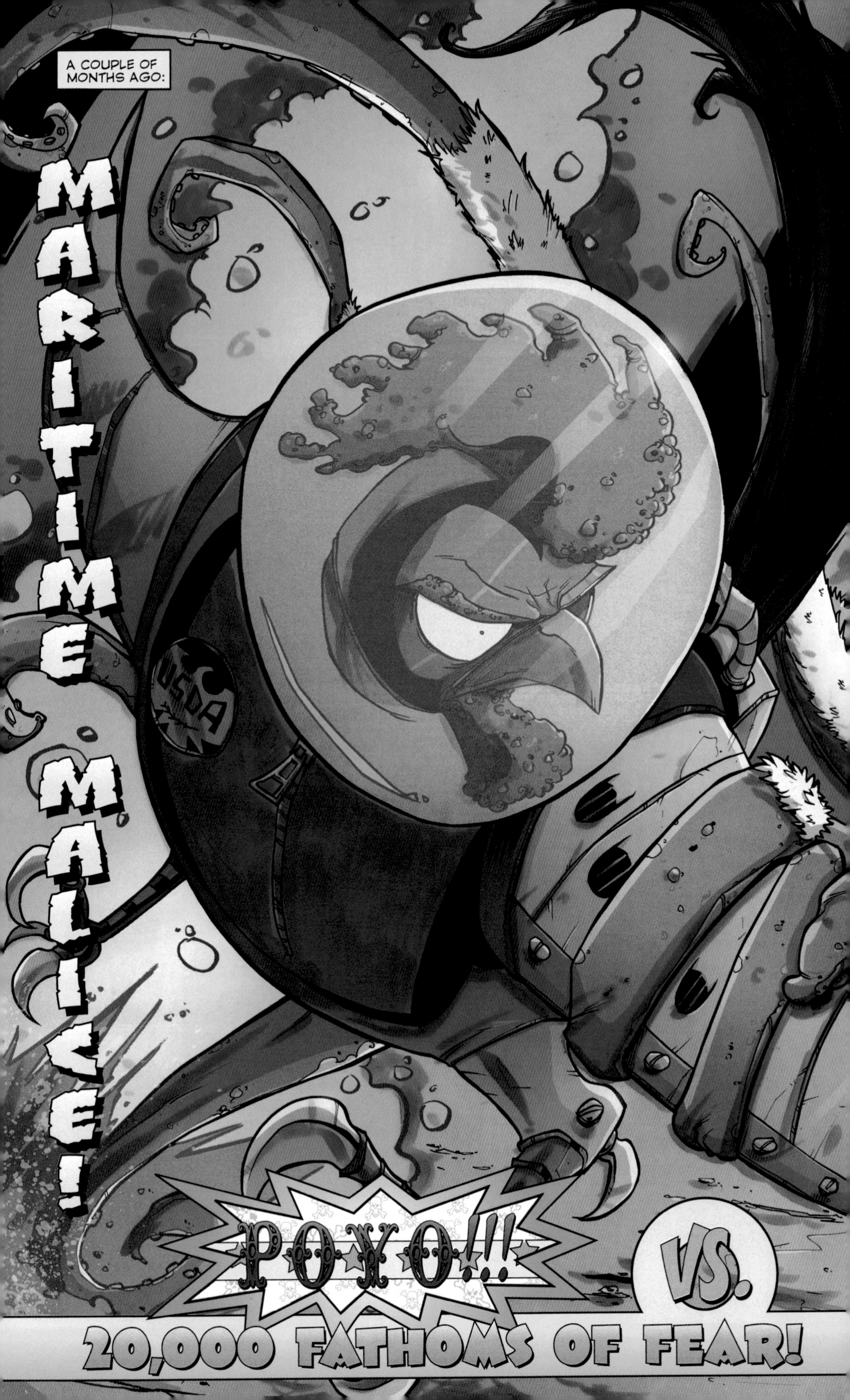
A COUPLE OF MONTHS AGO:
MARITIME MALICE!
USDA
POYO!!!
VS.
20,000 FATHOMS OF FEAR!

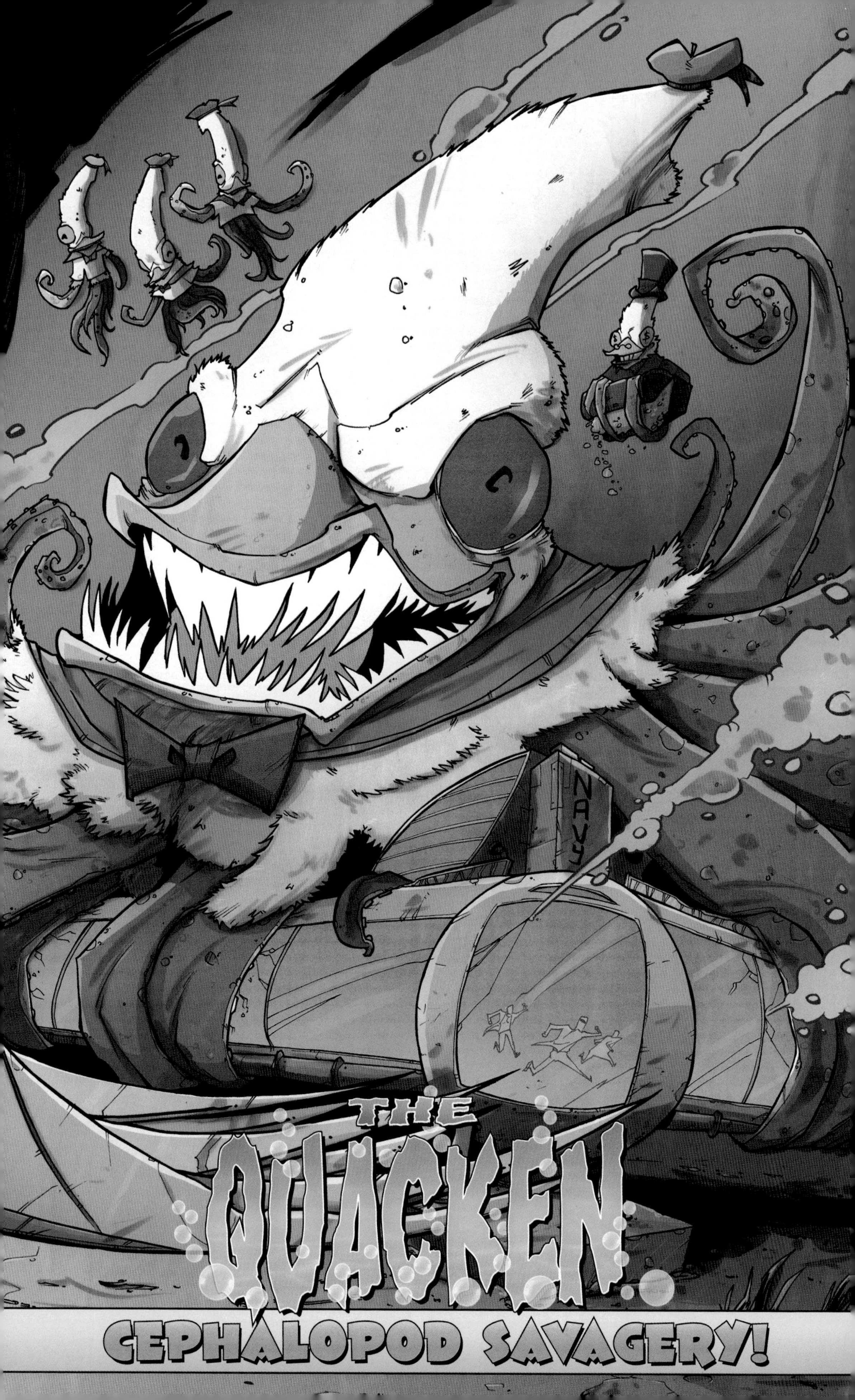
NAVY
THE
QUACKEN
CEPHALOPOD SAVAGERY!

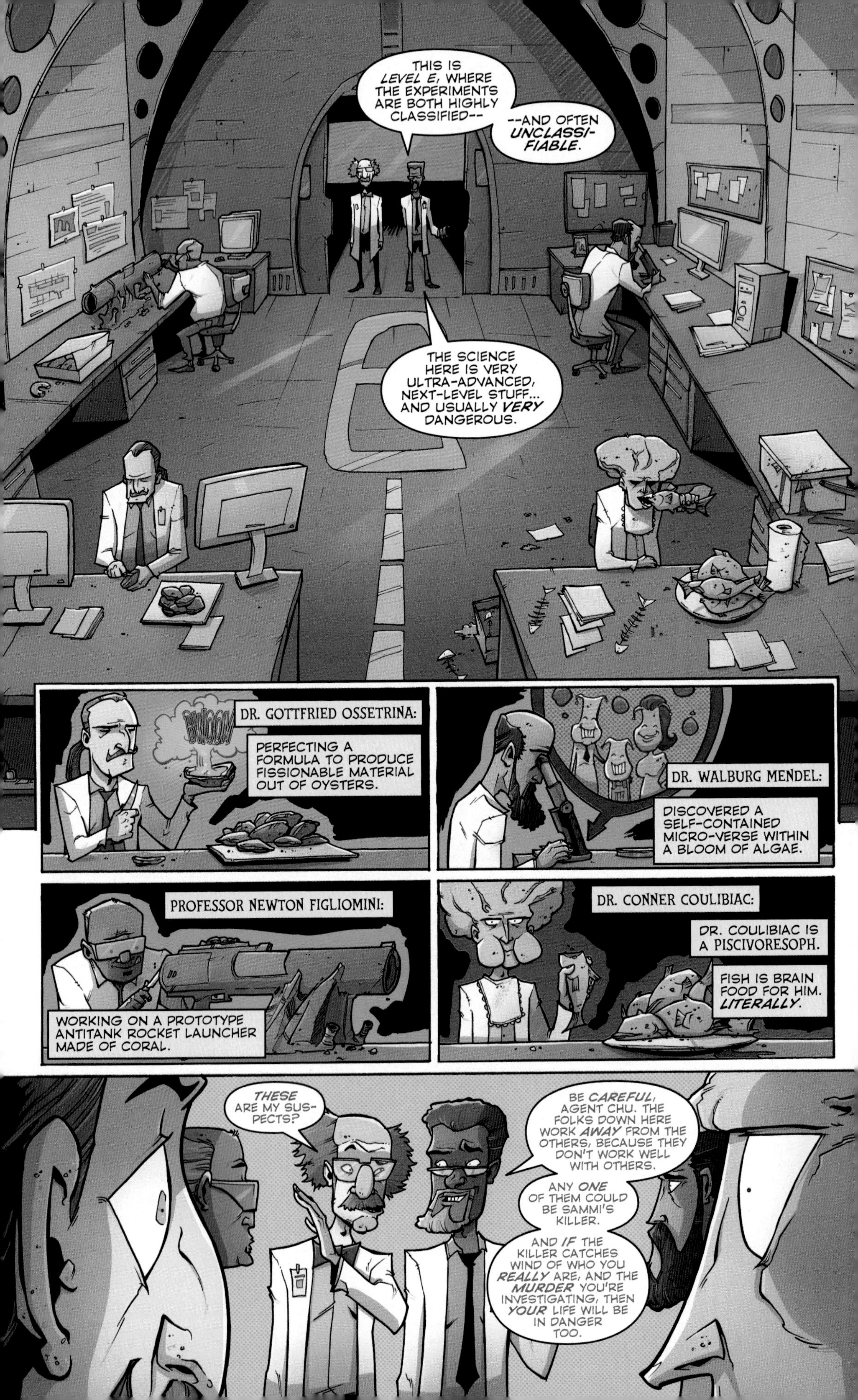
THIS IS LEVEL E, WHERE THE EXPERIMENTS ARE BOTH HIGHLY CLASSIFIED--
--AND OFTEN UNCLASSIFIABLE.
THE SCIENCE HERE IS VERY ULTRA-ADVANCED, NEXT-LEVEL STUFF... AND USUALLY VERY DANGEROUS.
DR. GOTTFRIED OSSETRINA:
BWOOM
PERFECTING A FORMULA TO PRODUCE FISSIONABLE MATERIAL OUT OF OYSTERS.
DR. WALBURG MENDEL:
DISCOVERED A SELF-CONTAINED MICRO-VERSE WITHIN A BLOOM OF ALGAE.
PROFESSOR NEWTON FIGLIOMINI:
WORKING ON A PROTOTYPE ANTITANK ROCKET LAUNCHER MADE OF CORAL.
DR. CONNER COULIBIAC:
DR. COULIBIAC IS A PISCIVORESOPH.
FISH IS BRAIN FOOD FOR HIM. LITERALLY.
THESE ARE MY SUSPECTS?
BE CAREFUL, AGENT CHU. THE FOLKS DOWN HERE WORK AWAY FROM THE OTHERS, BECAUSE THEY DON'T WORK WELL WITH OTHERS.
ANY ONE OF THEM COULD BE SAMMI'S KILLER.
AND IF THE KILLER CATCHES WIND OF WHO YOU REALLY ARE, AND THE MURDER YOU'RE INVESTIGATING, THEN YOUR LIFE WILL BE IN DANGER TOO.

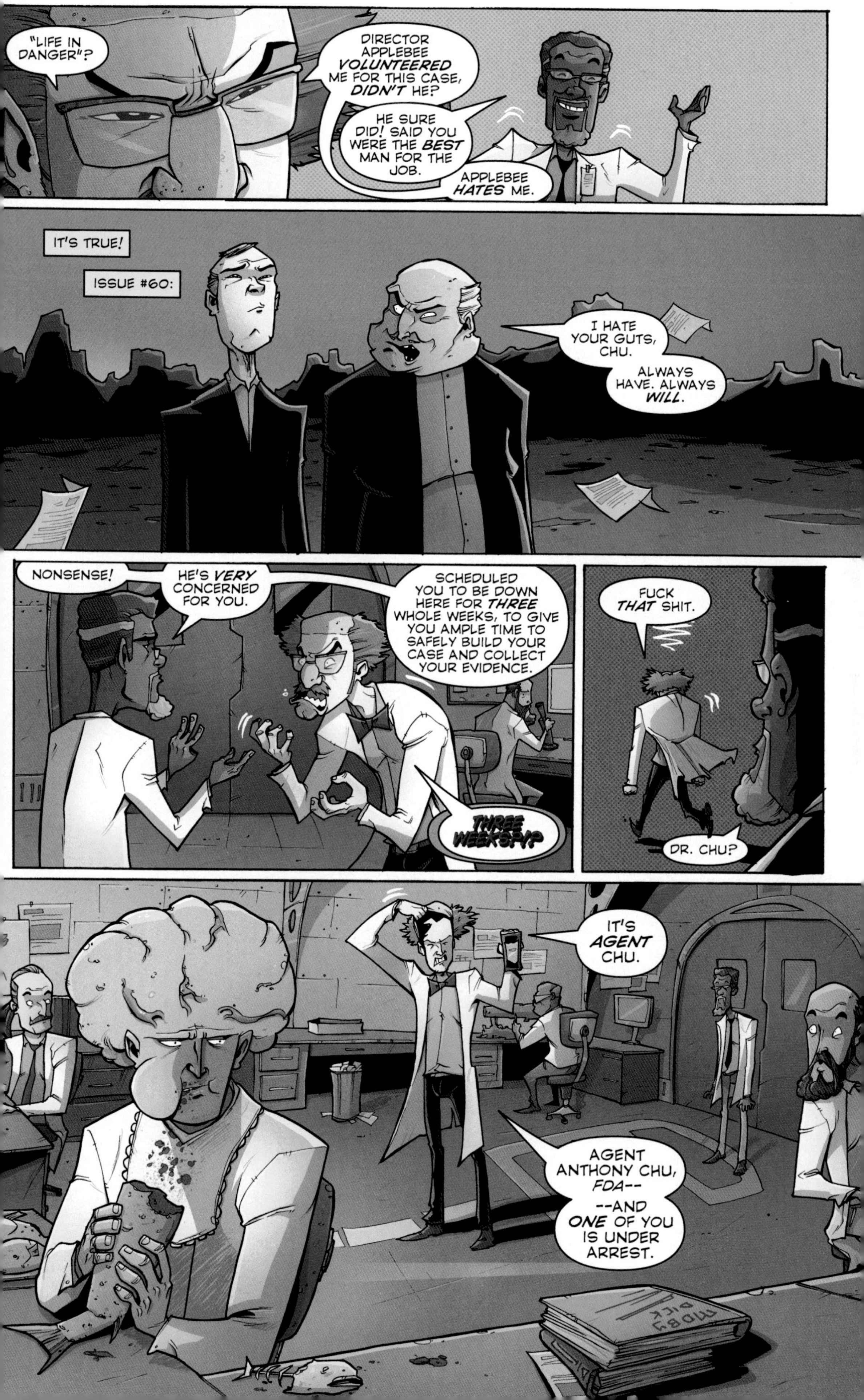
"LIFE IN DANGER"?
DIRECTOR APPLEBEE VOLUNTEERED ME FOR THIS CASE, DIDN'T HE?
HE SURE DID! SAID YOU WERE THE BEST MAN FOR THE JOB.
APPLEBEE HATES ME.
IT'S TRUE!
ISSUE #60:
I HATE YOUR GUTS, CHU.
ALWAYS HAVE. ALWAYS WILL.
NONSENSE!
HE'S VERY CONCERNED FOR YOU.
SCHEDULED YOU TO BE DOWN HERE FOR THREE WHOLE WEEKS, TO GIVE YOU AMPLE TIME TO SAFELY BUILD YOUR CASE AND COLLECT YOUR EVIDENCE.
THREE WEEKS?!?
FUCK THAT SHIT.
DR. CHU?
IT'S AGENT CHU.
AGENT ANTHONY CHU, FDA--
--AND ONE OF YOU IS UNDER ARREST.
MOBY DICK

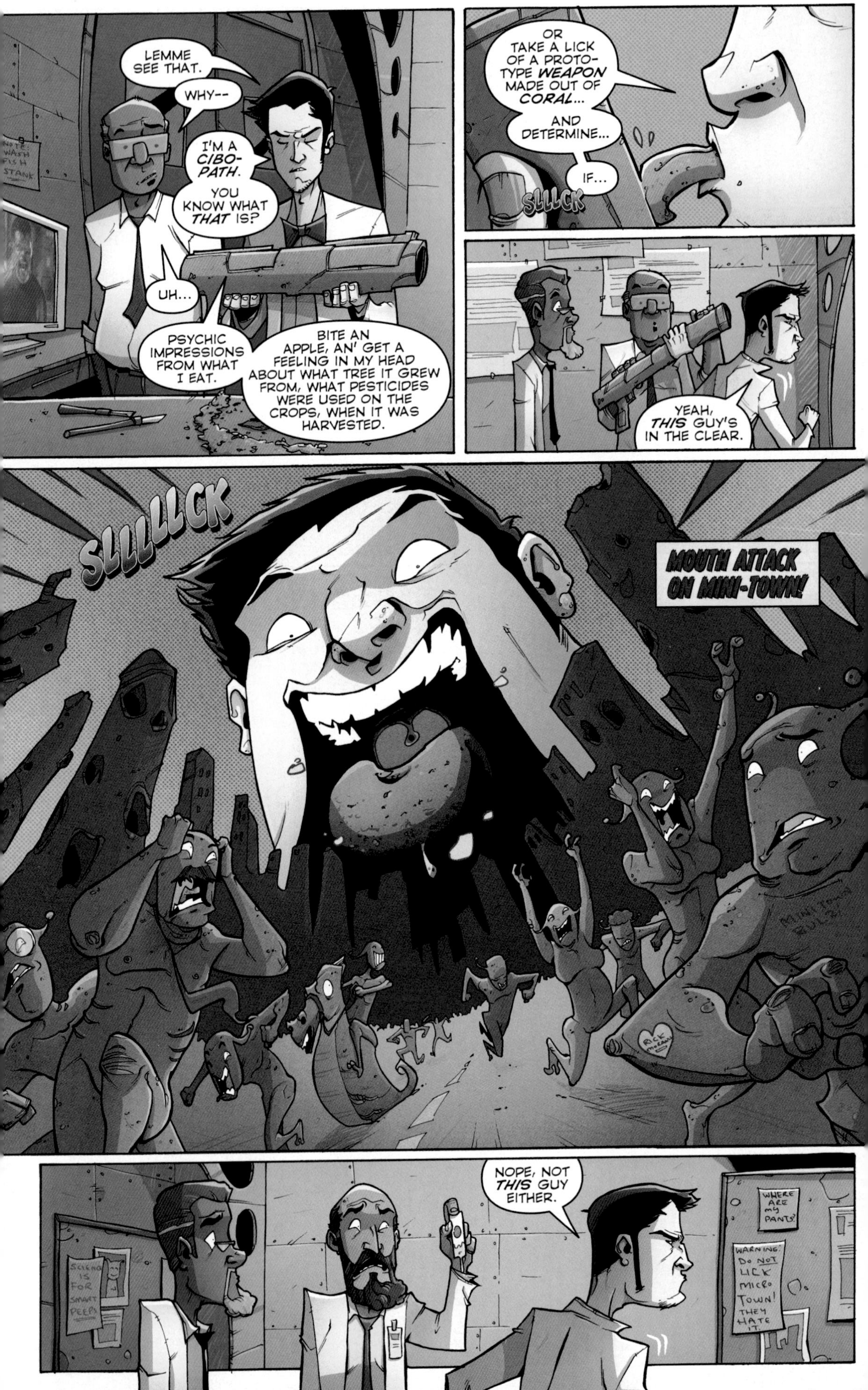
LEMME SEE THAT.
WHY--
I'M A *CIBO-PATH*.
YOU KNOW WHAT *THAT* IS?
UH...
PSYCHIC IMPRESSIONS FROM WHAT I EAT.
BITE AN APPLE, AN' GET A FEELING IN MY HEAD ABOUT WHAT TREE IT GREW FROM, WHAT PESTICIDES WERE USED ON THE CROPS, WHEN IT WAS HARVESTED.
NOTE: WASH FISH STANK
OR TAKE A LICK OF A PROTO-TYPE *WEAPON* MADE OUT OF *CORAL*...
AND DETERMINE...
IF...
SLLLCK
YEAH, *THIS* GUY'S IN THE CLEAR.
SLLLLLCK
MOUTH ATTACK ON MINI-TOWN!
NOPE, NOT *THIS* GUY EITHER.
SCIENCE IS FOR SMART PEEPS
WHERE ARE my PANTS?
WARNING: DO NOT LICK MICRO TOWN! THEY HATE IT.

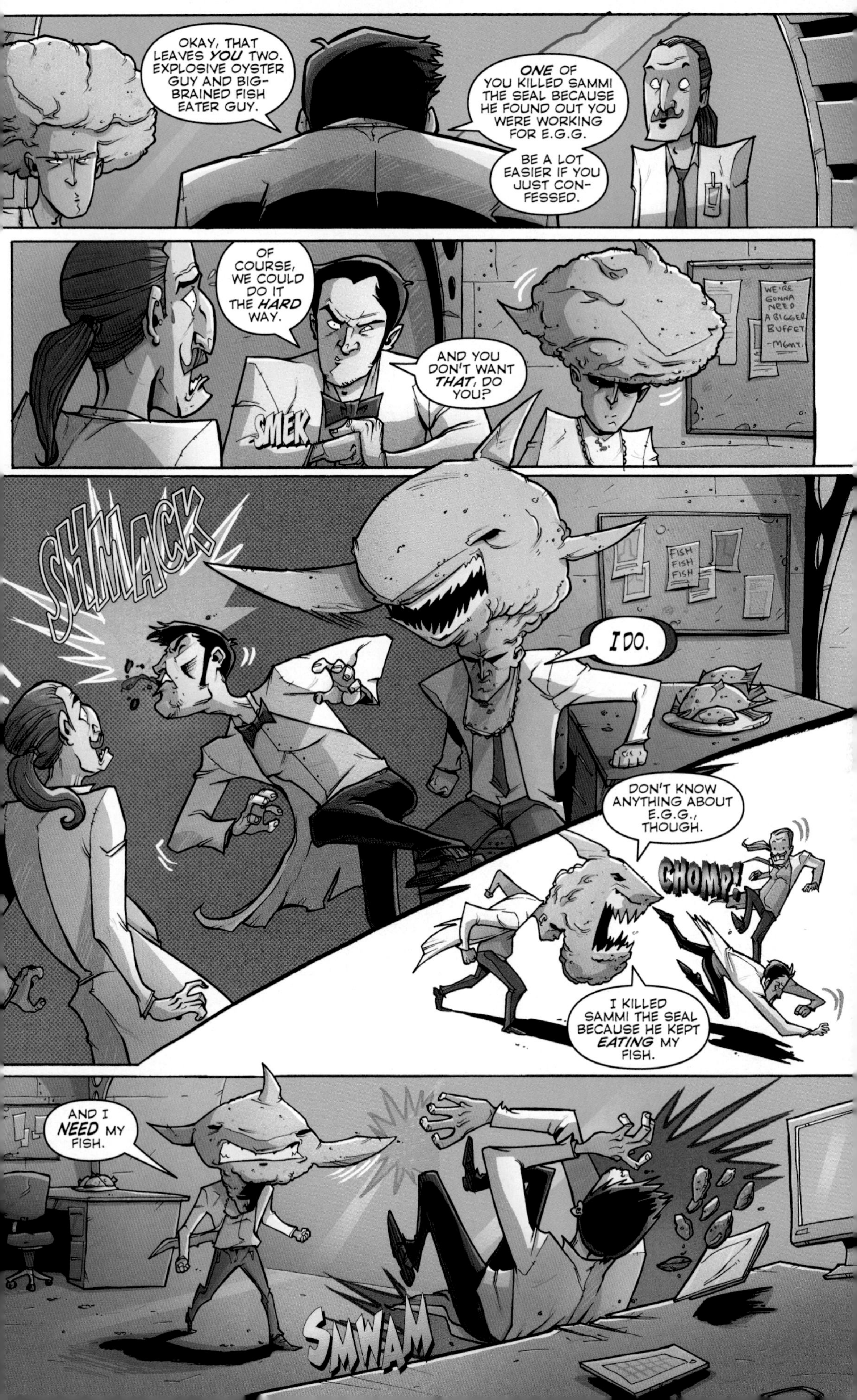
OKAY, THAT LEAVES YOU TWO. EXPLOSIVE OYSTER GUY AND BIG-BRAINED FISH EATER GUY.
ONE OF YOU KILLED SAMMI THE SEAL BECAUSE HE FOUND OUT YOU WERE WORKING FOR E.G.G.
BE A LOT EASIER IF YOU JUST CONFESSED.
OF COURSE, WE COULD DO IT THE HARD WAY.
AND YOU DON'T WANT THAT, DO YOU?
SMEK
WE'RE GONNA NEED A BIGGER BUFFET. -MGMT.
SHMACK
FISH FISH FISH
I DO.
DON'T KNOW ANYTHING ABOUT E.G.G., THOUGH.
CHOMP!
I KILLED SAMMI THE SEAL BECAUSE HE KEPT EATING MY FISH.
AND I NEED MY FISH.
SMWAM

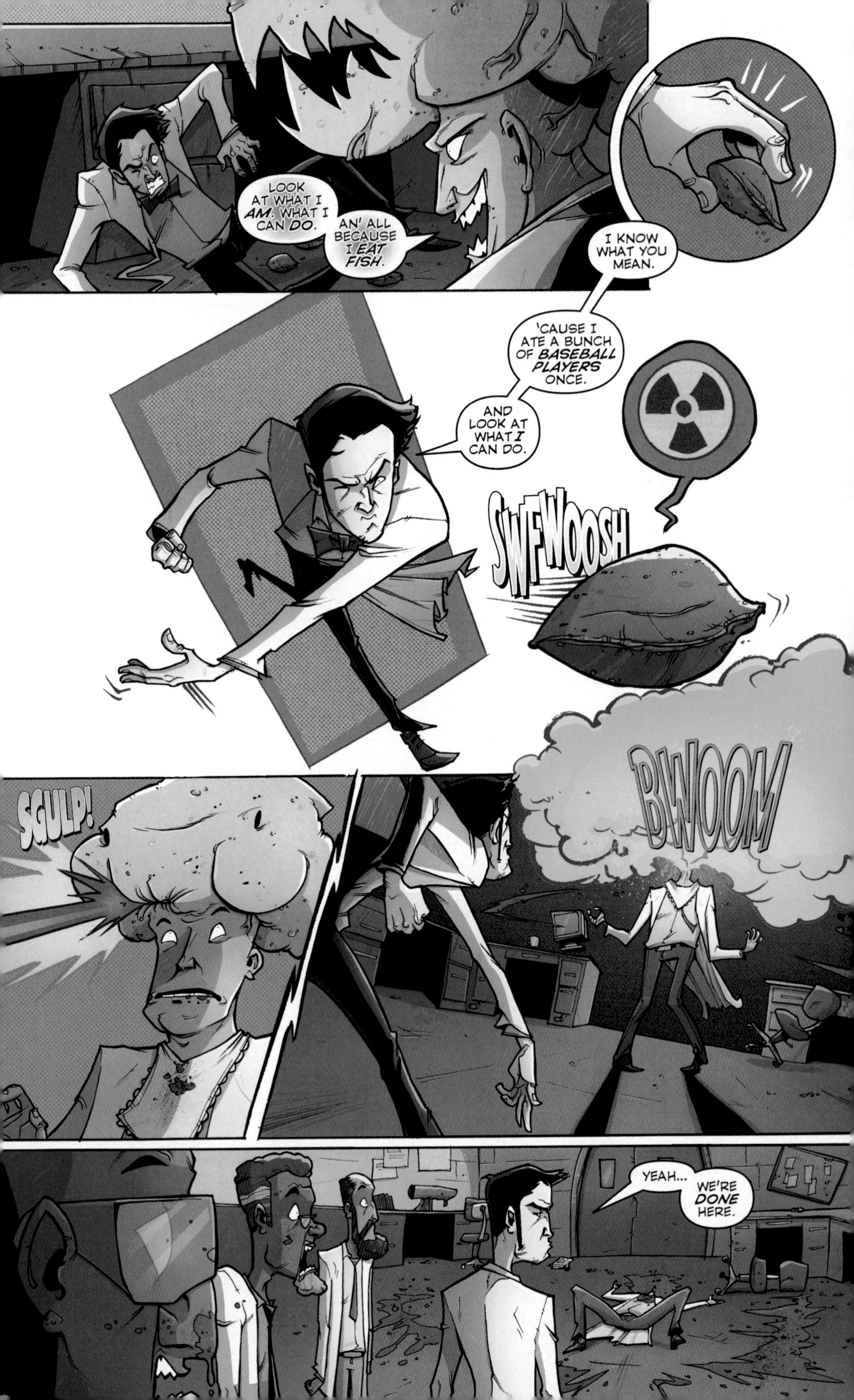
LOOK AT WHAT I AM. WHAT I CAN DO.
AN' ALL BECAUSE I EAT FISH.
I KNOW WHAT YOU MEAN.
'CAUSE I ATE A BUNCH OF BASEBALL PLAYERS ONCE.
AND LOOK AT WHAT I CAN DO.
SWFWOOSH
SGULP!
BWOOM
YEAH...
WE'RE DONE HERE.

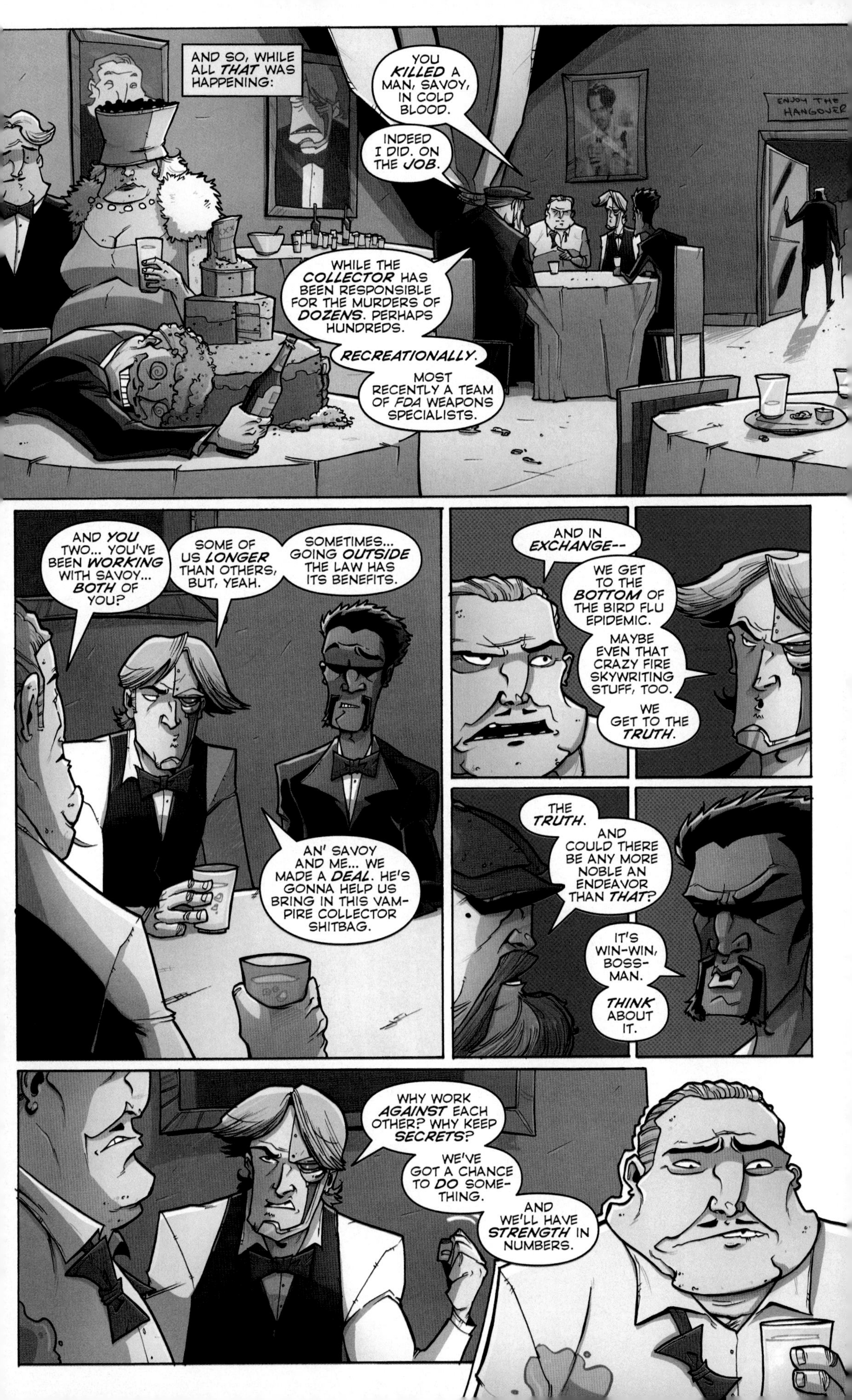
AND SO, WHILE ALL THAT WAS HAPPENING:
YOU KILLED A MAN, SAVOY, IN COLD BLOOD.
INDEED I DID. ON THE JOB.
ENJOY THE HANGOVER
WHILE THE COLLECTOR HAS BEEN RESPONSIBLE FOR THE MURDERS OF DOZENS. PERHAPS HUNDREDS.
RECREATIONALLY.
MOST RECENTLY A TEAM OF FDA WEAPONS SPECIALISTS.
AND YOU TWO... YOU'VE BEEN WORKING WITH SAVOY... BOTH OF YOU?
SOME OF US LONGER THAN OTHERS, BUT, YEAH.
SOMETIMES... GOING OUTSIDE THE LAW HAS ITS BENEFITS.
AN' SAVOY AND ME... WE MADE A DEAL. HE'S GONNA HELP US BRING IN THIS VAMPIRE COLLECTOR SHITBAG.
AND IN EXCHANGE--
WE GET TO THE BOTTOM OF THE BIRD FLU EPIDEMIC.
MAYBE EVEN THAT CRAZY FIRE SKYWRITING STUFF, TOO.
WE GET TO THE TRUTH.
THE TRUTH.
AND COULD THERE BE ANY MORE NOBLE AN ENDEAVOR THAN THAT?
IT'S WIN-WIN, BOSS-MAN.
THINK ABOUT IT.
WHY WORK AGAINST EACH OTHER? WHY KEEP SECRETS?
WE'VE GOT A CHANCE TO DO SOME-THING.
AND WE'LL HAVE STRENGTH IN NUMBERS.

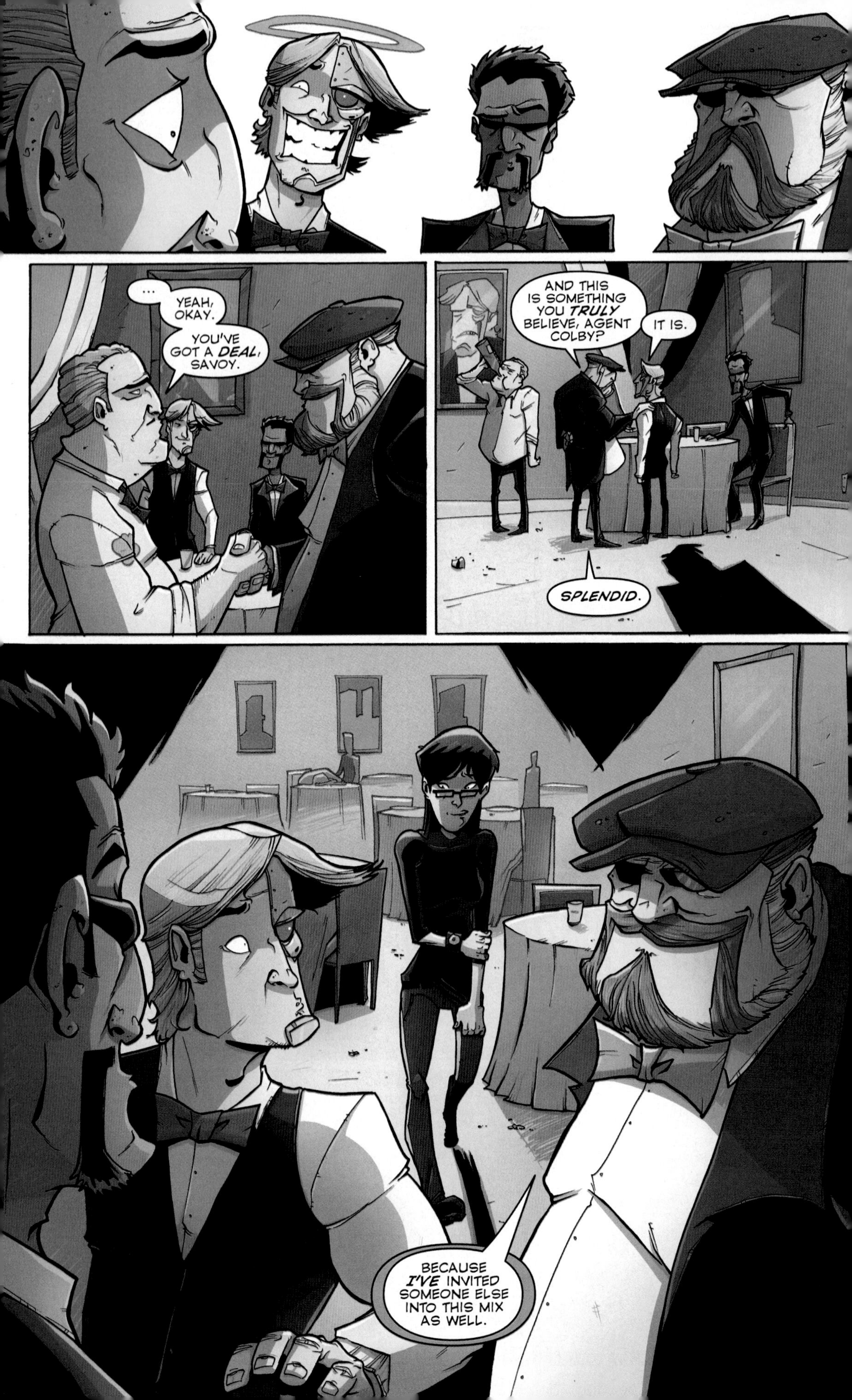
...
YEAH, OKAY.
YOU'VE GOT A DEAL, SAVOY.
AND THIS IS SOMETHING YOU TRULY BELIEVE, AGENT COLBY?
IT IS.
SPLENDID.
BECAUSE I'VE INVITED SOMEONE ELSE INTO THIS MIX AS WELL.

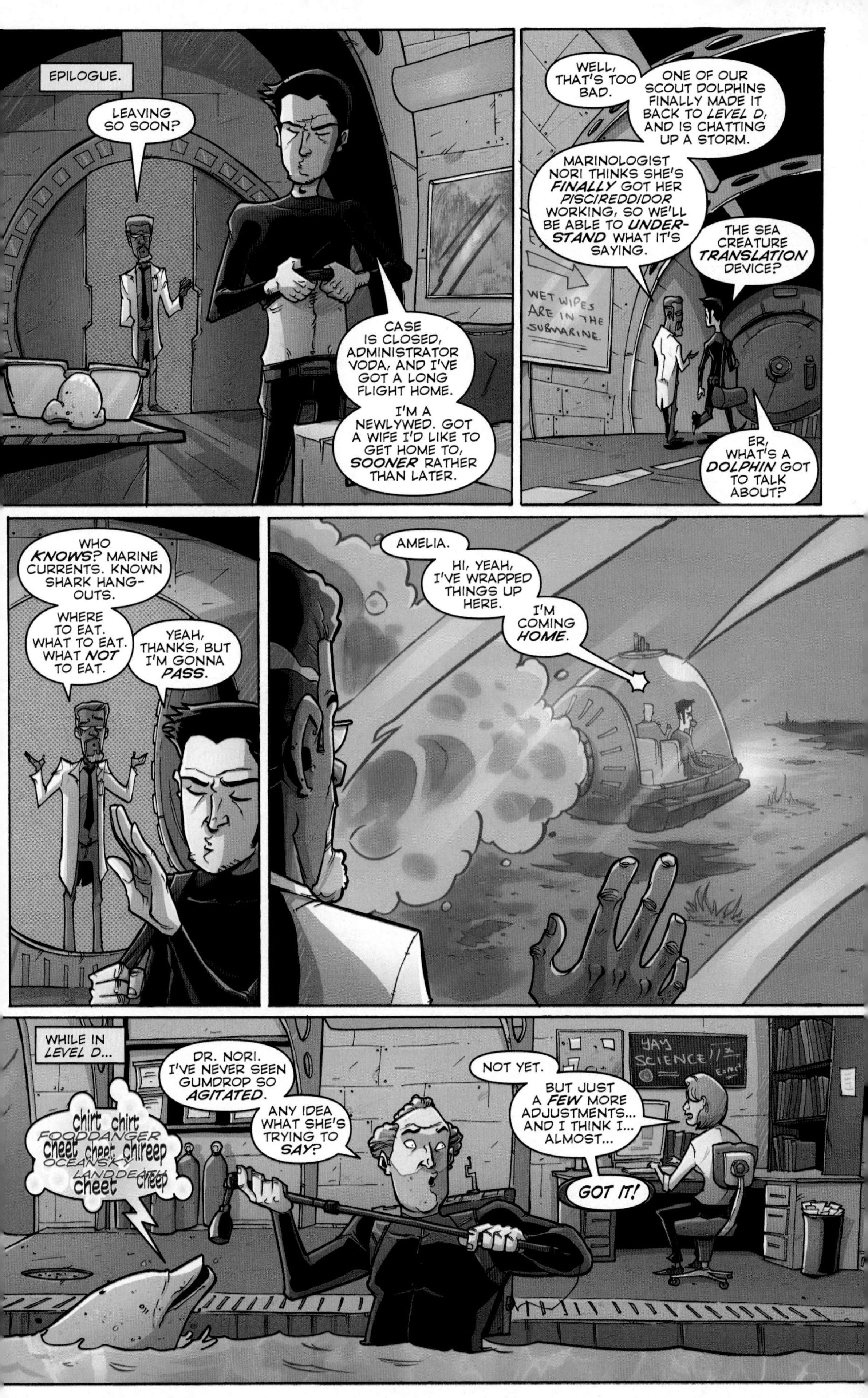
EPILOGUE.
LEAVING SO SOON?
CASE IS CLOSED, ADMINISTRATOR VODA, AND I'VE GOT A LONG FLIGHT HOME.
I'M A NEWLYWED. GOT A WIFE I'D LIKE TO GET HOME TO, *SOONER* RATHER THAN LATER.
WELL, THAT'S TOO BAD.
ONE OF OUR SCOUT DOLPHINS FINALLY MADE IT BACK TO *LEVEL D*, AND IS CHATTING UP A STORM.
MARINOLOGIST NORI THINKS SHE'S *FINALLY* GOT HER *PISCIREDDIDOR* WORKING, SO WE'LL BE ABLE TO *UNDERSTAND* WHAT IT'S SAYING.
WET WIPES ARE IN THE SUBMARINE.
THE SEA CREATURE *TRANSLATION* DEVICE?
ER, WHAT'S A *DOLPHIN* GOT TO TALK ABOUT?
WHO *KNOWS?* MARINE CURRENTS. KNOWN SHARK HANG-OUTS.
WHERE TO EAT. WHAT TO EAT. WHAT *NOT* TO EAT.
YEAH, THANKS, BUT I'M GONNA *PASS*.
AMELIA.
HI, YEAH, I'VE WRAPPED THINGS UP HERE.
I'M COMING *HOME*.
WHILE IN *LEVEL D*...
chirt chirt FOODDANGER cheet cheet chireep OCEANSKY LANDDEATH cheet cheep
DR. NORI. I'VE NEVER SEEN GUMDROP SO *AGITATED*.
ANY IDEA WHAT SHE'S TRYING TO *SAY*?
YAY SCIENCE!!
NOT YET.
BUT JUST A *FEW* MORE ADJUSTMENTS... AND I THINK I... ALMOST...
GOT IT!

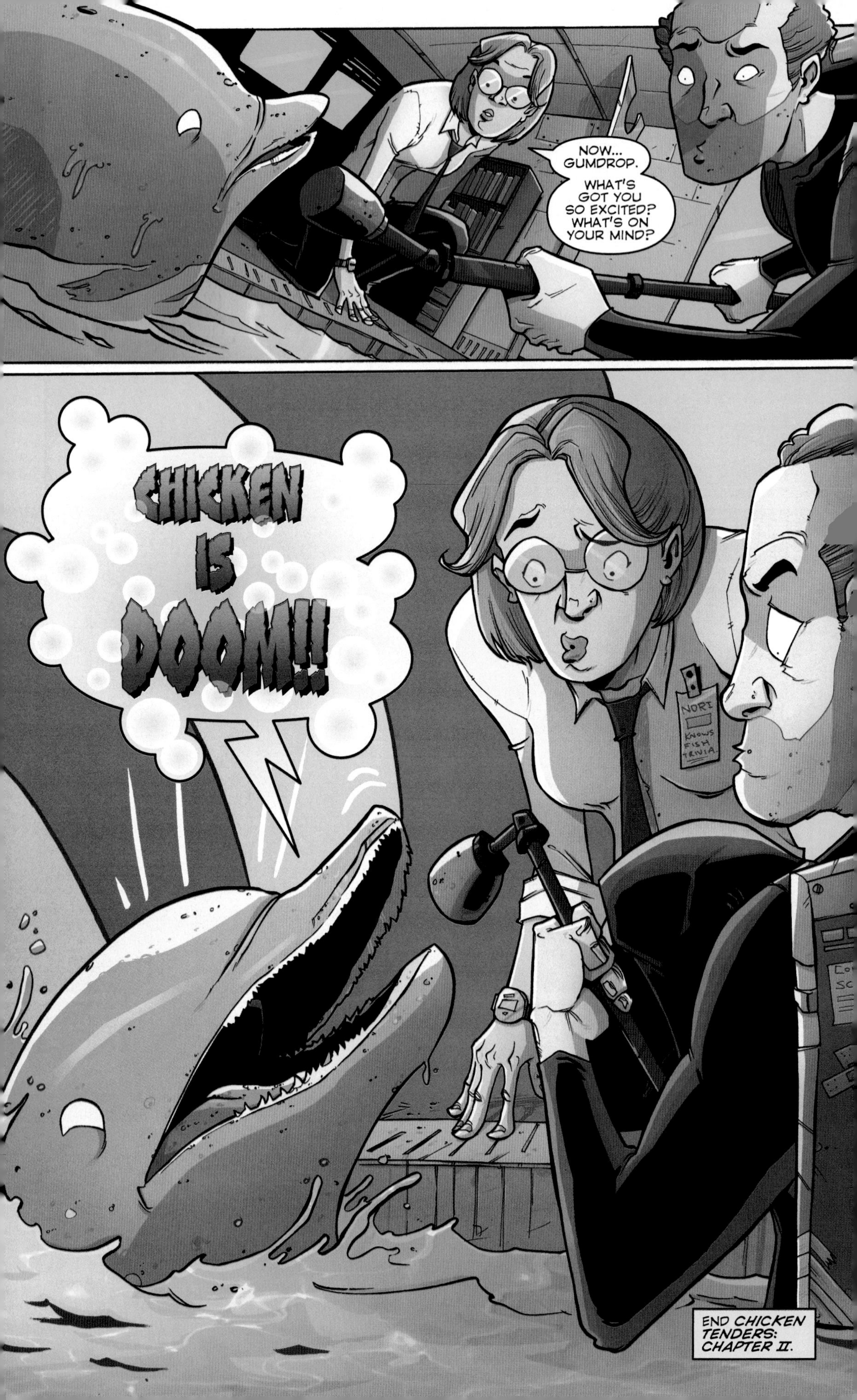
NOW... GUMDROP.
WHAT'S GOT YOU SO EXCITED? WHAT'S ON YOUR MIND?
CHICKEN IS DOOM!!
NORI KNOWS FISH TRIVIA
END CHICKEN TENDERS: CHAPTER II.

Interlude

Rob!

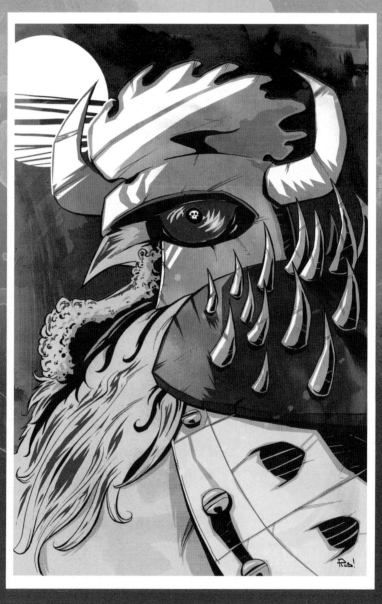

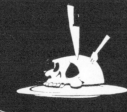

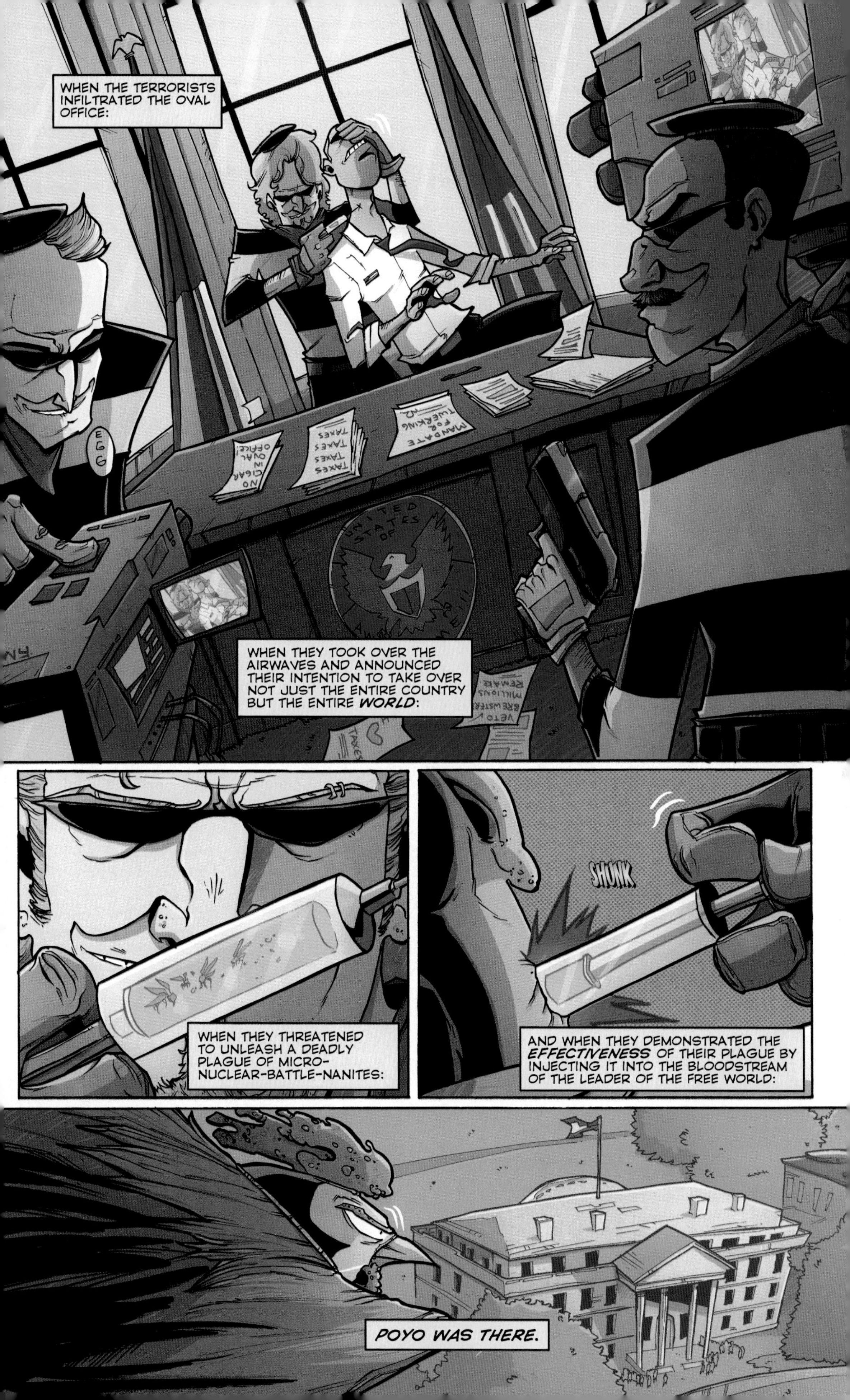
WHEN THE TERRORISTS INFILTRATED THE OVAL OFFICE:
EGG
NO CIGAR IN OVAL OFFICE!
TAXES TAXES TAXES
MANDATE FOR TWERKING
UNITED STATES OF
WHEN THEY TOOK OVER THE AIRWAVES AND ANNOUNCED THEIR INTENTION TO TAKE OVER NOT JUST THE ENTIRE COUNTRY BUT THE ENTIRE *WORLD*:
WHEN THEY THREATENED TO UNLEASH A DEADLY PLAGUE OF MICRO-NUCLEAR-BATTLE-NANITES:
SHUNK
AND WHEN THEY DEMONSTRATED THE *EFFECTIVENESS* OF THEIR PLAGUE BY INJECTING IT INTO THE BLOODSTREAM OF THE LEADER OF THE FREE WORLD:
POYO WAS THERE.

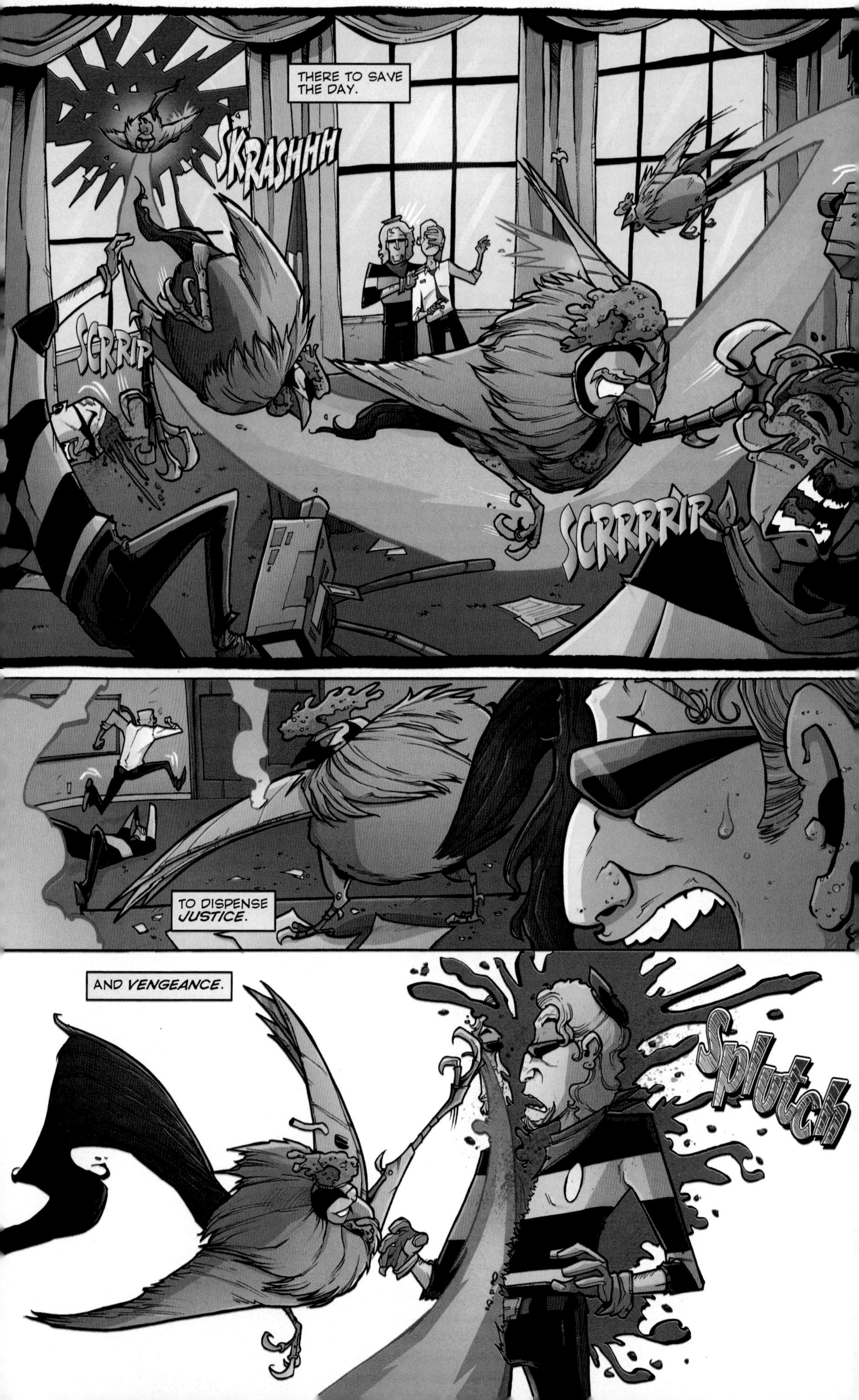
THERE TO SAVE THE DAY.
SKRASHHH
SCRRIP
SCRRRRIP
TO DISPENSE *JUSTICE*.
AND *VENGEANCE*.
Splutch

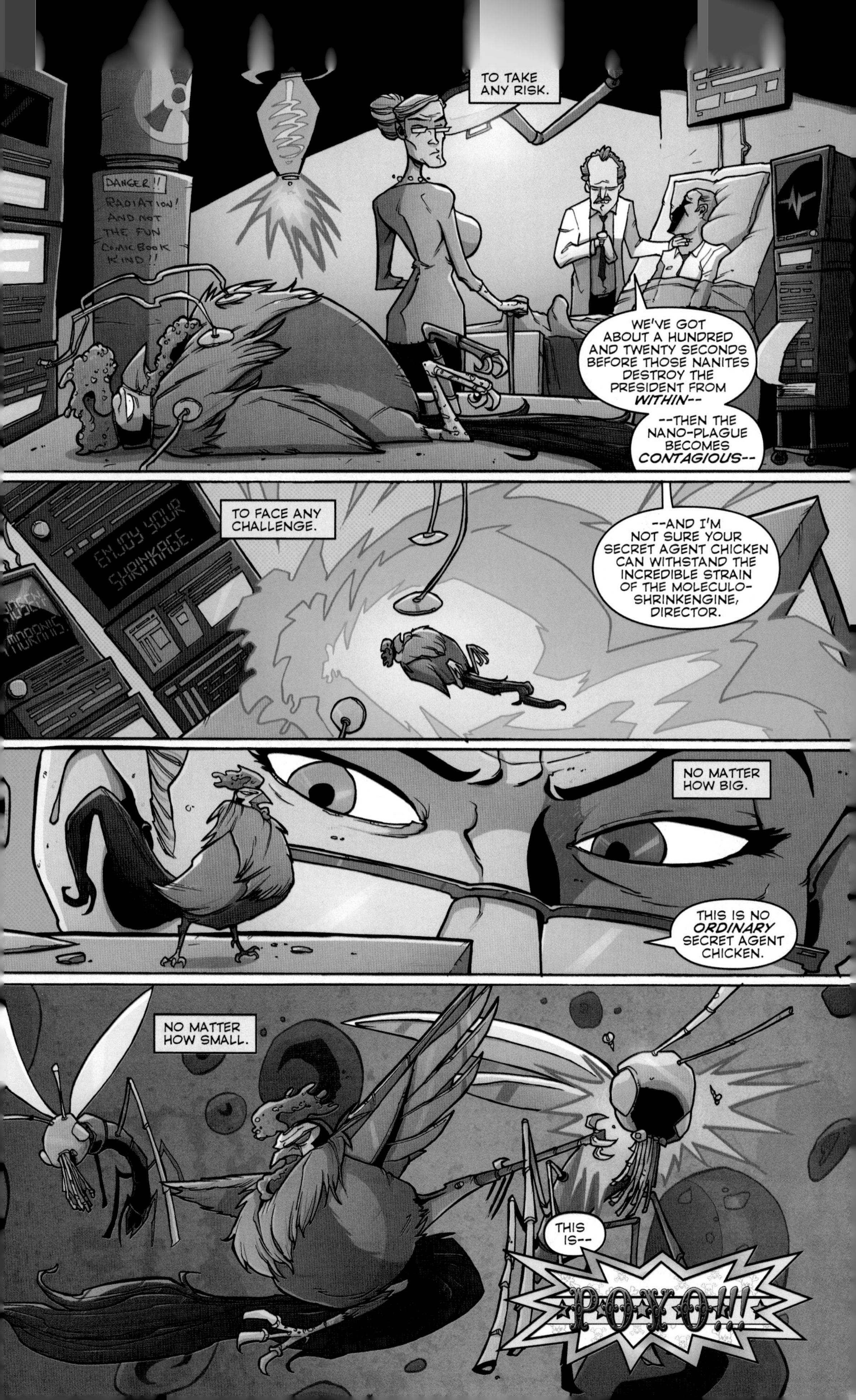
TO TAKE ANY RISK.
DANGER!! RADIATION! AND NOT THE FUN COMICBOOK KIND!!
WE'VE GOT ABOUT A HUNDRED AND TWENTY SECONDS BEFORE THOSE NANITES DESTROY THE PRESIDENT FROM *WITHIN*--
--THEN THE NANO-PLAGUE BECOMES *CONTAGIOUS*--
TO FACE ANY CHALLENGE.
ENJOY YOUR SHRINKAGE.
--AND I'M NOT SURE YOUR SECRET AGENT CHICKEN CAN WITHSTAND THE INCREDIBLE STRAIN OF THE MOLECULO-SHRINKENGINE, DIRECTOR.
NO MATTER HOW BIG.
THIS IS NO *ORDINARY* SECRET AGENT CHICKEN.
NO MATTER HOW SMALL.
THIS IS--
POYO!!!

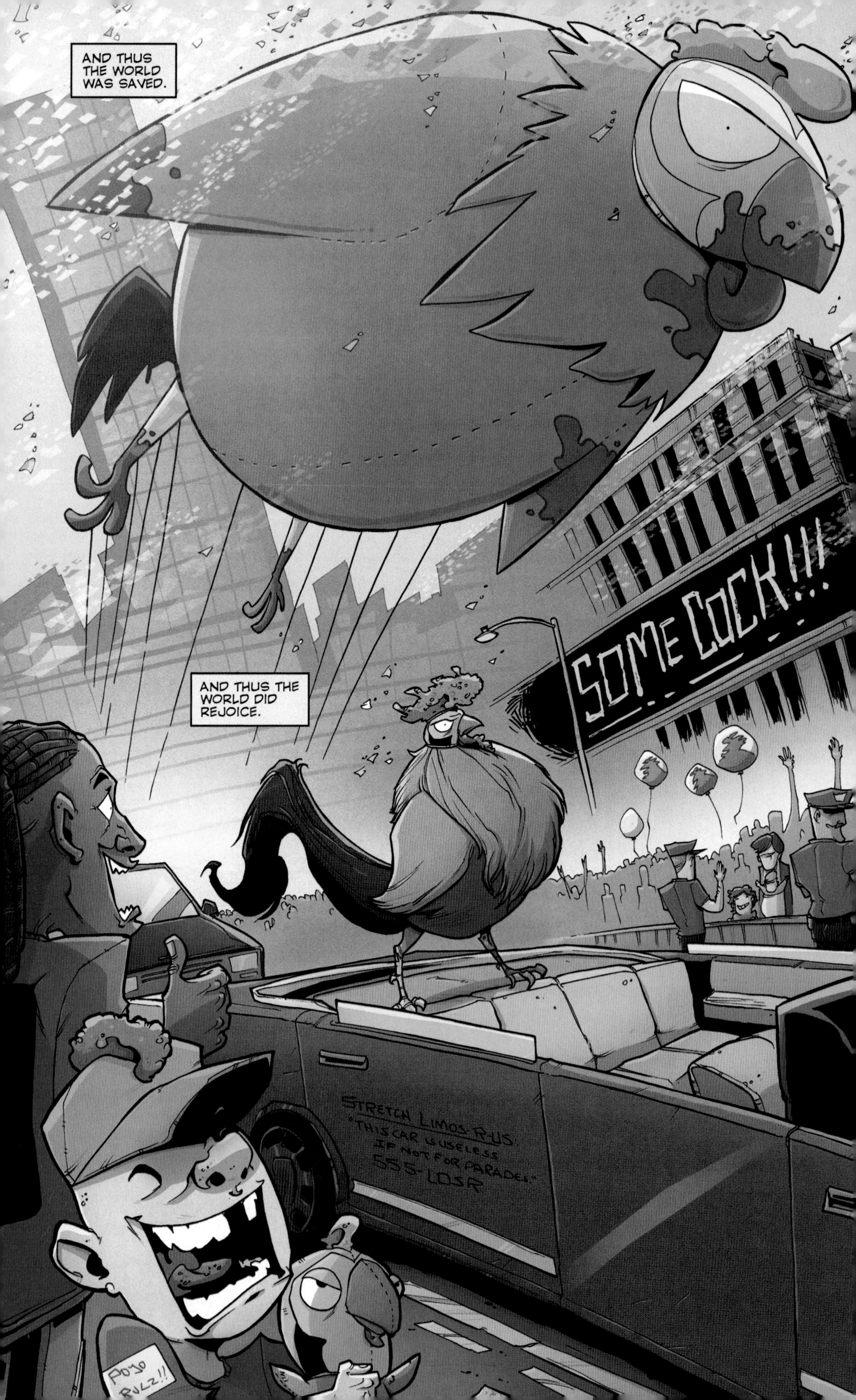
AND THUS THE WORLD WAS SAVED.
SOME COCK!!!
AND THUS THE WORLD DID REJOICE.
STRETCH LIMOS-R-US
"THIS CAR IS USELESS IF NOT FOR PARADES."
555-LOSR
POJO RULZ!!

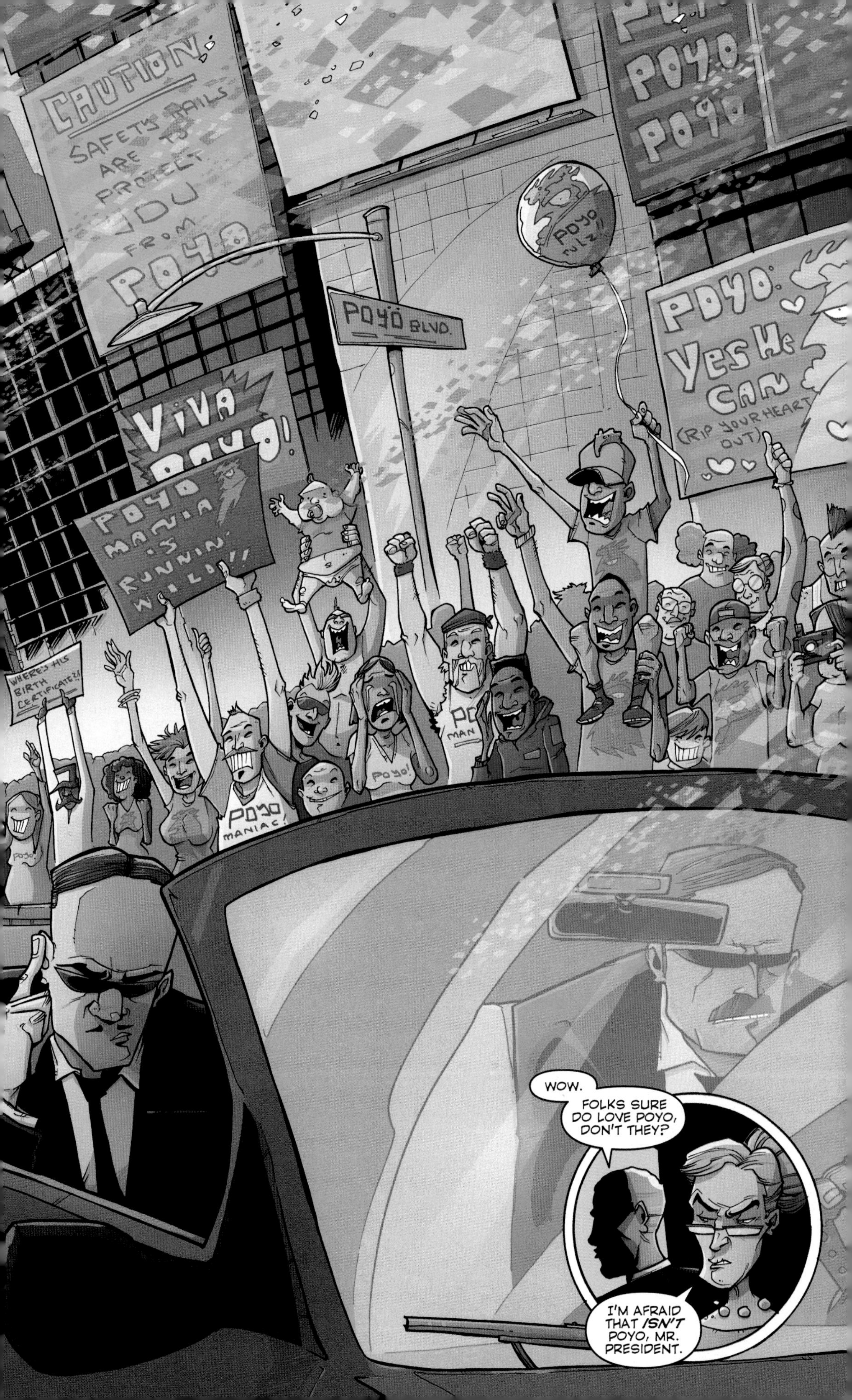
CAUTION
SAFETY RAILS ARE TO PROTECT YOU FROM POYO
POYO
POYO
POYO BLVD.
POYO RULZ!!
POYO: YES HE CAN (RIP YOUR HEART OUT)
VIVA
POYO MANIA IS RUNNIN' WILD!!
WHERE'S HIS BIRTH CERTIFICATE?!!
POYO MANIAC!
POYO!
WOW.
FOLKS SURE DO LOVE POYO, DON'T THEY?
I'M AFRAID THAT *ISN'T* POYO, MR. PRESIDENT.

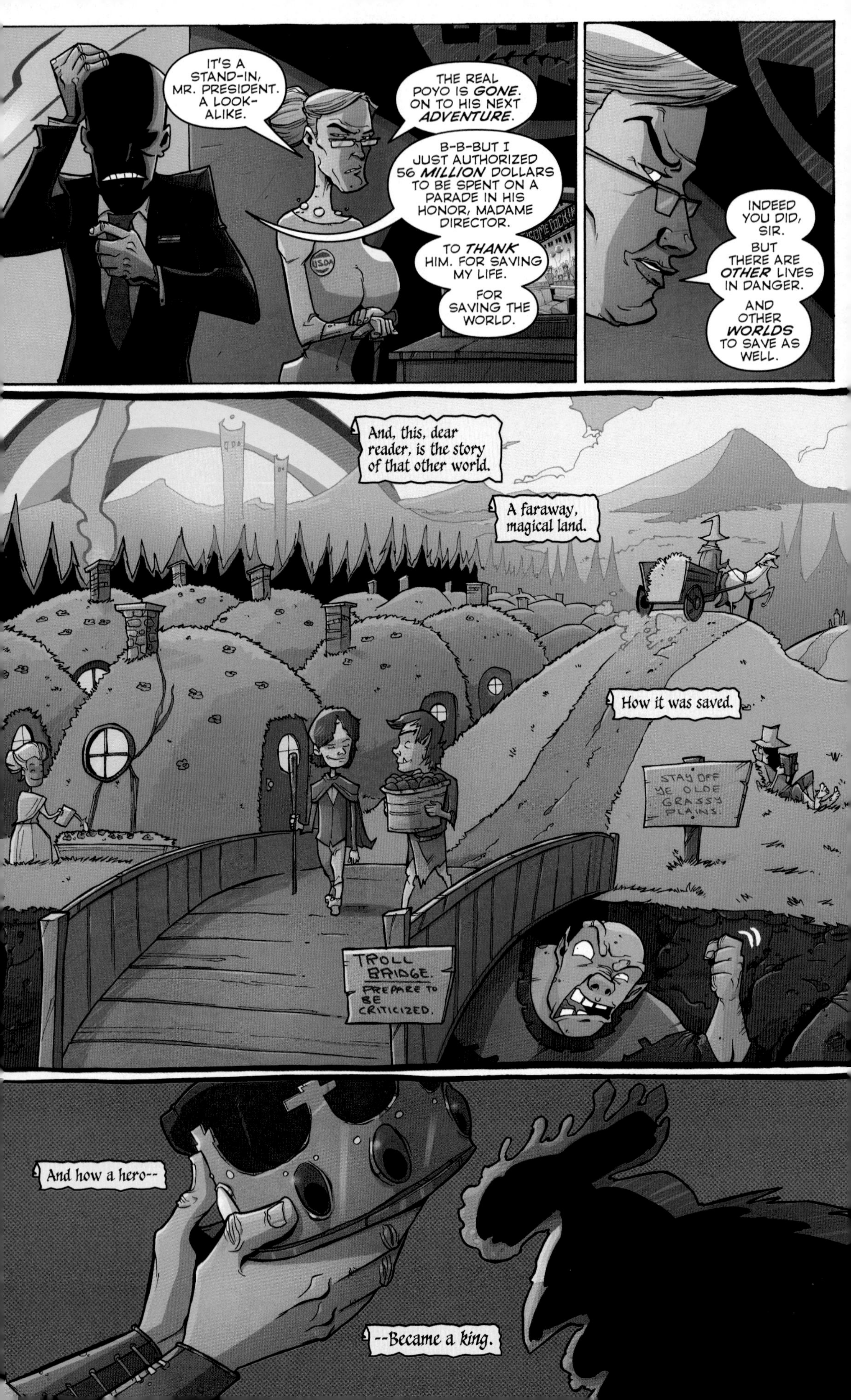

IT'S A STAND-IN, MR. PRESIDENT. A LOOK-ALIKE.
THE REAL POYO IS GONE. ON TO HIS NEXT ADVENTURE.
B-B-BUT I JUST AUTHORIZED 56 MILLION DOLLARS TO BE SPENT ON A PARADE IN HIS HONOR, MADAME DIRECTOR.
TO THANK HIM. FOR SAVING MY LIFE.
FOR SAVING THE WORLD.
INDEED YOU DID, SIR.
BUT THERE ARE OTHER LIVES IN DANGER.
AND OTHER WORLDS TO SAVE AS WELL.
And, this, dear reader, is the story of that other world.
A faraway, magical land.
How it was saved.
STAY OFF YE OLDE GRASSY PLAINS.
TROLL BRIDGE. PREPARE TO BE CRITICIZED.
And how a hero--
--Became a king.

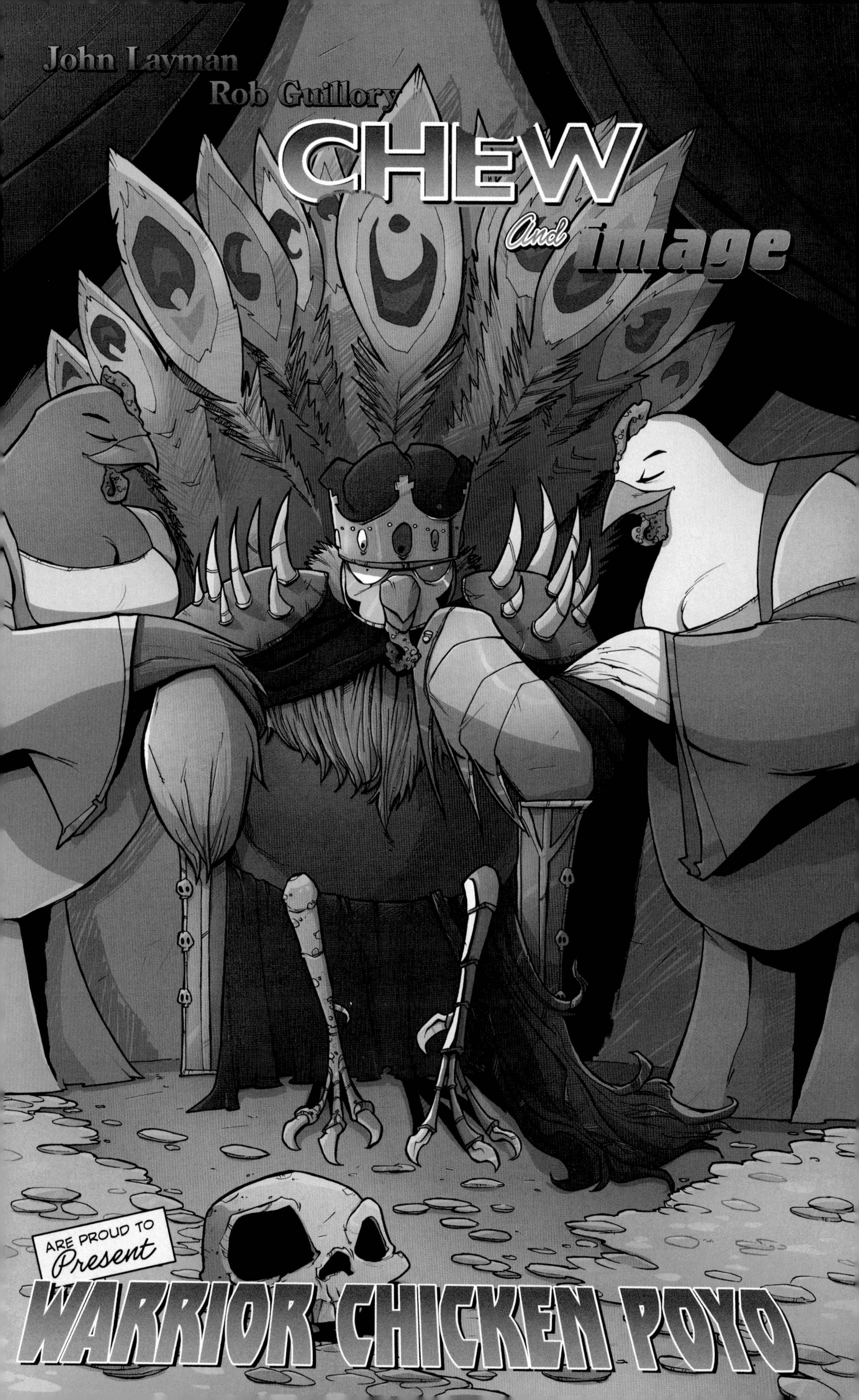
John Layman
Rob Guillory
CHEW
And image
ARE PROUD TO Present
WARRIOR CHICKEN POYO

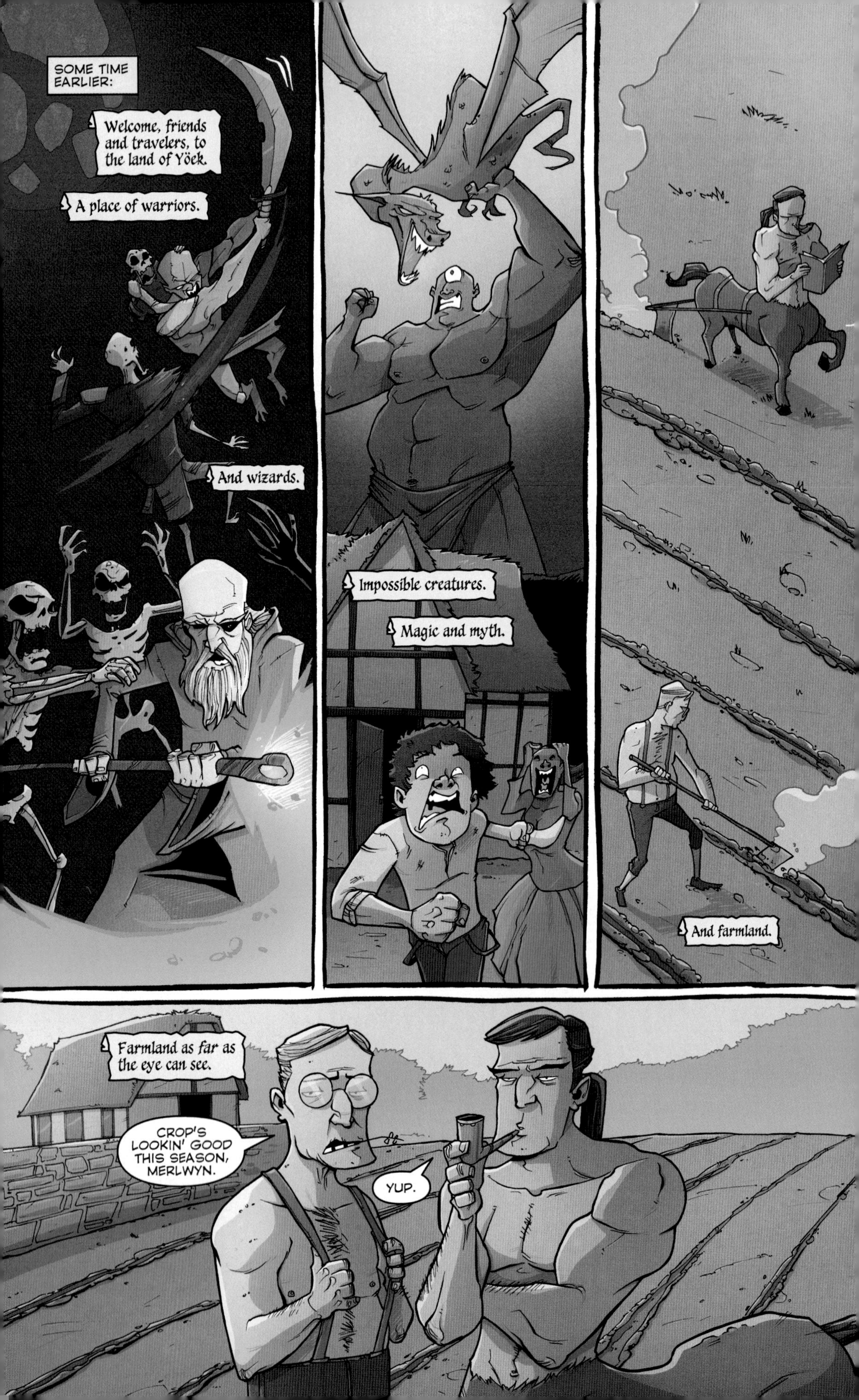
SOME TIME EARLIER:
Welcome, friends and travelers, to the land of Yöek.
A place of warriors.
And wizards.
Impossible creatures.
Magic and myth.
And farmland.
Farmland as far as the eye can see.
CROP'S LOOKIN' GOOD THIS SEASON, MERLWYN.
YUP.

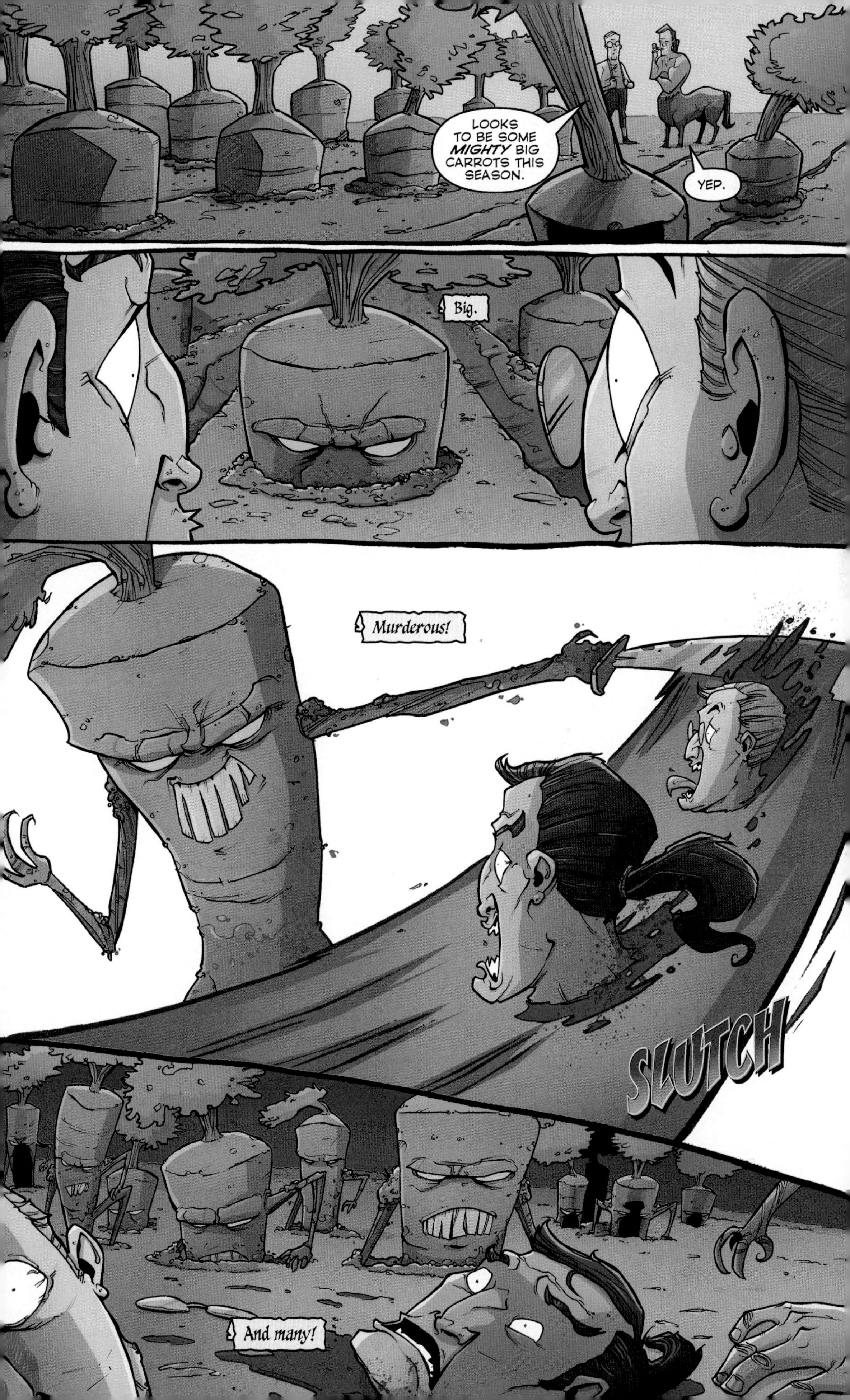
LOOKS TO BE SOME *MIGHTY* BIG CARROTS THIS SEASON.
YEP.
Big.
Murderous!
SLUTCH
And many!

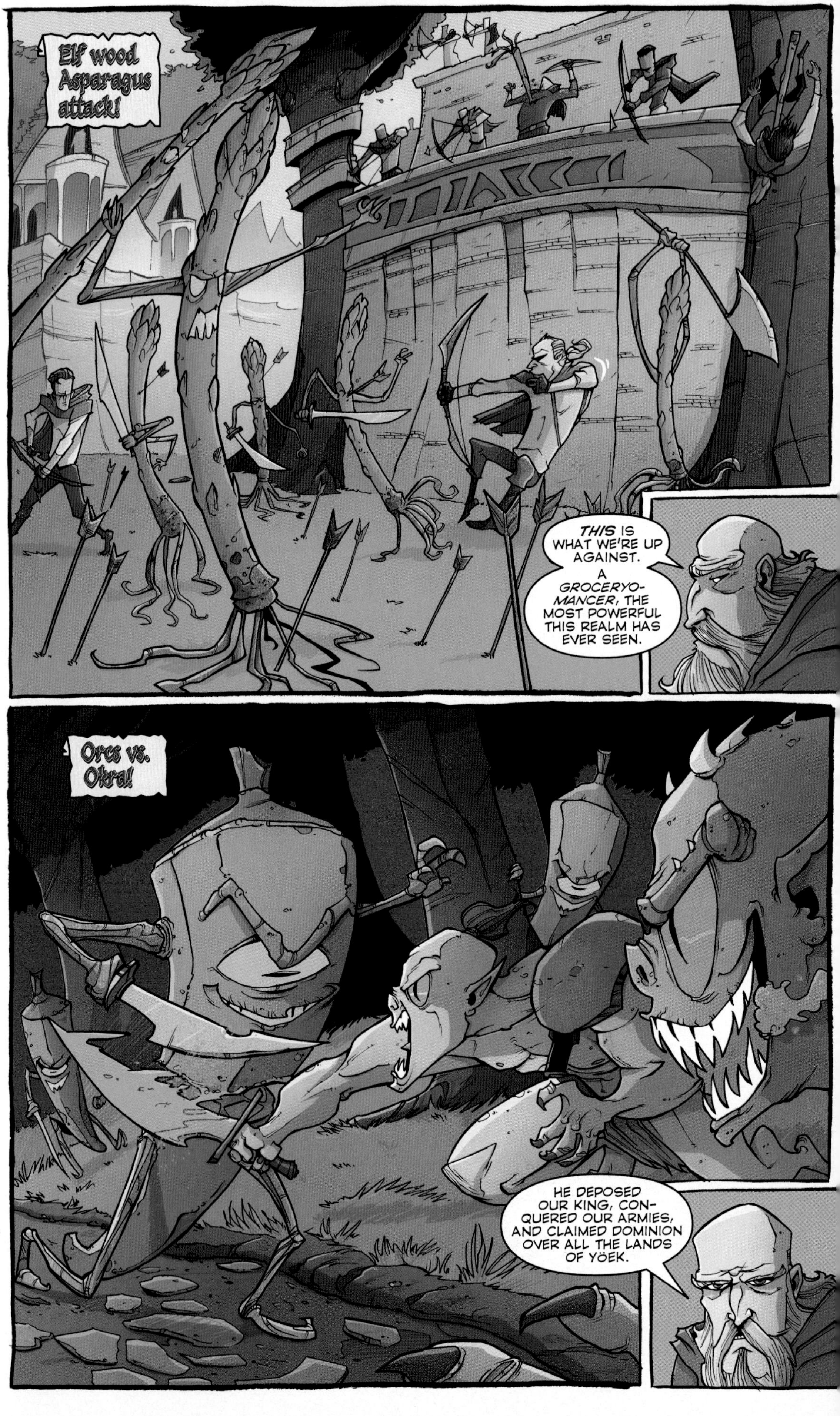
Elf wood Asparagus attack!
THIS IS WHAT WE'RE UP AGAINST.
A GROCERYO-MANCER, THE MOST POWERFUL THIS REALM HAS EVER SEEN.
Orcs vs. Okra!
HE DEPOSED OUR KING, CON-QUERED OUR ARMIES, AND CLAIMED DOMINION OVER ALL THE LANDS OF YÖEK.

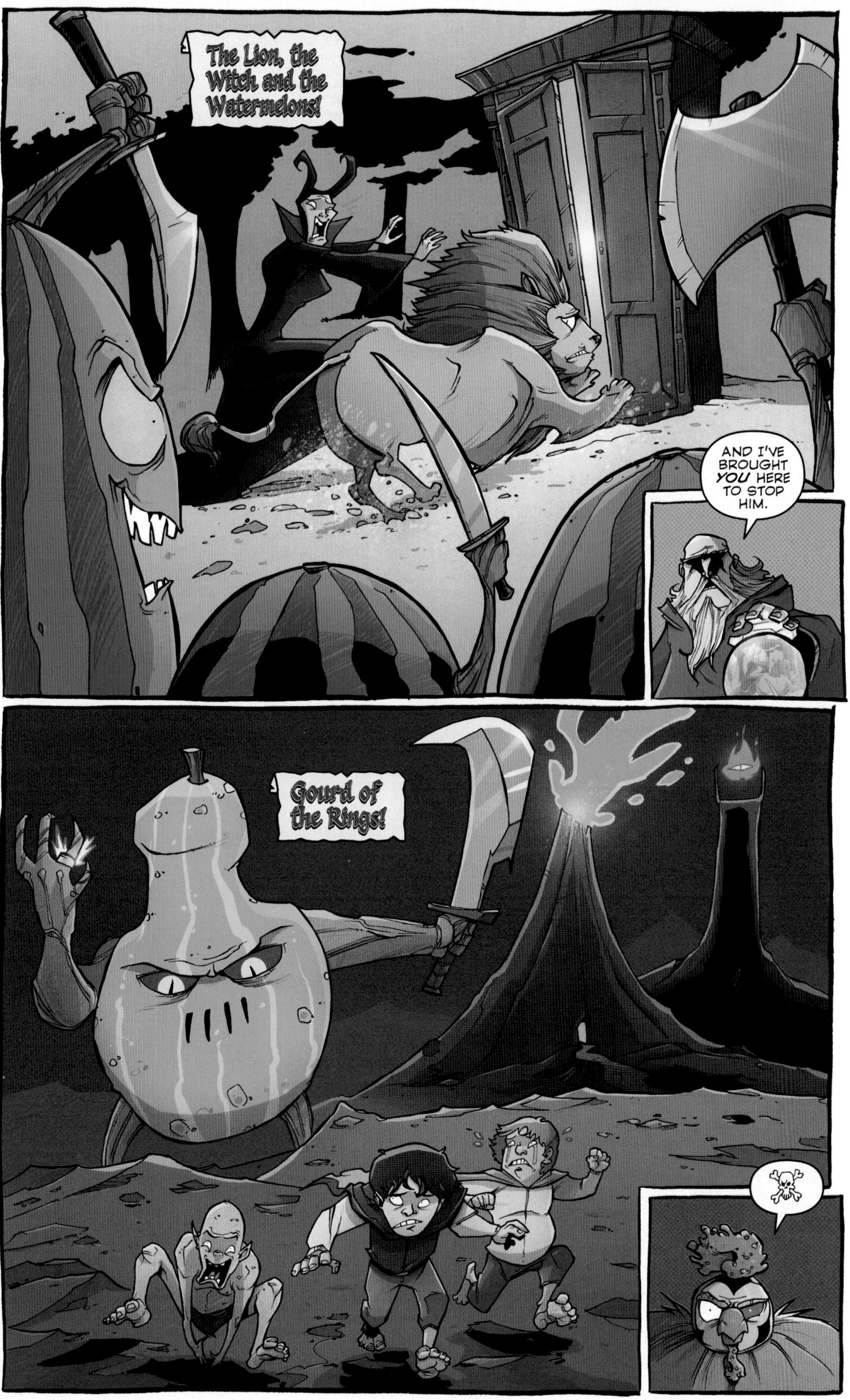

The Lion, the Witch and the Watermelons!
AND I'VE BROUGHT YOU HERE TO STOP HIM.
Gourd of the Rings!

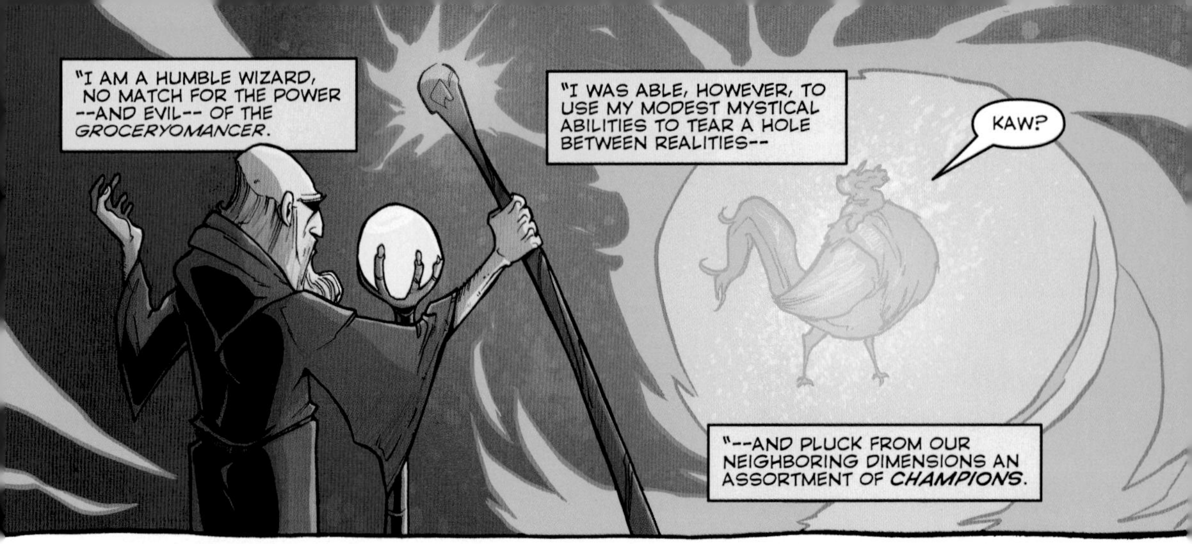
"I AM A HUMBLE WIZARD, NO MATCH FOR THE POWER --AND EVIL-- OF THE GROCERYOMANCER.
"I WAS ABLE, HOWEVER, TO USE MY MODEST MYSTICAL ABILITIES TO TEAR A HOLE BETWEEN REALITIES--
KAW?
"--AND PLUCK FROM OUR NEIGHBORING DIMENSIONS AN ASSORTMENT OF CHAMPIONS.

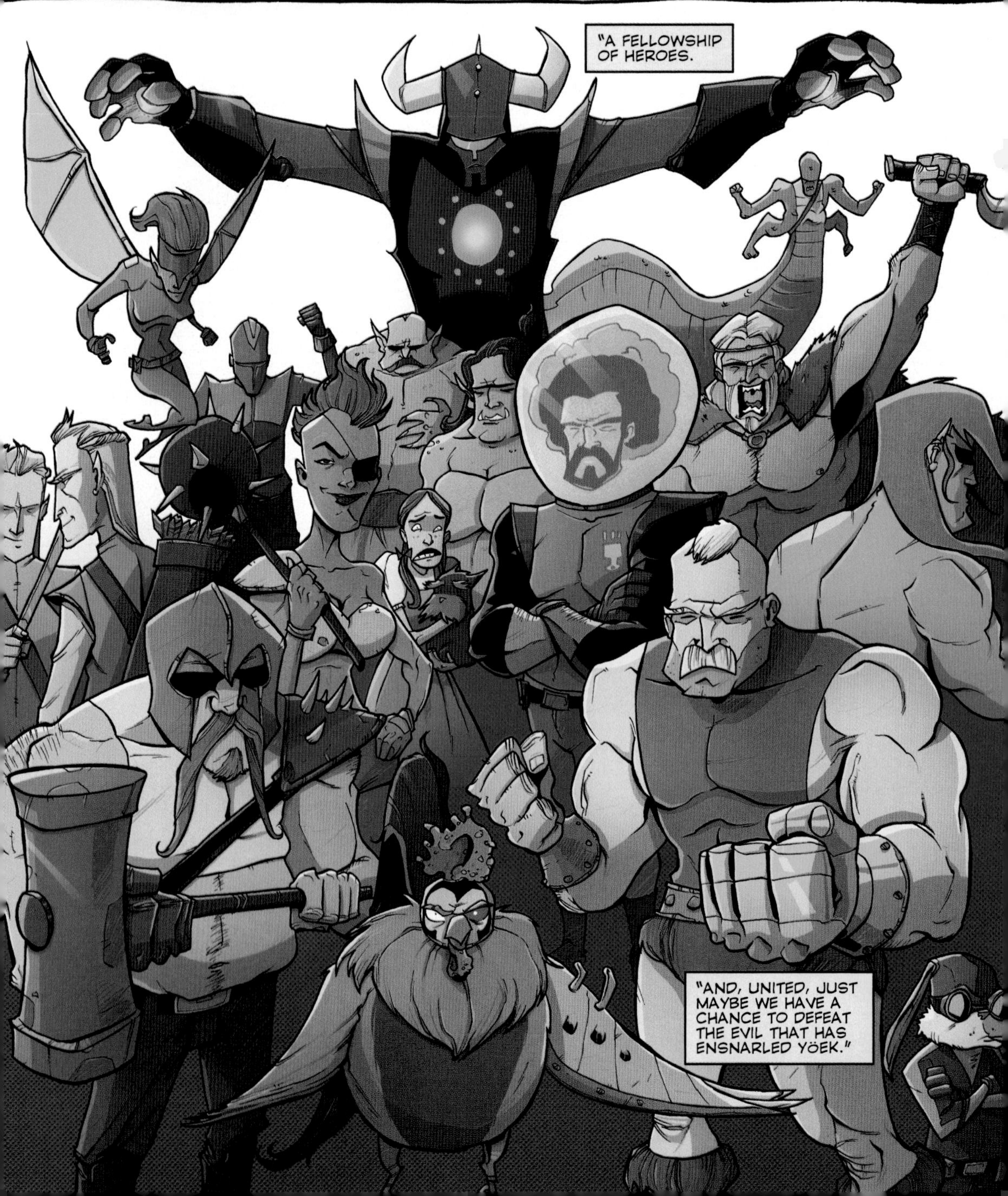
"A FELLOWSHIP OF HEROES.
"AND, UNITED, JUST MAYBE WE HAVE A CHANCE TO DEFEAT THE EVIL THAT HAS ENSNARLED YÖEK."

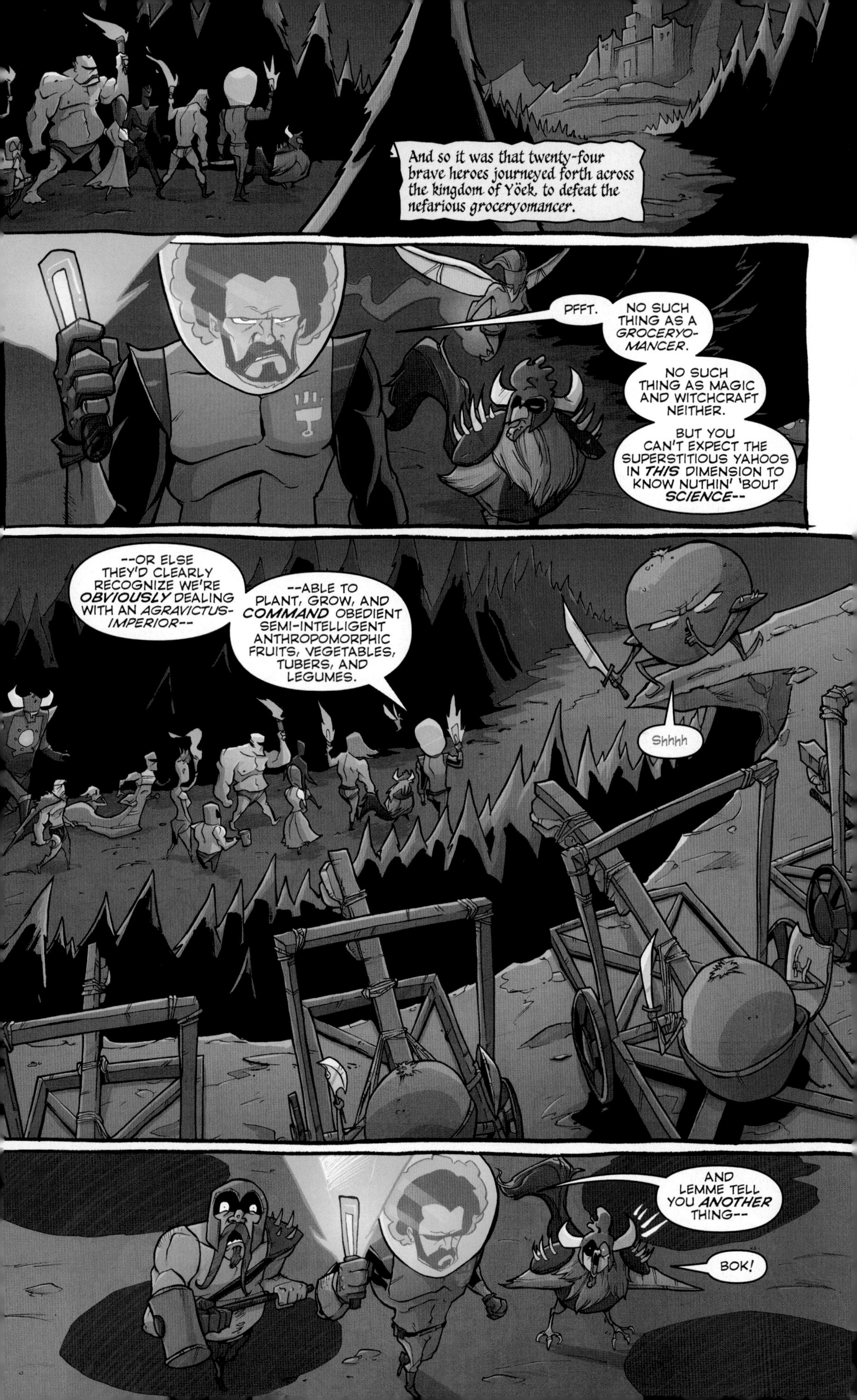
And so it was that twenty-four brave heroes journeyed forth across the kingdom of Yöek, to defeat the nefarious groceryomancer.
PFFT.
NO SUCH THING AS A GROCERYO-MANCER.
NO SUCH THING AS MAGIC AND WITCHCRAFT NEITHER.
BUT YOU CAN'T EXPECT THE SUPERSTITIOUS YAHOOS IN THIS DIMENSION TO KNOW NUTHIN' 'BOUT SCIENCE--
--OR ELSE THEY'D CLEARLY RECOGNIZE WE'RE OBVIOUSLY DEALING WITH AN AGRAVICTUS-IMPERIOR--
--ABLE TO PLANT, GROW, AND COMMAND OBEDIENT SEMI-INTELLIGENT ANTHROPOMORPHIC FRUITS, VEGETABLES, TUBERS, AND LEGUMES.
Shhhh
AND LEMME TELL YOU ANOTHER THING--
BOK!

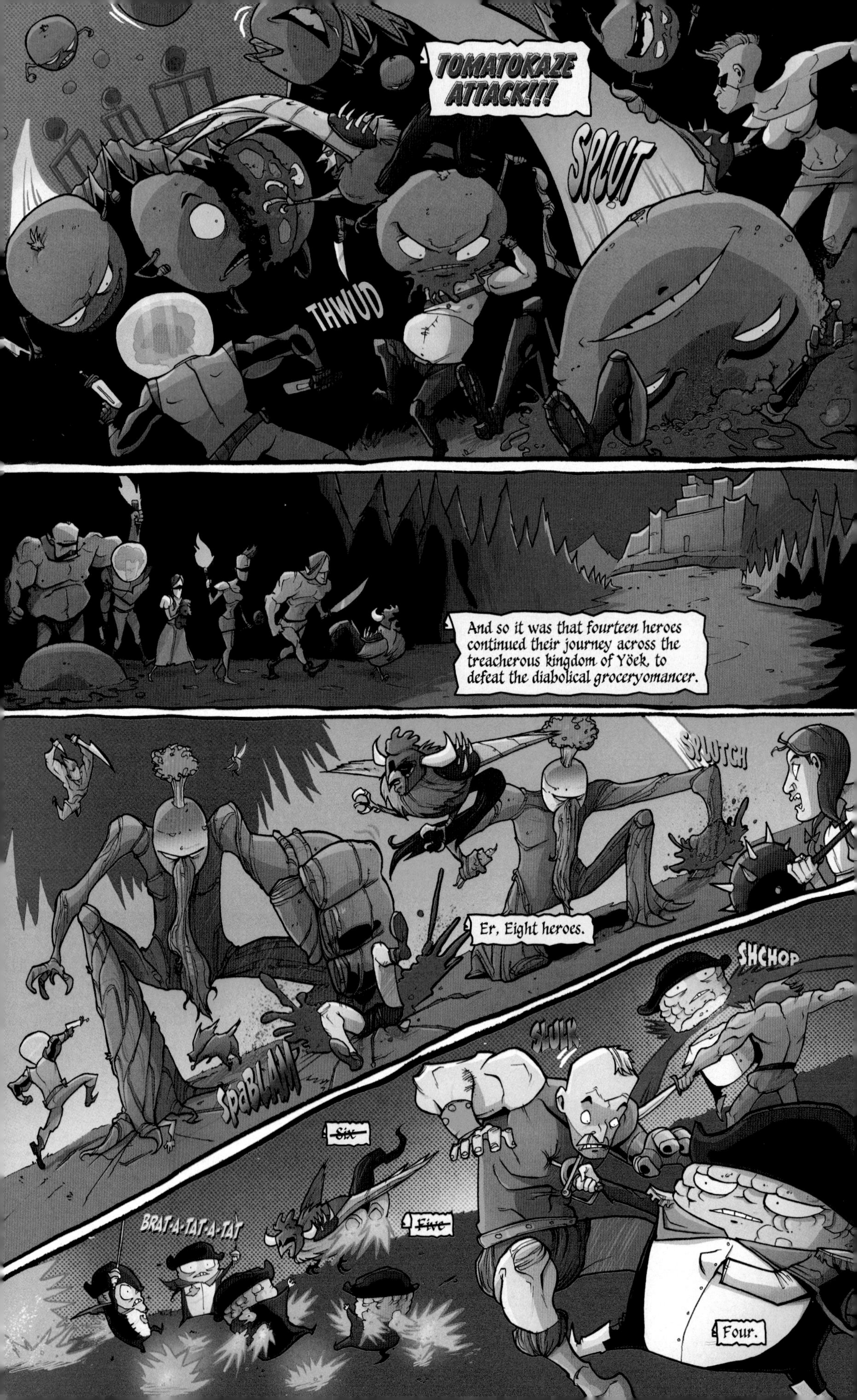
TOMATOKAZE ATTACK!!!
SPLUT
THWUD
And so it was that *fourteen* heroes continued their journey across the treacherous kingdom of Yöek, to defeat the diabolical *groceryomancer*.
SPLUTCH
Er, Eight heroes.
SHCHOP
SPaBLAM
SHUR
~~Six~~
BRAT-A-TAT-A-TAT
~~Five~~
Four.

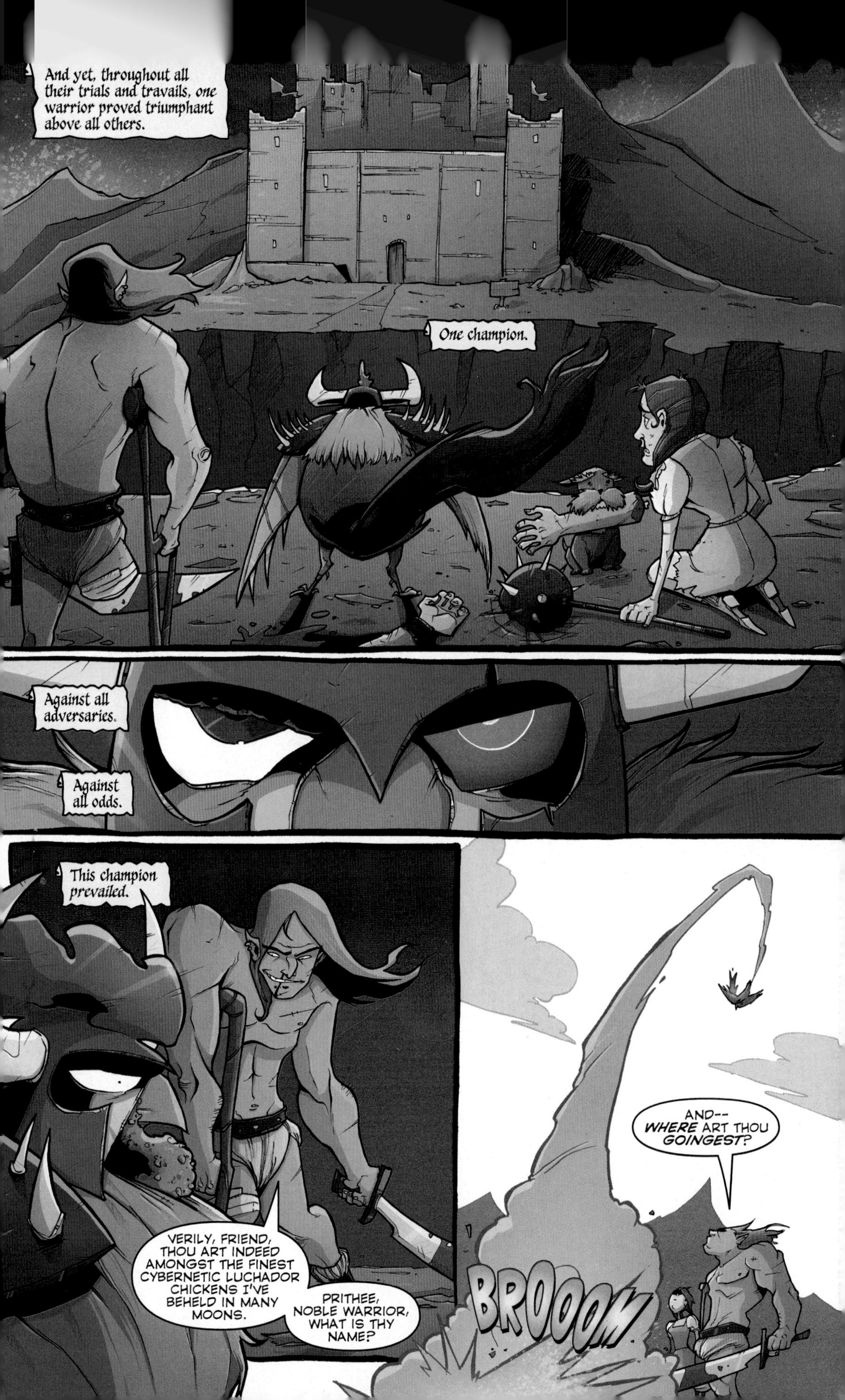
And yet, throughout all their trials and travails, one warrior proved triumphant above all others.
One champion.
Against all adversaries.
Against all odds.
This champion prevailed.
VERILY, FRIEND, THOU ART INDEED AMONGST THE FINEST CYBERNETIC LUCHADOR CHICKENS I'VE BEHELD IN MANY MOONS.
PRITHEE, NOBLE WARRIOR, WHAT IS THY NAME?
BROOOOM
AND-- WHERE ART THOU GOINGEST?

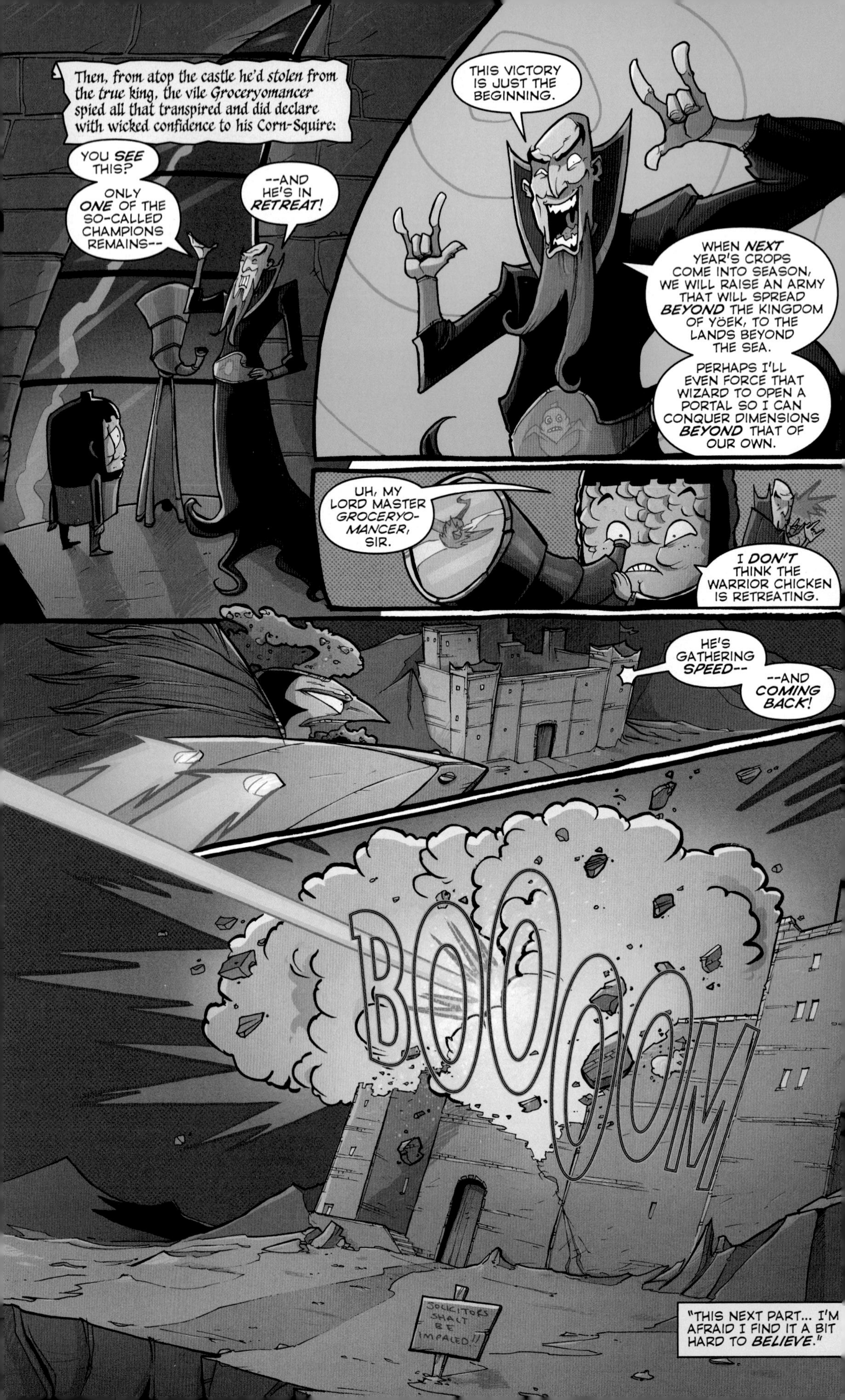
Then, from atop the castle he'd *stolen* from the *true king*, the vile *Groceryomancer* spied all that transpired and did declare with wicked confidence to his Corn-Squire:
YOU **SEE** THIS?
ONLY **ONE** OF THE SO-CALLED CHAMPIONS REMAINS--
--AND HE'S IN **RETREAT!**
THIS VICTORY IS JUST THE BEGINNING.
WHEN **NEXT** YEAR'S CROPS COME INTO SEASON, WE WILL RAISE AN ARMY THAT WILL SPREAD **BEYOND** THE KINGDOM OF YÖEK, TO THE LANDS BEYOND THE SEA.
PERHAPS I'LL EVEN FORCE THAT WIZARD TO OPEN A PORTAL SO I CAN CONQUER DIMENSIONS **BEYOND** THAT OF OUR OWN.
UH, MY LORD MASTER *GROCERYOMANCER*, SIR.
I **DON'T** THINK THE WARRIOR CHICKEN IS RETREATING.
HE'S GATHERING **SPEED**--
--AND **COMING BACK!**
BOOOOOM
SOLICITORS SHALT BE IMPALED!!
"THIS NEXT PART... I'M AFRAID I FIND IT A BIT HARD TO **BELIEVE**."

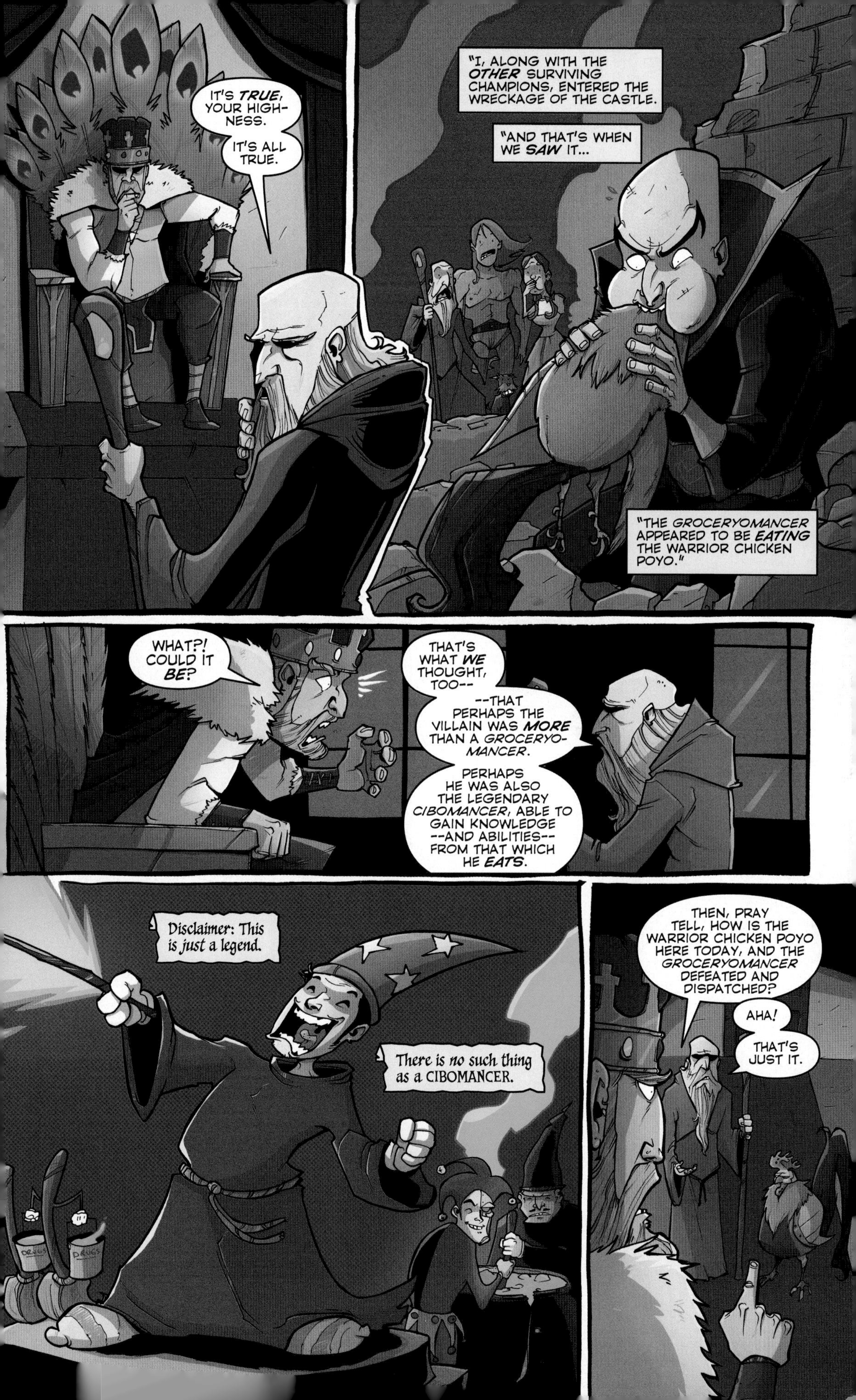
IT'S TRUE, YOUR HIGHNESS.
IT'S ALL TRUE.
"I, ALONG WITH THE OTHER SURVIVING CHAMPIONS, ENTERED THE WRECKAGE OF THE CASTLE.
"AND THAT'S WHEN WE SAW IT...
"THE GROCERYOMANCER APPEARED TO BE EATING THE WARRIOR CHICKEN POYO."
WHAT?! COULD IT BE?
THAT'S WHAT WE THOUGHT, TOO--
--THAT PERHAPS THE VILLAIN WAS MORE THAN A GROCERYO-MANCER.
PERHAPS HE WAS ALSO THE LEGENDARY CIBOMANCER, ABLE TO GAIN KNOWLEDGE --AND ABILITIES-- FROM THAT WHICH HE EATS.
Disclaimer: This is just a legend.
There is no such thing as a CIBOMANCER.
THEN, PRAY TELL, HOW IS THE WARRIOR CHICKEN POYO HERE TODAY, AND THE GROCERYOMANCER DEFEATED AND DISPATCHED?
AHA!
THAT'S JUST IT.

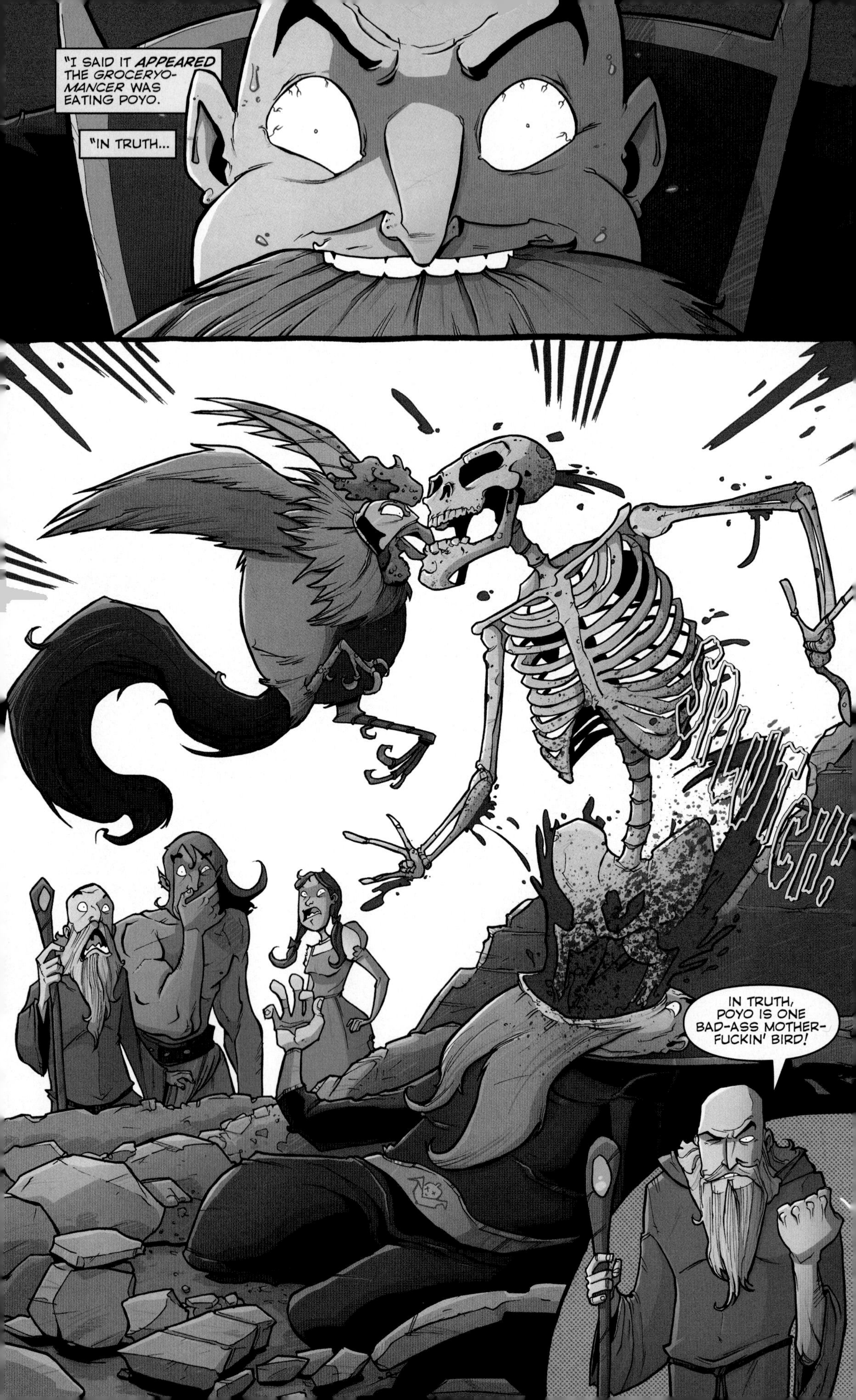
"I SAID IT APPEARED THE GROCERYO-MANCER WAS EATING POYO.
"IN TRUTH...
SPLUTCH!
IN TRUTH, POYO IS ONE BAD-ASS MOTHER-FUCKIN' BIRD!

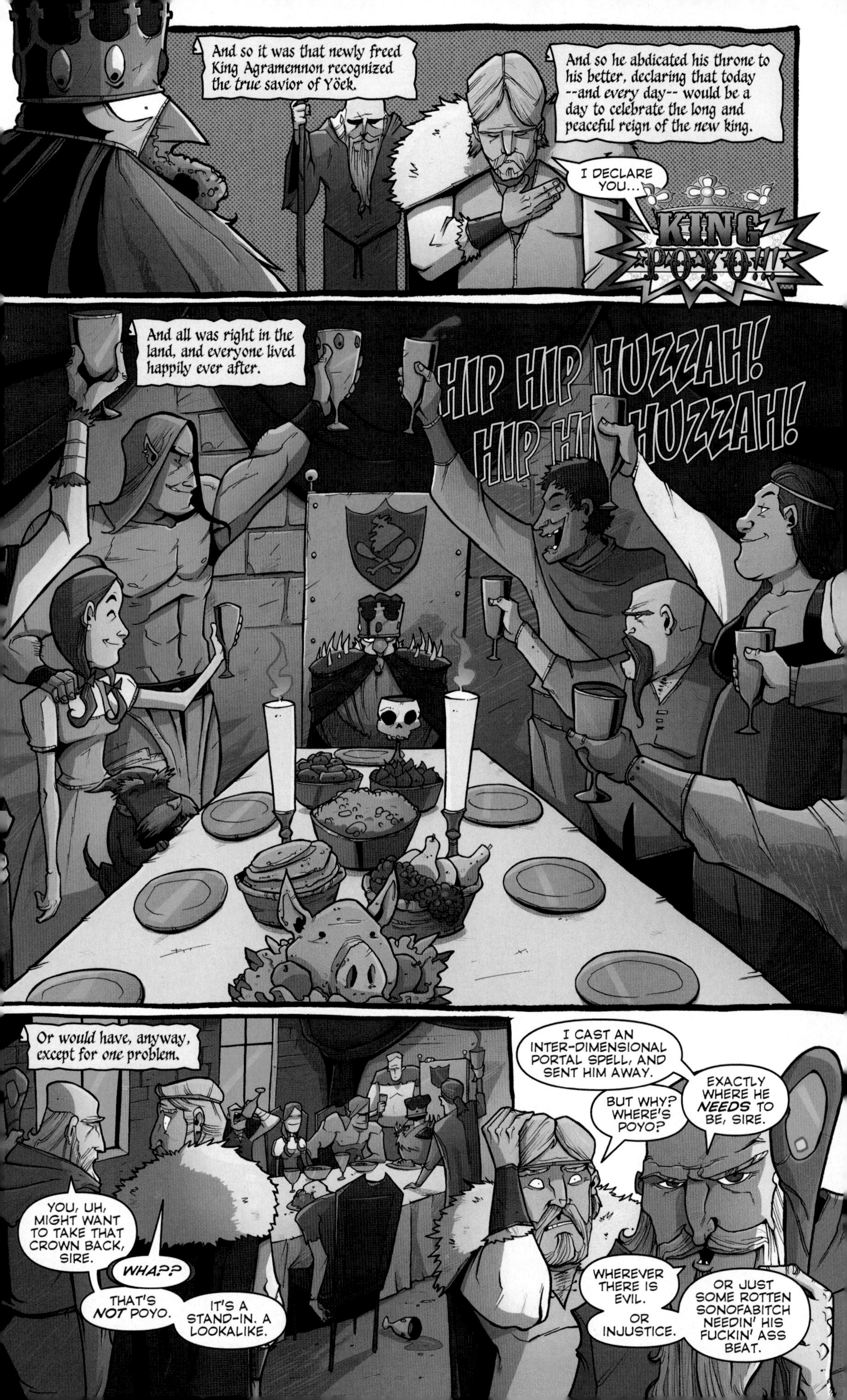
And so it was that newly freed King Agramemnon recognized the *true* savior of Yöek.
And so he abdicated his throne to his better, declaring that today --and every day-- would be a day to celebrate the long and peaceful reign of the *new* king.
I DECLARE YOU...
KING POYO!!!
And all was right in the land, and everyone lived happily ever after.
HIP HIP HUZZAH!
HIP HIP HUZZAH!
Or would have, anyway, except for *one* problem.
YOU, UH, MIGHT WANT TO TAKE THAT CROWN BACK, SIRE.
WHA??
THAT'S NOT POYO.
IT'S A STAND-IN. A LOOKALIKE.
I CAST AN INTER-DIMENSIONAL PORTAL SPELL, AND SENT HIM AWAY.
BUT WHY? WHERE'S POYO?
EXACTLY WHERE HE NEEDS TO BE, SIRE.
WHEREVER THERE IS EVIL.
OR INJUSTICE.
OR JUST SOME ROTTEN SONOFABITCH NEEDIN' HIS FUCKIN' ASS BEAT.

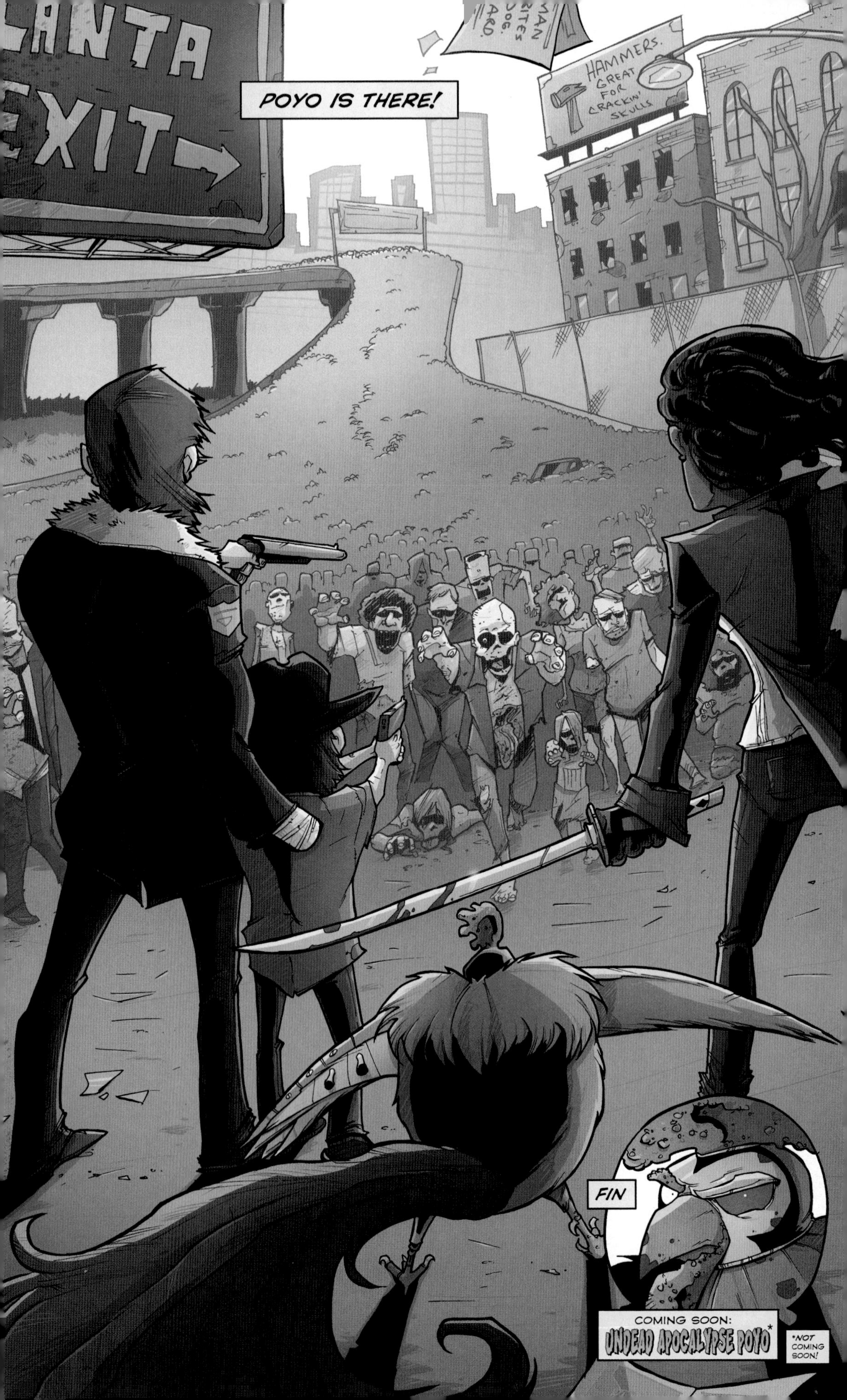

POYO IS THERE!
EXIT
HAMMERS. GREAT FOR CRACKIN' SKULLS
FIN
COMING SOON:
UNDEAD APOCALYPSE POYO*
*NOT COMING SOON!

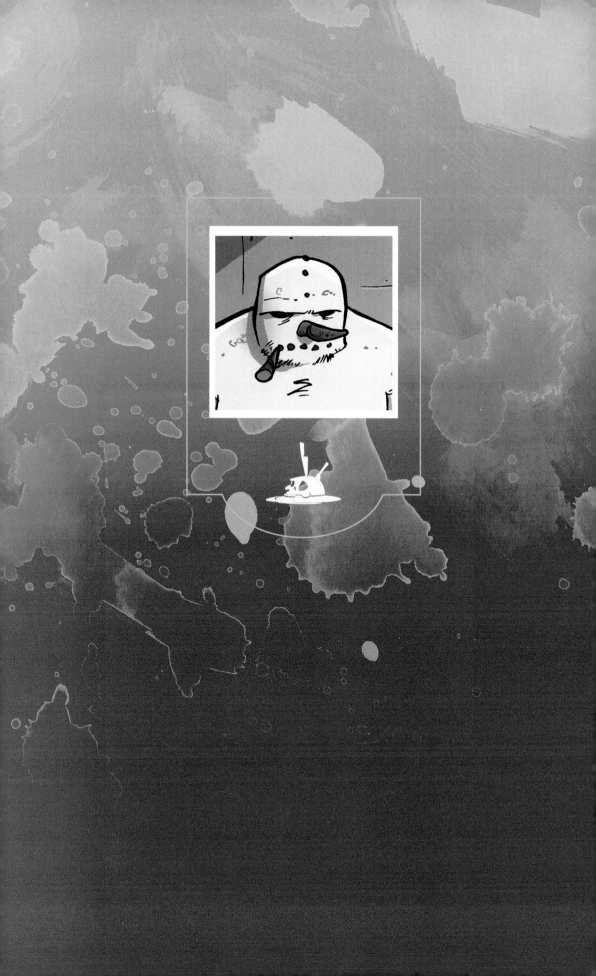

Chapter 3

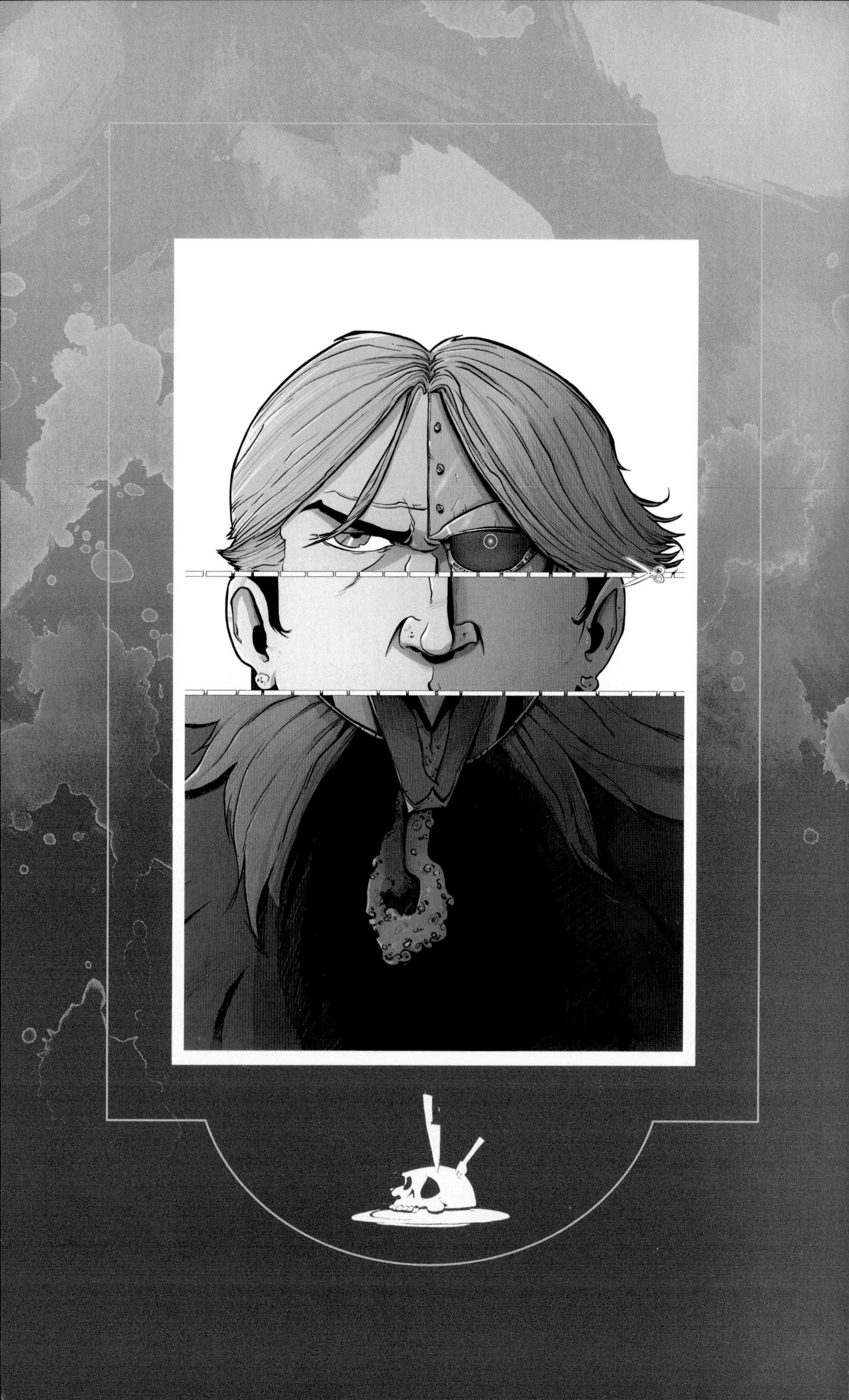

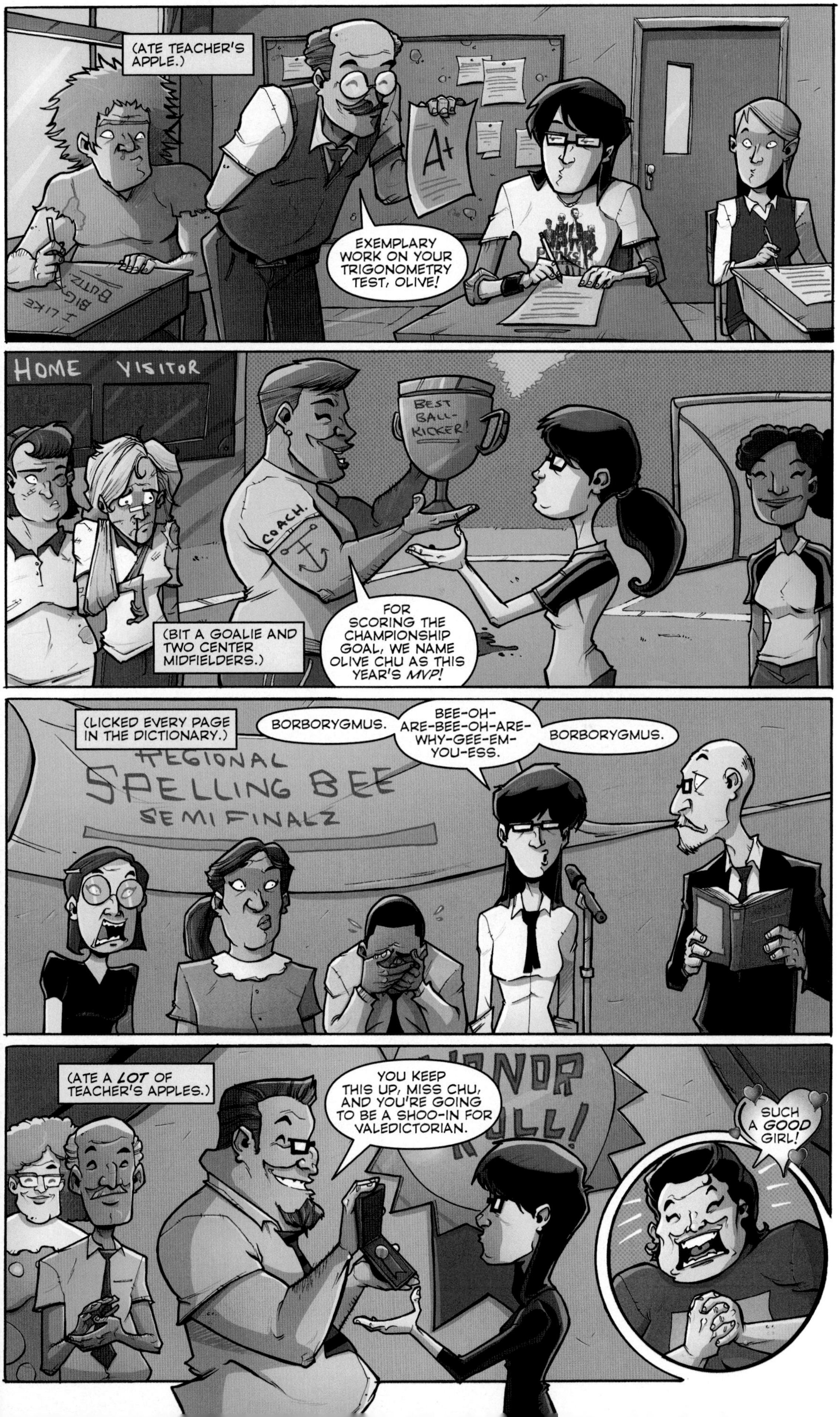

(ATE TEACHER'S APPLE.)
I LIKE BIG BUTZ.
A+
EXEMPLARY WORK ON YOUR TRIGONOMETRY TEST, OLIVE!
HOME VISITOR
BEST BALL-KICKER!
COACH.
FOR SCORING THE CHAMPIONSHIP GOAL, WE NAME OLIVE CHU AS THIS YEAR'S *MVP!*
(BIT A GOALIE AND TWO CENTER MIDFIELDERS.)
(LICKED EVERY PAGE IN THE DICTIONARY.)
BORBORYGMUS.
BEE-OH-ARE-BEE-OH-ARE-WHY-GEE-EM-YOU-ESS.
BORBORYGMUS.
REGIONAL SPELLING BEE SEMIFINALZ
(ATE A *LOT* OF TEACHER'S APPLES.)
YOU KEEP THIS UP, MISS CHU, AND YOU'RE GOING TO BE A SHOO-IN FOR VALEDICTORIAN.
SUCH A *GOOD* GIRL!

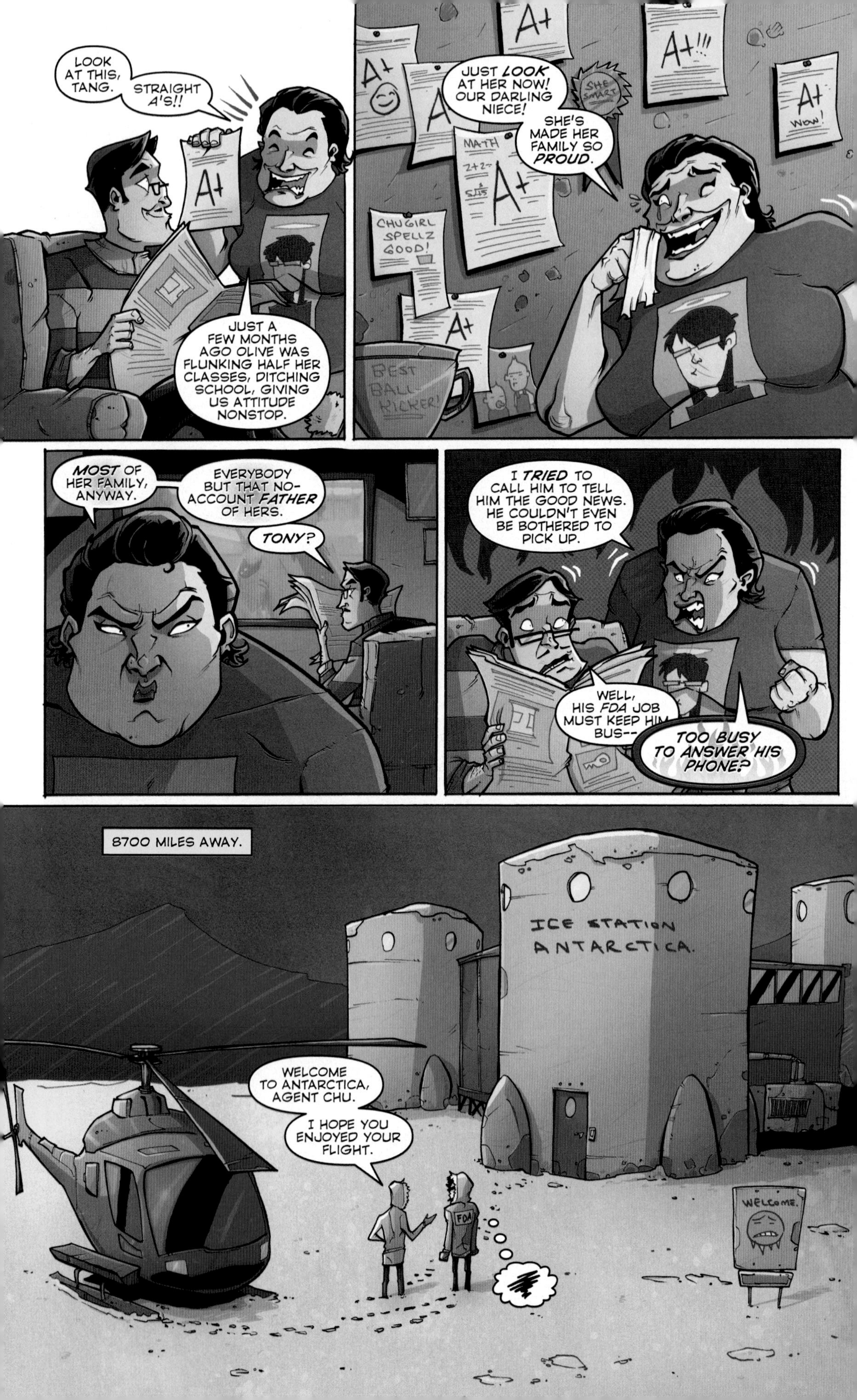

LOOK AT THIS, TANG.
STRAIGHT A'S!!
A+
JUST A FEW MONTHS AGO OLIVE WAS FLUNKING HALF HER CLASSES, DITCHING SCHOOL, GIVING US ATTITUDE NONSTOP.
JUST LOOK AT HER NOW! OUR DARLING NIECE!
SHE'S MADE HER FAMILY SO PROUD.
A+!!!
A+ WOW!
SHE SMART
MATH
CHUGIRL SPELLZ GOOD!
BEST BALL-KICKER!
MOST OF HER FAMILY, ANYWAY.
EVERYBODY BUT THAT NO-ACCOUNT FATHER OF HERS.
TONY?
I TRIED TO CALL HIM TO TELL HIM THE GOOD NEWS. HE COULDN'T EVEN BE BOTHERED TO PICK UP.
WELL, HIS FDA JOB MUST KEEP HIM BUS--
TOO BUSY TO ANSWER HIS PHONE?
8700 MILES AWAY.
ICE STATION ANTARCTICA.
WELCOME TO ANTARCTICA, AGENT CHU.
I HOPE YOU ENJOYED YOUR FLIGHT.
FDA
WELCOME.

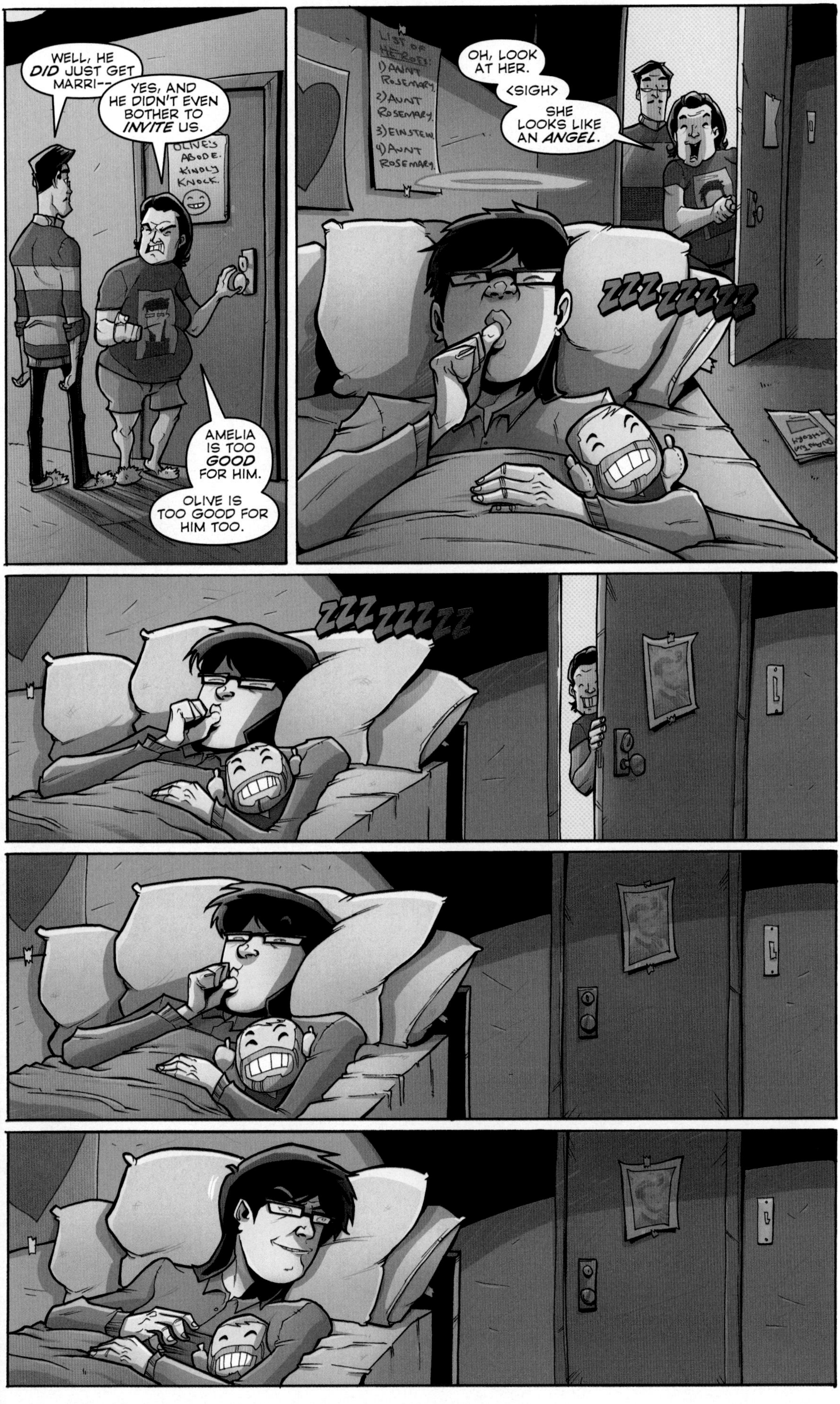
WELL, HE DID JUST GET MARRI--
YES, AND HE DIDN'T EVEN BOTHER TO INVITE US.
OLIVE'S ABODE. KINDLY KNOCK.
AMELIA IS TOO GOOD FOR HIM.
OLIVE IS TOO GOOD FOR HIM TOO.
LIST OF HEROES: 1) AUNT ROSEMARY. 2) AUNT ROSEMARY. 3) EINSTEIN. 4) AUNT ROSEMARY.
OH, LOOK AT HER.
<SIGH>
SHE LOOKS LIKE AN ANGEL.
ZZZZZZZZ
ZZZZZZZZ

SCIENCE BAD. EINSTEIN AWESOME.

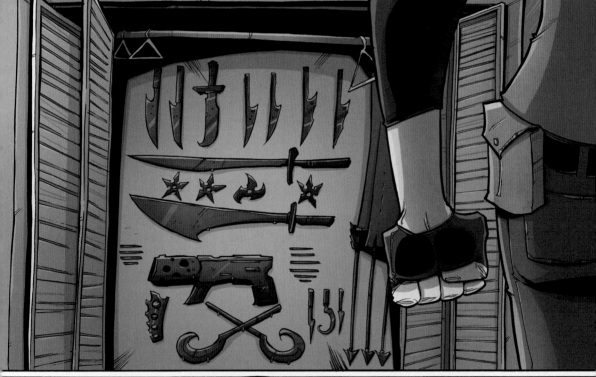

SERIOUSLY? *OLIVE CHU?*

SWEET LITTLE FOUR-EYED TOOTHPICK OLIVE CHU?

YOU THINK SHE'S *READY* FOR THIS, FATMAN?

I'LL LET *YOU* BE THE JUDGE, AGENT COLBY.

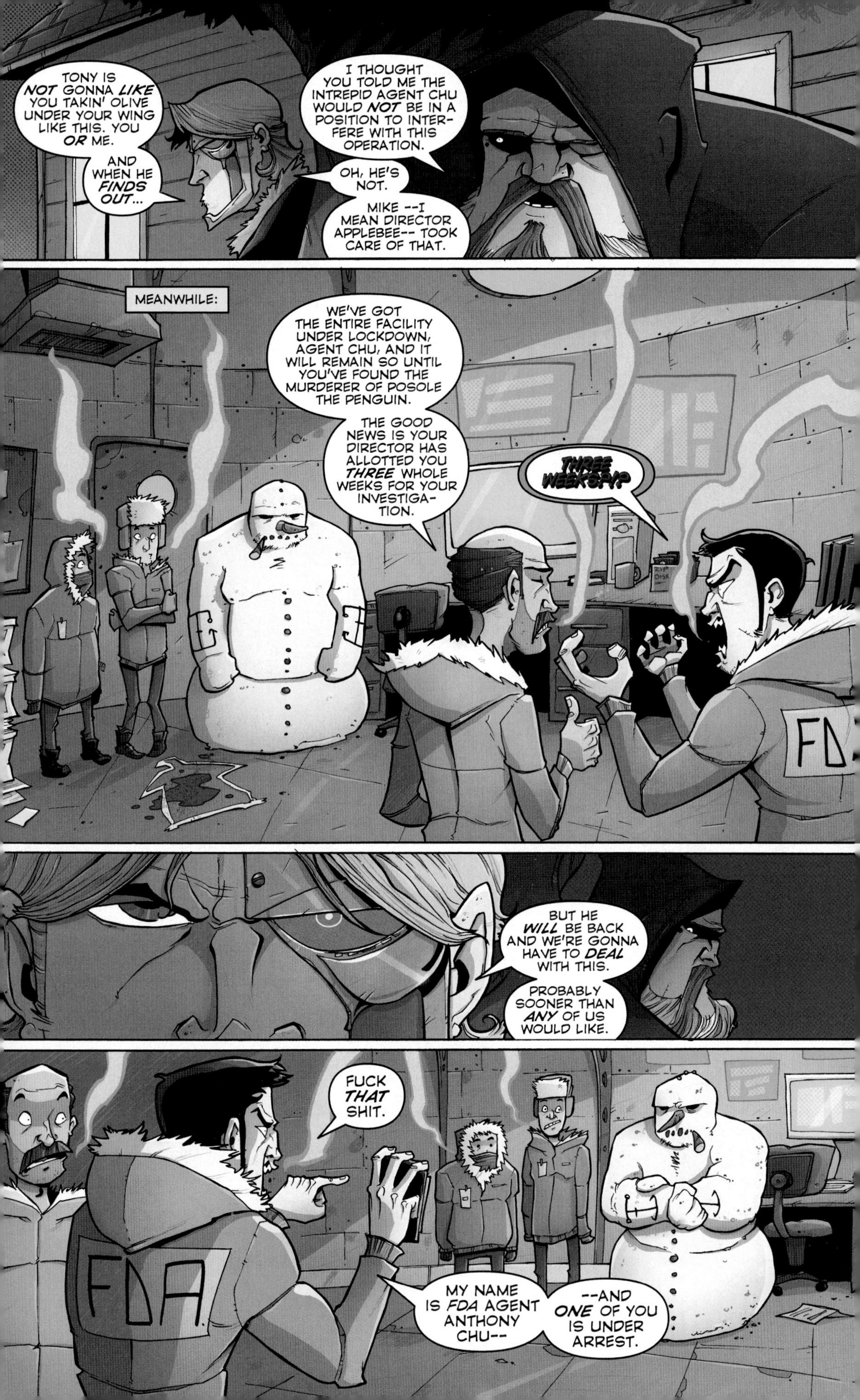
TONY IS NOT GONNA LIKE YOU TAKIN' OLIVE UNDER YOUR WING LIKE THIS. YOU OR ME.
AND WHEN HE FINDS OUT...
I THOUGHT YOU TOLD ME THE INTREPID AGENT CHU WOULD NOT BE IN A POSITION TO INTERFERE WITH THIS OPERATION.
OH, HE'S NOT.
MIKE --I MEAN DIRECTOR APPLEBEE-- TOOK CARE OF THAT.
MEANWHILE:
WE'VE GOT THE ENTIRE FACILITY UNDER LOCKDOWN, AGENT CHU, AND IT WILL REMAIN SO UNTIL YOU'VE FOUND THE MURDERER OF POSOLE THE PENGUIN.
THE GOOD NEWS IS YOUR DIRECTOR HAS ALLOTTED YOU THREE WHOLE WEEKS FOR YOUR INVESTIGATION.
THREE WEEKS?!?
BUT HE WILL BE BACK AND WE'RE GONNA HAVE TO DEAL WITH THIS.
PROBABLY SOONER THAN ANY OF US WOULD LIKE.
FUCK THAT SHIT.
MY NAME IS FDA AGENT ANTHONY CHU--
--AND ONE OF YOU IS UNDER ARREST.

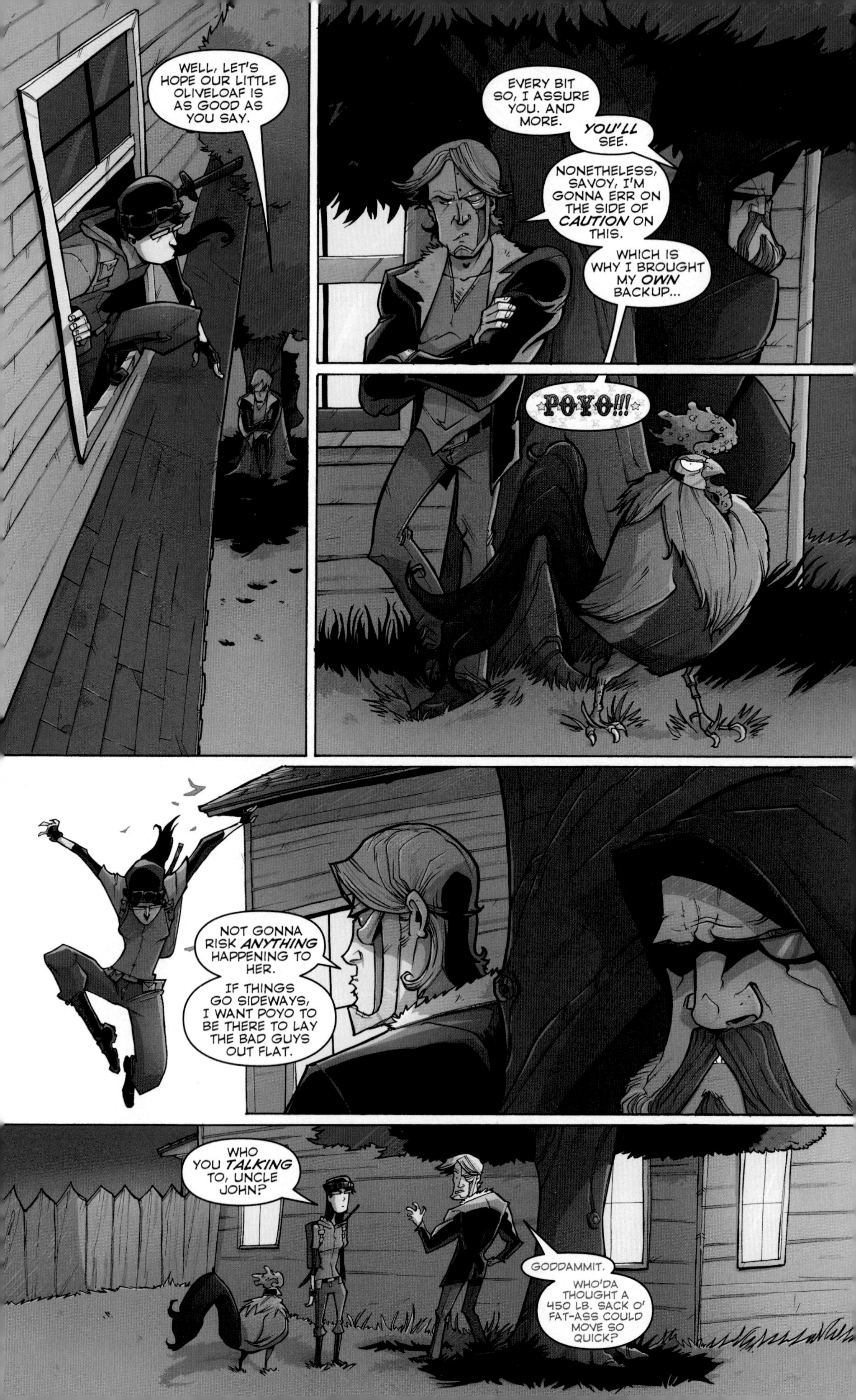
WELL, LET'S HOPE OUR LITTLE OLIVELOAF IS AS GOOD AS YOU SAY.
EVERY BIT SO, I ASSURE YOU. AND MORE. YOU'LL SEE.
NONETHELESS, SAVOY, I'M GONNA ERR ON THE SIDE OF CAUTION ON THIS.
WHICH IS WHY I BROUGHT MY OWN BACKUP...
POYO!!!
NOT GONNA RISK ANYTHING HAPPENING TO HER.
IF THINGS GO SIDEWAYS, I WANT POYO TO BE THERE TO LAY THE BAD GUYS OUT FLAT.
WHO YOU TALKING TO, UNCLE JOHN?
GODDAMMIT.
WHO'DA THOUGHT A 450 LB. SACK O' FAT-ASS COULD MOVE SO QUICK?

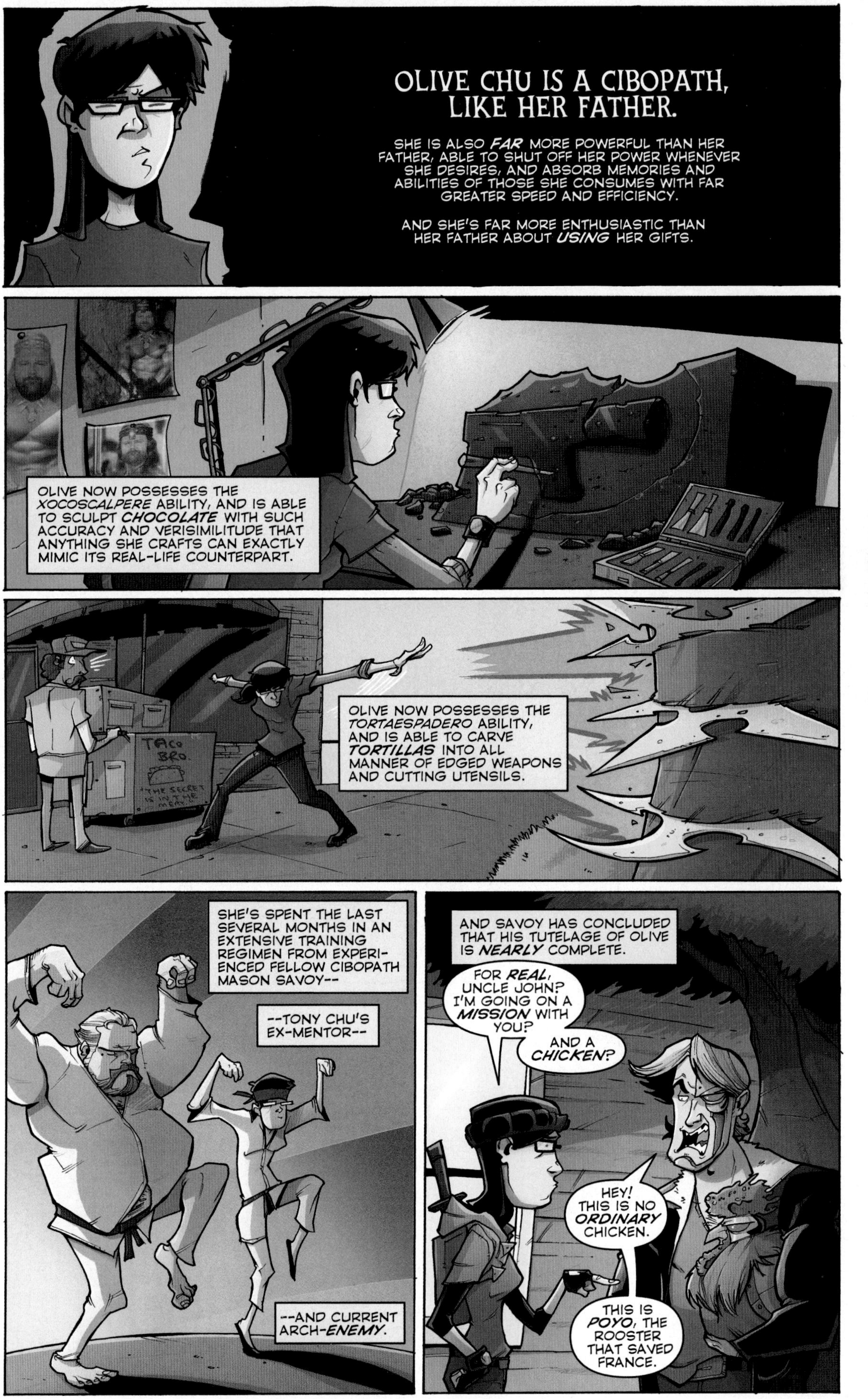
OLIVE CHU IS A CIBOPATH, LIKE HER FATHER.
SHE IS ALSO *FAR* MORE POWERFUL THAN HER FATHER, ABLE TO SHUT OFF HER POWER WHENEVER SHE DESIRES, AND ABSORB MEMORIES AND ABILITIES OF THOSE SHE CONSUMES WITH FAR GREATER SPEED AND EFFICIENCY.
AND SHE'S FAR MORE ENTHUSIASTIC THAN HER FATHER ABOUT *USING* HER GIFTS.
OLIVE NOW POSSESSES THE *XOCOSCALPERE* ABILITY, AND IS ABLE TO SCULPT ***CHOCOLATE*** WITH SUCH ACCURACY AND VERISIMILITUDE THAT ANYTHING SHE CRAFTS CAN EXACTLY MIMIC ITS REAL-LIFE COUNTERPART.
TACO BRO.
OLIVE NOW POSSESSES THE *TORTAESPADERO* ABILITY, AND IS ABLE TO CARVE ***TORTILLAS*** INTO ALL MANNER OF EDGED WEAPONS AND CUTTING UTENSILS.
SHE'S SPENT THE LAST SEVERAL MONTHS IN AN EXTENSIVE TRAINING REGIMEN FROM EXPERI-ENCED FELLOW CIBOPATH MASON SAVOY--
--TONY CHU'S EX-MENTOR--
--AND CURRENT ARCH-***ENEMY***.
AND SAVOY HAS CONCLUDED THAT HIS TUTELAGE OF OLIVE IS ***NEARLY*** COMPLETE.
FOR ***REAL***, UNCLE JOHN? I'M GOING ON A ***MISSION*** WITH YOU?
AND A ***CHICKEN***?
HEY! THIS IS NO ***ORDINARY*** CHICKEN.
THIS IS ***POYO***, THE ROOSTER THAT SAVED FRANCE.

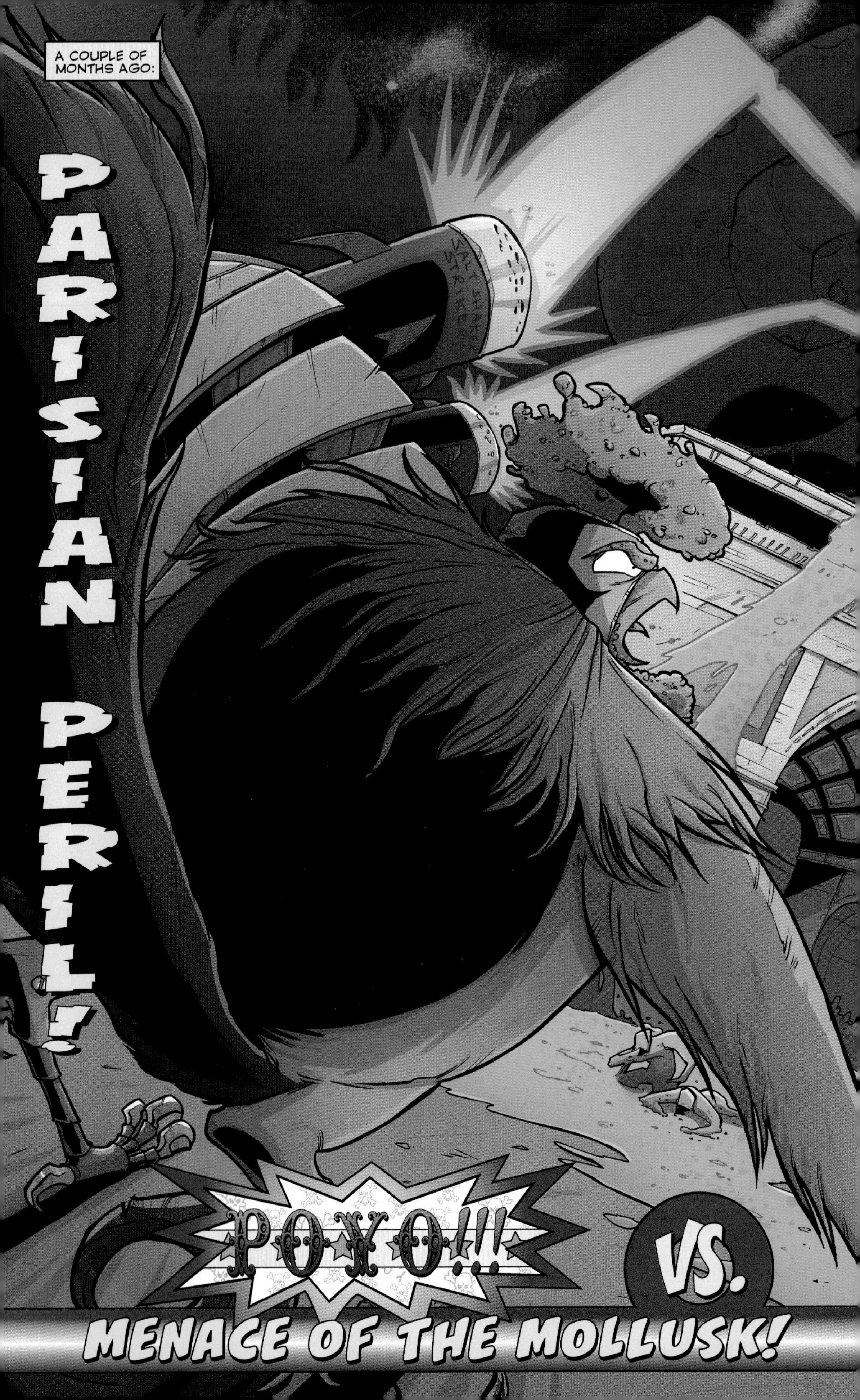
A COUPLE OF MONTHS AGO:
PARISIAN PERIL!
SALT SHAKER STRIKER
POYO!!!
VS.
MENACE OF THE MOLLUSK!

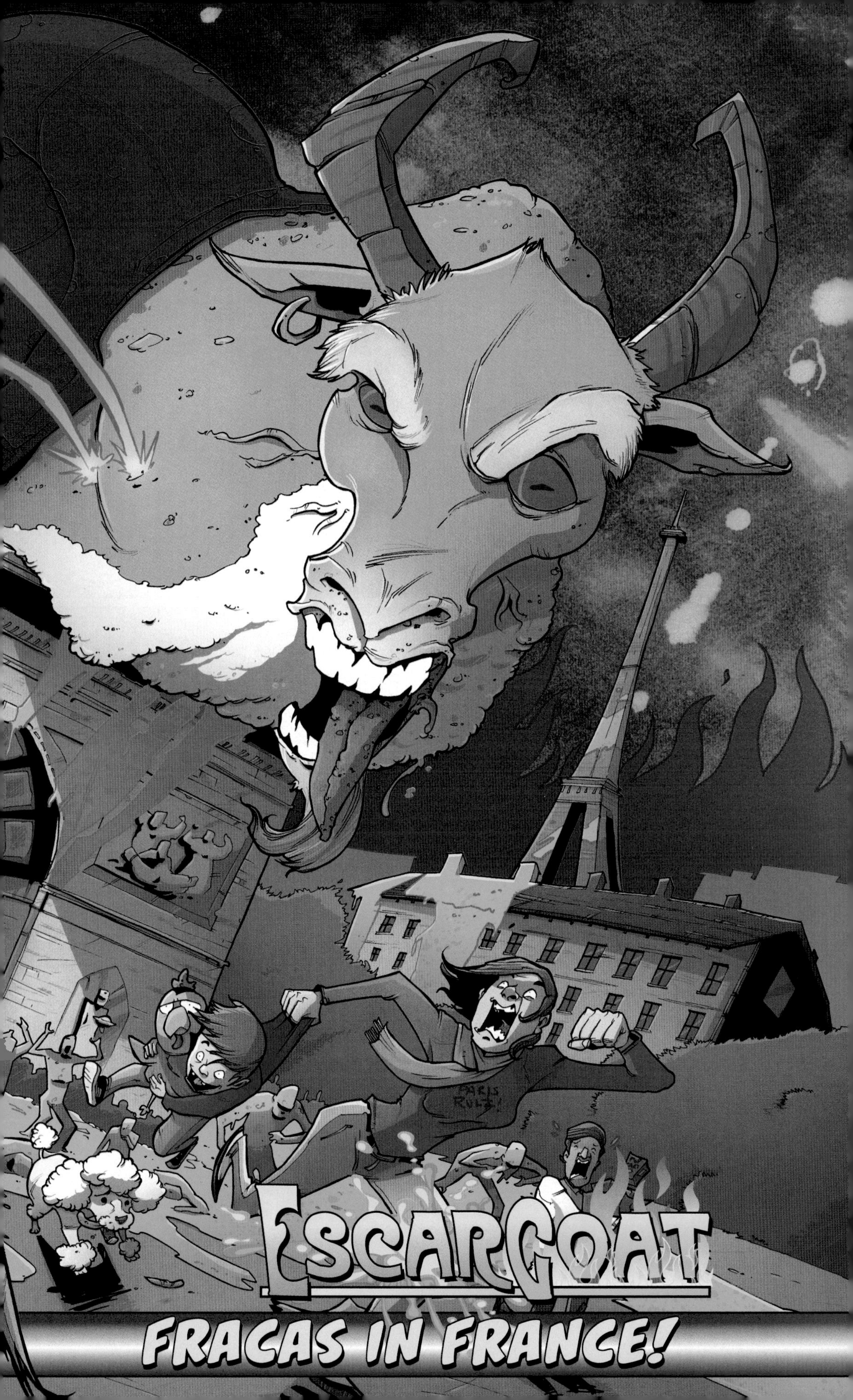
ESCARGOAT
FRACAS IN FRANCE!

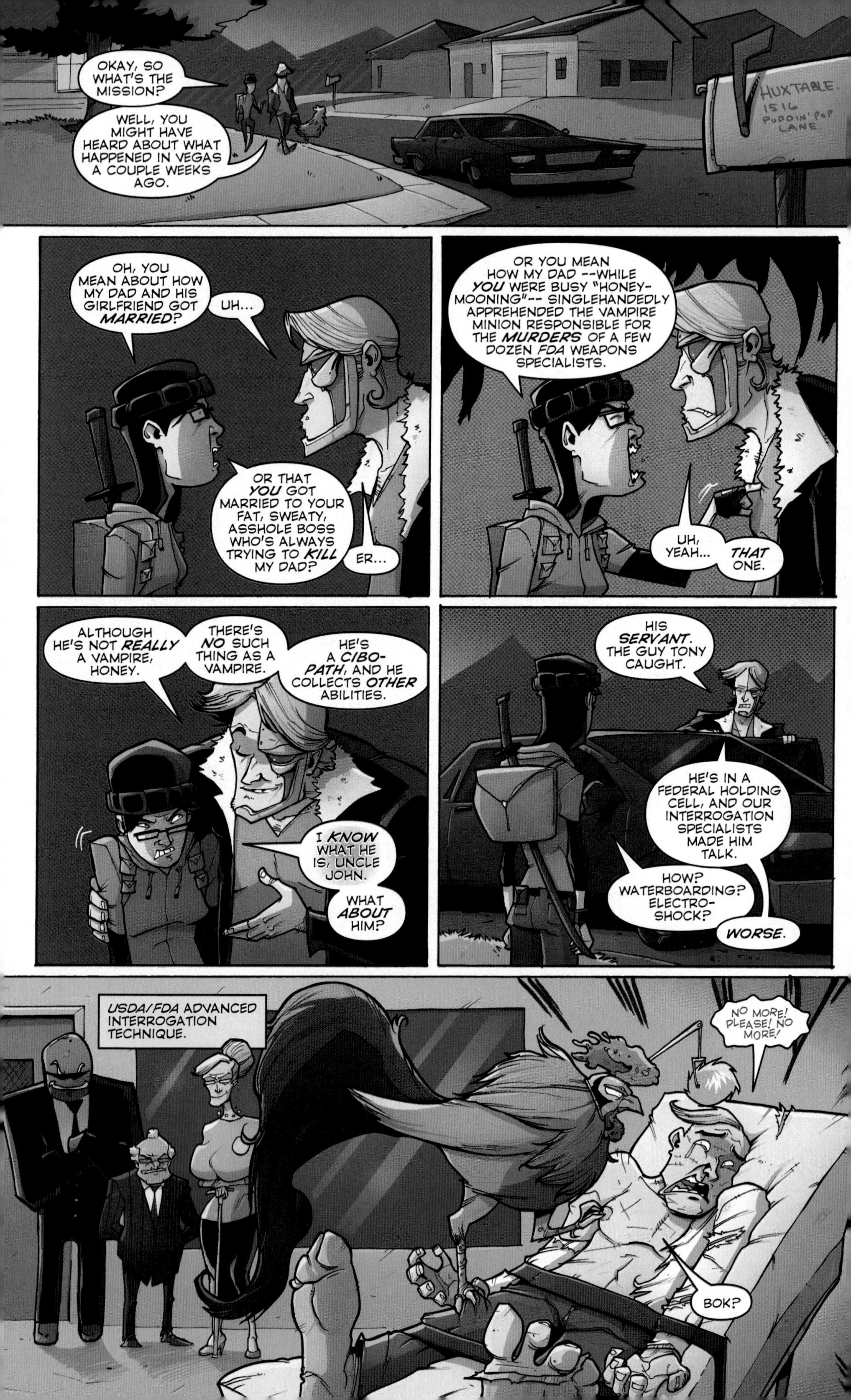

OKAY, SO WHAT'S THE MISSION?
WELL, YOU MIGHT HAVE HEARD ABOUT WHAT HAPPENED IN VEGAS A COUPLE WEEKS AGO.
HUXTABLE. 1516 PUDDIN' POP LANE
OH, YOU MEAN ABOUT HOW MY DAD AND HIS GIRLFRIEND GOT *MARRIED*?
UH...
OR THAT *YOU* GOT MARRIED TO YOUR FAT, SWEATY, ASSHOLE BOSS WHO'S ALWAYS TRYING TO *KILL* MY DAD?
ER...
OR YOU MEAN HOW MY DAD --WHILE *YOU* WERE BUSY "HONEY-MOONING"-- SINGLEHANDEDLY APPREHENDED THE VAMPIRE MINION RESPONSIBLE FOR THE *MURDERS* OF A FEW DOZEN *FDA* WEAPONS SPECIALISTS.
UH, YEAH... *THAT* ONE.
ALTHOUGH HE'S NOT *REALLY* A VAMPIRE, HONEY.
THERE'S *NO* SUCH THING AS A VAMPIRE.
HE'S A *CIBO-PATH*, AND HE COLLECTS *OTHER* ABILITIES.
I *KNOW* WHAT HE IS, UNCLE JOHN.
WHAT *ABOUT* HIM?
HIS *SERVANT*. THE GUY TONY CAUGHT.
HE'S IN A FEDERAL HOLDING CELL, AND OUR INTERROGATION SPECIALISTS MADE HIM TALK.
HOW? WATERBOARDING? ELECTRO-SHOCK?
WORSE.
USDA/FDA ADVANCED INTERROGATION TECHNIQUE.
NO MORE! PLEASE! NO MORE!
BOK?

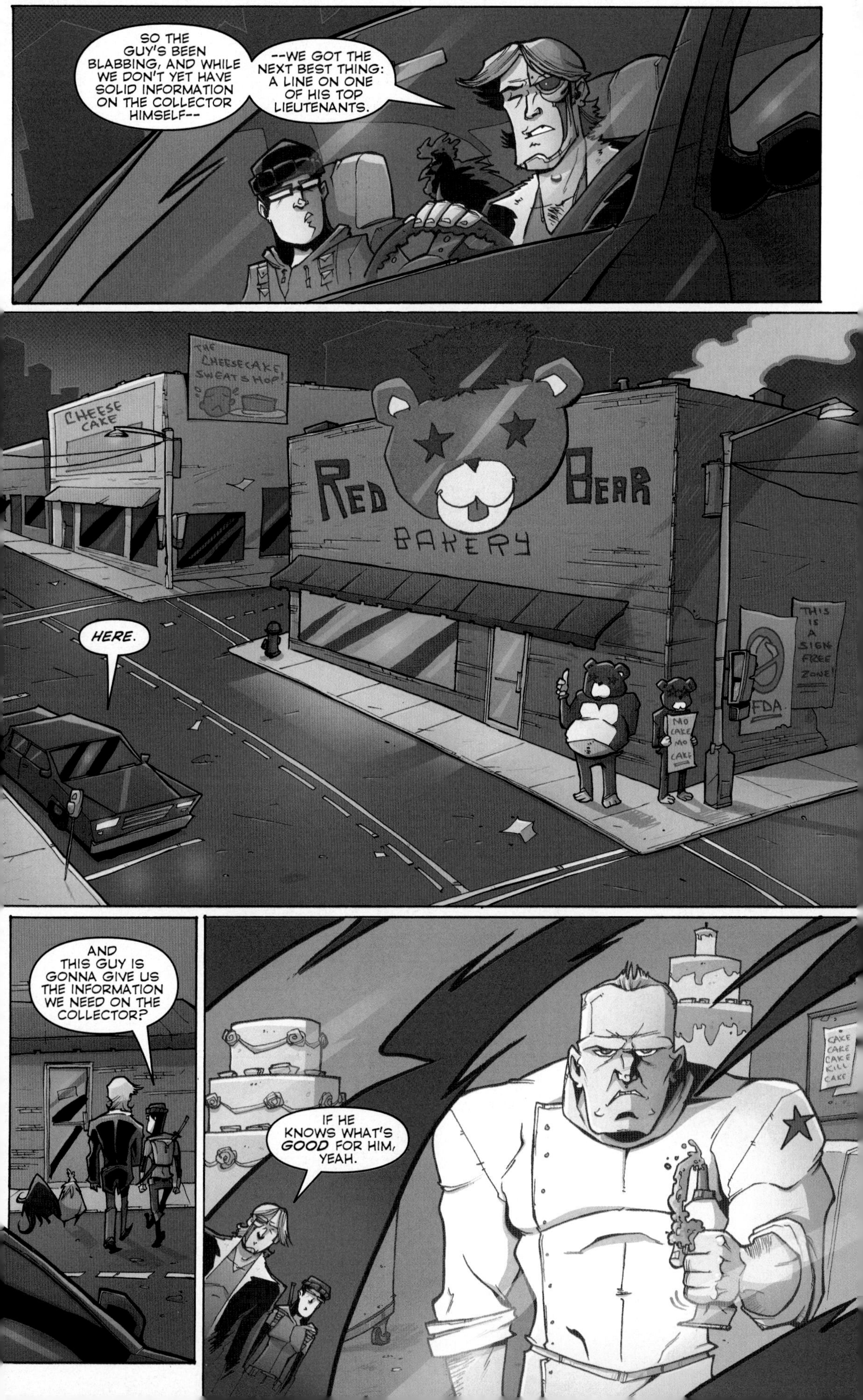
SO THE GUY'S BEEN BLABBING, AND WHILE WE DON'T YET HAVE SOLID INFORMATION ON THE COLLECTOR HIMSELF--
--WE GOT THE NEXT BEST THING: A LINE ON ONE OF HIS TOP LIEUTENANTS.
CHEESE CAKE
THE CHEESECAKE SWEATSHOP!
RED BEAR BAKERY
THIS IS A SIGN-FREE ZONE!
FDA
NO CAKE NO CAKE
HERE.
AND THIS GUY IS GONNA GIVE US THE INFORMATION WE NEED ON THE COLLECTOR?
CAKE CAKE CAKE KILL CAKE
IF HE KNOWS WHAT'S *GOOD* FOR HIM, YEAH.

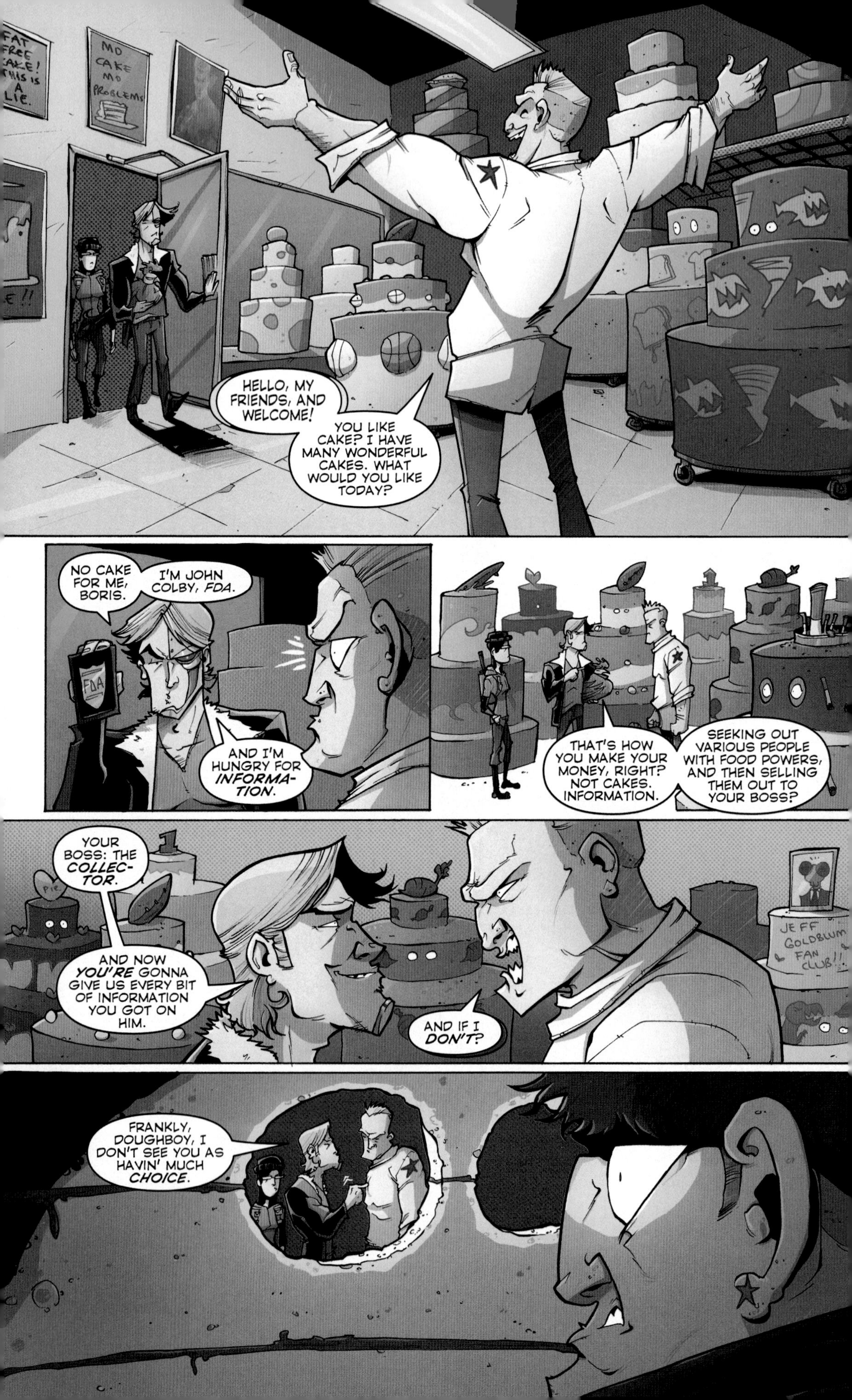
FAT FREE CAKE! THIS IS A LIE.
MO CAKE MO PROBLEMS
HELLO, MY FRIENDS, AND WELCOME!
YOU LIKE CAKE? I HAVE MANY WONDERFUL CAKES. WHAT WOULD YOU LIKE TODAY?
NO CAKE FOR ME, BORIS.
I'M JOHN COLBY, *FDA*.
FDA
AND I'M HUNGRY FOR *INFORMATION*.
THAT'S HOW YOU MAKE YOUR MONEY, RIGHT? NOT CAKES. INFORMATION.
SEEKING OUT VARIOUS PEOPLE WITH FOOD POWERS, AND THEN SELLING THEM OUT TO YOUR BOSS?
YOUR BOSS: THE *COLLECTOR*.
AND NOW *YOU'RE* GONNA GIVE US EVERY BIT OF INFORMATION YOU GOT ON HIM.
JEFF GOLDBLUM FAN CLUB!!
AND IF I *DON'T*?
FRANKLY, DOUGHBOY, I DON'T SEE YOU AS HAVIN' MUCH *CHOICE*.

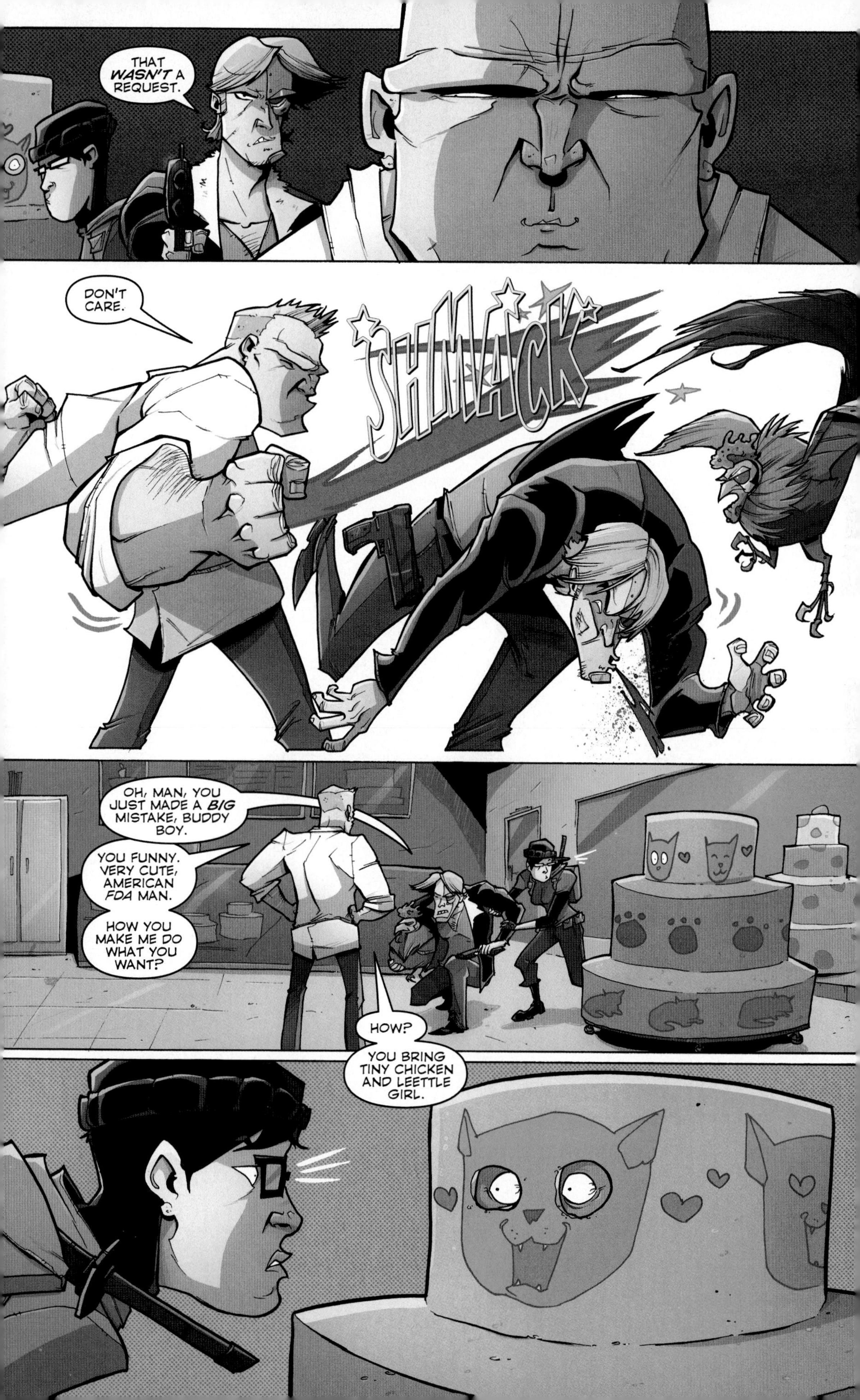
THAT *WASN'T* A REQUEST.
DON'T CARE.
SHMACK
OH, MAN, YOU JUST MADE A *BIG* MISTAKE, BUDDY BOY.
YOU FUNNY. VERY CUTE, AMERICAN *FDA* MAN.
HOW YOU MAKE ME DO WHAT YOU WANT?
HOW?
YOU BRING TINY CHICKEN AND LEETTLE GIRL.

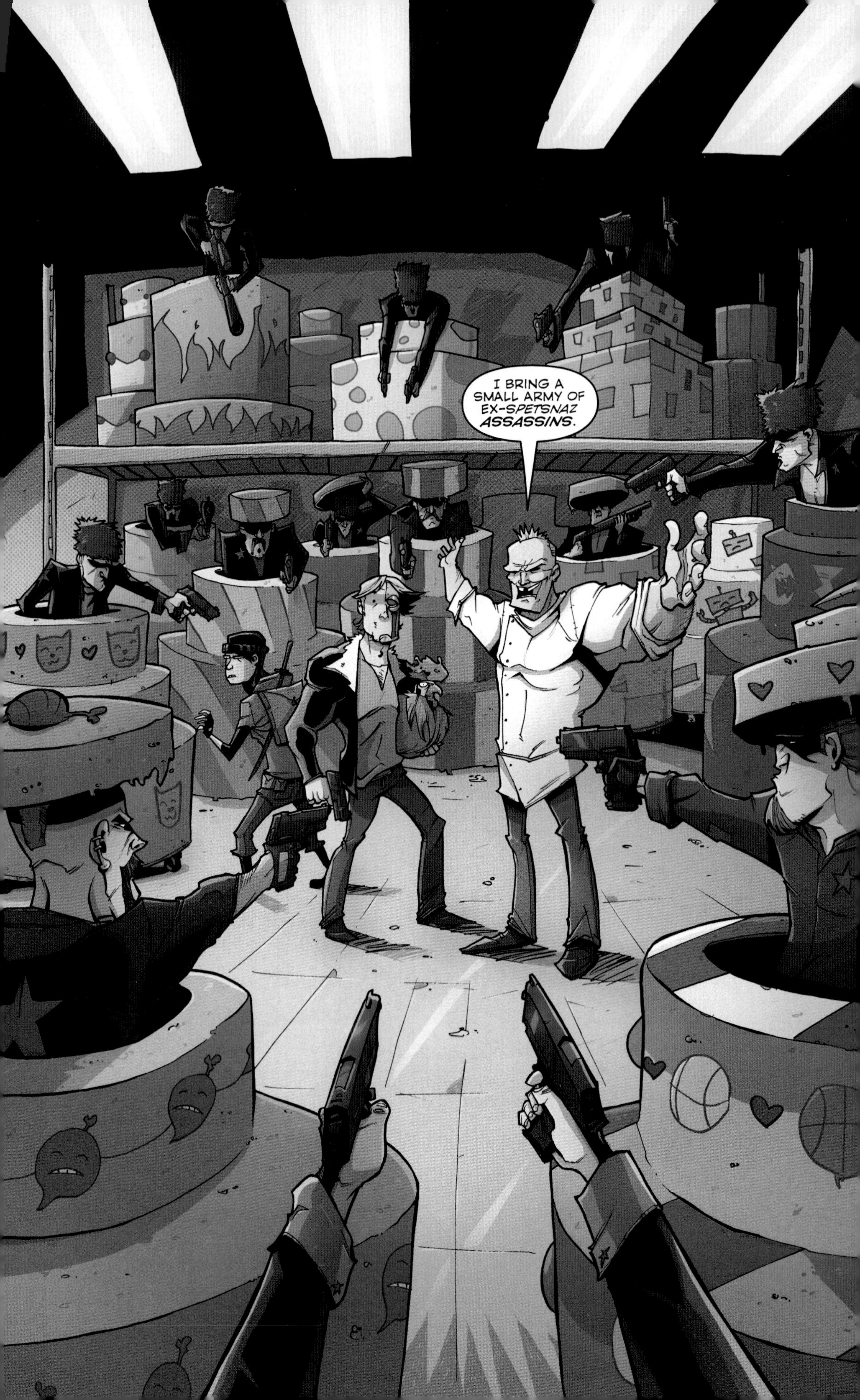
I BRING A SMALL ARMY OF EX-*SPETSNAZ* ***ASSASSINS***.

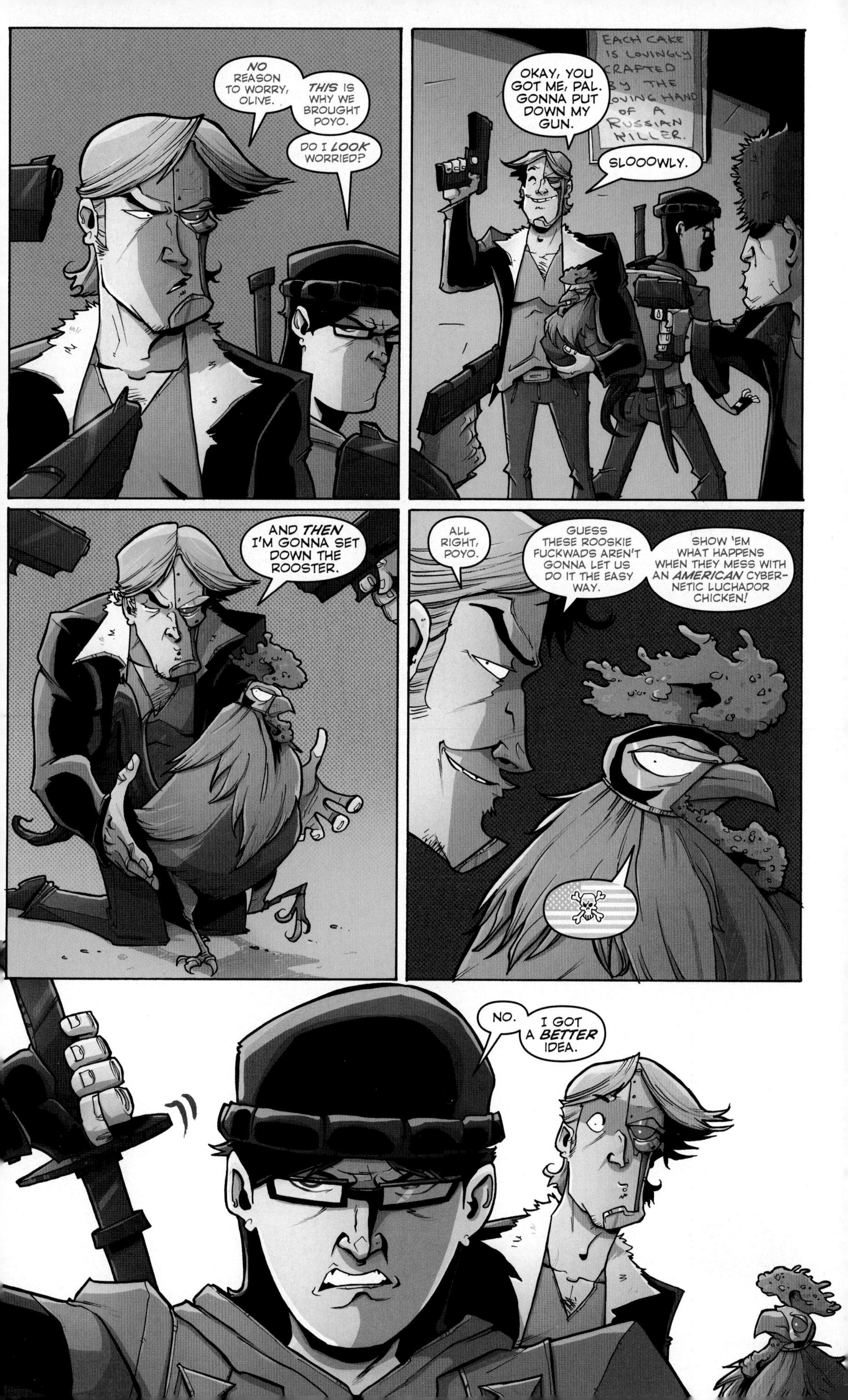
NO REASON TO WORRY, OLIVE.
THIS IS WHY WE BROUGHT POYO.
DO I LOOK WORRIED?
EACH CAKE IS LOVINGLY CRAFTED BY THE LOVING HAND OF A RUSSIAN KILLER.
OKAY, YOU GOT ME, PAL. GONNA PUT DOWN MY GUN.
SLOOOWLY.
AND THEN I'M GONNA SET DOWN THE ROOSTER.
ALL RIGHT, POYO.
GUESS THESE ROOSKIE FUCKWADS AREN'T GONNA LET US DO IT THE EASY WAY.
SHOW 'EM WHAT HAPPENS WHEN THEY MESS WITH AN AMERICAN CYBERNETIC LUCHADOR CHICKEN!
NO.
I GOT A BETTER IDEA.

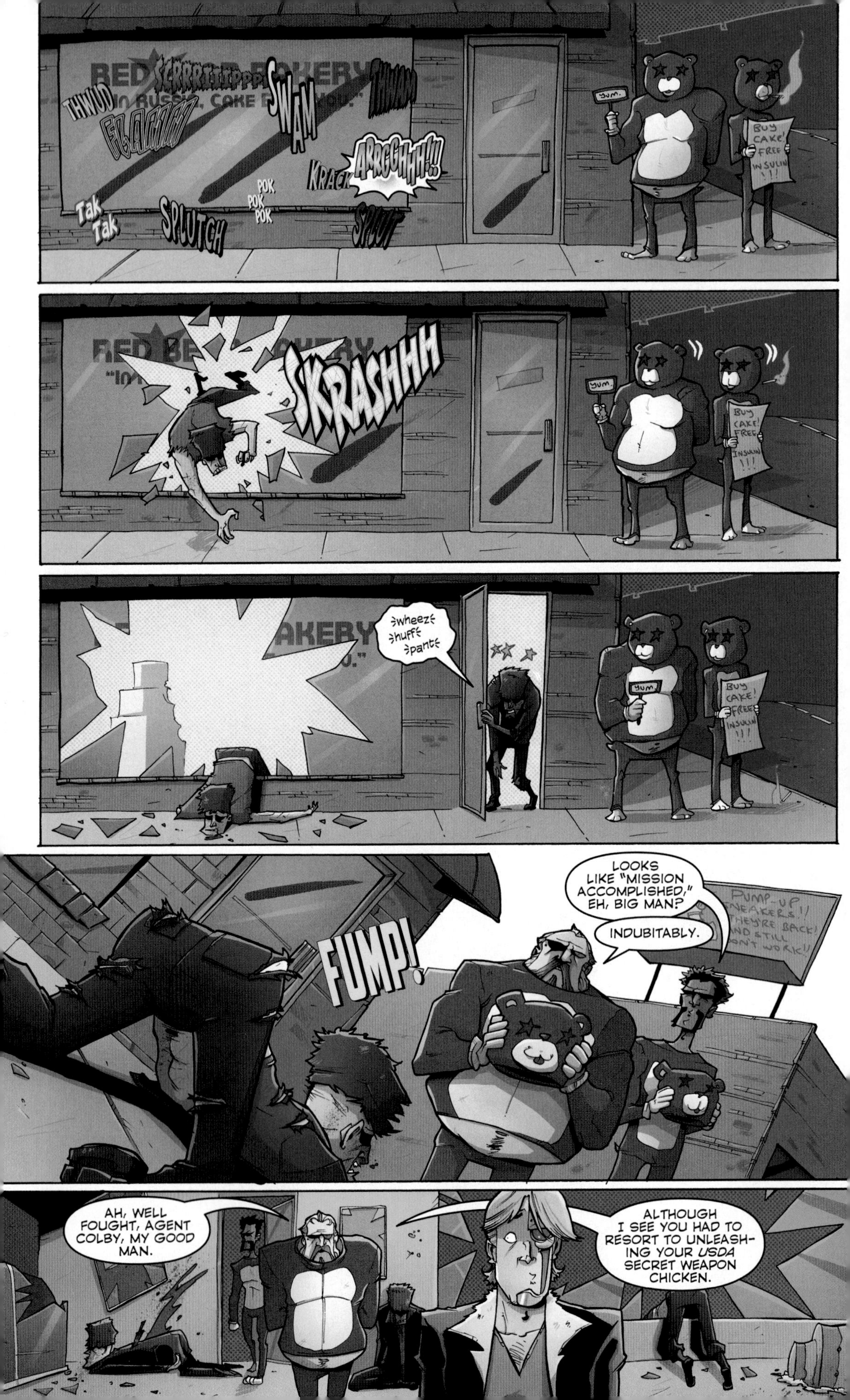
THWUD
SWAM
KRACK
ARRGGHHH!!!
Tak Tak
SPLUTCH
POK POK POK
YUM.
BUY CAKE! FREE INSULIN!!!
SKRASHHH
YUM.
BUY CAKE! FREE INSULIN!!!
wheez huff pant
YUM.
BUY CAKE! FREE INSULIN!!!
FUMP!
LOOKS LIKE "MISSION ACCOMPLISHED," EH, BIG MAN?
INDUBITABLY.
PUMP-UP
AH, WELL FOUGHT, AGENT COLBY, MY GOOD MAN.
ALTHOUGH I SEE YOU HAD TO RESORT TO UNLEASHING YOUR *USDA* SECRET WEAPON CHICKEN.

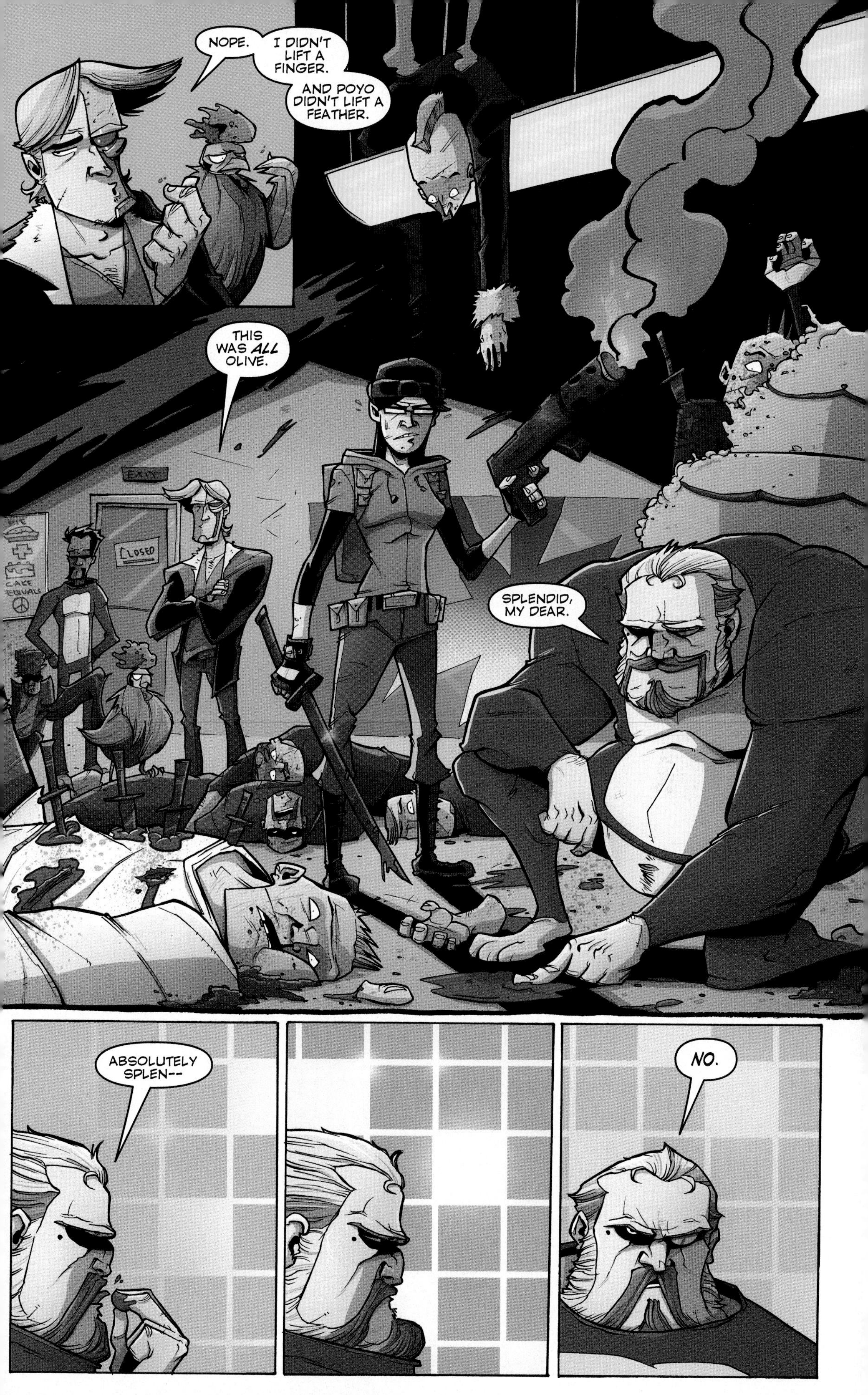
NOPE.
I DIDN'T LIFT A FINGER.
AND POYO DIDN'T LIFT A FEATHER.
THIS WAS ALL OLIVE.
EXIT
CLOSED
SPLENDID, MY DEAR.
ABSOLUTELY SPLEN--
NO.

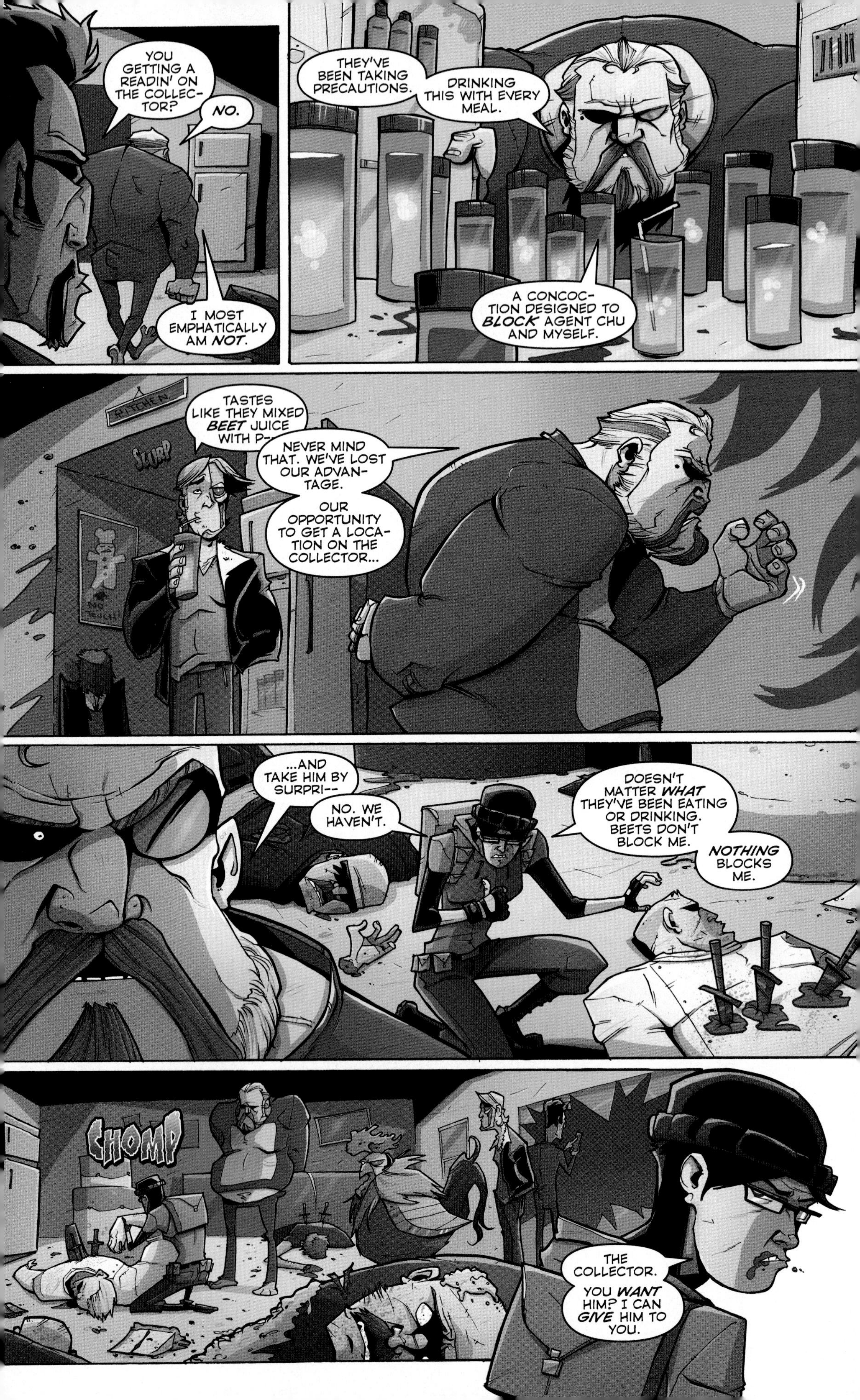
YOU GETTING A READIN' ON THE COLLECTOR?
NO.
I MOST EMPHATICALLY AM NOT.
THEY'VE BEEN TAKING PRECAUTIONS.
DRINKING THIS WITH EVERY MEAL.
A CONCOCTION DESIGNED TO BLOCK AGENT CHU AND MYSELF.
KITCHEN
TASTES LIKE THEY MIXED BEET JUICE WITH P--
SLURP
NEVER MIND THAT. WE'VE LOST OUR ADVANTAGE.
OUR OPPORTUNITY TO GET A LOCATION ON THE COLLECTOR...
NO TOUCH!
...AND TAKE HIM BY SURPRI--
NO. WE HAVEN'T.
DOESN'T MATTER WHAT THEY'VE BEEN EATING OR DRINKING. BEETS DON'T BLOCK ME.
NOTHING BLOCKS ME.
CHOMP
THE COLLECTOR.
YOU WANT HIM? I CAN GIVE HIM TO YOU.

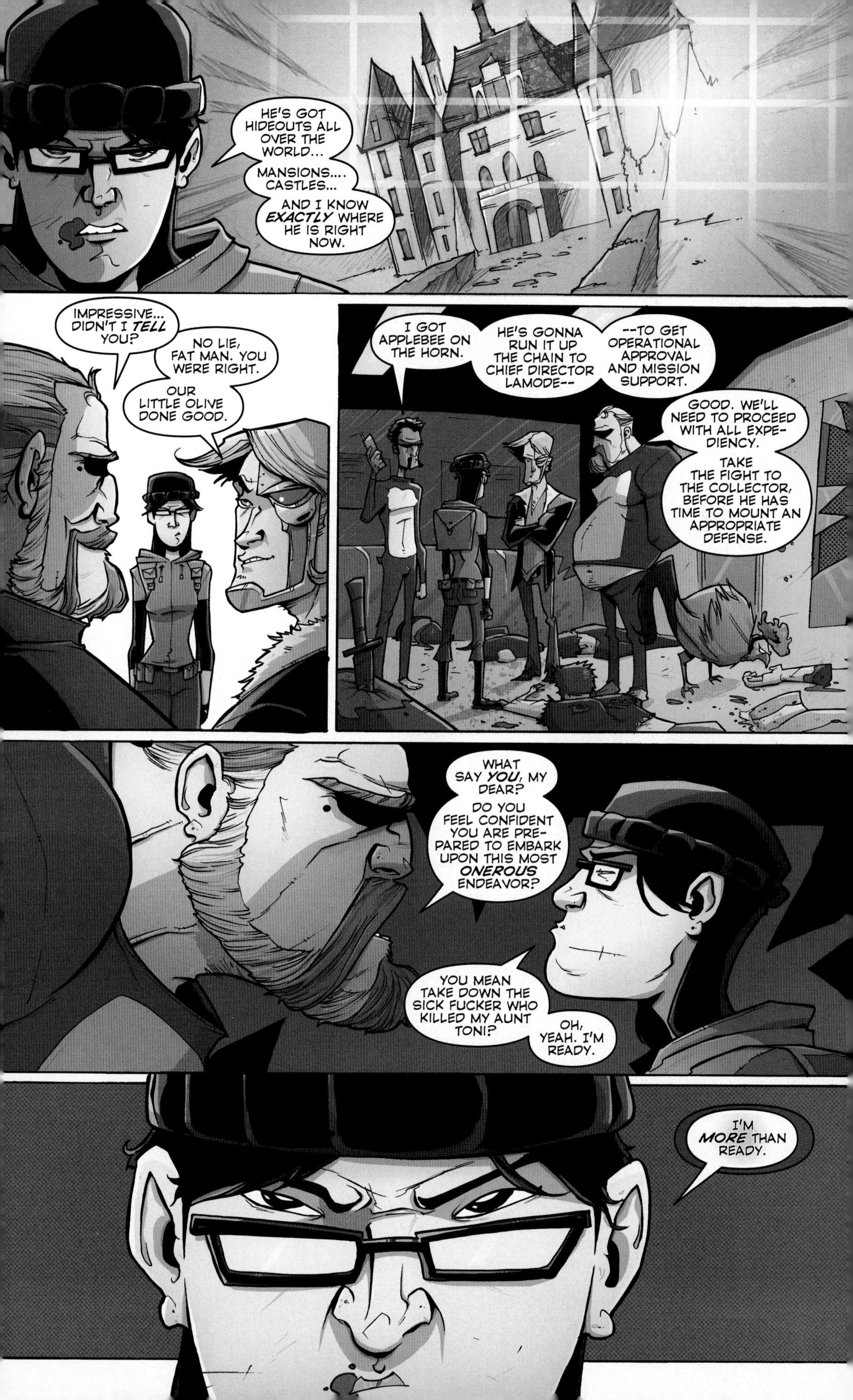
HE'S GOT HIDEOUTS ALL OVER THE WORLD...
MANSIONS.... CASTLES...
AND I KNOW *EXACTLY* WHERE HE IS RIGHT NOW.
IMPRESSIVE... DIDN'T I *TELL* YOU?
NO LIE, FAT MAN. YOU WERE RIGHT.
OUR LITTLE OLIVE DONE GOOD.
I GOT APPLEBEE ON THE HORN.
HE'S GONNA RUN IT UP THE CHAIN TO CHIEF DIRECTOR LAMODE--
--TO GET OPERATIONAL APPROVAL AND MISSION SUPPORT.
GOOD. WE'LL NEED TO PROCEED WITH ALL EXPE-DIENCY.
TAKE THE FIGHT TO THE COLLECTOR, BEFORE HE HAS TIME TO MOUNT AN APPROPRIATE DEFENSE.
WHAT SAY *YOU*, MY DEAR?
DO YOU FEEL CONFIDENT YOU ARE PRE-PARED TO EMBARK UPON THIS MOST *ONEROUS* ENDEAVOR?
YOU MEAN TAKE DOWN THE SICK FUCKER WHO KILLED MY AUNT TONI?
OH, YEAH. I'M READY.
I'M *MORE* THAN READY.

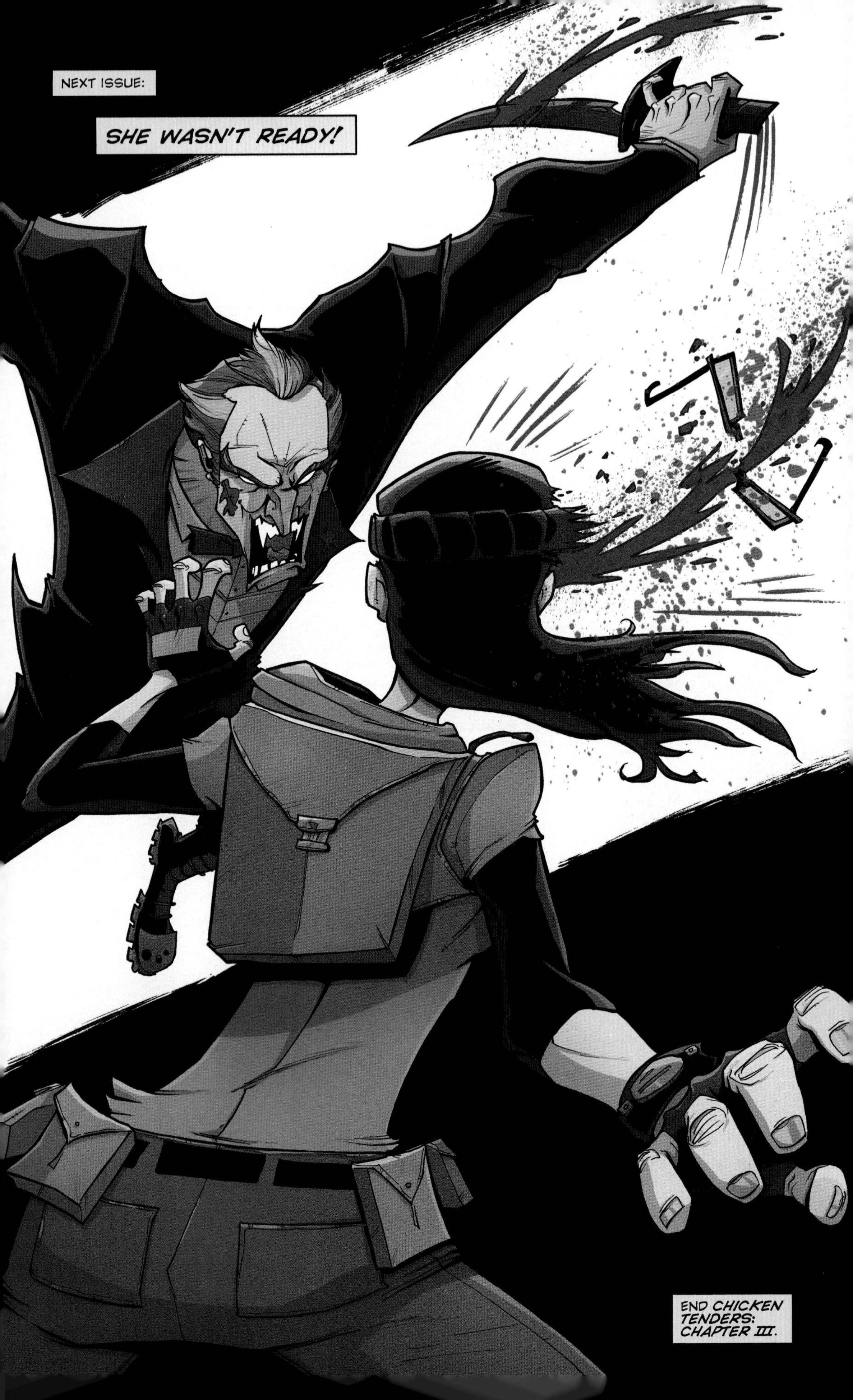
NEXT ISSUE:
SHE WASN'T READY!
END CHICKEN TENDERS: CHAPTER III.

Chapter 4

ROB!

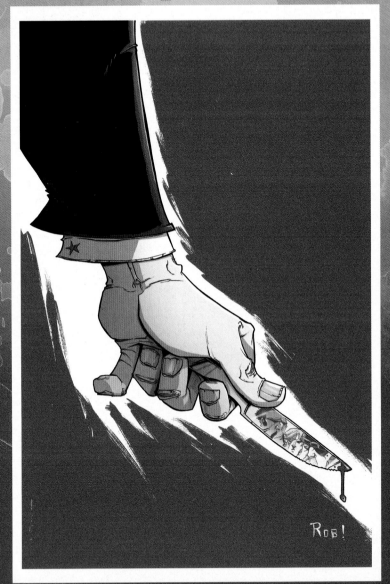

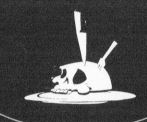

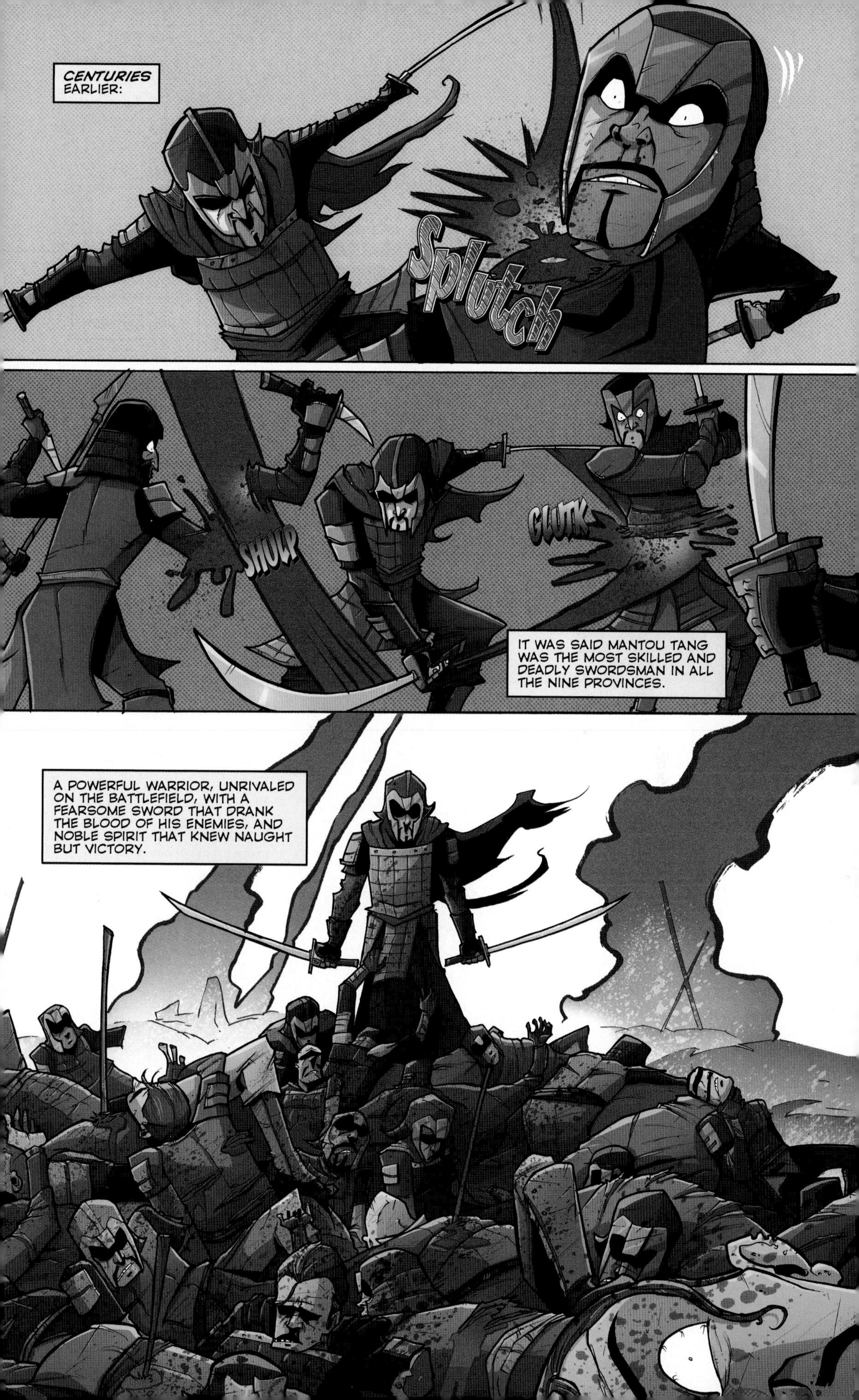
CENTURIES EARLIER:
SPLUTCH
SHULP
GLUTK
IT WAS SAID MANTOU TANG WAS THE MOST SKILLED AND DEADLY SWORDSMAN IN ALL THE NINE PROVINCES.
A POWERFUL WARRIOR, UNRIVALED ON THE BATTLEFIELD, WITH A FEARSOME SWORD THAT DRANK THE BLOOD OF HIS ENEMIES, AND NOBLE SPIRIT THAT KNEW NAUGHT BUT VICTORY.

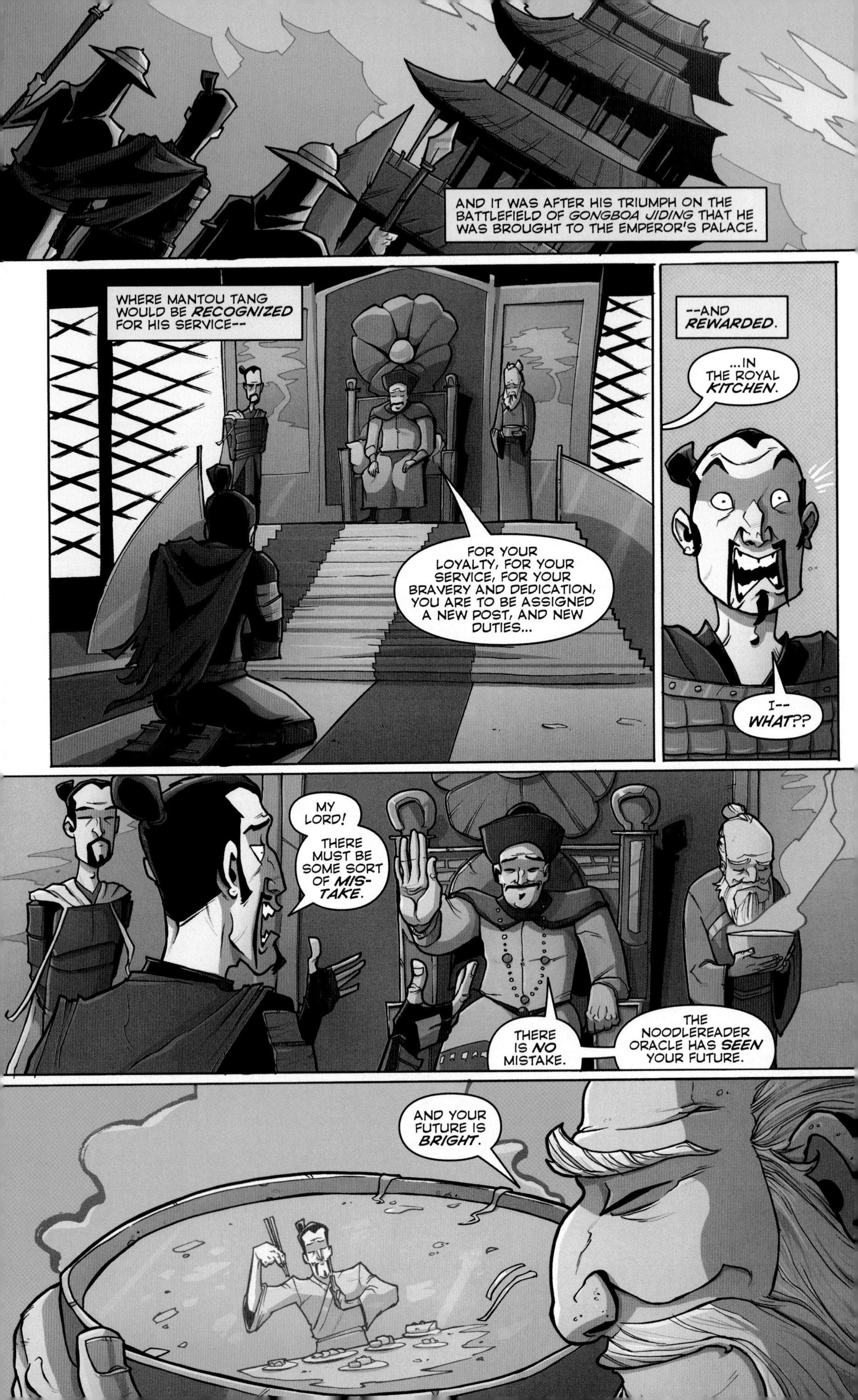
AND IT WAS AFTER HIS TRIUMPH ON THE BATTLEFIELD OF *GONGBOA JIDING* THAT HE WAS BROUGHT TO THE EMPEROR'S PALACE.
WHERE MANTOU TANG WOULD BE *RECOGNIZED* FOR HIS SERVICE--
FOR YOUR LOYALTY, FOR YOUR SERVICE, FOR YOUR BRAVERY AND DEDICATION, YOU ARE TO BE ASSIGNED A NEW POST, AND NEW DUTIES...
--AND *REWARDED*.
...IN THE ROYAL *KITCHEN*.
I-- *WHAT??*
MY *LORD!*
THERE MUST BE SOME SORT OF *MIS-TAKE*.
THERE IS *NO* MISTAKE.
THE NOODLEREADER ORACLE HAS *SEEN* YOUR FUTURE.
AND YOUR FUTURE IS *BRIGHT*.

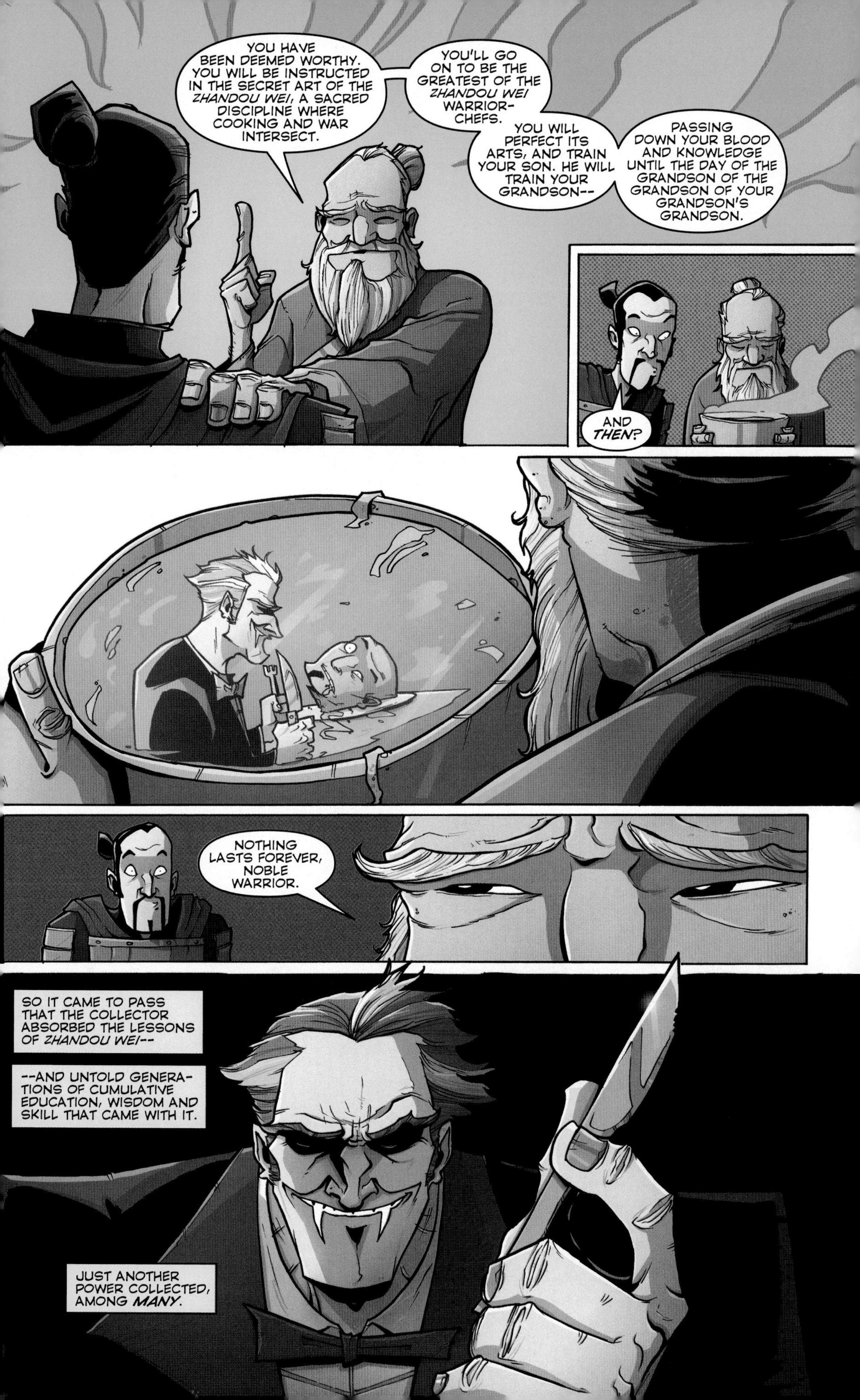
YOU HAVE BEEN DEEMED WORTHY. YOU WILL BE INSTRUCTED IN THE SECRET ART OF THE *ZHANDOU WEI*, A SACRED DISCIPLINE WHERE COOKING AND WAR INTERSECT.
YOU'LL GO ON TO BE THE GREATEST OF THE *ZHANDOU WEI* WARRIOR-CHEFS.
YOU WILL PERFECT ITS ARTS, AND TRAIN YOUR SON. HE WILL TRAIN YOUR GRANDSON--
PASSING DOWN YOUR BLOOD AND KNOWLEDGE UNTIL THE DAY OF THE GRANDSON OF THE GRANDSON OF YOUR GRANDSON'S GRANDSON.
AND *THEN*?
NOTHING LASTS FOREVER, NOBLE WARRIOR.
SO IT CAME TO PASS THAT THE COLLECTOR ABSORBED THE LESSONS OF *ZHANDOU WEI*--
--AND UNTOLD GENERATIONS OF CUMULATIVE EDUCATION, WISDOM AND SKILL THAT CAME WITH IT.
JUST ANOTHER POWER COLLECTED, AMONG *MANY*.

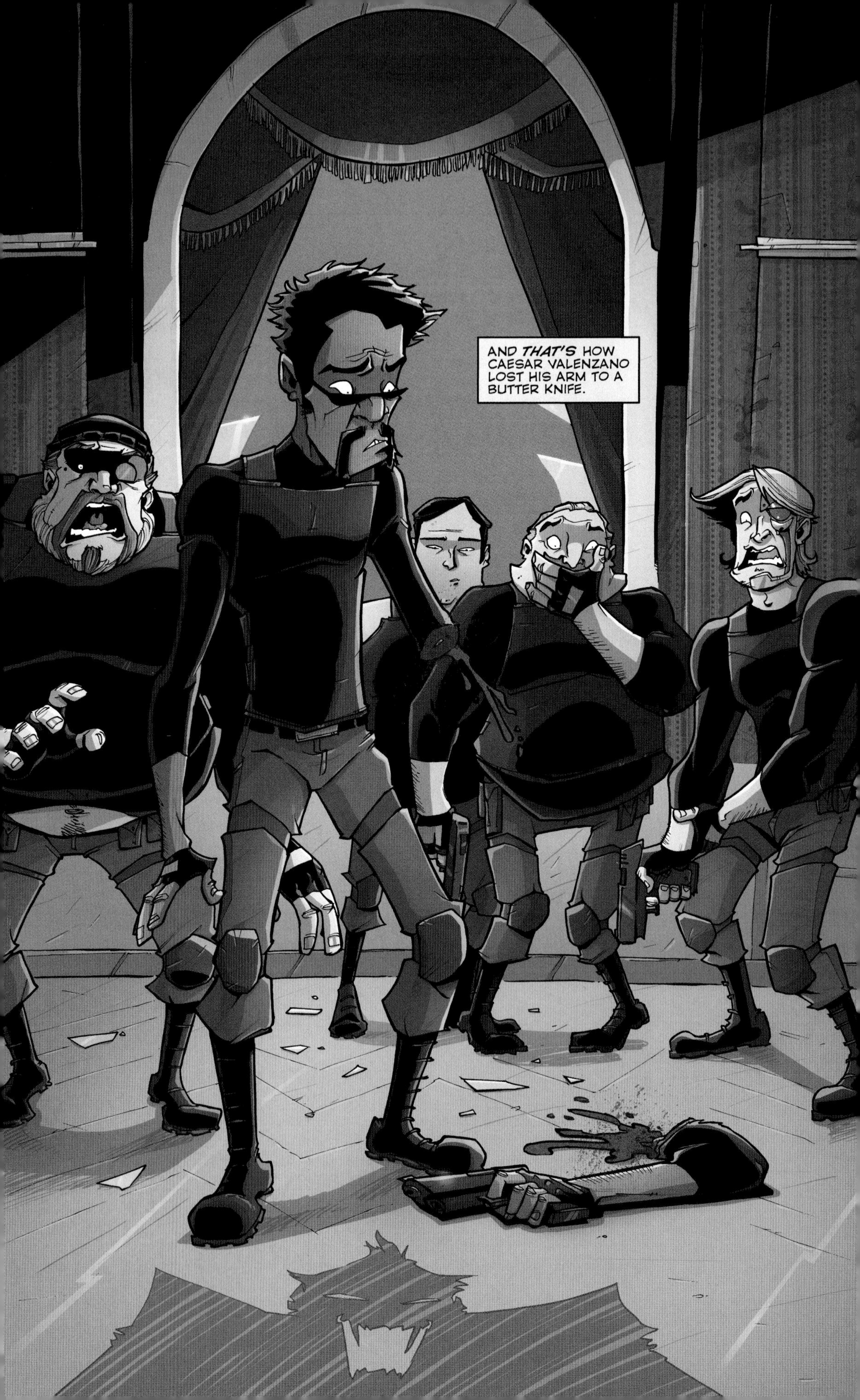
AND *THAT'S* HOW CAESAR VALENZANO LOST HIS ARM TO A BUTTER KNIFE.

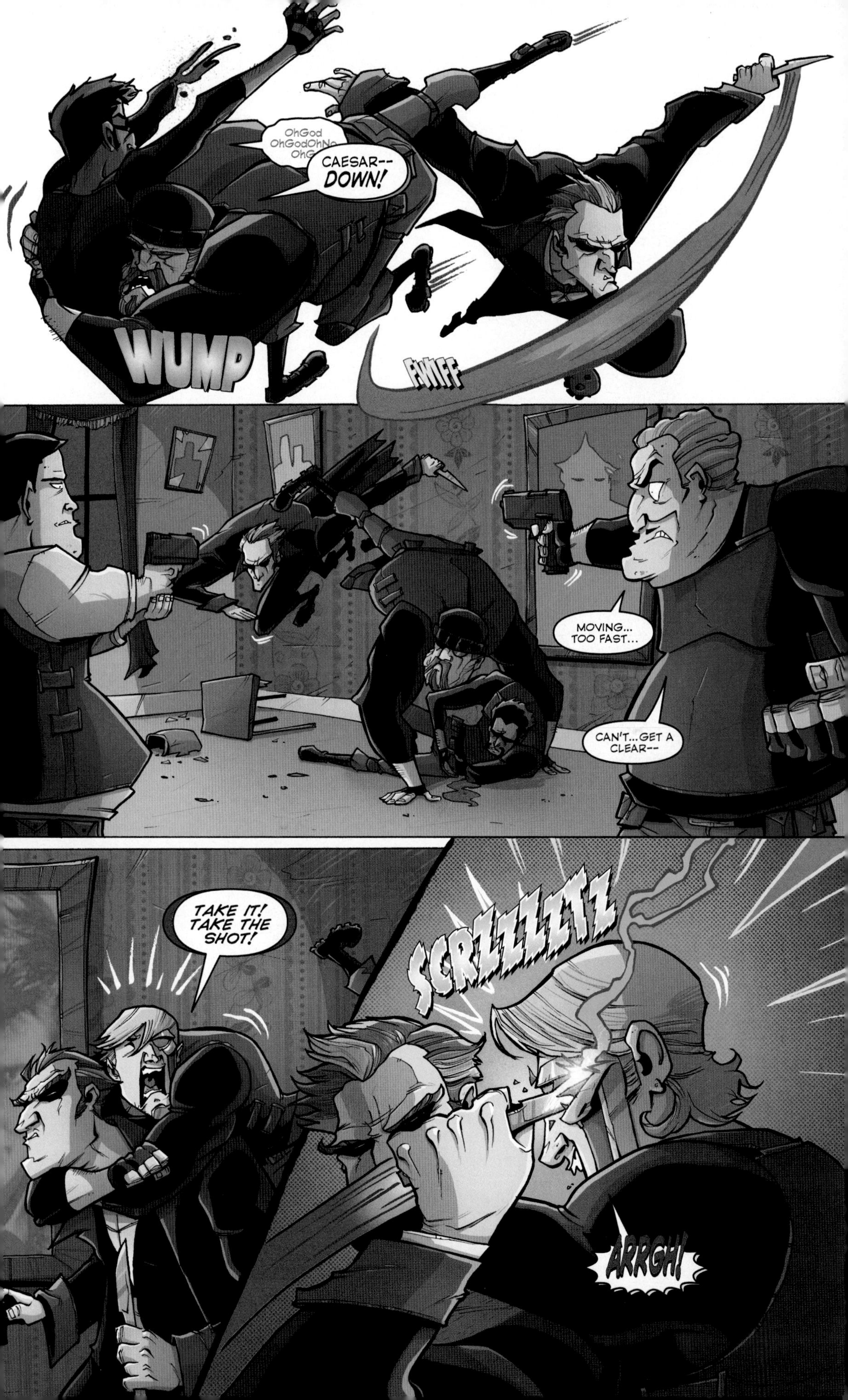
OhGod OhGodOhNo OhG
CAESAR-- DOWN!
WUMP
FWIFF
MOVING... TOO FAST...
CAN'T...GET A CLEAR--
TAKE IT! TAKE THE SHOT!
SCRZZZZZTZ
ARRGH!

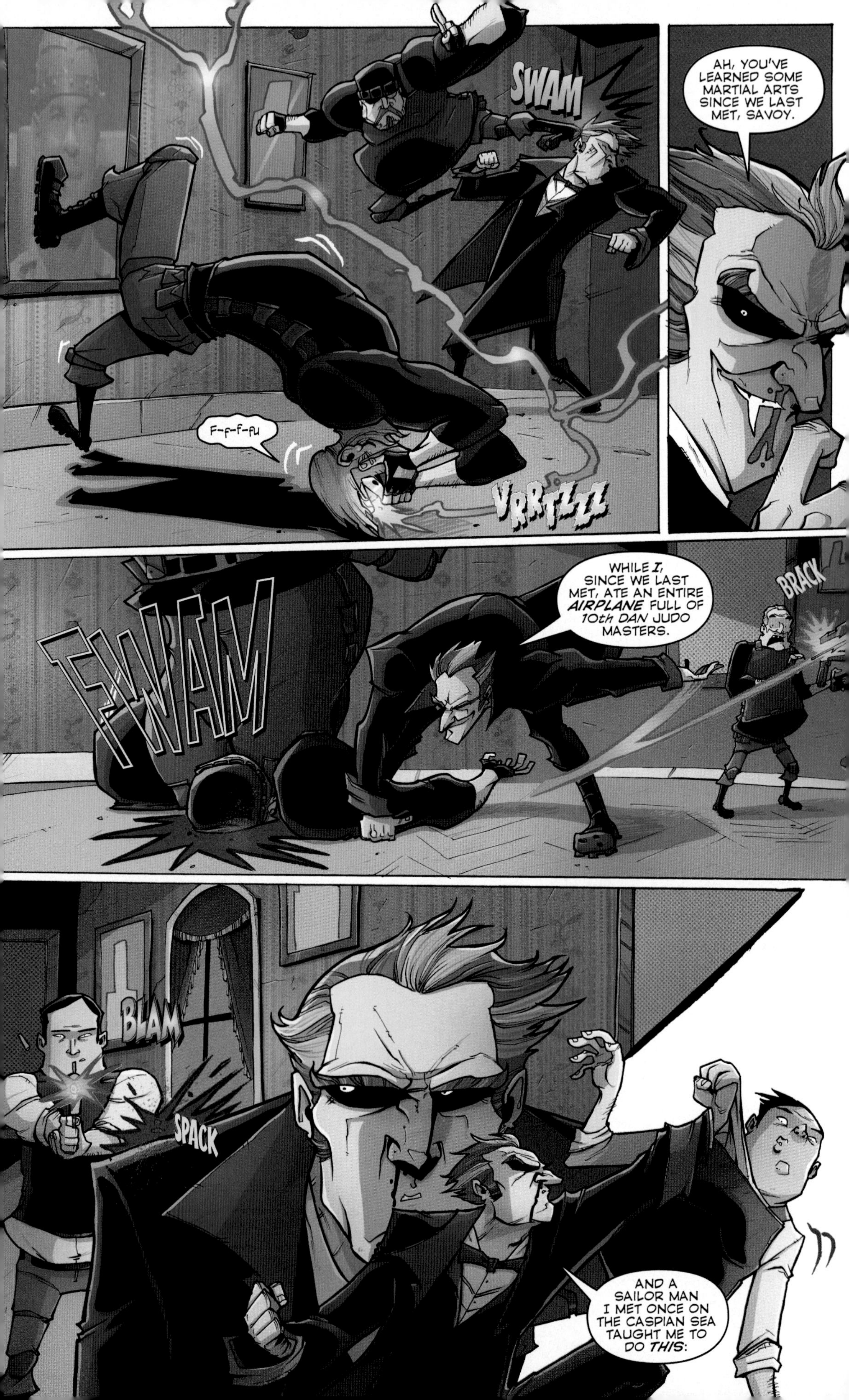
SWAM
F-f-f-fu
VRRTZZZ
AH, YOU'VE LEARNED SOME MARTIAL ARTS SINCE WE LAST MET, SAVOY.
FWAM
WHILE I, SINCE WE LAST MET, ATE AN ENTIRE AIRPLANE FULL OF 10th DAN JUDO MASTERS.
BRACK
BLAM
SPACK
AND A SAILOR MAN I MET ONCE ON THE CASPIAN SEA TAUGHT ME TO DO THIS:

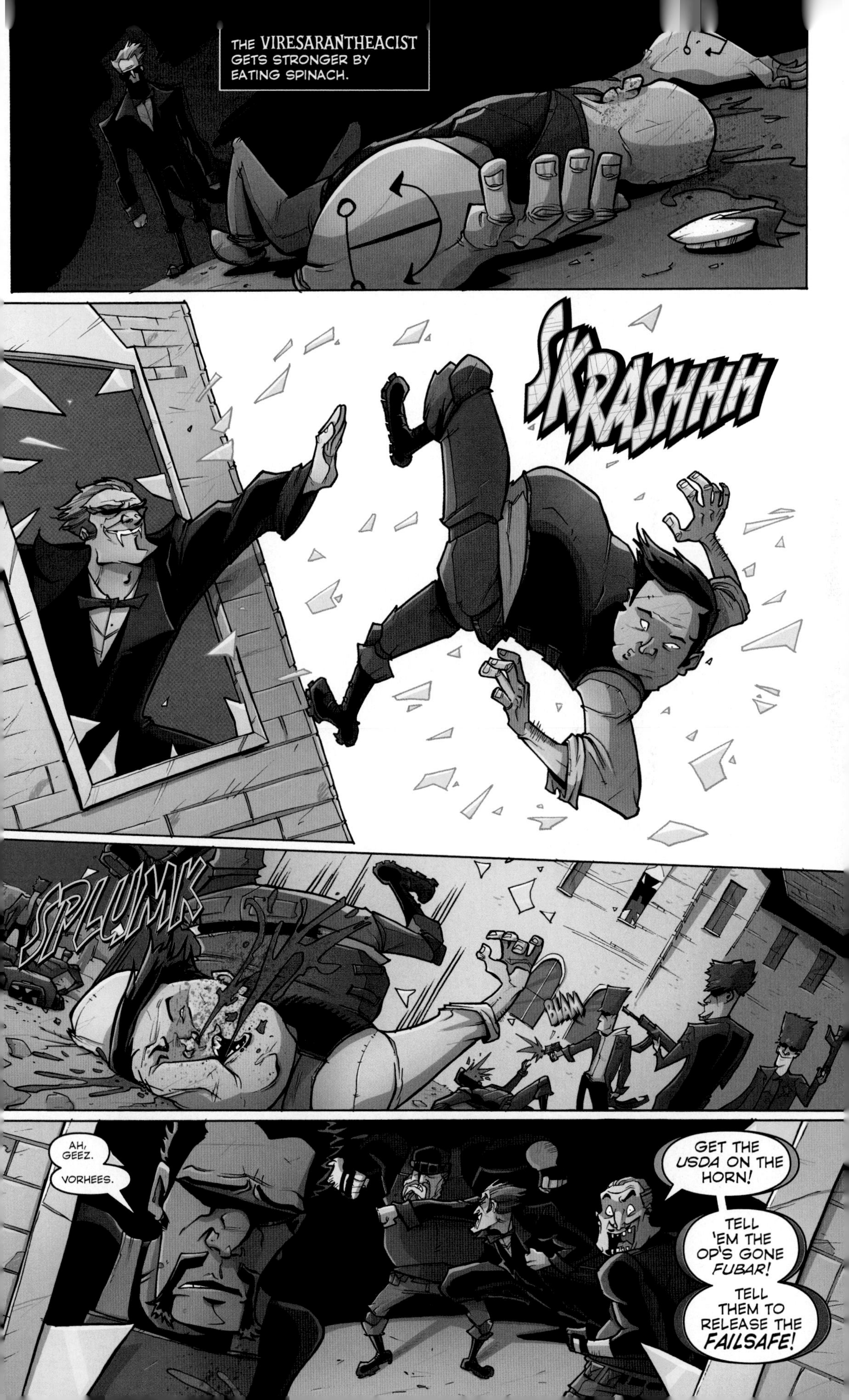
THE VIRESARANTHEACIST GETS STRONGER BY EATING SPINACH.
SKRASHHH
SPLUMK
BLAM
AH, GEEZ.
VORHEES.
GET THE USDA ON THE HORN!
TELL 'EM THE OP'S GONE FUBAR!
TELL THEM TO RELEASE THE FAILSAFE!

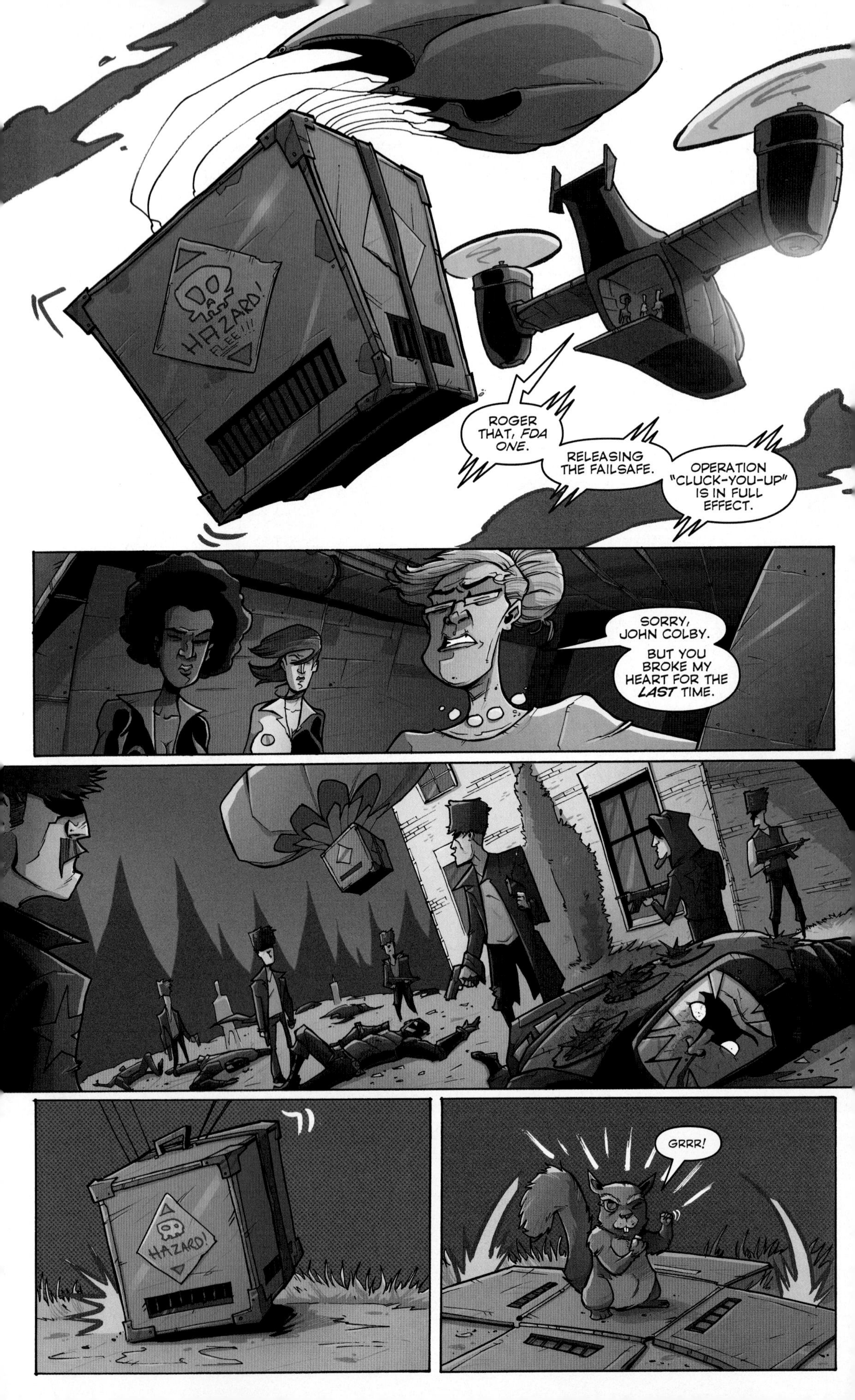
HAZARD!
FLEE!!!
ROGER THAT, FDA ONE.
RELEASING THE FAILSAFE.
OPERATION "CLUCK-YOU-UP" IS IN FULL EFFECT.
SORRY, JOHN COLBY.
BUT YOU BROKE MY HEART FOR THE LAST TIME.
HAZARD!
GRRR!

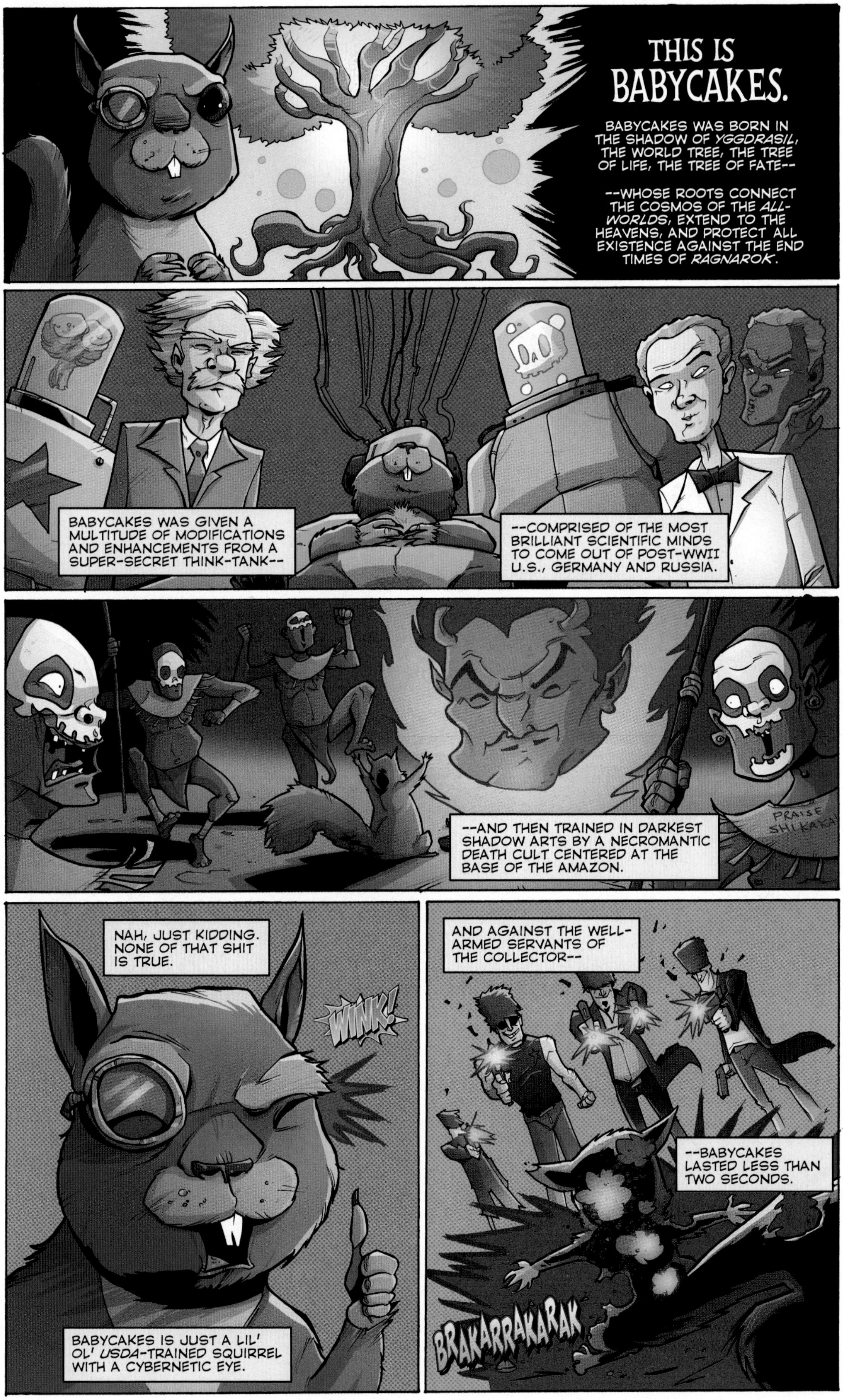
THIS IS BABYCAKES.
BABYCAKES WAS BORN IN THE SHADOW OF *YGGDRASIL*, THE WORLD TREE, THE TREE OF LIFE, THE TREE OF FATE--
--WHOSE ROOTS CONNECT THE COSMOS OF THE *ALL-WORLDS*, EXTEND TO THE HEAVENS, AND PROTECT ALL EXISTENCE AGAINST THE END TIMES OF *RAGNAROK*.
BABYCAKES WAS GIVEN A MULTITUDE OF MODIFICATIONS AND ENHANCEMENTS FROM A SUPER-SECRET THINK-TANK--
--COMPRISED OF THE MOST BRILLIANT SCIENTIFIC MINDS TO COME OUT OF POST-WWII U.S., GERMANY AND RUSSIA.
PRAISE SHIKAKA
--AND THEN TRAINED IN DARKEST SHADOW ARTS BY A NECROMANTIC DEATH CULT CENTERED AT THE BASE OF THE AMAZON.
NAH, JUST KIDDING. NONE OF THAT SHIT IS TRUE.
WINK!
BABYCAKES IS JUST A LIL' OL' *USDA*-TRAINED SQUIRREL WITH A CYBERNETIC EYE.
AND AGAINST THE WELL-ARMED SERVANTS OF THE COLLECTOR--
--BABYCAKES LASTED LESS THAN TWO SECONDS.
BRAKARRAKARAK

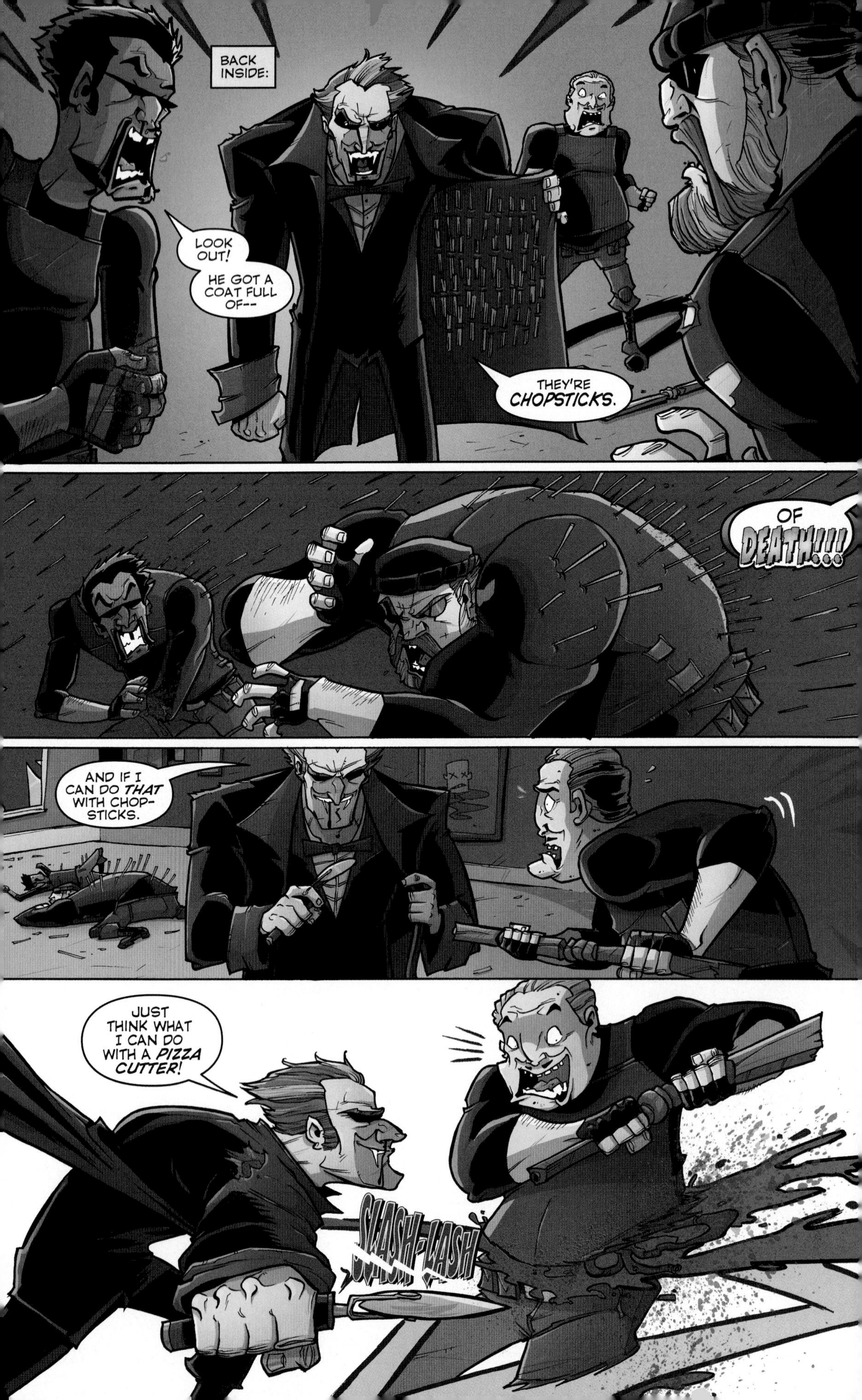

BACK INSIDE:
LOOK OUT!
HE GOT A COAT FULL OF--
THEY'RE *CHOPSTICKS.*
OF DEATH!!!
AND IF I CAN DO *THAT* WITH CHOP-STICKS.
JUST THINK WHAT I CAN DO WITH A *PIZZA CUTTER!*
SLASH-LASH

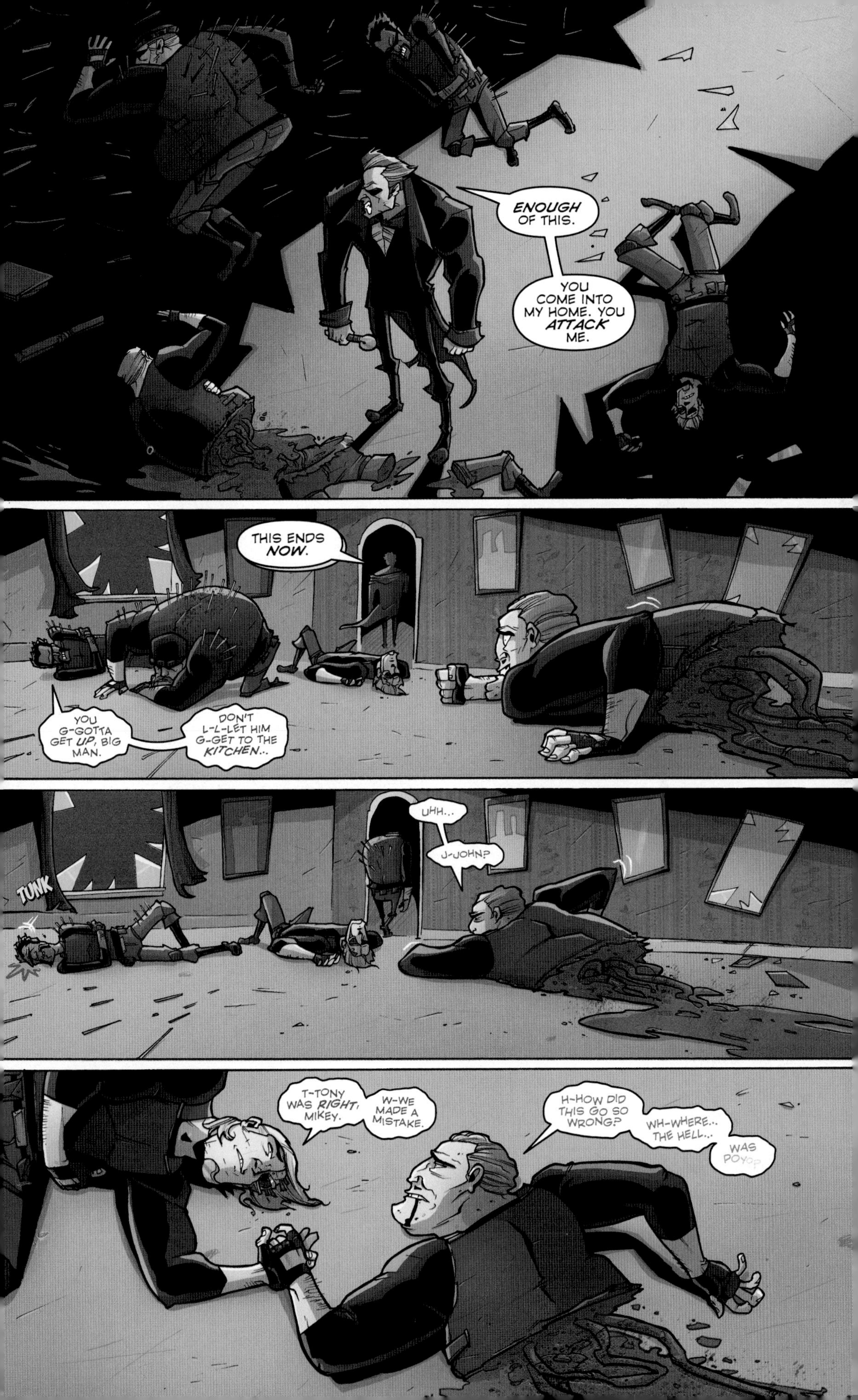

ENOUGH OF THIS.
YOU COME INTO MY HOME. YOU ATTACK ME.
THIS ENDS NOW.
YOU G-GOTTA GET UP, BIG MAN.
DON'T L-L-LET HIM G-GET TO THE KITCHEN...
TUNK
UHH...
J-JOHN?
T-TONY WAS RIGHT, MIKEY.
W-WE MADE A MISTAKE.
H-HOW DID THIS GO SO WRONG?
WH-WHERE... THE HELL...
WAS POYOP

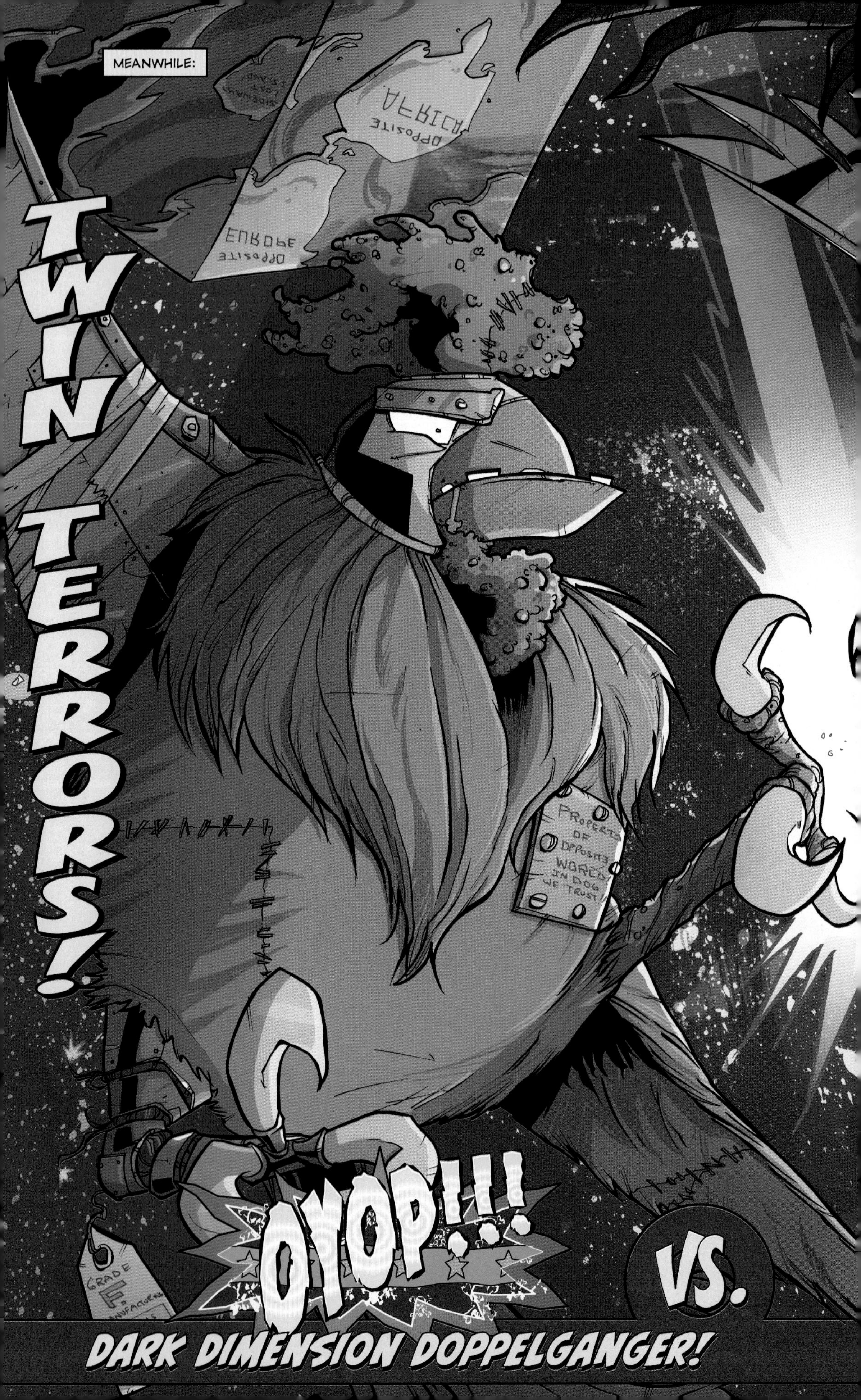
MEANWHILE:
TWIN TERRORS!
PROPERTY OF OPPOSITE WORLD IN DOG WE TRUST!
OYOP!!!
VS.
DARK DIMENSION DOPPELGANGER!

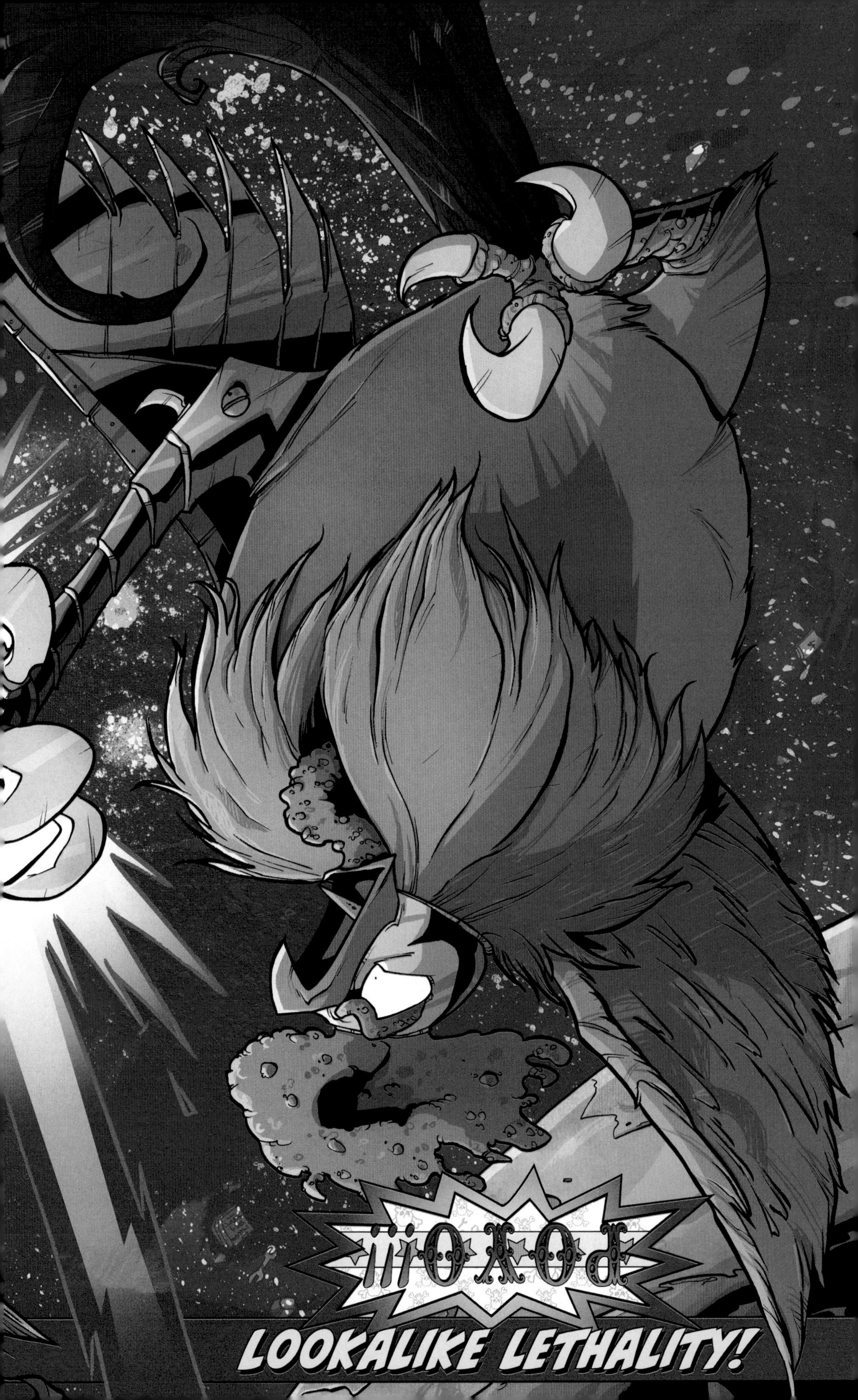

POXO!!
LOOKALIKE LETHALITY!

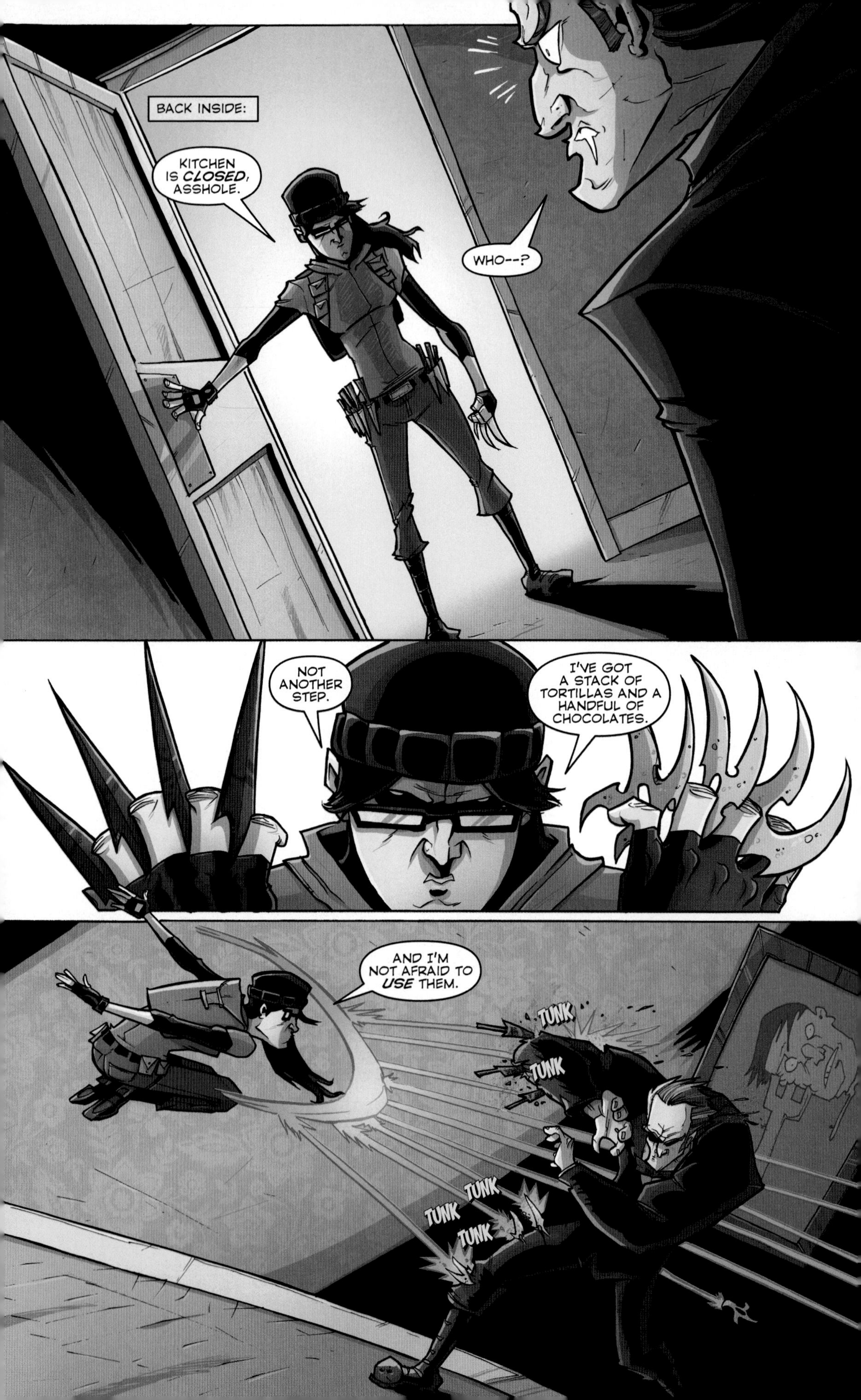
BACK INSIDE:
KITCHEN IS *CLOSED*, ASSHOLE.
WHO--?
NOT ANOTHER STEP.
I'VE GOT A STACK OF TORTILLAS AND A HANDFUL OF CHOCOLATES.
AND I'M NOT AFRAID TO *USE* THEM.
TUNK
TUNK
TUNK
TUNK
TUNK

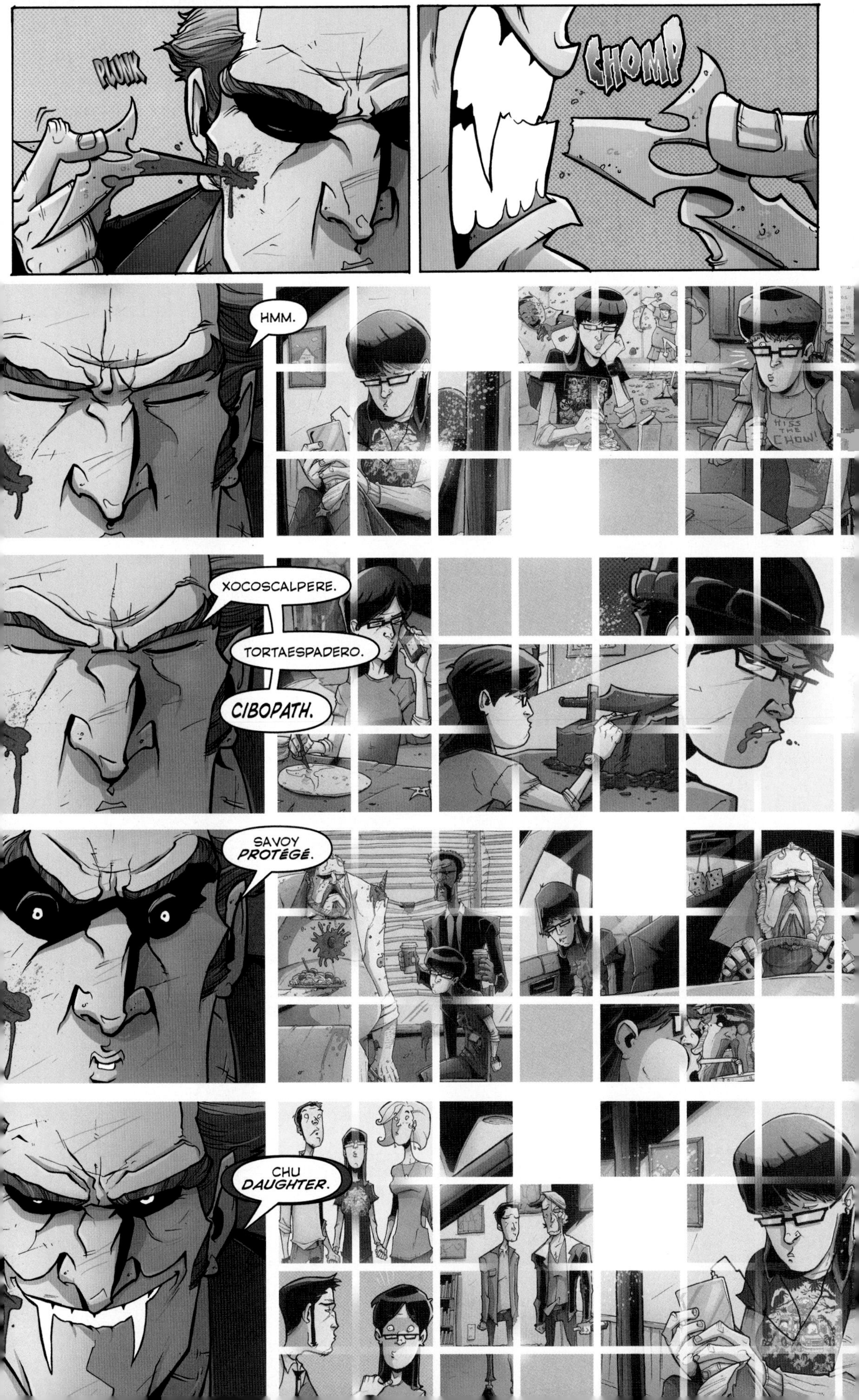

PLUNK
CHOMP
HMM.
HISS THE CHOW!
XOCOSCALPERE.
TORTAESPADERO.
CIBOPATH.
SAVOY PROTÉGÉ.
CHU DAUGHTER.

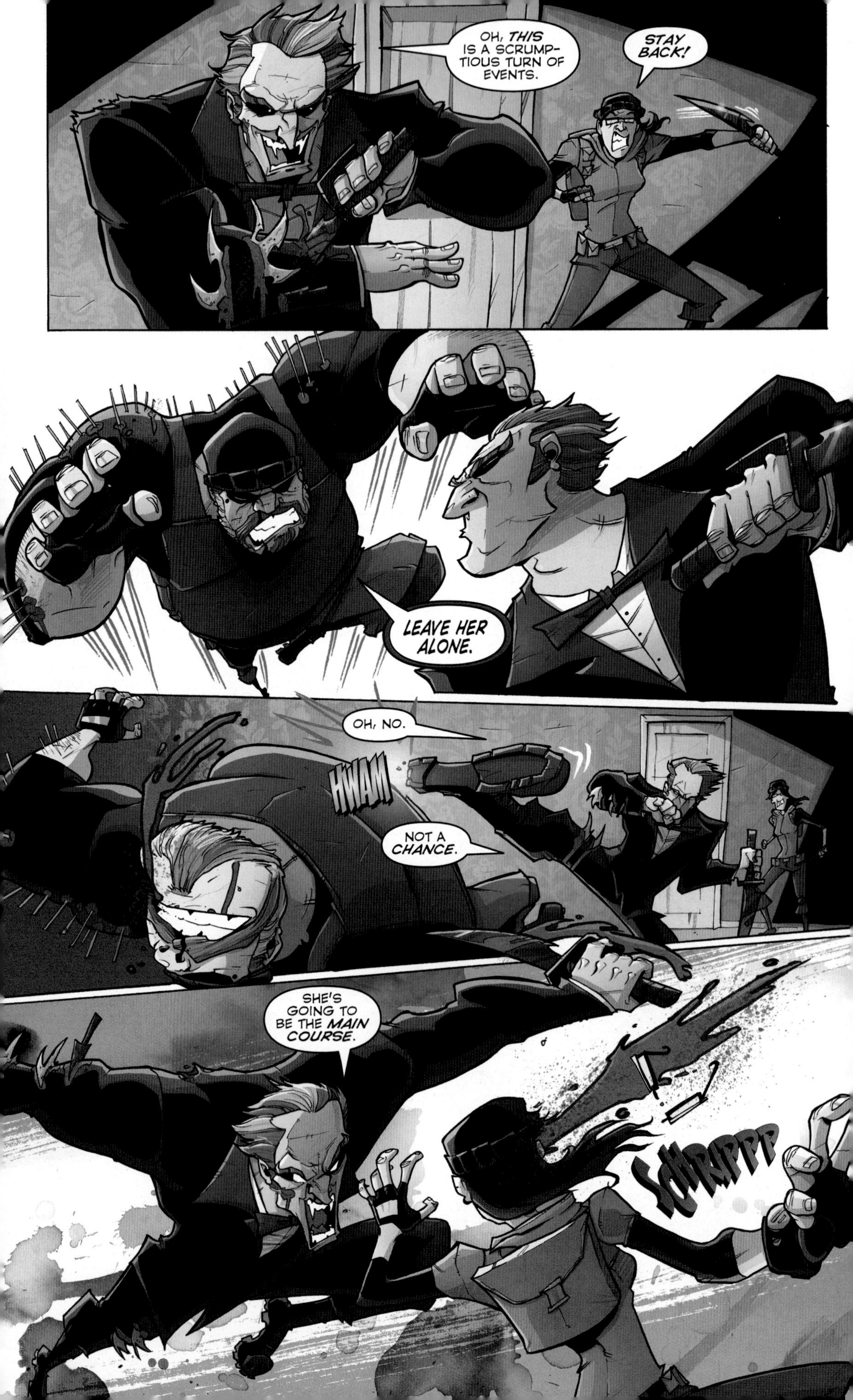
OH, *THIS* IS A SCRUMP-TIOUS TURN OF EVENTS.
STAY BACK!
LEAVE HER ALONE.
OH, NO.
HWAM
NOT A *CHANCE*.
SHE'S GOING TO BE THE *MAIN COURSE*.
SCHRIPPP

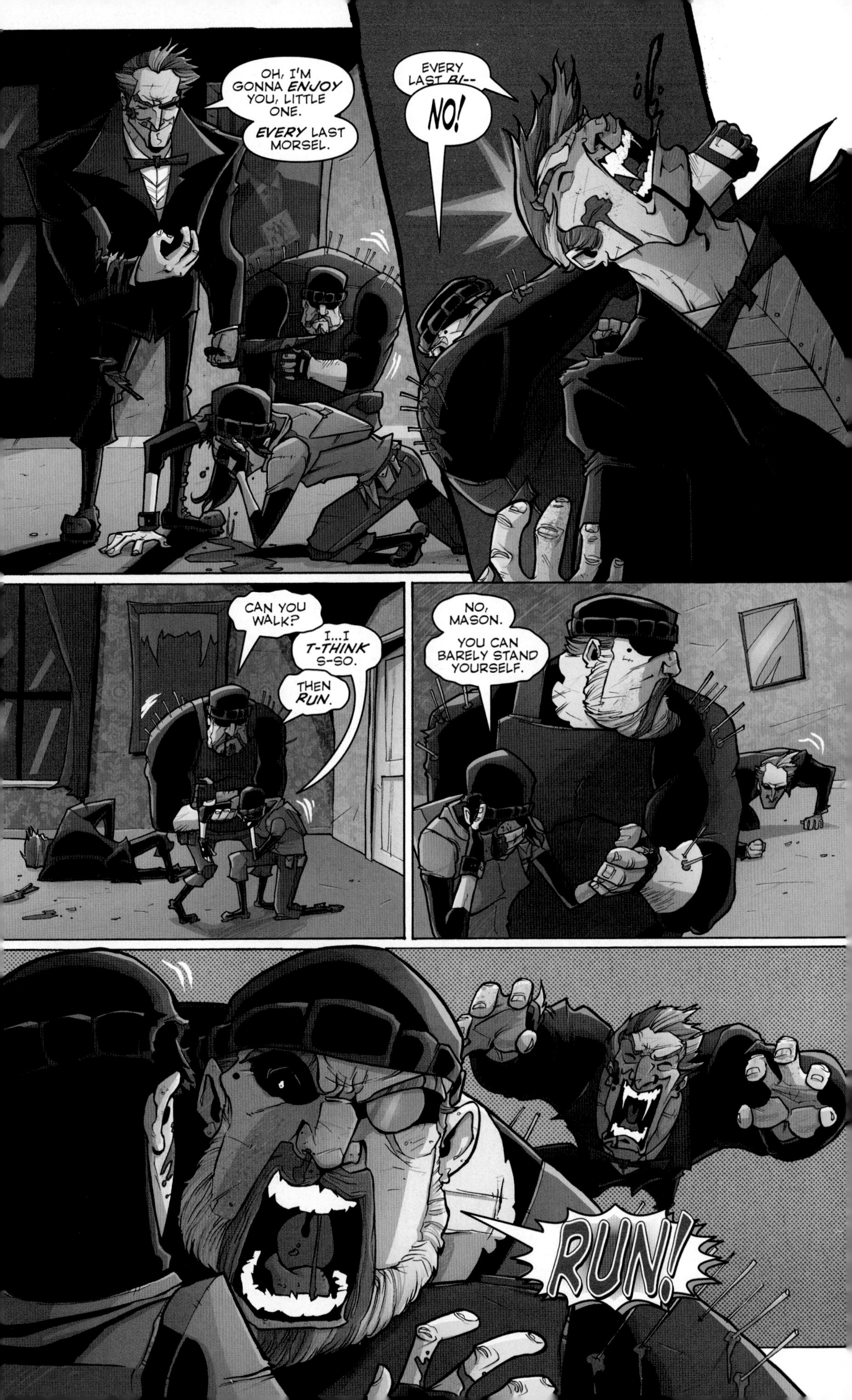
OH, I'M GONNA ENJOY YOU, LITTLE ONE.
EVERY LAST MORSEL.
EVERY LAST B/--
NO!
CAN YOU WALK?
I...I T-THINK S-SO.
THEN RUN.
NO, MASON.
YOU CAN BARELY STAND YOURSELF.
RUN!

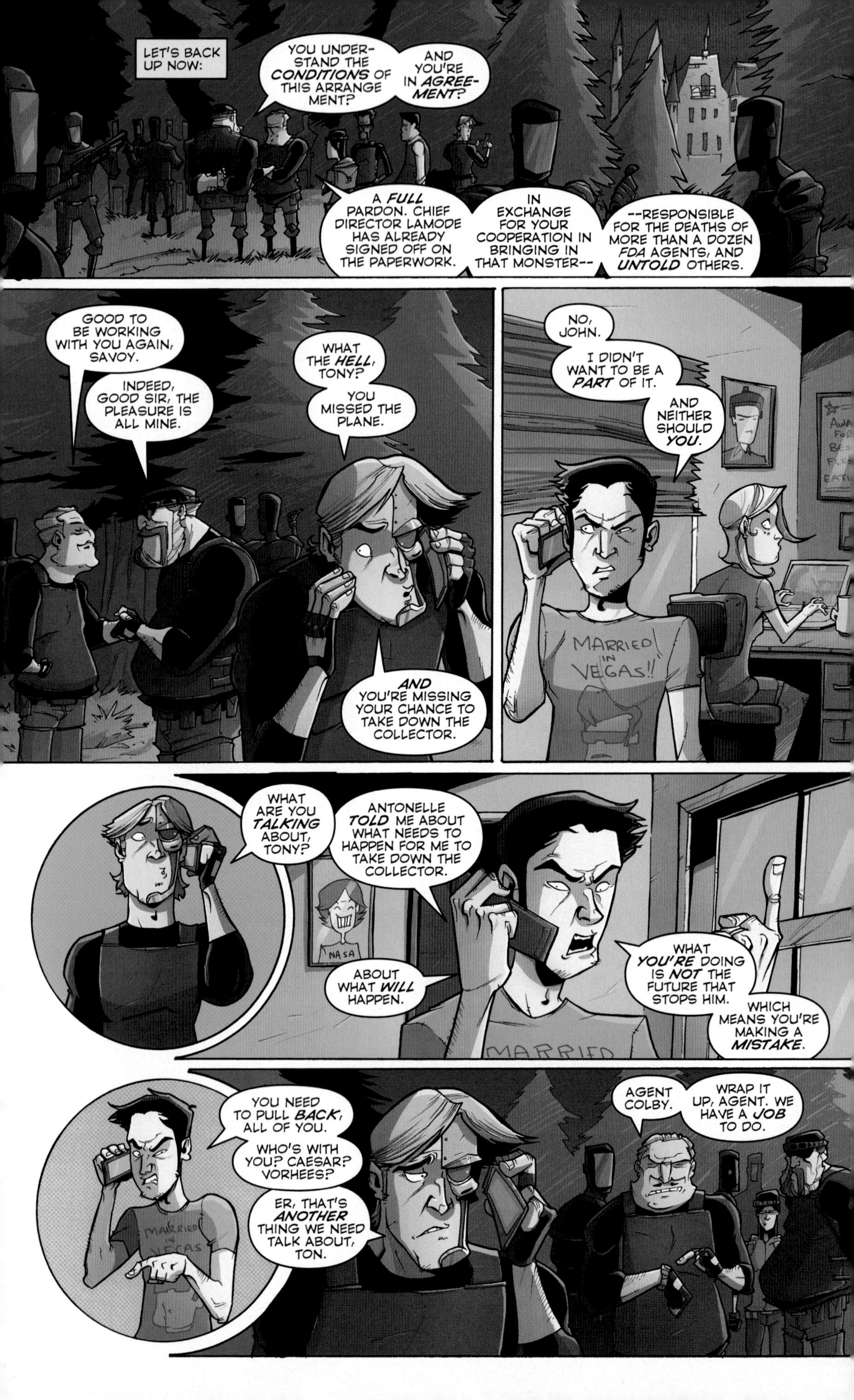
LET'S BACK UP NOW:
YOU UNDERSTAND THE CONDITIONS OF THIS ARRANGEMENT?
AND YOU'RE IN AGREEMENT?
A FULL PARDON. CHIEF DIRECTOR LAMODE HAS ALREADY SIGNED OFF ON THE PAPERWORK.
IN EXCHANGE FOR YOUR COOPERATION IN BRINGING IN THAT MONSTER--
--RESPONSIBLE FOR THE DEATHS OF MORE THAN A DOZEN FDA AGENTS, AND UNTOLD OTHERS.
GOOD TO BE WORKING WITH YOU AGAIN, SAVOY.
INDEED, GOOD SIR, THE PLEASURE IS ALL MINE.
WHAT THE HELL, TONY?
YOU MISSED THE PLANE.
AND YOU'RE MISSING YOUR CHANCE TO TAKE DOWN THE COLLECTOR.
NO, JOHN.
I DIDN'T WANT TO BE A PART OF IT.
AND NEITHER SHOULD YOU.
MARRIED IN VEGAS!!
WHAT ARE YOU TALKING ABOUT, TONY?
ANTONELLE TOLD ME ABOUT WHAT NEEDS TO HAPPEN FOR ME TO TAKE DOWN THE COLLECTOR.
NASA
ABOUT WHAT WILL HAPPEN.
WHAT YOU'RE DOING IS NOT THE FUTURE THAT STOPS HIM.
WHICH MEANS YOU'RE MAKING A MISTAKE.
YOU NEED TO PULL BACK, ALL OF YOU.
WHO'S WITH YOU? CAESAR? VORHEES?
ER, THAT'S ANOTHER THING WE NEED TALK ABOUT, TON.
AGENT COLBY.
WRAP IT UP, AGENT. WE HAVE A JOB TO DO.

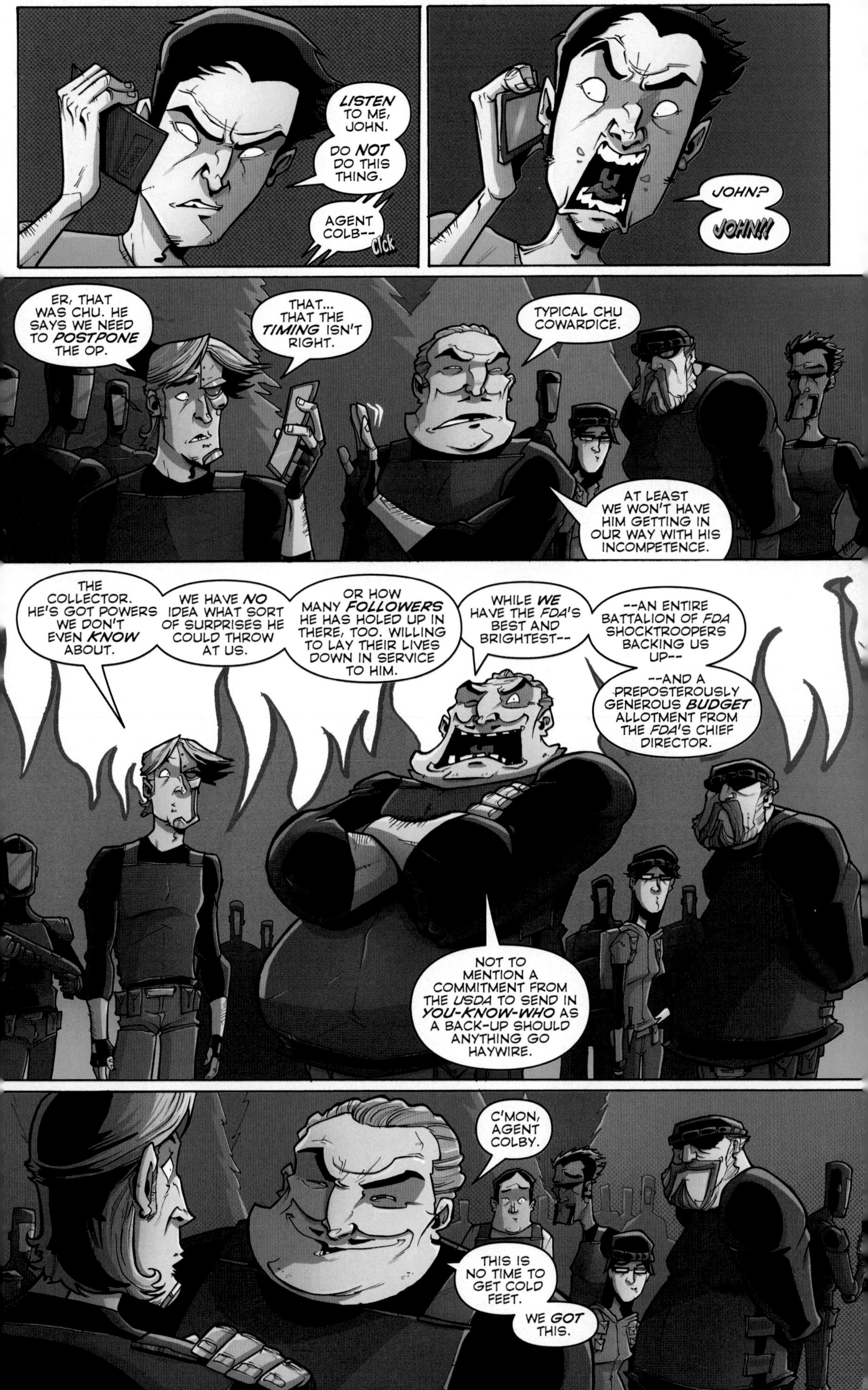
LISTEN TO ME, JOHN.
DO NOT DO THIS THING.
AGENT COLB--
CLCK
JOHN?
JOHN!!
ER, THAT WAS CHU. HE SAYS WE NEED TO POSTPONE THE OP.
THAT... THAT THE TIMING ISN'T RIGHT.
TYPICAL CHU COWARDICE.
AT LEAST WE WON'T HAVE HIM GETTING IN OUR WAY WITH HIS INCOMPETENCE.
THE COLLECTOR. HE'S GOT POWERS WE DON'T EVEN KNOW ABOUT.
WE HAVE NO IDEA WHAT SORT OF SURPRISES HE COULD THROW AT US.
OR HOW MANY FOLLOWERS HE HAS HOLED UP IN THERE, TOO. WILLING TO LAY THEIR LIVES DOWN IN SERVICE TO HIM.
WHILE WE HAVE THE FDA'S BEST AND BRIGHTEST--
--AN ENTIRE BATTALION OF FDA SHOCKTROOPERS BACKING US UP--
--AND A PREPOSTEROUSLY GENEROUS BUDGET ALLOTMENT FROM THE FDA'S CHIEF DIRECTOR.
NOT TO MENTION A COMMITMENT FROM THE USDA TO SEND IN YOU-KNOW-WHO AS A BACK-UP SHOULD ANYTHING GO HAYWIRE.
C'MON, AGENT COLBY.
THIS IS NO TIME TO GET COLD FEET.
WE GOT THIS.

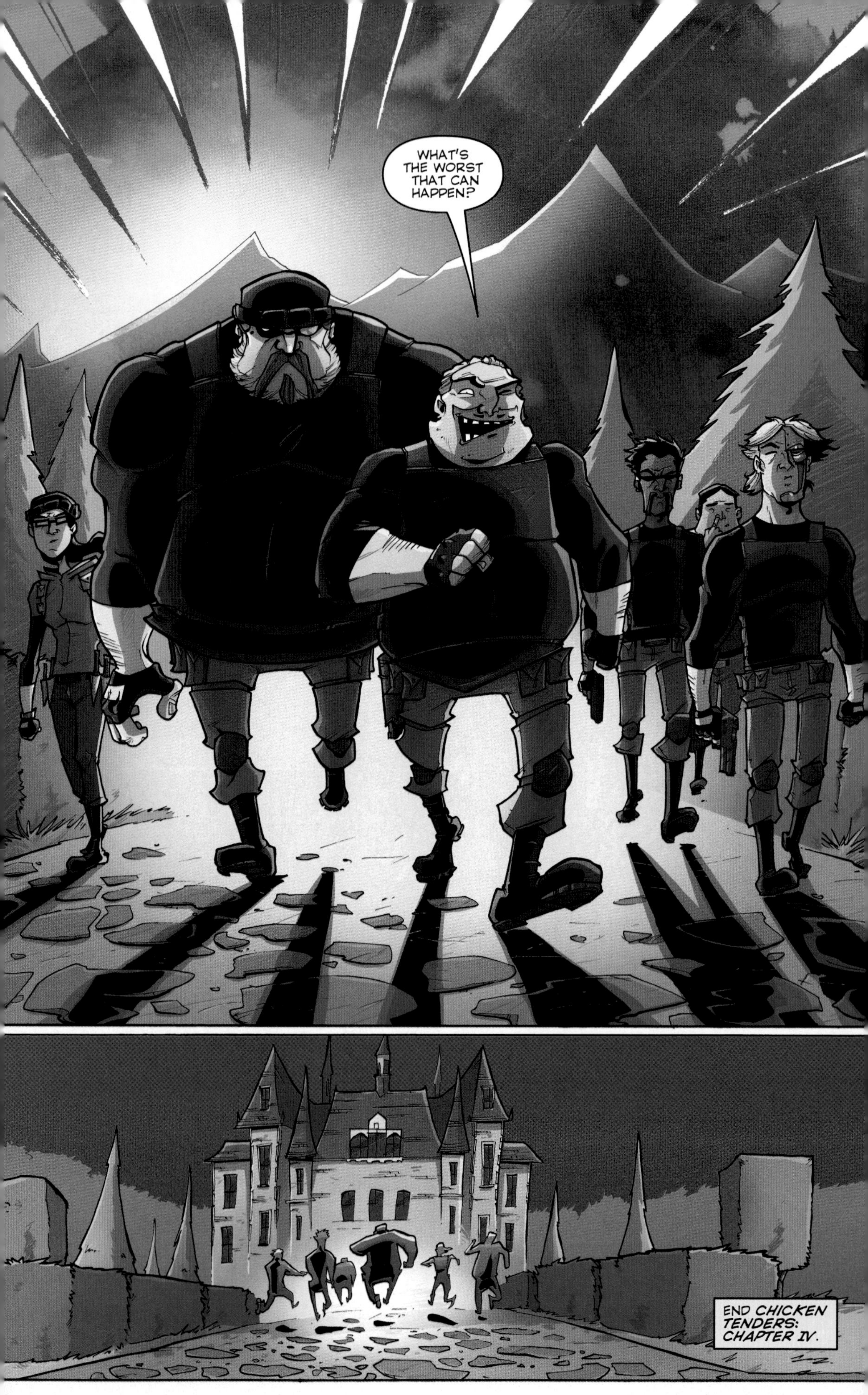
WHAT'S THE WORST THAT CAN HAPPEN?
END CHICKEN TENDERS: CHAPTER IV.

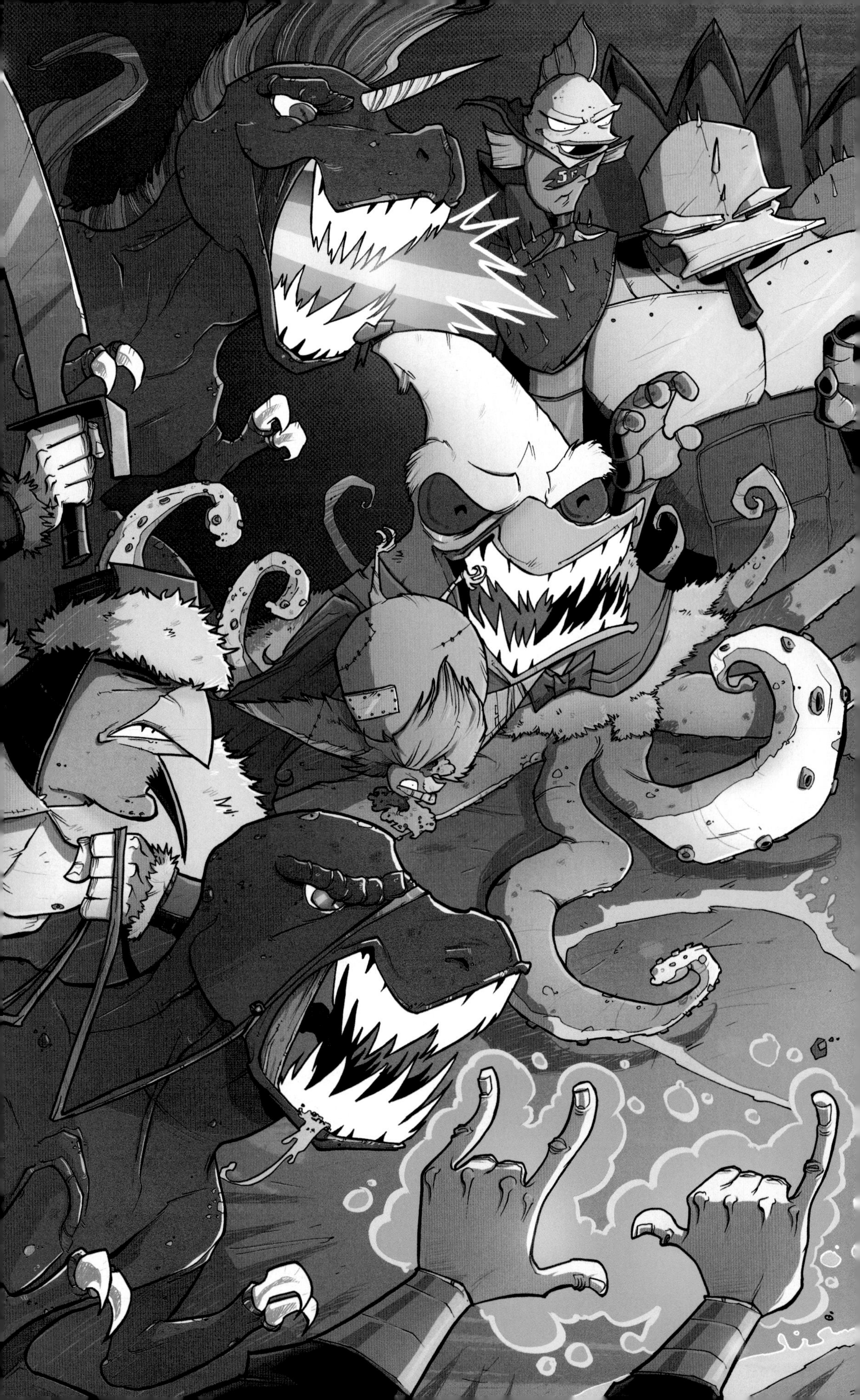

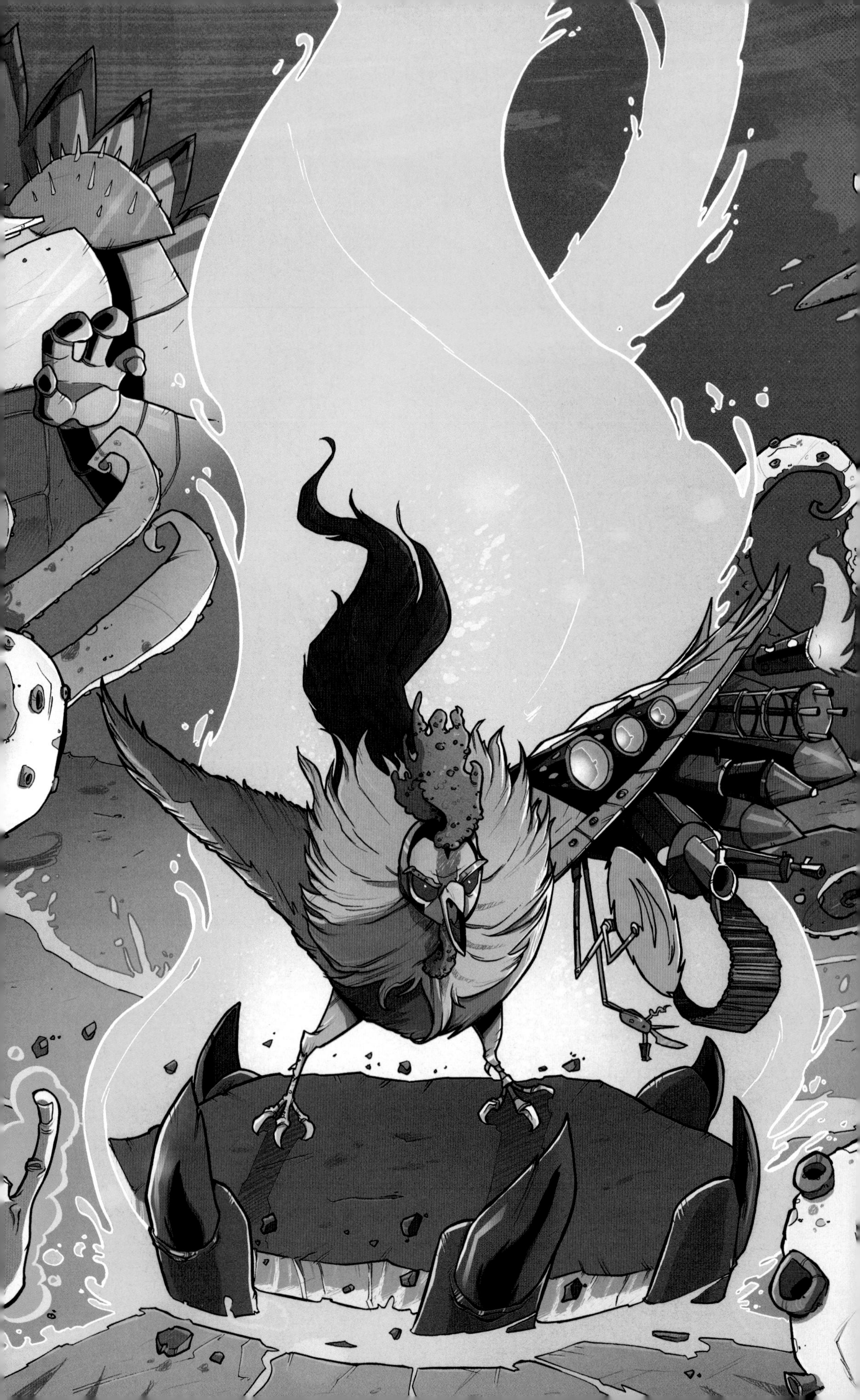

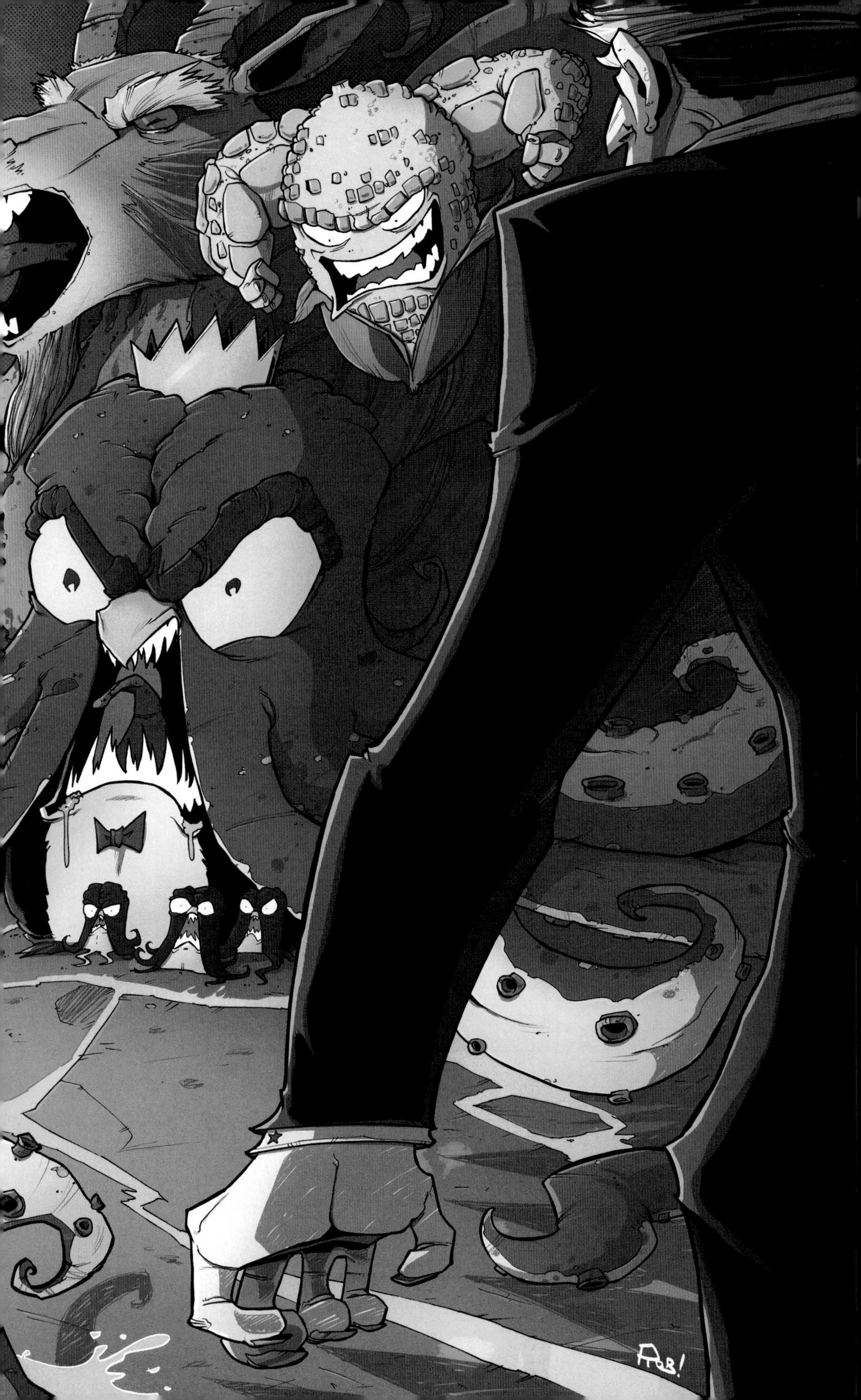

Chapter 5

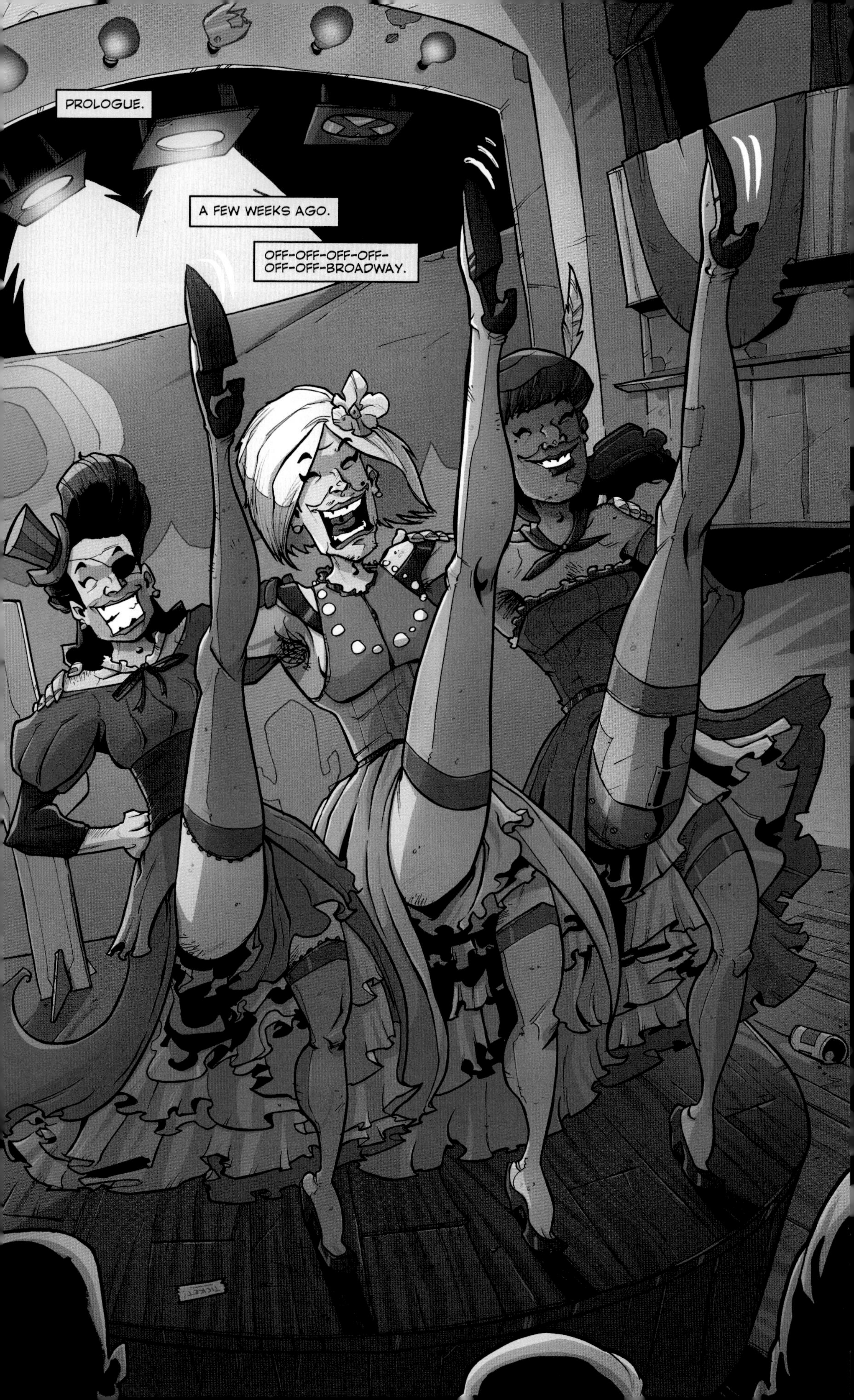
PROLOGUE.
A FEW WEEKS AGO.
OFF-OFF-OFF-OFF-
OFF-OFF-BROADWAY.

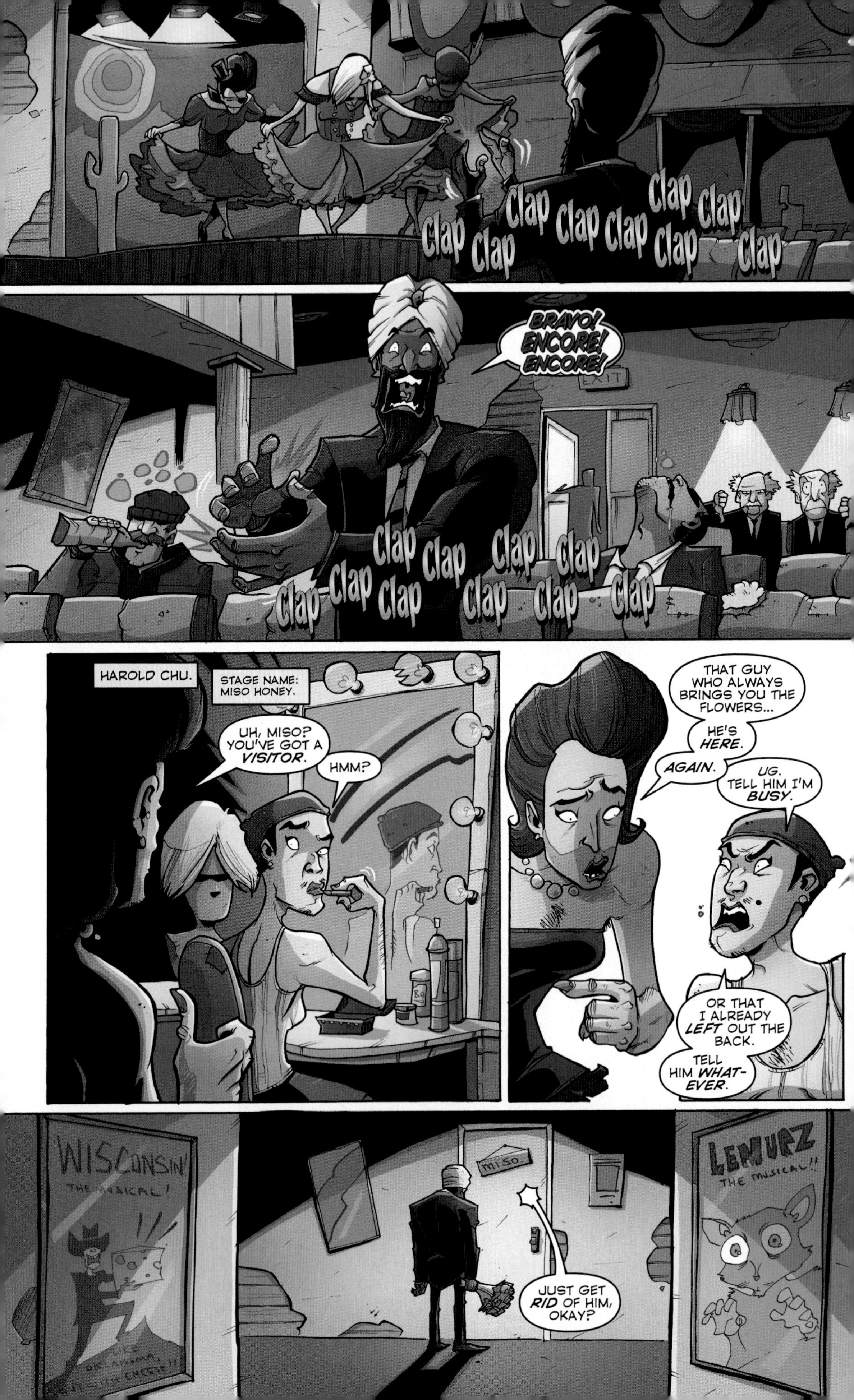
Clap Clap Clap Clap Clap Clap Clap Clap Clap
BRAVO! ENCORE! ENCORE!
Clap Clap Clap Clap Clap Clap Clap Clap Clap Clap
HAROLD CHU.
STAGE NAME: MISO HONEY.
UH, MISO? YOU'VE GOT A VISITOR.
HMM?
THAT GUY WHO ALWAYS BRINGS YOU THE FLOWERS...
HE'S HERE.
AGAIN.
UG. TELL HIM I'M BUSY.
OR THAT I ALREADY LEFT OUT THE BACK.
TELL HIM WHAT-EVER.
WISCONSIN' THE MUSICAL!
LIKE OKLAHOMA, BUT WITH CHEESE!!
MISO
LEMURZ THE MUSICAL!!
JUST GET RID OF HIM, OKAY?

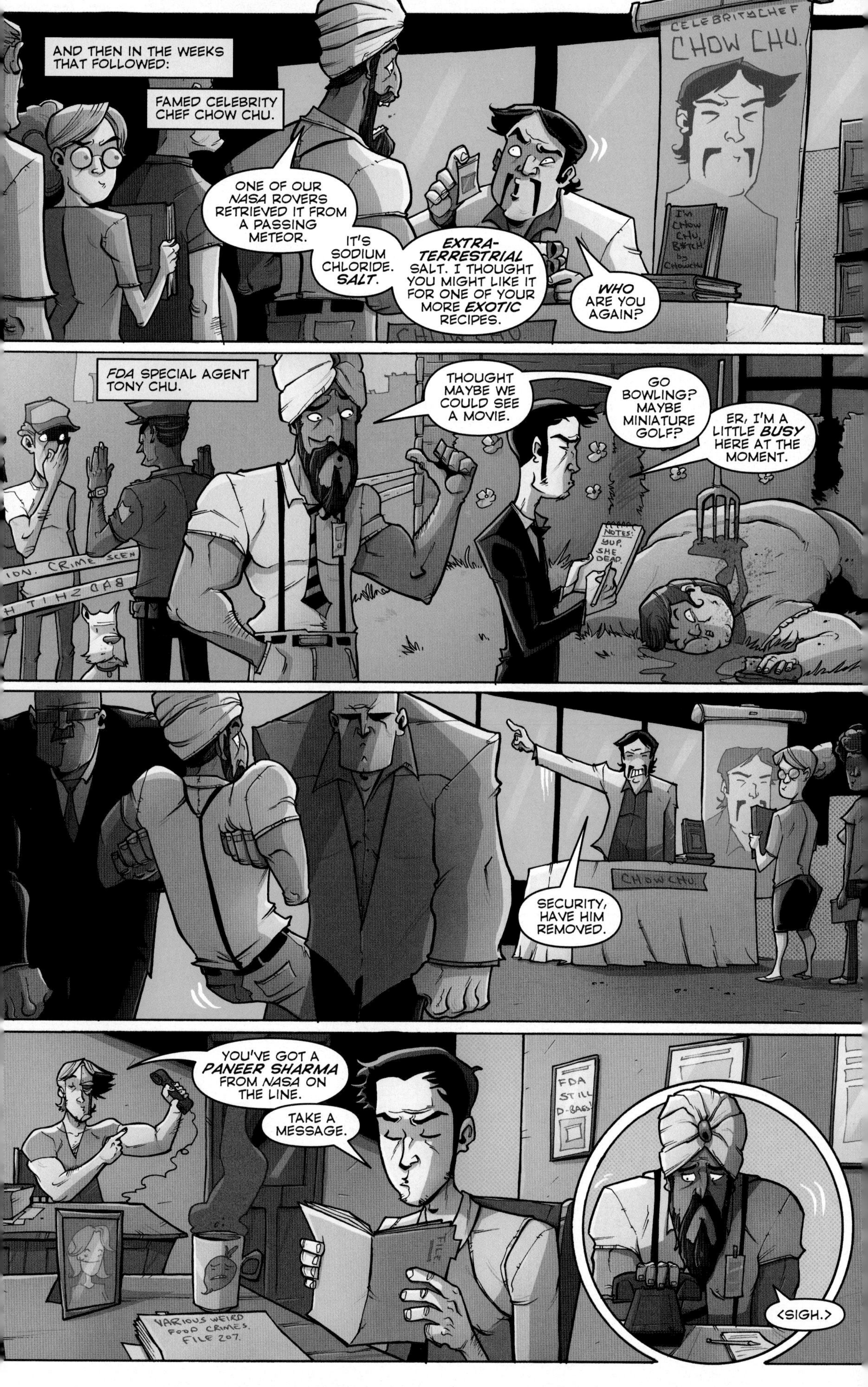

AND THEN IN THE WEEKS THAT FOLLOWED:
FAMED CELEBRITY CHEF CHOW CHU.
CELEBRITY CHEF CHOW CHU.
ONE OF OUR NASA ROVERS RETRIEVED IT FROM A PASSING METEOR.
IT'S SODIUM CHLORIDE. SALT.
EXTRA-TERRESTRIAL SALT. I THOUGHT YOU MIGHT LIKE IT FOR ONE OF YOUR MORE EXOTIC RECIPES.
WHO ARE YOU AGAIN?
FDA SPECIAL AGENT TONY CHU.
THOUGHT MAYBE WE COULD SEE A MOVIE.
GO BOWLING? MAYBE MINIATURE GOLF?
ER, I'M A LITTLE BUSY HERE AT THE MOMENT.
NOTES: YUP, SHE DEAD.
CHOW CHU
SECURITY, HAVE HIM REMOVED.
YOU'VE GOT A PANEER SHARMA FROM NASA ON THE LINE.
TAKE A MESSAGE.
FDA STILL D-BAGS!
VARIOUS WEIRD FOOD CRIMES. FILE 207.
<SIGH.>

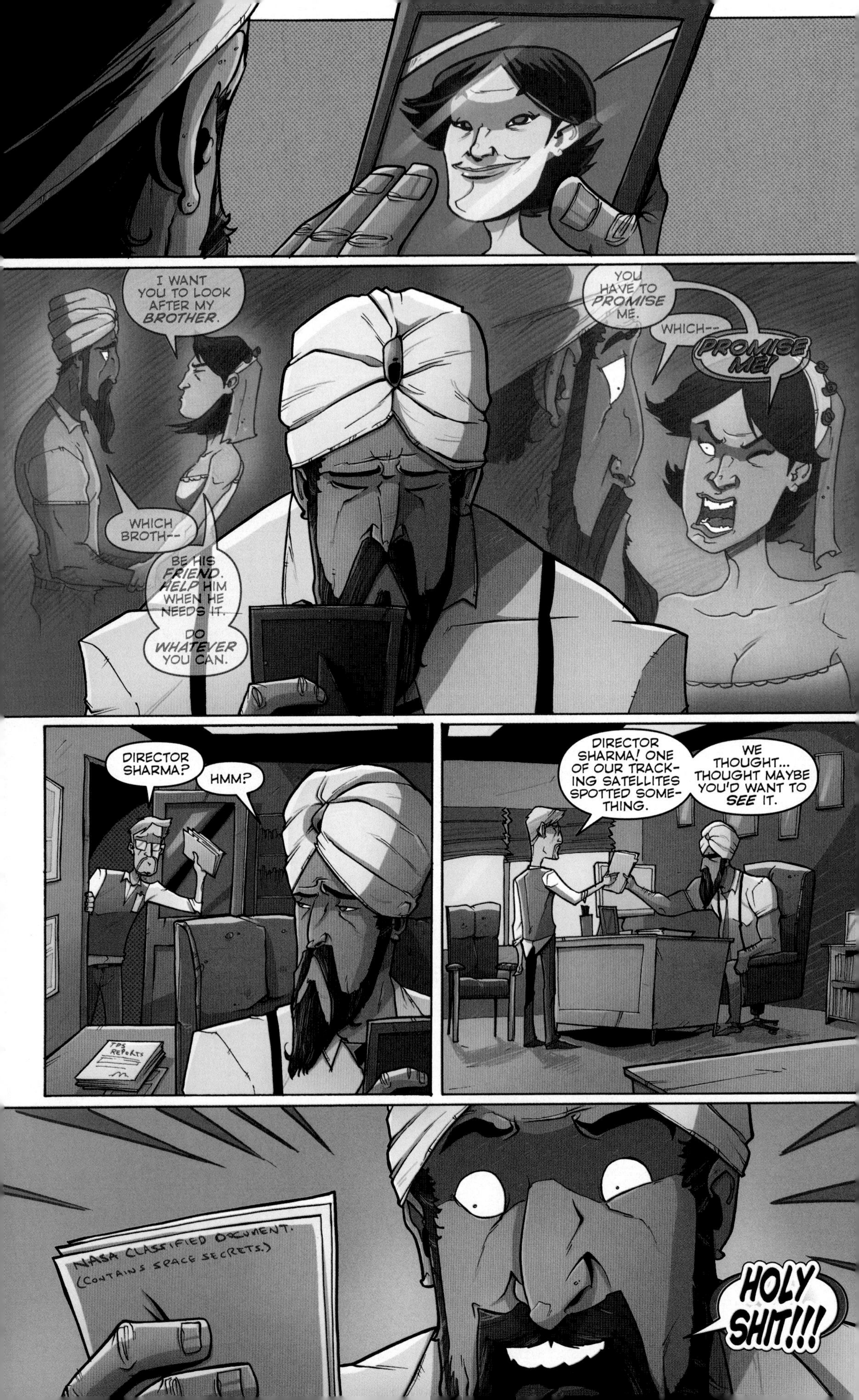
I WANT YOU TO LOOK AFTER MY BROTHER.
WHICH BROTH--
BE HIS FRIEND. HELP HIM WHEN HE NEEDS IT.
DO WHATEVER YOU CAN.
YOU HAVE TO PROMISE ME.
WHICH--
PROMISE ME!
DIRECTOR SHARMA?
HMM?
TPS REPORTS
DIRECTOR SHARMA! ONE OF OUR TRACK-ING SATELLITES SPOTTED SOME-THING.
WE THOUGHT... THOUGHT MAYBE YOU'D WANT TO SEE IT.
NASA CLASSIFIED DOCUMENT.
(CONTAINS SPACE SECRETS.)
HOLY SHIT!!!

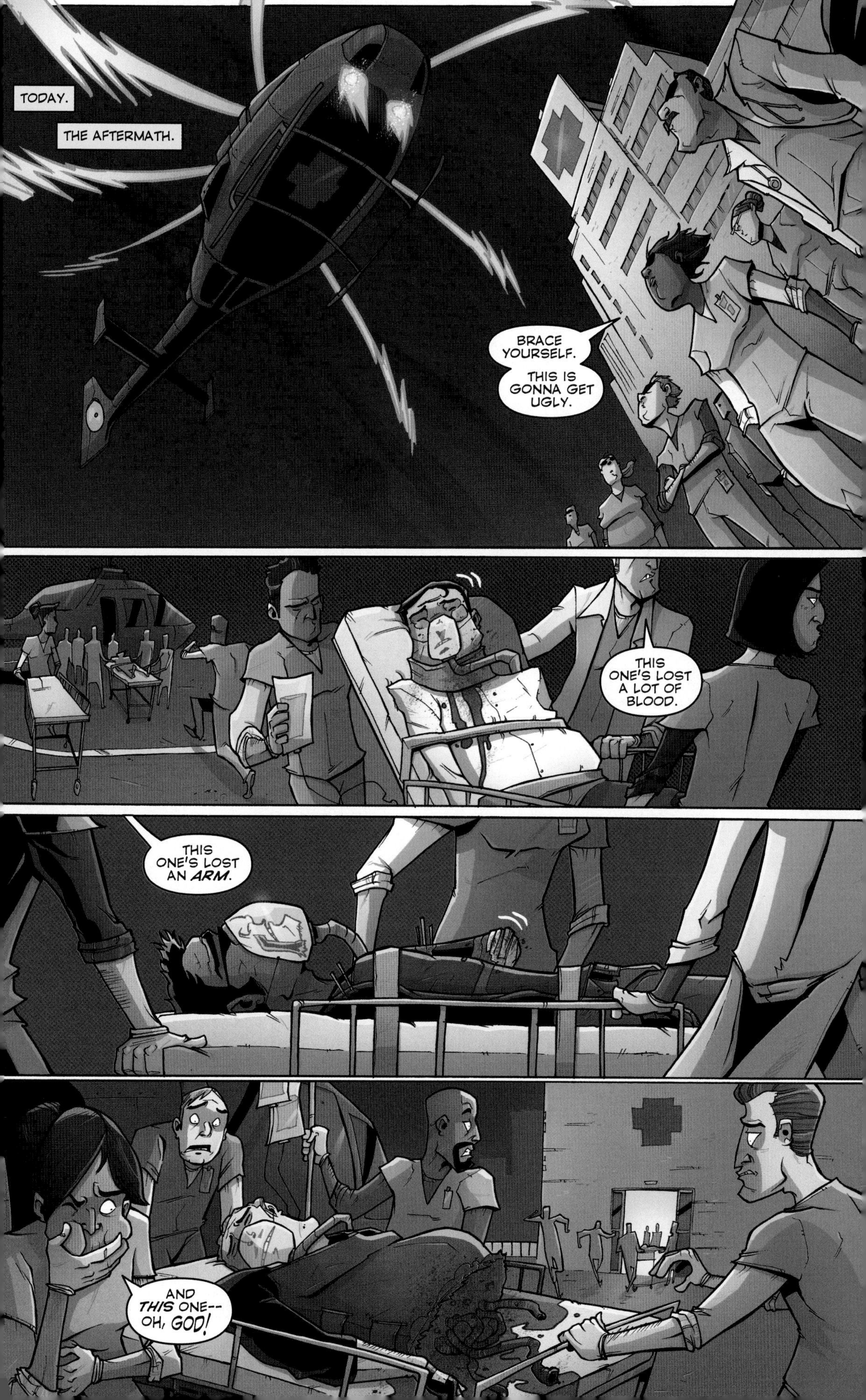
TODAY.
THE AFTERMATH.
BRACE YOURSELF. THIS IS GONNA GET UGLY.
THIS ONE'S LOST A LOT OF BLOOD.
THIS ONE'S LOST AN *ARM*.
AND *THIS* ONE-- OH, *GOD*!

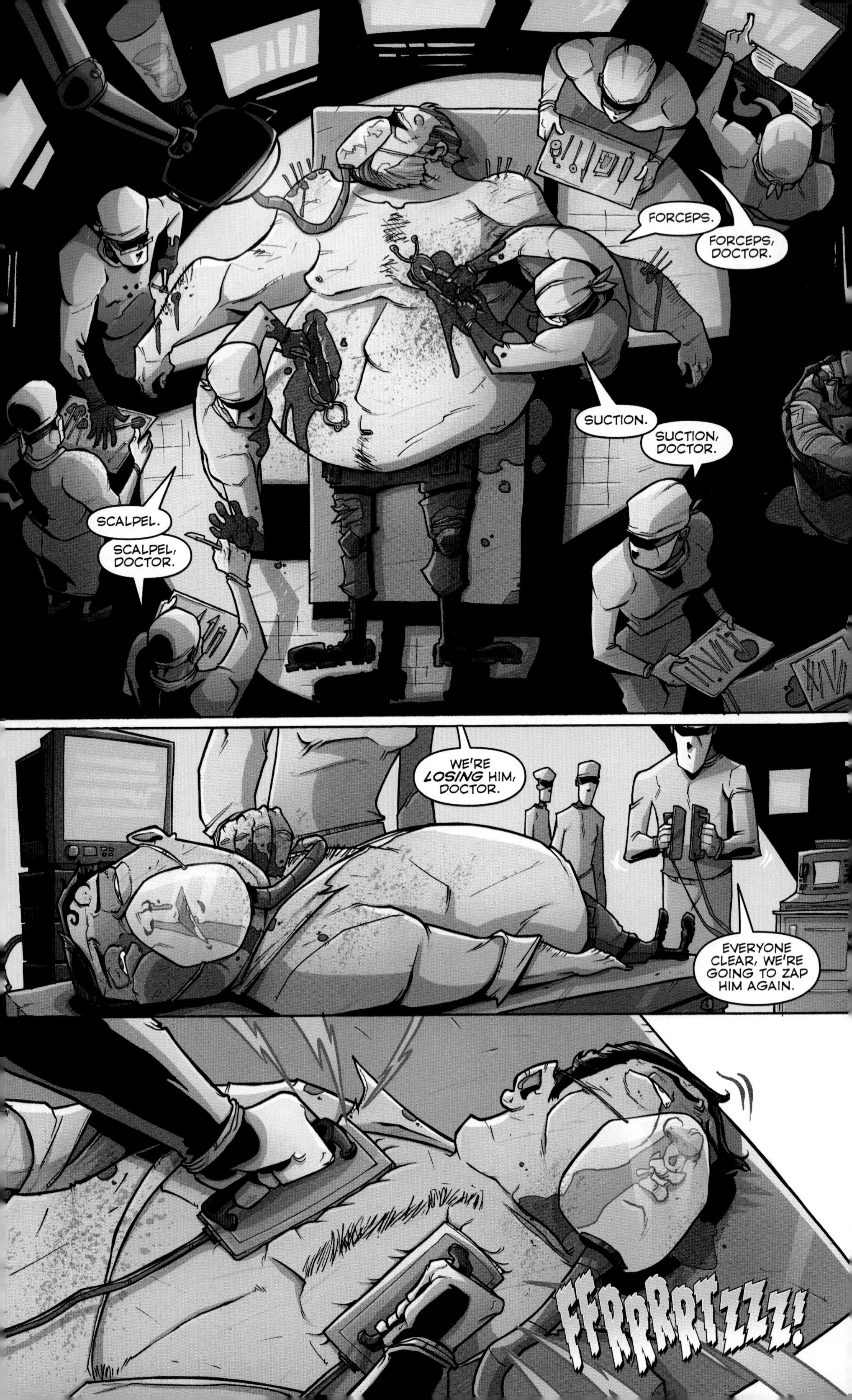
FORCEPS.
FORCEPS, DOCTOR.
SUCTION.
SUCTION, DOCTOR.
SCALPEL.
SCALPEL, DOCTOR.
WE'RE *LOSING* HIM, DOCTOR.
EVERYONE CLEAR, WE'RE GOING TO ZAP HIM AGAIN.
FFRRRRTZZZZ!

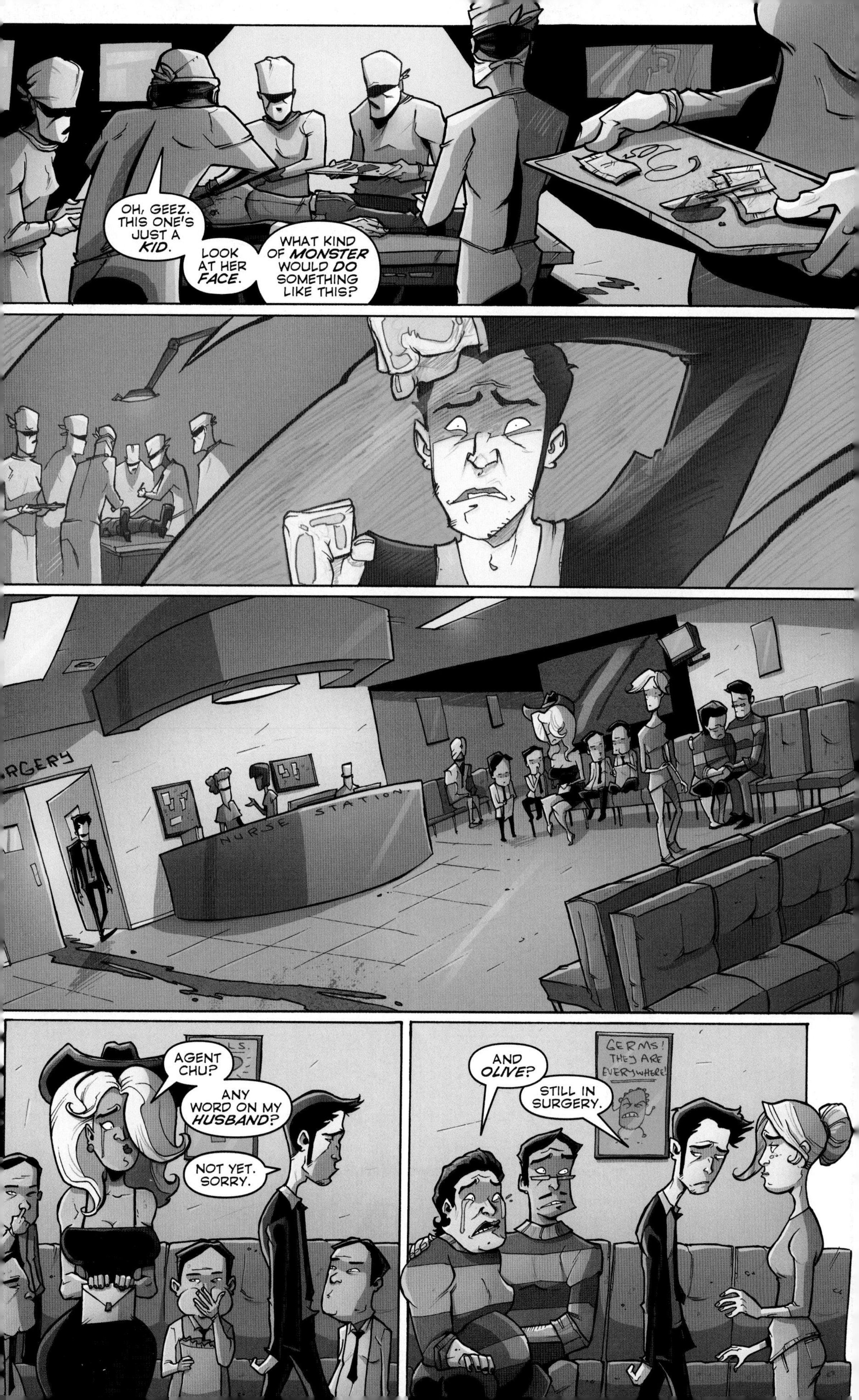

OH, GEEZ. THIS ONE'S JUST A *KID*.
LOOK AT HER *FACE*.
WHAT KIND OF *MONSTER* WOULD *DO* SOMETHING LIKE THIS?
NURSE STATION
AGENT CHU?
ANY WORD ON MY *HUSBAND*?
NOT YET. SORRY.
GERMS! THEY ARE EVERYWHERE!
AND *OLIVE*?
STILL IN SURGERY.

TONY?

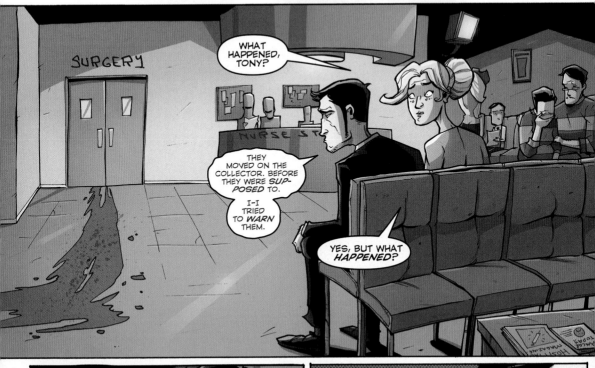

SURGERY

WHAT HAPPENED, TONY?

THEY MOVED ON THE COLLECTOR. BEFORE THEY WERE *SUPPOSED* TO.

I-I TRIED TO *WARN* THEM.

YES, BUT WHAT *HAPPENED?*

THANK YOU.

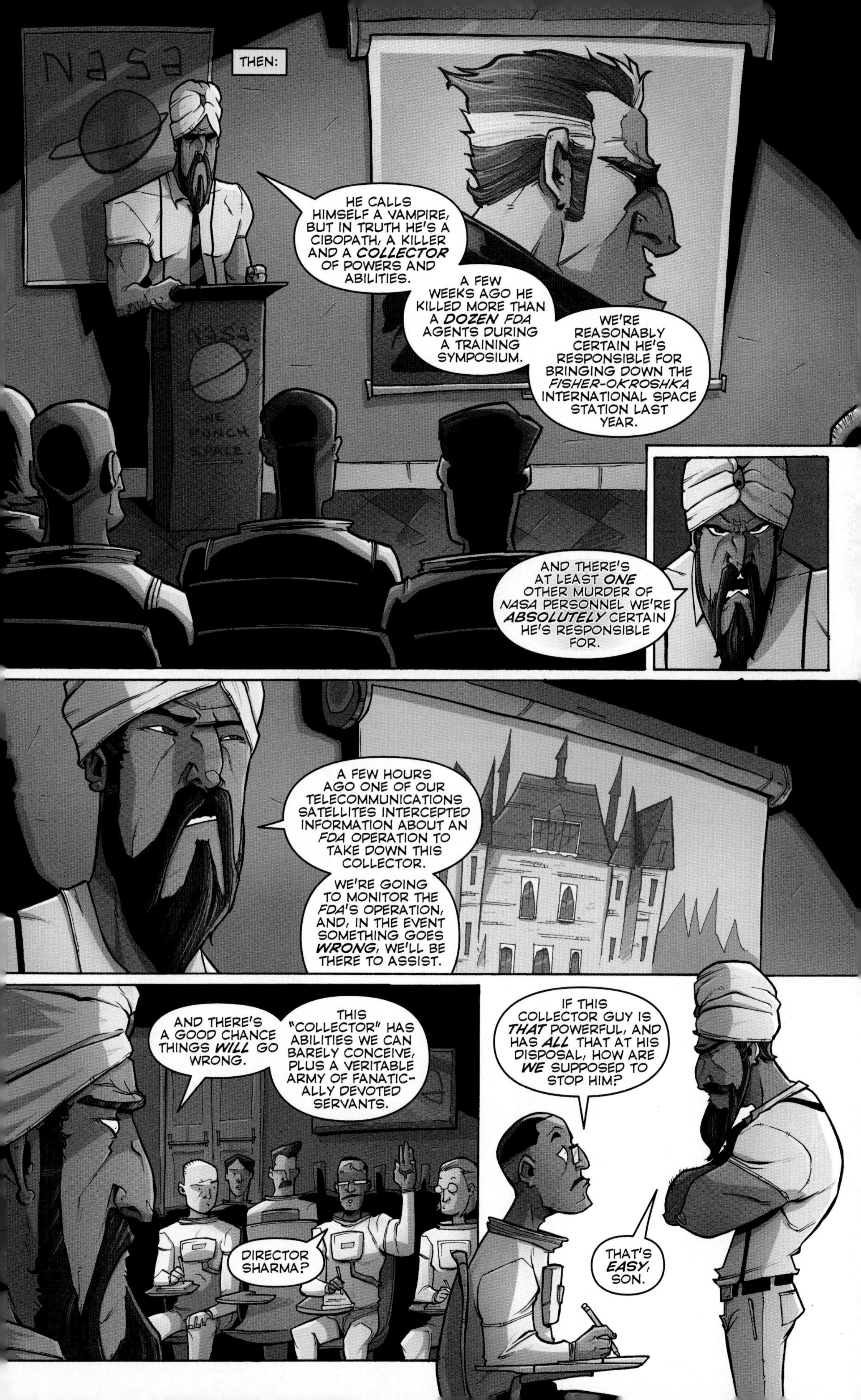
THEN:
HE CALLS HIMSELF A VAMPIRE, BUT IN TRUTH HE'S A CIBOPATH, A KILLER AND A *COLLECTOR* OF POWERS AND ABILITIES.
A FEW WEEKS AGO HE KILLED MORE THAN A ***DOZEN*** *FDA* AGENTS DURING A TRAINING SYMPOSIUM.
WE'RE REASONABLY CERTAIN HE'S RESPONSIBLE FOR BRINGING DOWN THE *FISHER-OKROSHKA* INTERNATIONAL SPACE STATION LAST YEAR.
NASA
WE PUNCH SPACE.
AND THERE'S AT LEAST ***ONE*** OTHER MURDER OF *NASA* PERSONNEL WE'RE ***ABSOLUTELY*** CERTAIN HE'S RESPONSIBLE FOR.
A FEW HOURS AGO ONE OF OUR TELECOMMUNICATIONS SATELLITES INTERCEPTED INFORMATION ABOUT AN *FDA* OPERATION TO TAKE DOWN THIS COLLECTOR.
WE'RE GOING TO MONITOR THE *FDA*'S OPERATION, AND, IN THE EVENT SOMETHING GOES ***WRONG***, WE'LL BE THERE TO ASSIST.
AND THERE'S A GOOD CHANCE THINGS ***WILL*** GO WRONG.
THIS "COLLECTOR" HAS ABILITIES WE CAN BARELY CONCEIVE, PLUS A VERITABLE ARMY OF FANATICALLY DEVOTED SERVANTS.
DIRECTOR SHARMA?
IF THIS COLLECTOR GUY IS ***THAT*** POWERFUL, AND HAS ***ALL*** THAT AT HIS DISPOSAL, HOW ARE ***WE*** SUPPOSED TO STOP HIM?
THAT'S ***EASY***, SON.

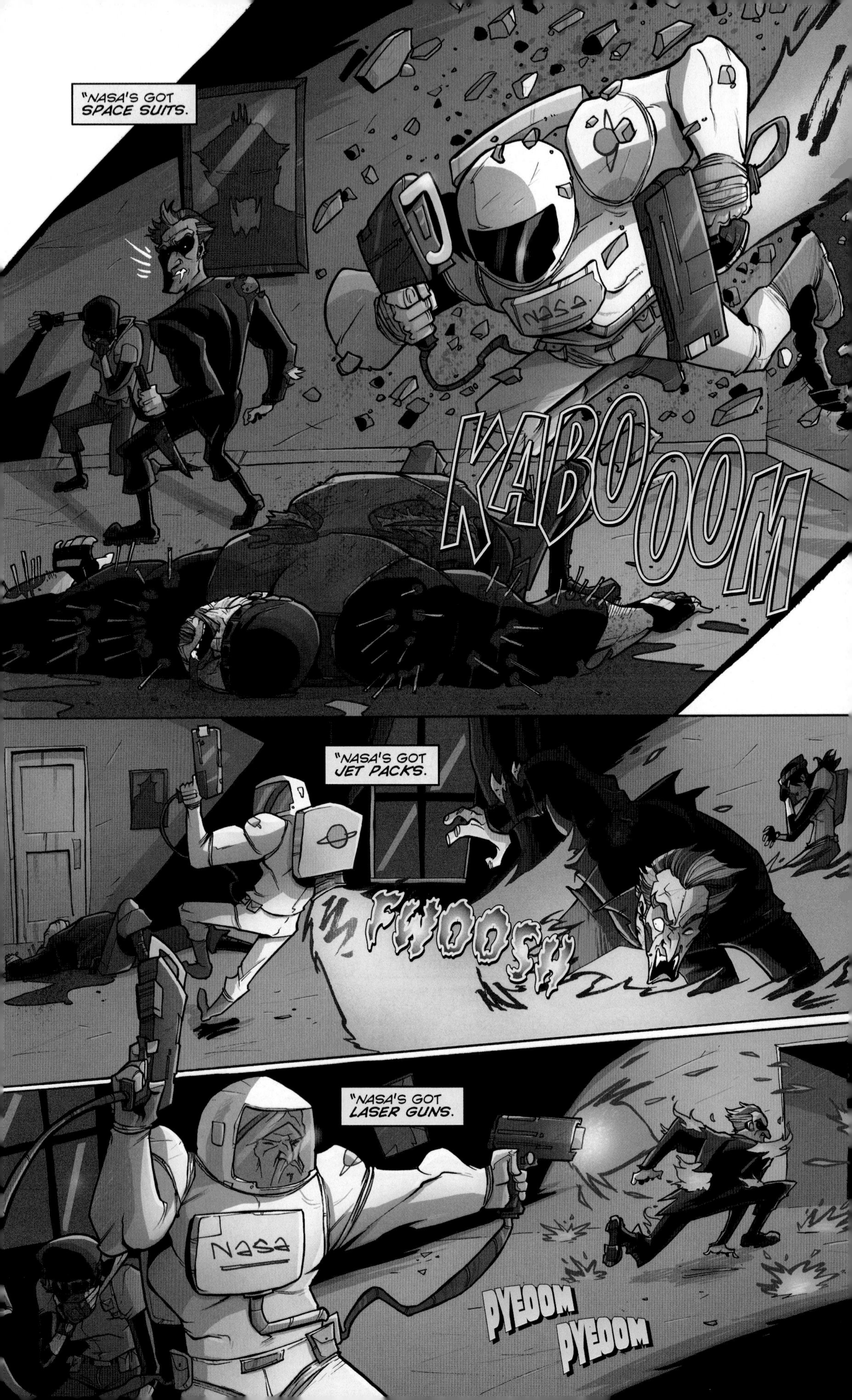
"NASA'S GOT SPACE SUITS.
KABOOOOM
"NASA'S GOT JET PACKS.
FWOOSH
"NASA'S GOT LASER GUNS.
PYEOOM
PYEOOM

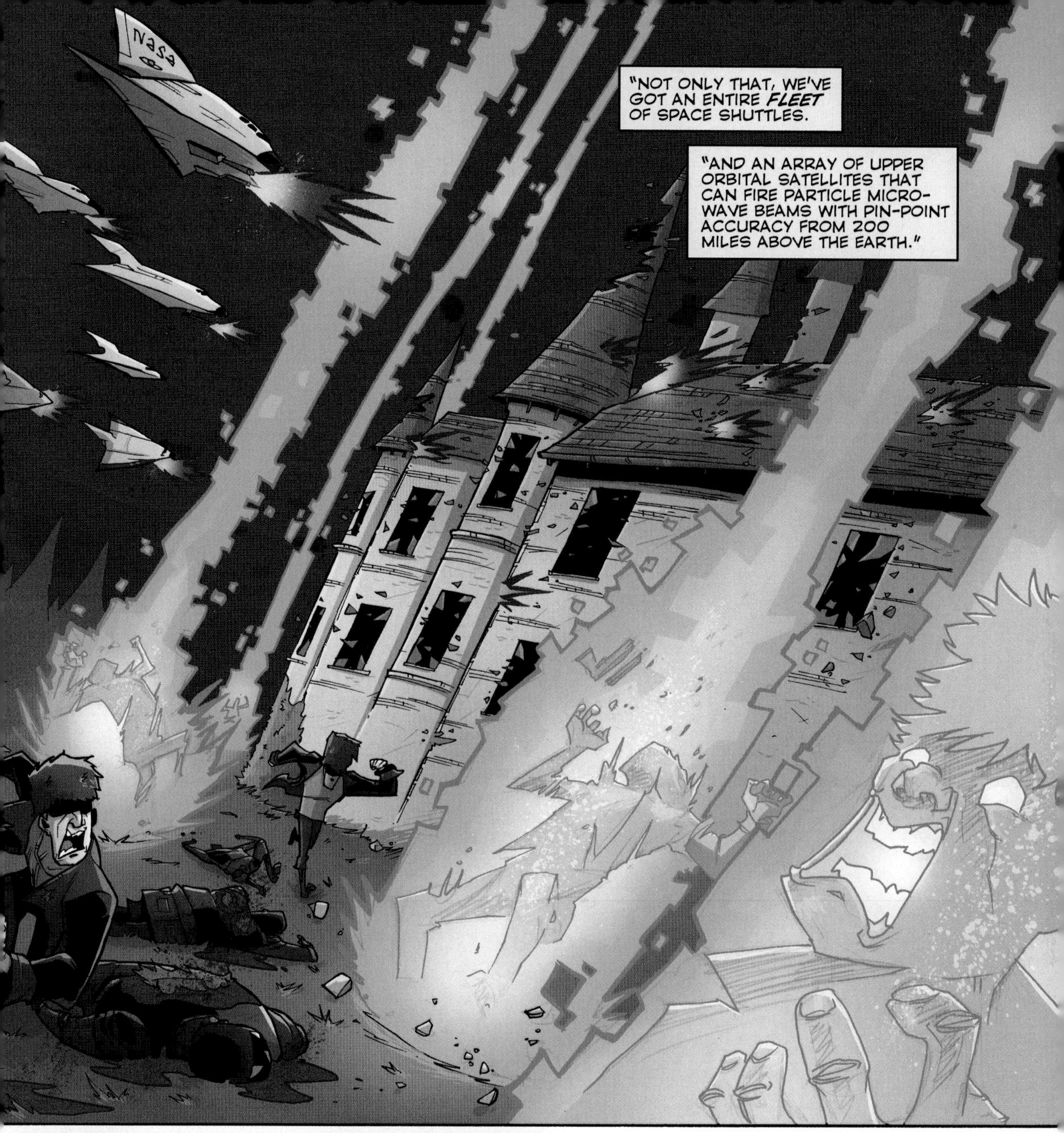
"NOT ONLY THAT, WE'VE GOT AN ENTIRE *FLEET* OF SPACE SHUTTLES.
"AND AN ARRAY OF UPPER ORBITAL SATELLITES THAT CAN FIRE PARTICLE MICRO-WAVE BEAMS WITH PIN-POINT ACCURACY FROM 200 MILES ABOVE THE EARTH."
NASA

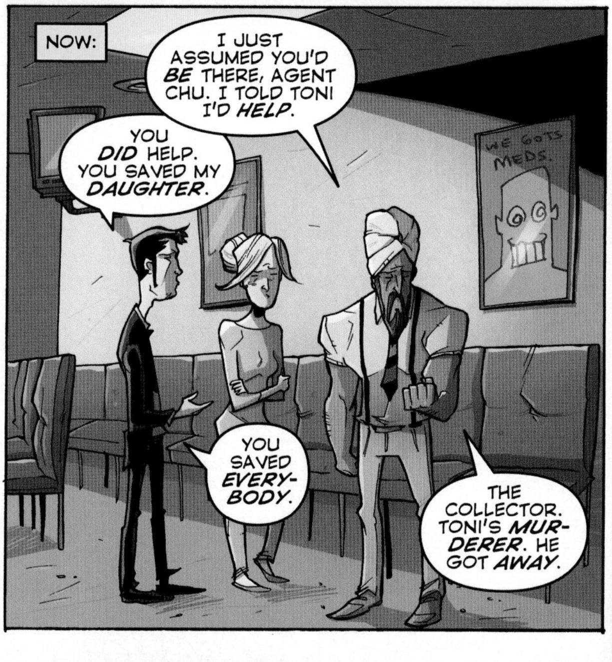
NOW:
I JUST ASSUMED YOU'D *BE* THERE, AGENT CHU. I TOLD TONI I'D *HELP*.
YOU *DID* HELP. YOU SAVED MY *DAUGHTER*.
WE GOTS MEDS.
YOU SAVED *EVERY-BODY*.
THE COLLECTOR. TONI'S *MUR-DERER*. HE GOT *AWAY*.

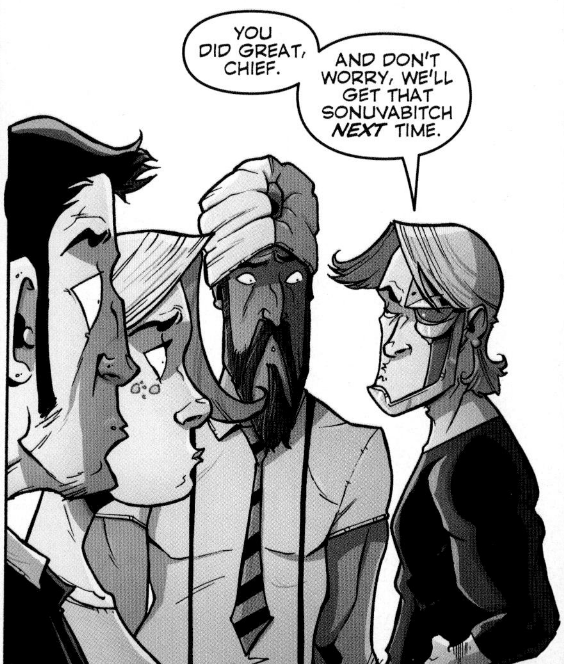
YOU DID GREAT, CHIEF.
AND DON'T WORRY, WE'LL GET THAT SONUVABITCH *NEXT* TIME.

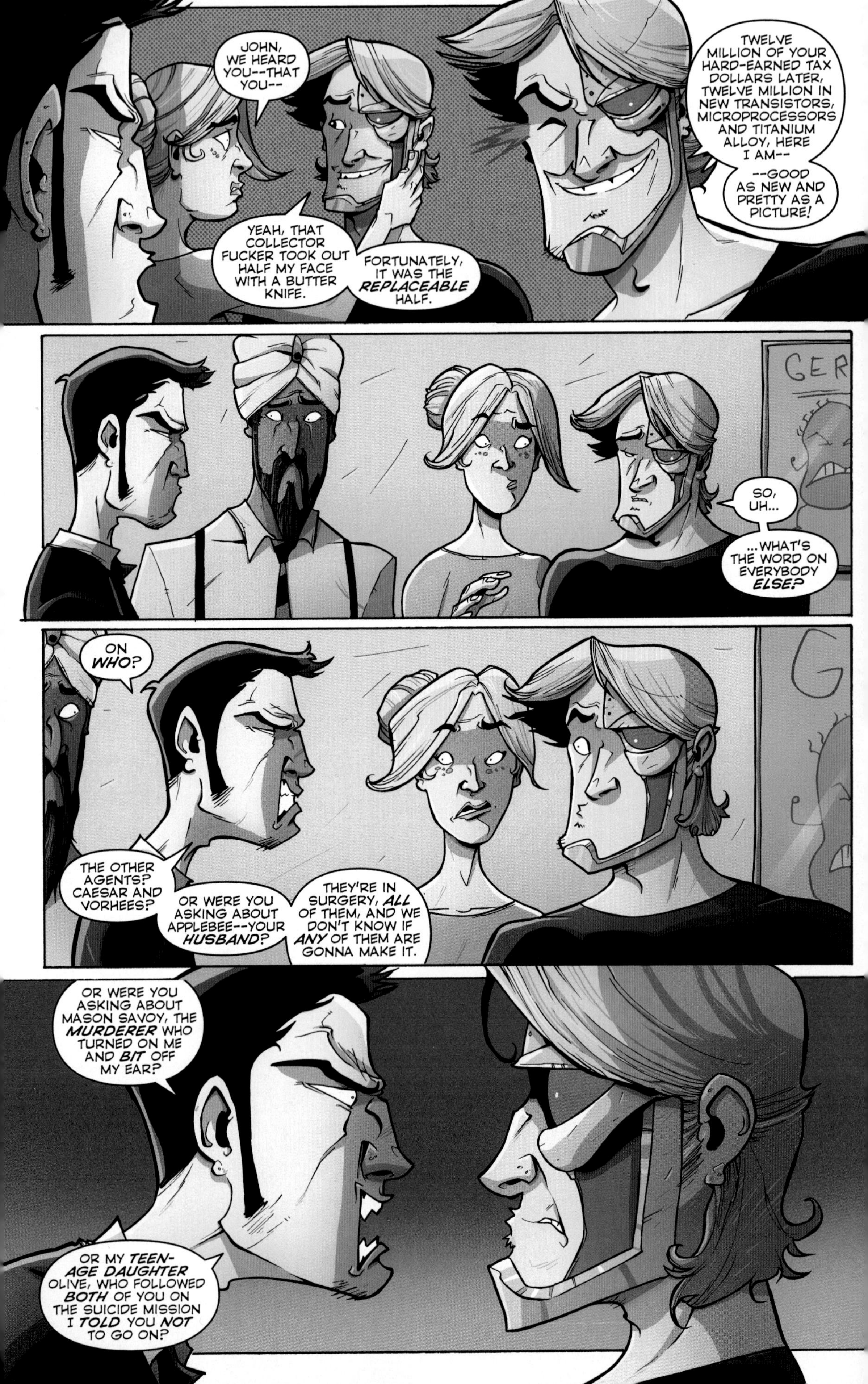
JOHN, WE HEARD YOU--THAT YOU--
YEAH, THAT COLLECTOR FUCKER TOOK OUT HALF MY FACE WITH A BUTTER KNIFE.
FORTUNATELY, IT WAS THE REPLACEABLE HALF.
TWELVE MILLION OF YOUR HARD-EARNED TAX DOLLARS LATER, TWELVE MILLION IN NEW TRANSISTORS, MICROPROCESSORS AND TITANIUM ALLOY, HERE I AM--
--GOOD AS NEW AND PRETTY AS A PICTURE!
SO, UH...
...WHAT'S THE WORD ON EVERYBODY ELSE?
GER
ON WHO?
THE OTHER AGENTS? CAESAR AND VORHEES?
OR WERE YOU ASKING ABOUT APPLEBEE--YOUR HUSBAND?
THEY'RE IN SURGERY, ALL OF THEM, AND WE DON'T KNOW IF ANY OF THEM ARE GONNA MAKE IT.
OR WERE YOU ASKING ABOUT MASON SAVOY, THE MURDERER WHO TURNED ON ME AND BIT OFF MY EAR?
OR MY TEEN-AGE DAUGHTER OLIVE, WHO FOLLOWED BOTH OF YOU ON THE SUICIDE MISSION I TOLD YOU NOT TO GO ON?

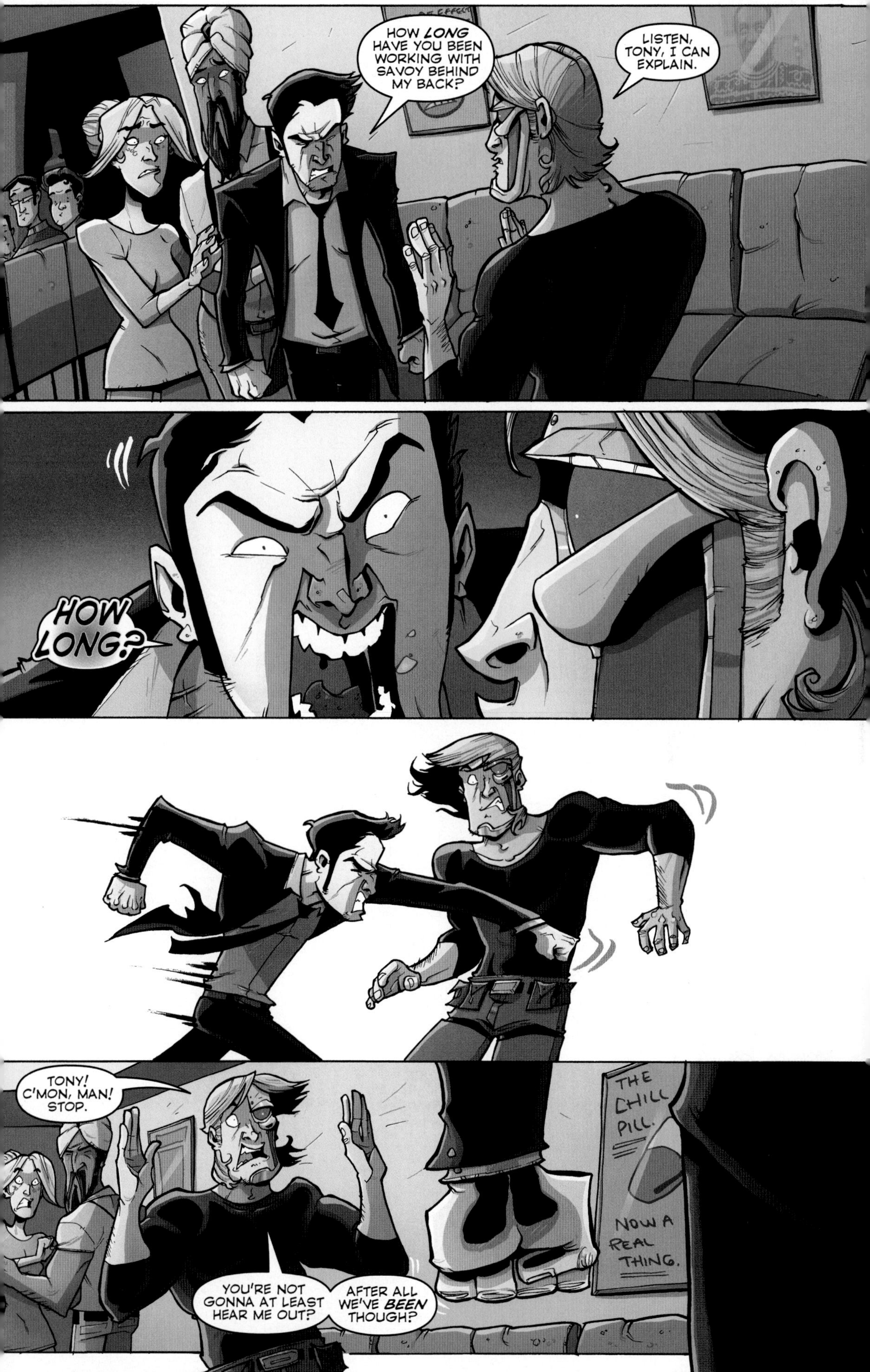
HOW LONG HAVE YOU BEEN WORKING WITH SAVOY BEHIND MY BACK?
LISTEN, TONY, I CAN EXPLAIN.
HOW LONG?
TONY! C'MON, MAN! STOP.
THE CHILL PILL.
NOW A REAL THING.
YOU'RE NOT GONNA AT LEAST HEAR ME OUT?
AFTER ALL WE'VE BEEN THOUGH?

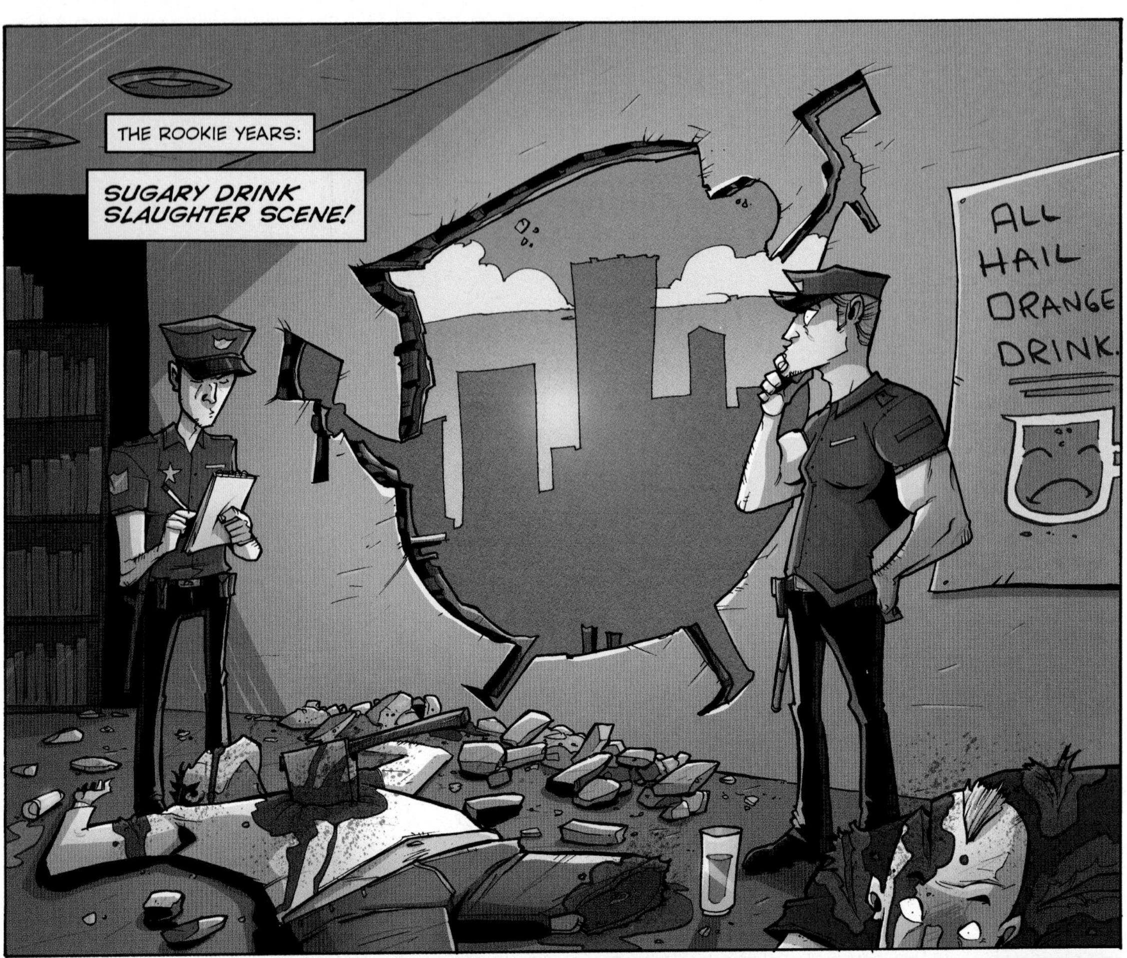

THE ROOKIE YEARS:
SUGARY DRINK SLAUGHTER SCENE!
ALL HAIL ORANGE DRINK.

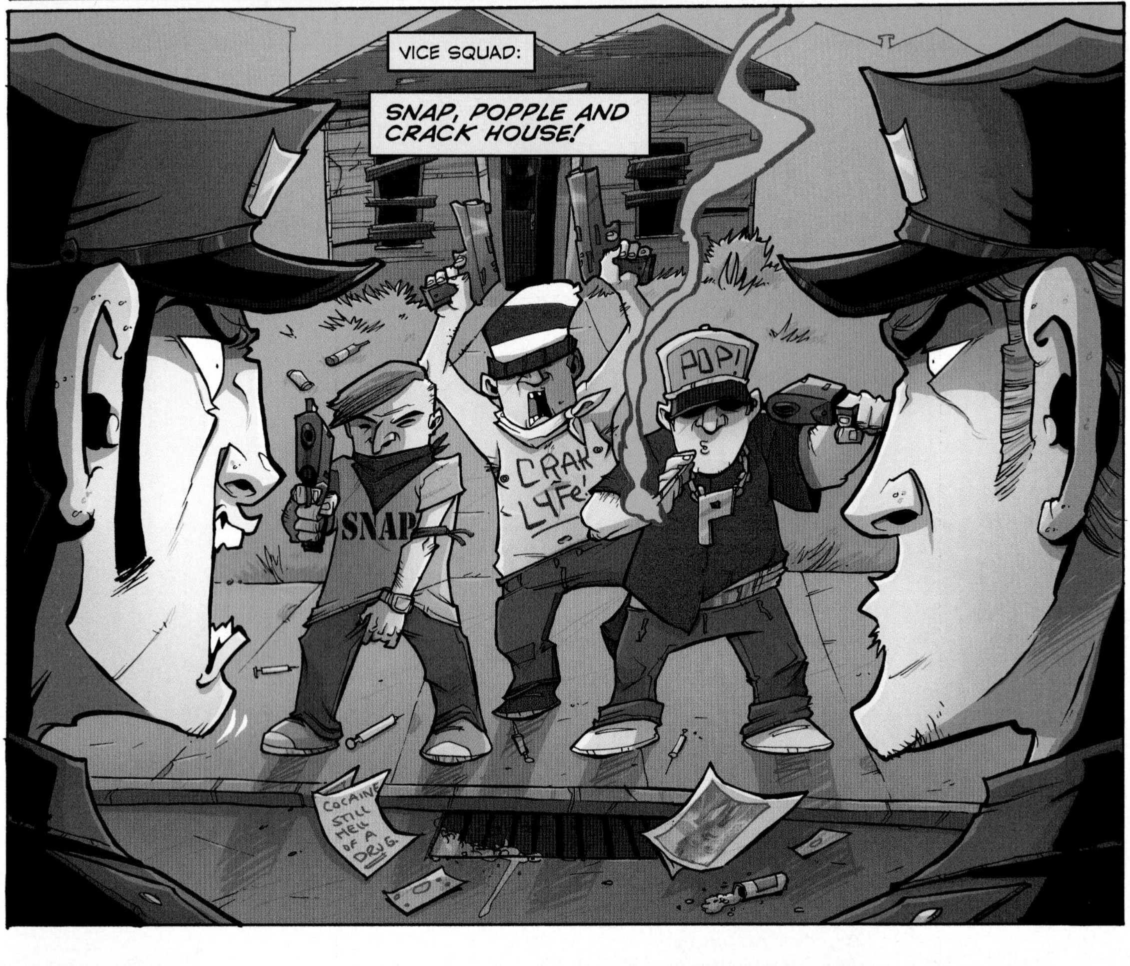

VICE SQUAD:
SNAP, POPPLE AND CRACK HOUSE!
SNAP
CRAK LYFe
POP!
P
COCAINE STILL HELL OF A DRUG.

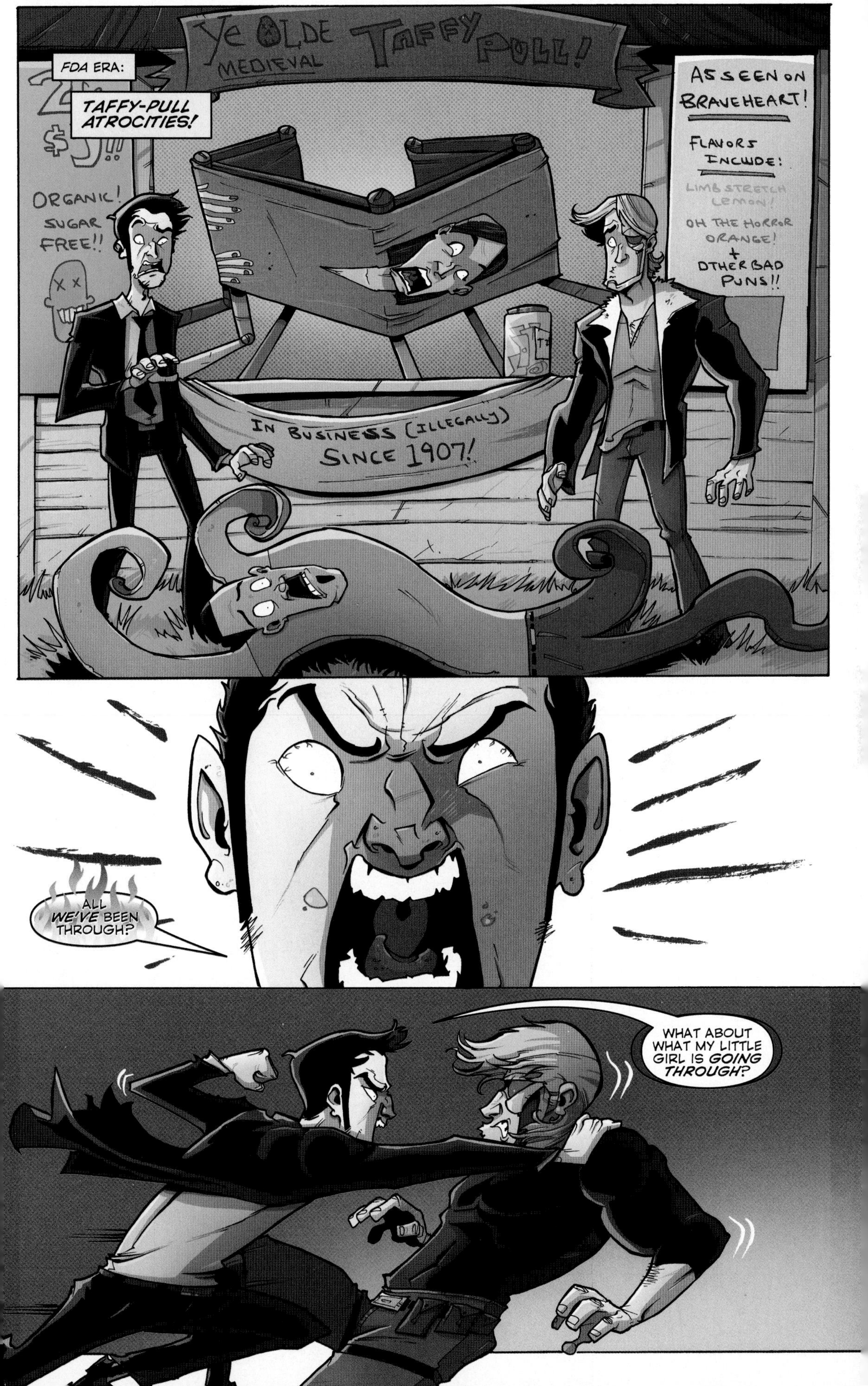
FDA ERA:
TAFFY-PULL ATROCITIES!
YE OLDE MEDIEVAL TAFFY PULL!
ORGANIC! SUGAR FREE!!
AS SEEN ON BRAVEHEART!
FLAVORS INCLUDE:
LIMB STRETCH LEMON!
OH THE HORROR ORANGE!
+ OTHER BAD PUNS!!
IN BUSINESS (ILLEGALLY) SINCE 1907!
ALL *WE'VE* BEEN THROUGH?
WHAT ABOUT WHAT MY LITTLE GIRL IS *GOING THROUGH*?

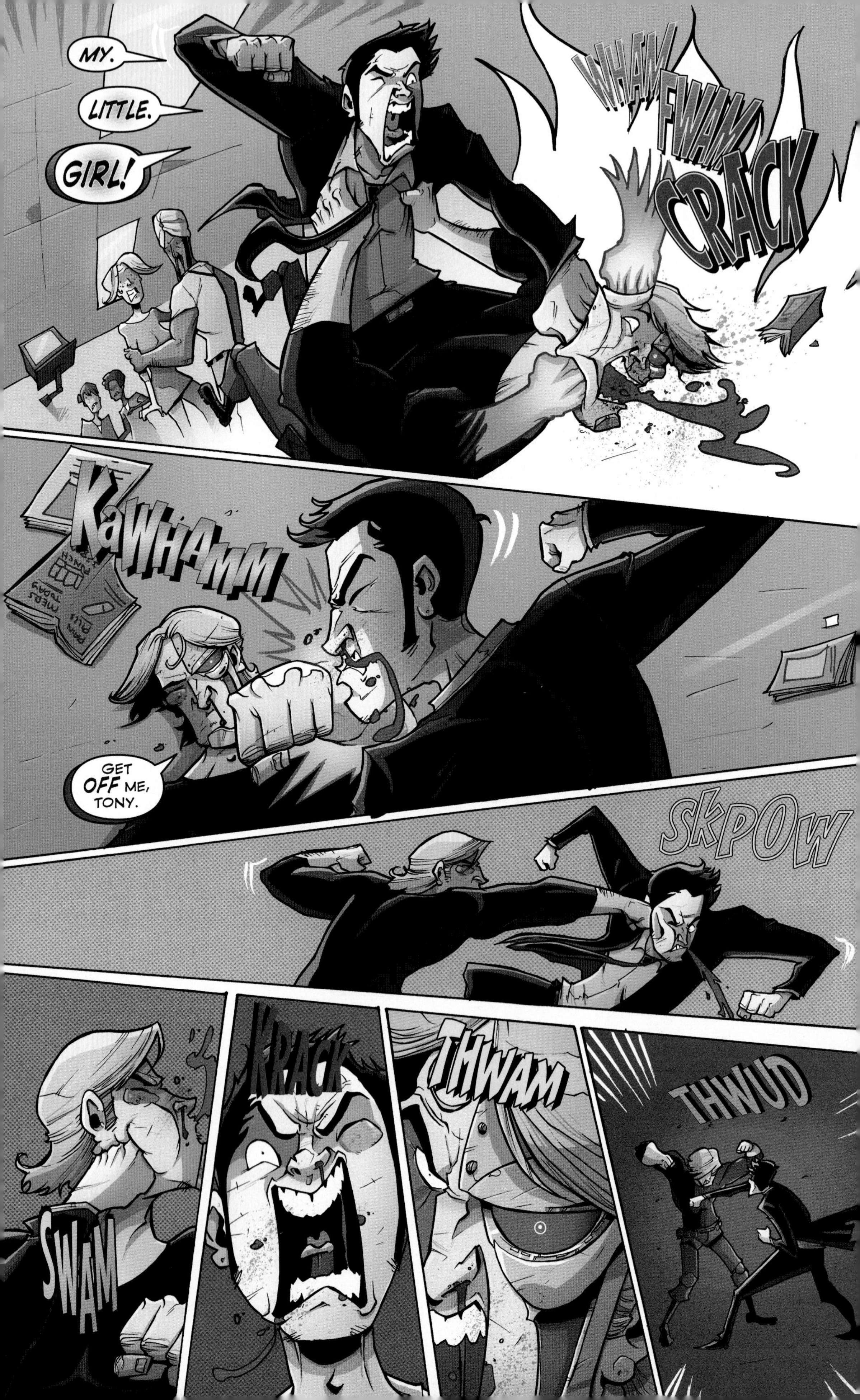
MY.
LITTLE.
GIRL!
WHAM
FWAM
CRACK
KaWHAMM
PAIN PILLS MEDS TODAY
PUNCH
GET OFF ME, TONY.
SKPOW
SWAM
KRACK
THWAM
THWUD

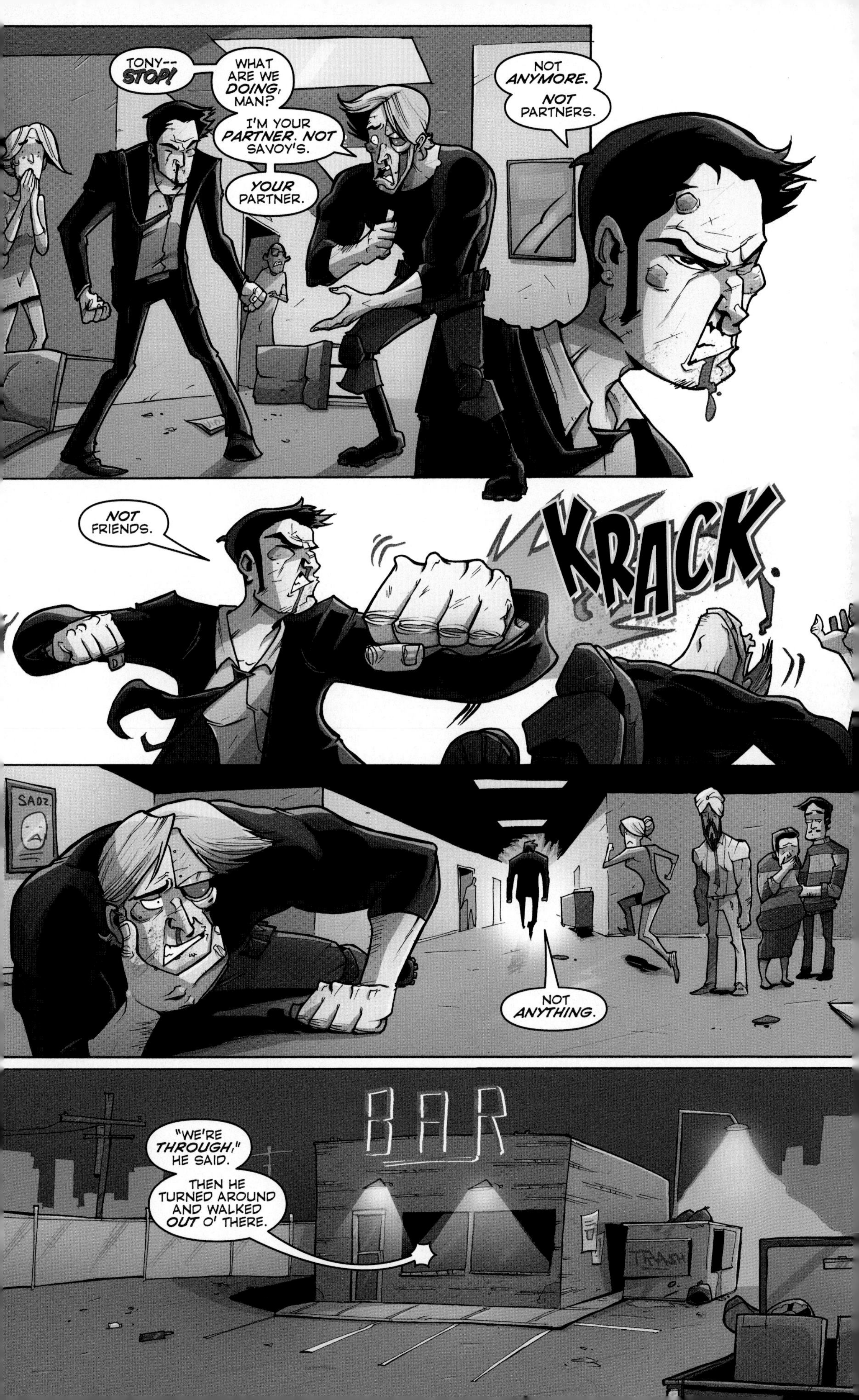
TONY-- STOP!
WHAT ARE WE DOING, MAN?
I'M YOUR PARTNER. NOT SAVOY'S.
YOUR PARTNER.
NOT ANYMORE.
NOT PARTNERS.
NOT FRIENDS.
KRACK.
NOT ANYTHING.
BAR
"WE'RE THROUGH," HE SAID.
THEN HE TURNED AROUND AND WALKED OUT O' THERE.

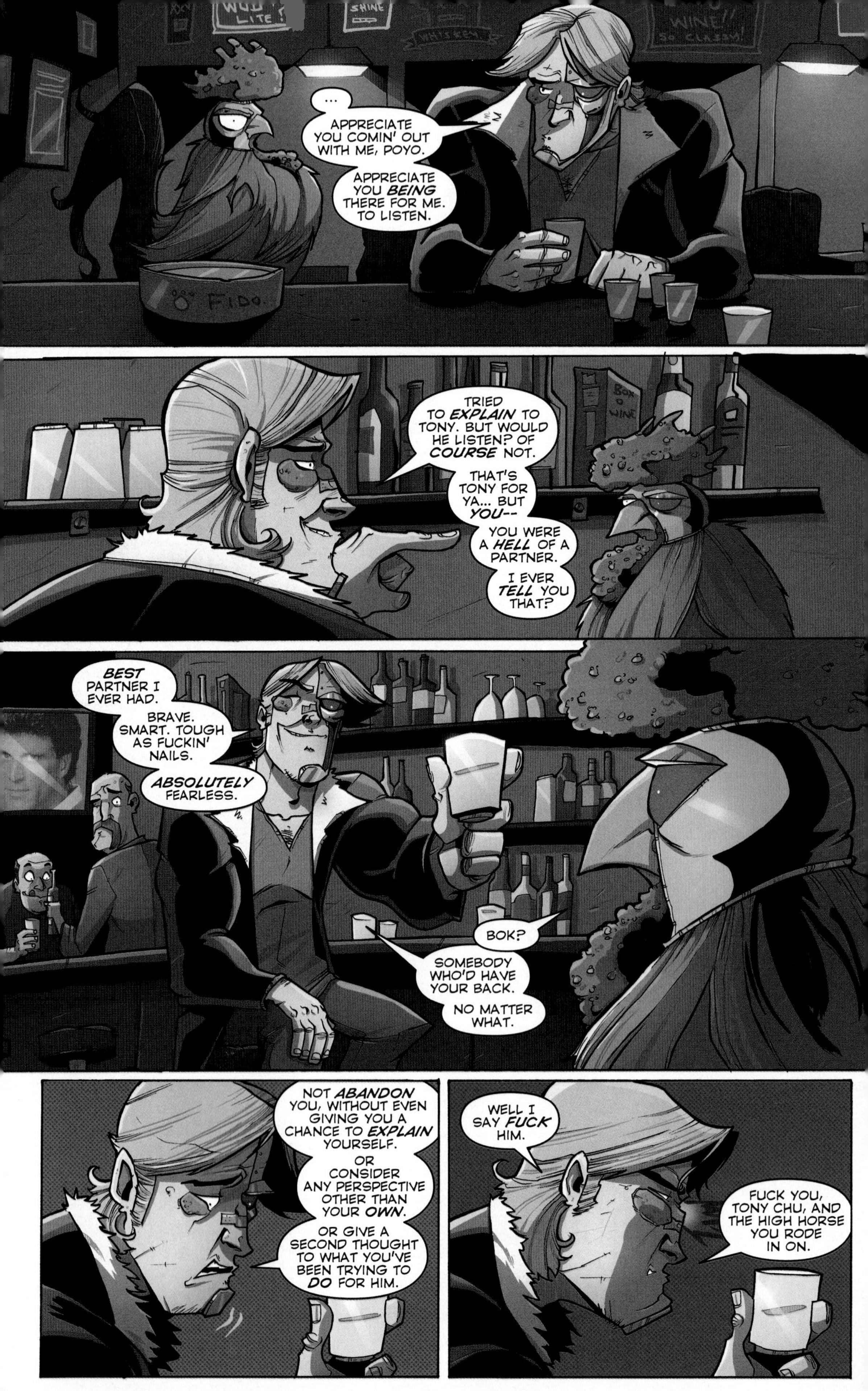
...
APPRECIATE YOU COMIN' OUT WITH ME, POYO.
APPRECIATE YOU *BEING* THERE FOR ME. TO LISTEN.
TRIED TO *EXPLAIN* TO TONY. BUT WOULD HE LISTEN? OF *COURSE* NOT.
THAT'S TONY FOR YA... BUT *YOU*--
YOU WERE A *HELL* OF A PARTNER.
I EVER *TELL* YOU THAT?
BEST PARTNER I EVER HAD.
BRAVE. SMART. TOUGH AS FUCKIN' NAILS.
ABSOLUTELY FEARLESS.
BOK?
SOMEBODY WHO'D HAVE YOUR BACK.
NO MATTER WHAT.
NOT *ABANDON* YOU, WITHOUT EVEN GIVING YOU A CHANCE TO *EXPLAIN* YOURSELF.
OR CONSIDER ANY PERSPECTIVE OTHER THAN YOUR *OWN*.
OR GIVE A SECOND THOUGHT TO WHAT YOU'VE BEEN TRYING TO *DO* FOR HIM.
WELL I SAY *FUCK* HIM.
FUCK YOU, TONY CHU, AND THE HIGH HORSE YOU RODE IN ON.

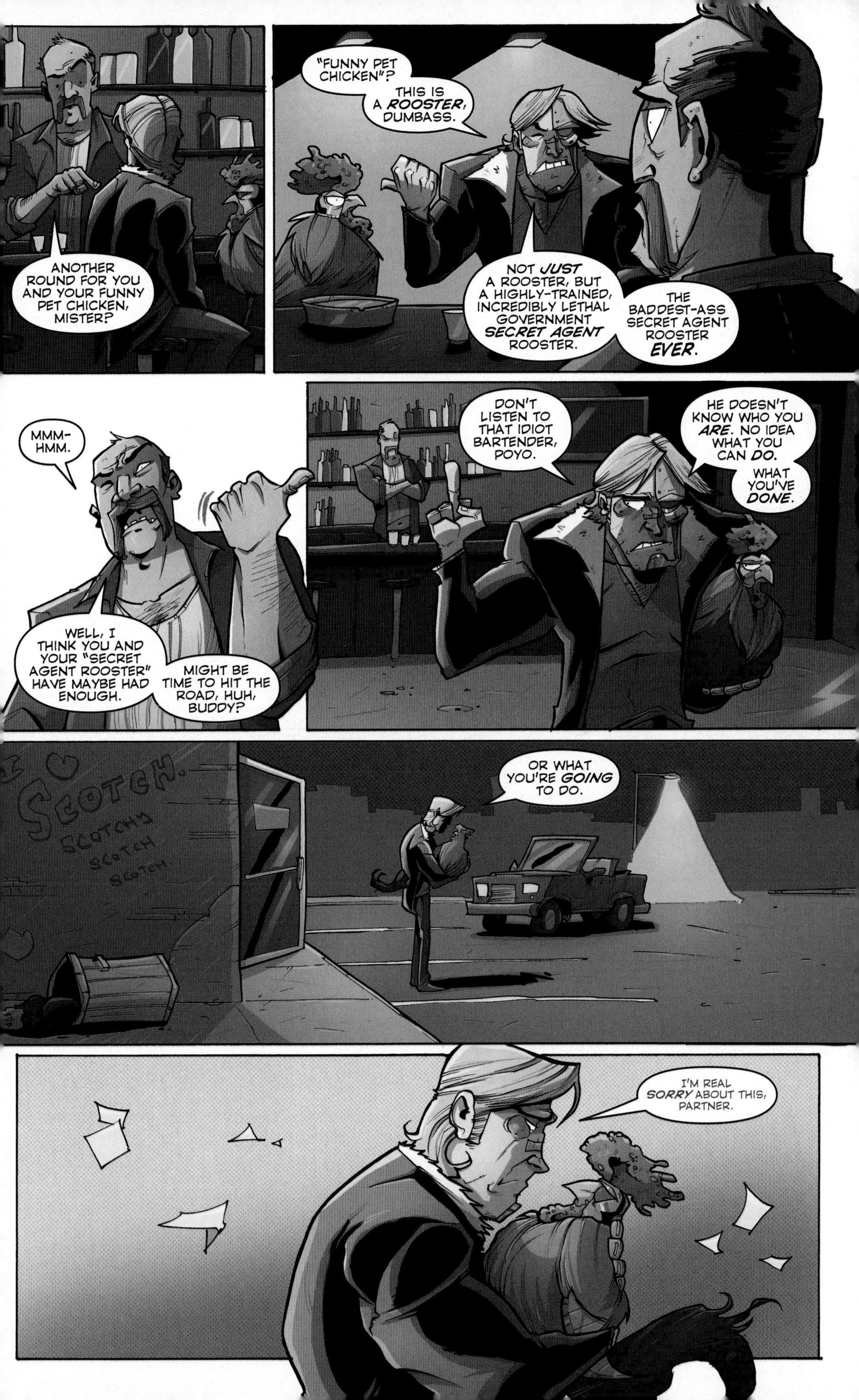
ANOTHER ROUND FOR YOU AND YOUR FUNNY PET CHICKEN, MISTER?
"FUNNY PET CHICKEN"?
THIS IS A ROOSTER, DUMBASS.
NOT JUST A ROOSTER, BUT A HIGHLY-TRAINED, INCREDIBLY LETHAL GOVERNMENT SECRET AGENT ROOSTER.
THE BADDEST-ASS SECRET AGENT ROOSTER EVER.
MMM-HMM.
WELL, I THINK YOU AND YOUR "SECRET AGENT ROOSTER" HAVE MAYBE HAD ENOUGH.
MIGHT BE TIME TO HIT THE ROAD, HUH, BUDDY?
DON'T LISTEN TO THAT IDIOT BARTENDER, POYO.
HE DOESN'T KNOW WHO YOU ARE. NO IDEA WHAT YOU CAN DO.
WHAT YOU'VE DONE.
SCOTCH.
SCOTCH
SCOTCH
SCOTCH.
OR WHAT YOU'RE GOING TO DO.
I'M REAL SORRY ABOUT THIS, PARTNER.

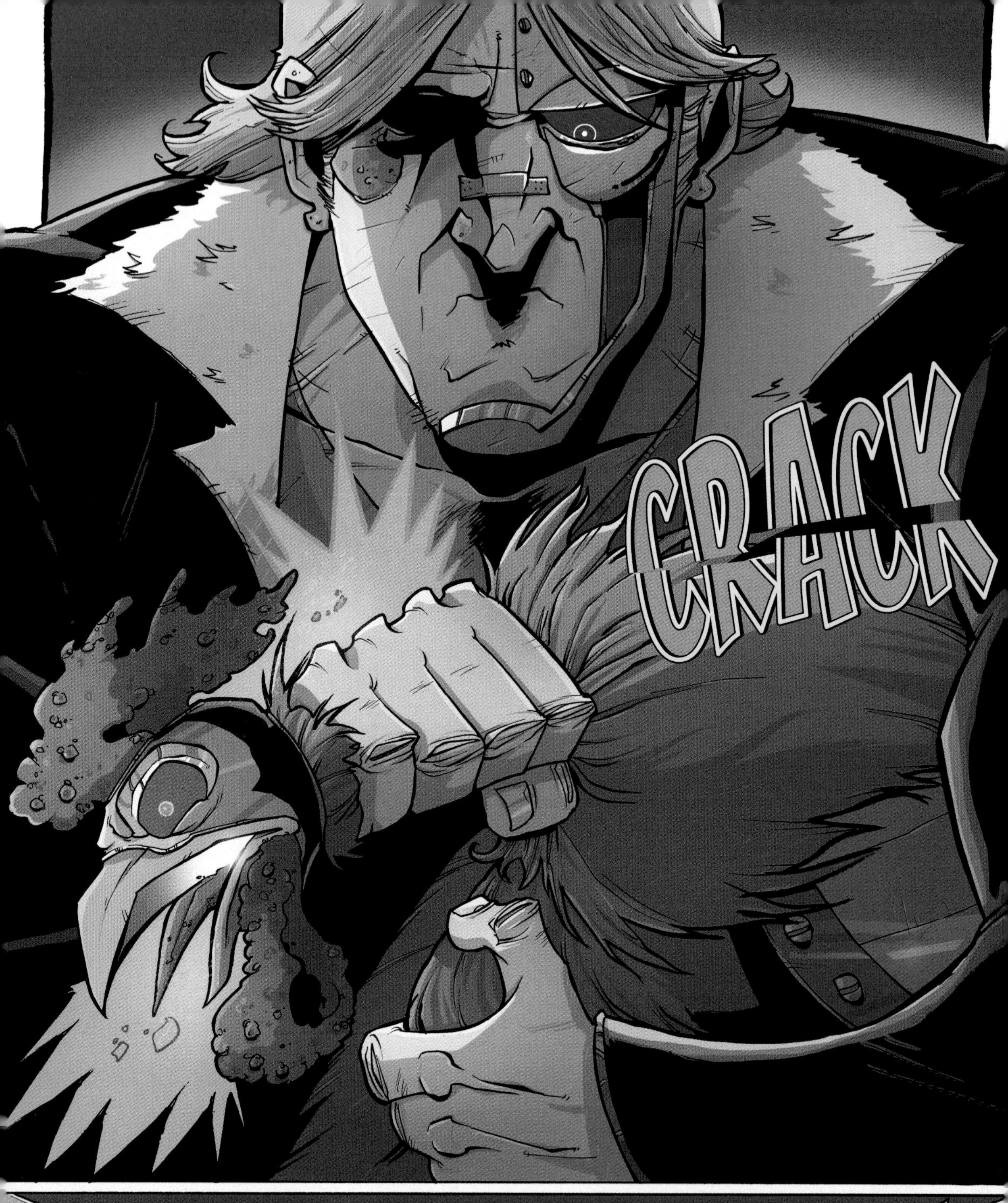
CRACK

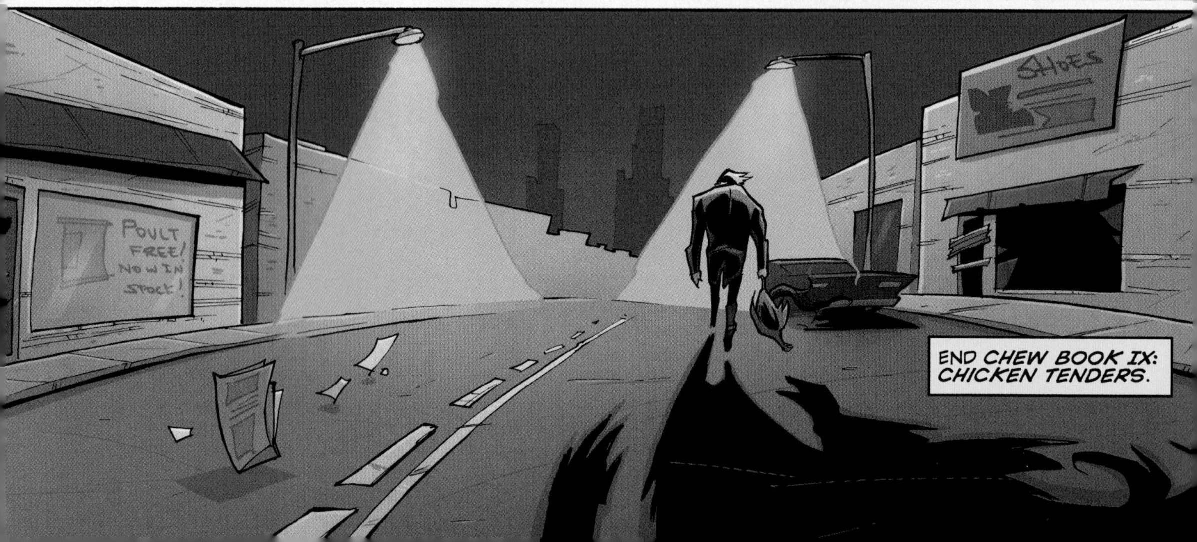
POULT FREE! NOW IN STOCK!
SHOES
END CHEW BOOK IX: CHICKEN TENDERS.

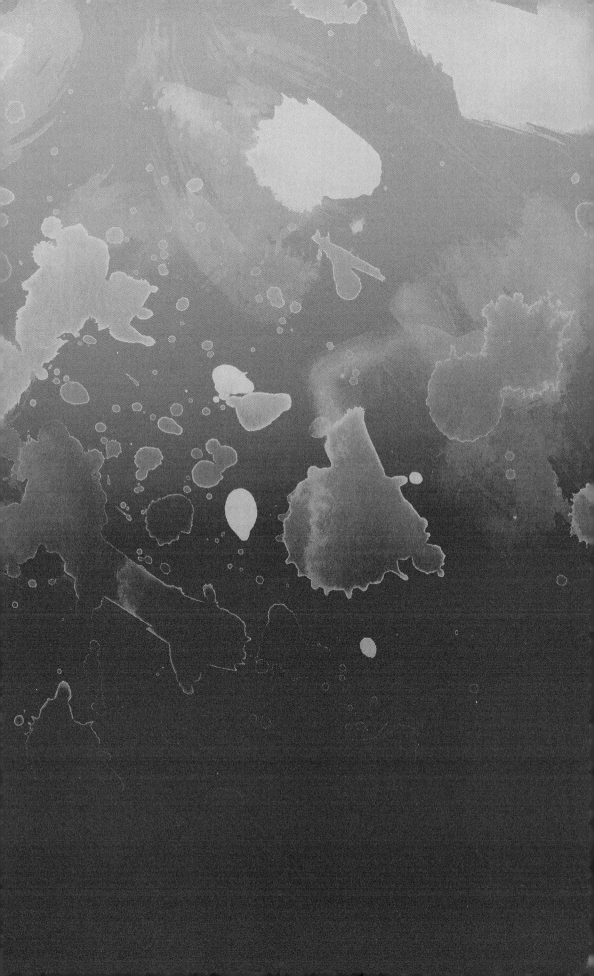

GALLERY

KODY
CHAMBERLAIN
@KodyChamberlain

CHRIS BURNHAM
@TheBurnham
&
DAVID BARON
@myzombies

IRENE STRYCHALSKI
@RenieDraws
reniedraws.tumblr.com

DANIEL WARREN
JOHNSON
@danielwarrenart

RAY FAWKES
@rayfawkes

PAUL HANLEY
paulhanley.deviantart.com

RYAN BROWNE
@RyanBrowneArt

DAN GOLDMAN
@dan_goldman
redlightproperties.com

SINA GRACE
@sinagrace
&
SHAUN STEVEN STRUBLE
@struble

JEREMY BASTIAN
@JeremyBastian

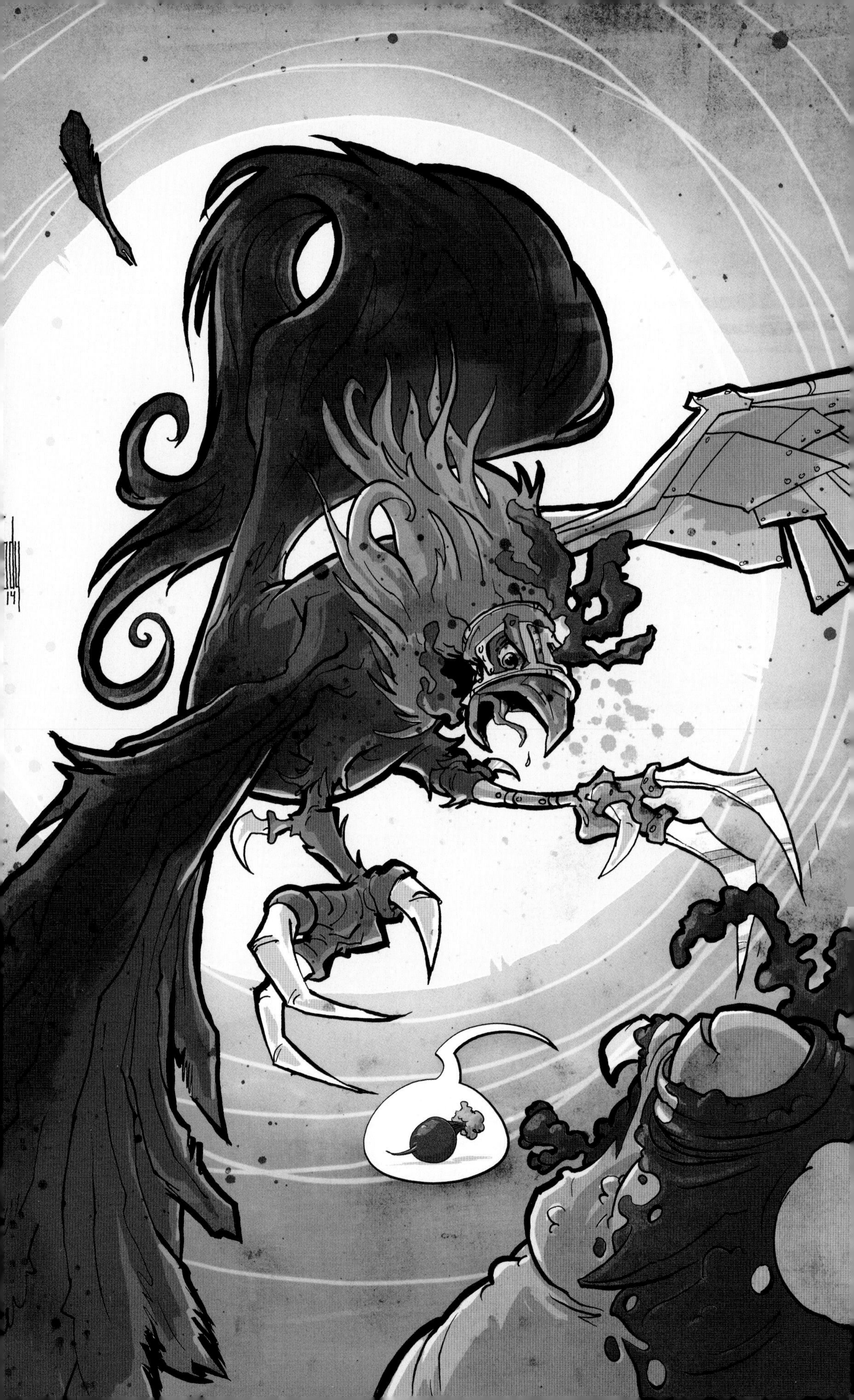

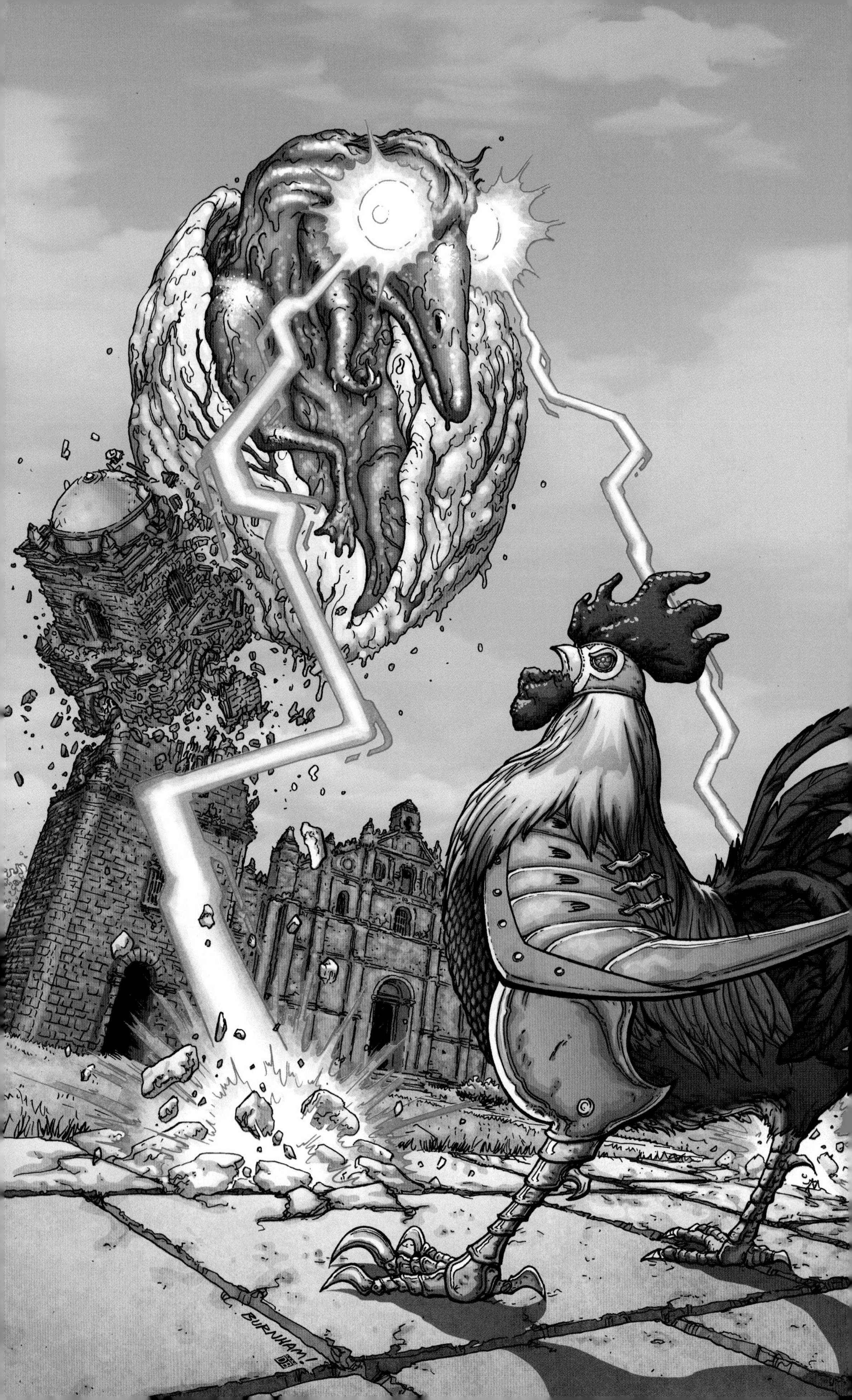
BURNHAM!

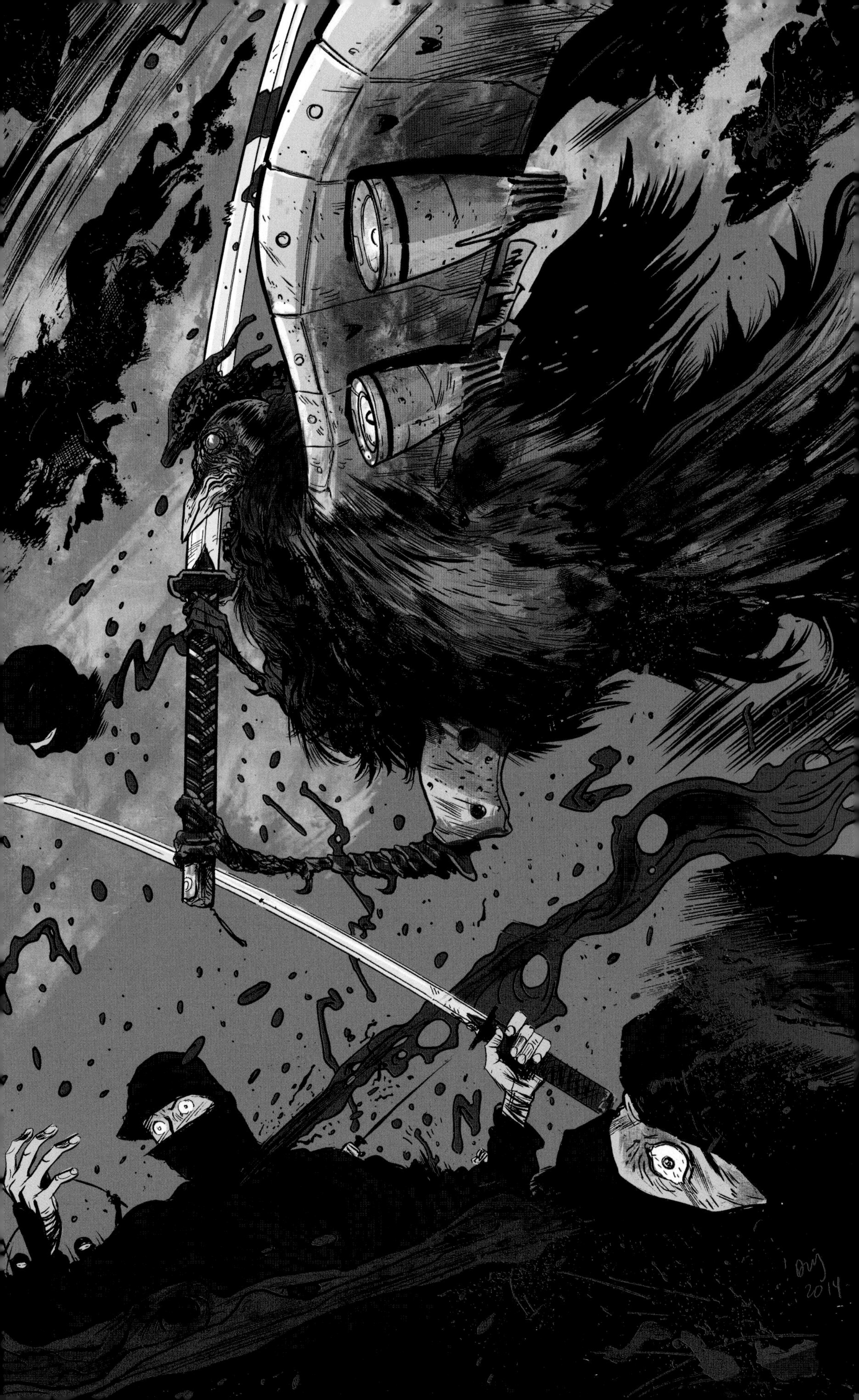

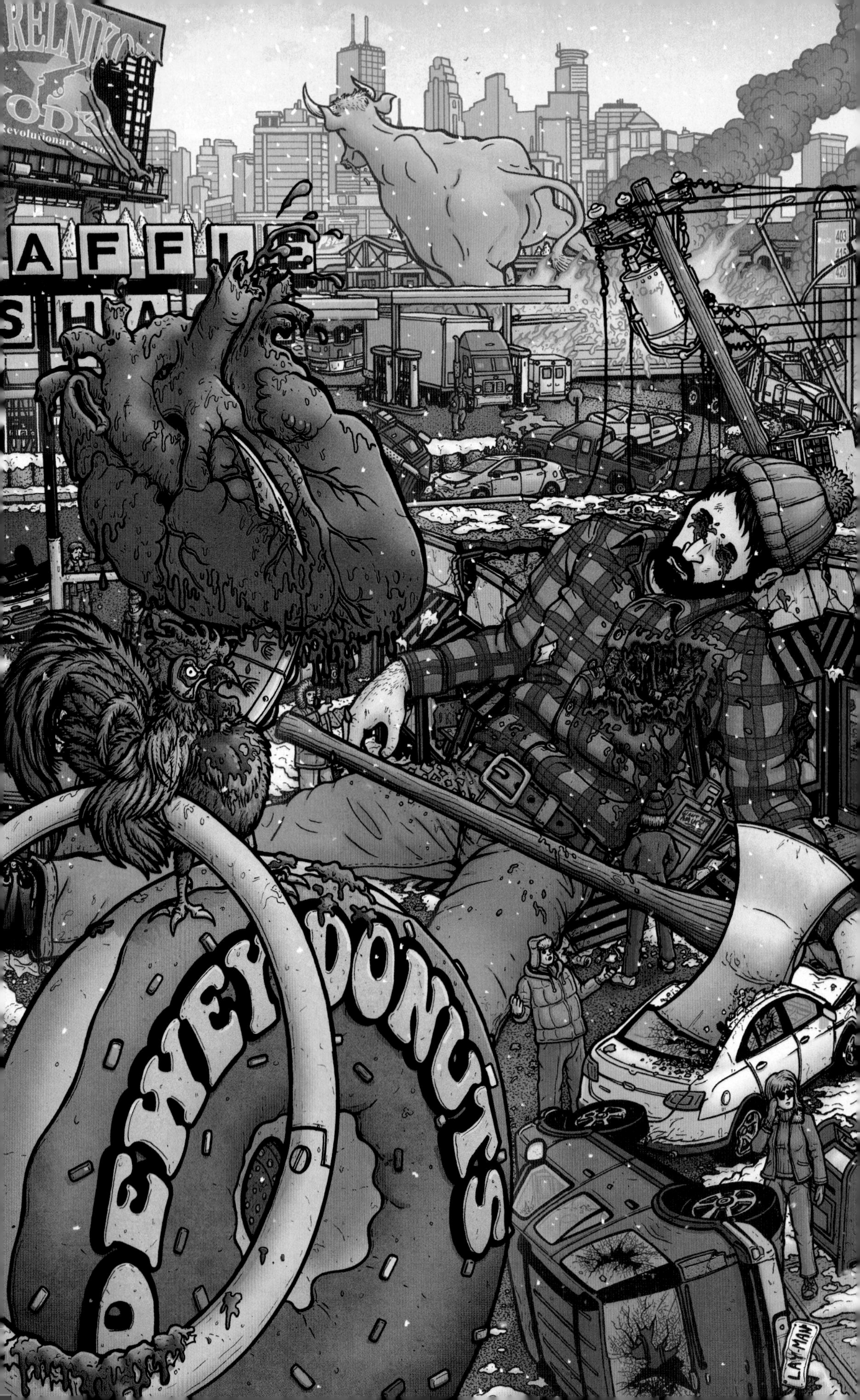

Revolutionary
403
415
420
DONUTS

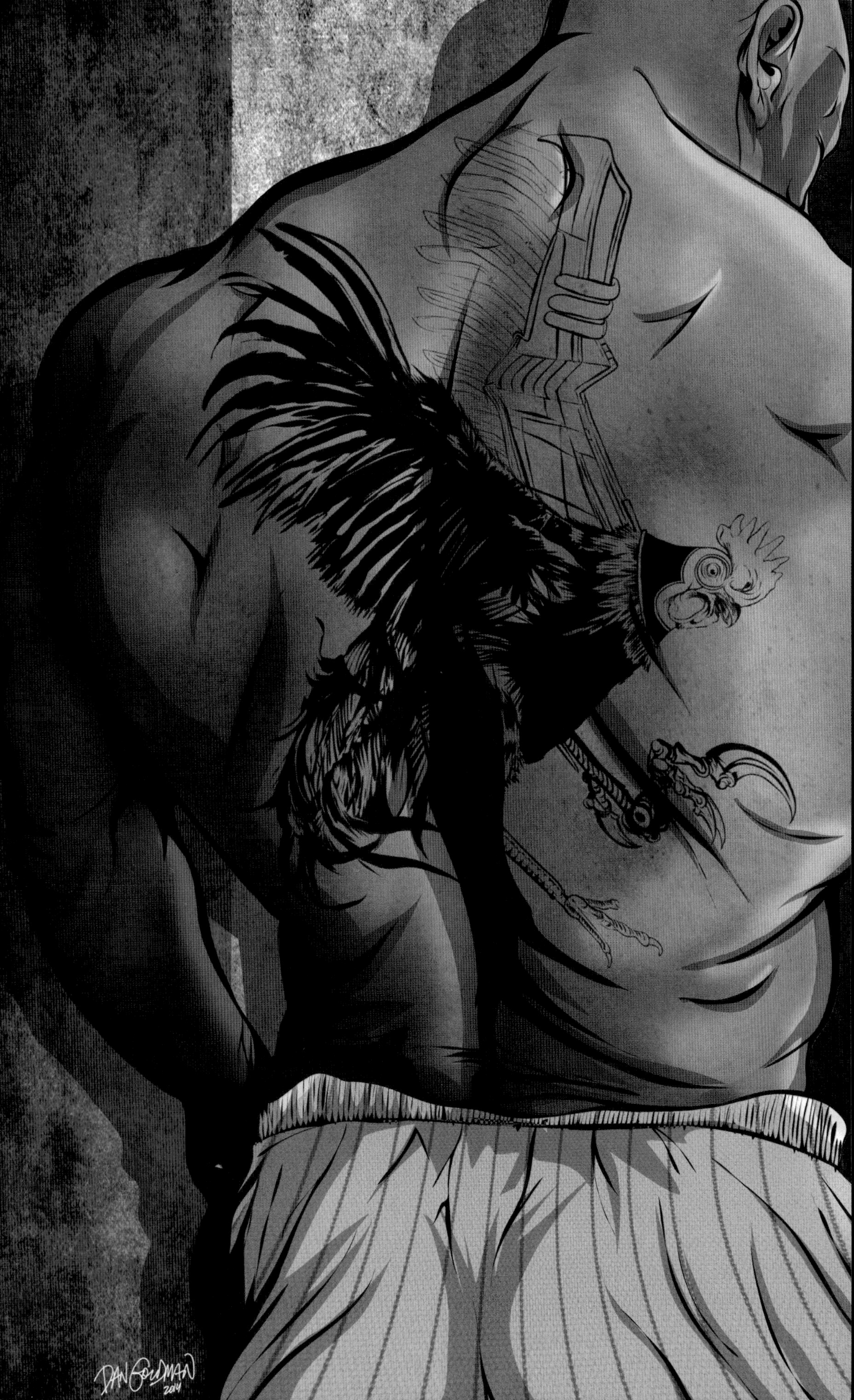
DAN GOLDMAN
2014

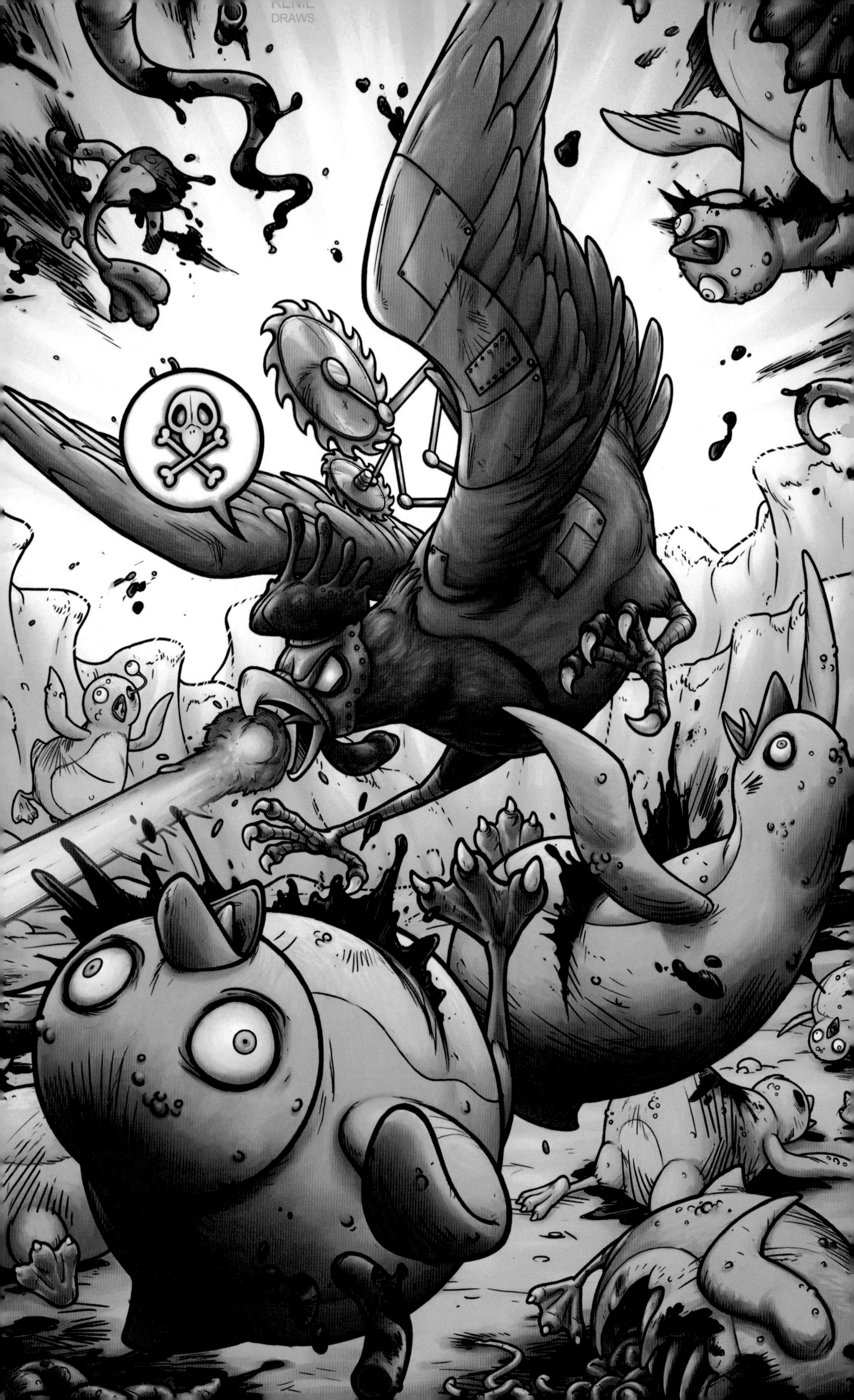
DRAWS

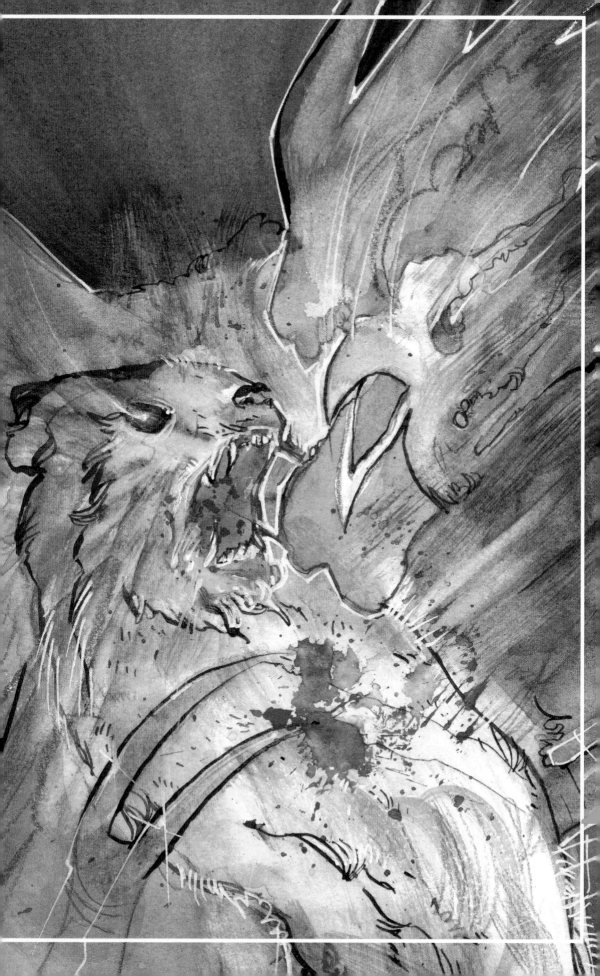

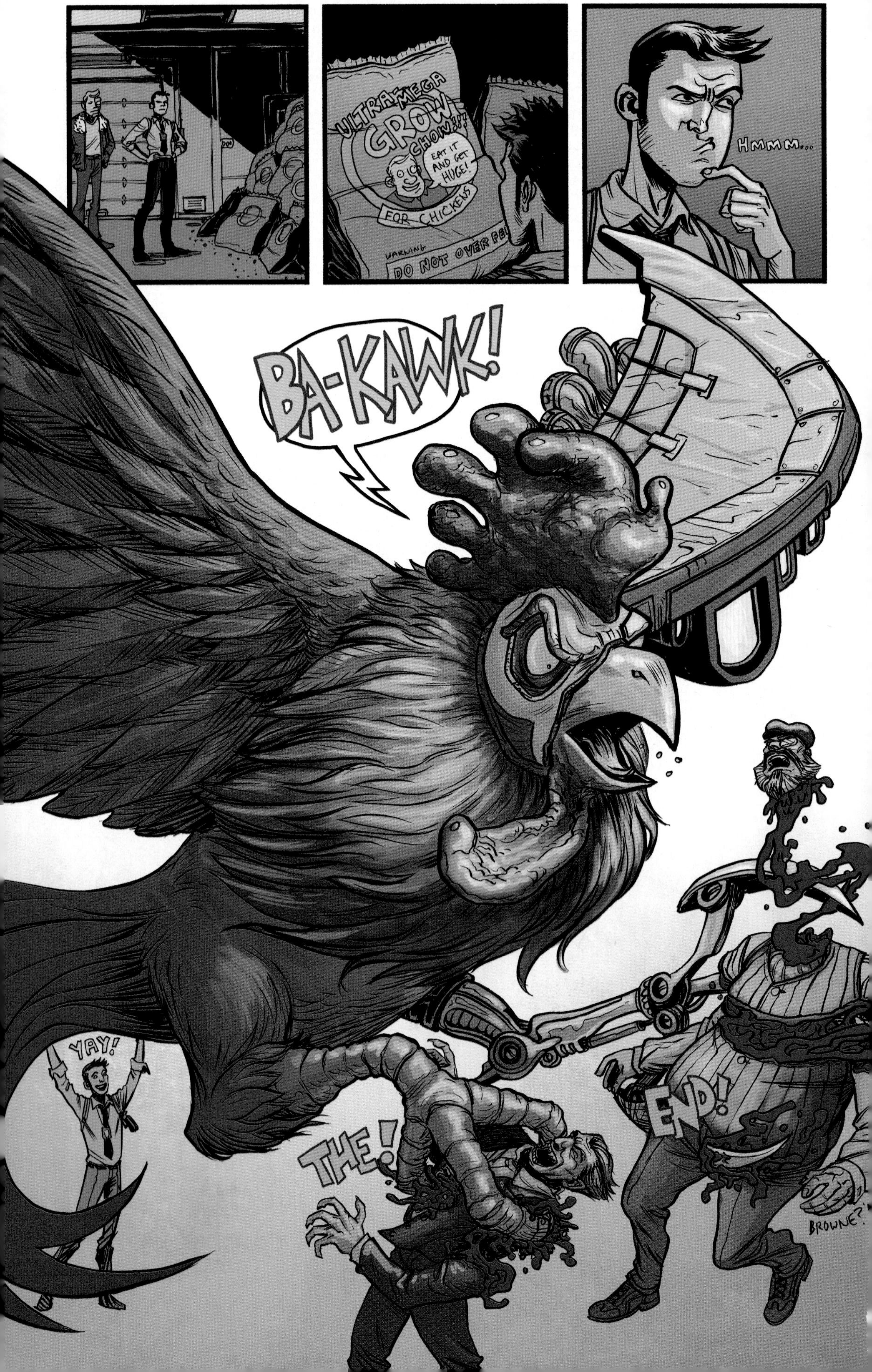
ULTRA MEGA GROW CHOW!!!
EAT IT AND GET HUGE!
FOR CHICKENS
WARNING
DO NOT OVER
HMMM...
BA-KAWK!
YAY!
THE!
END!
BROWNE?

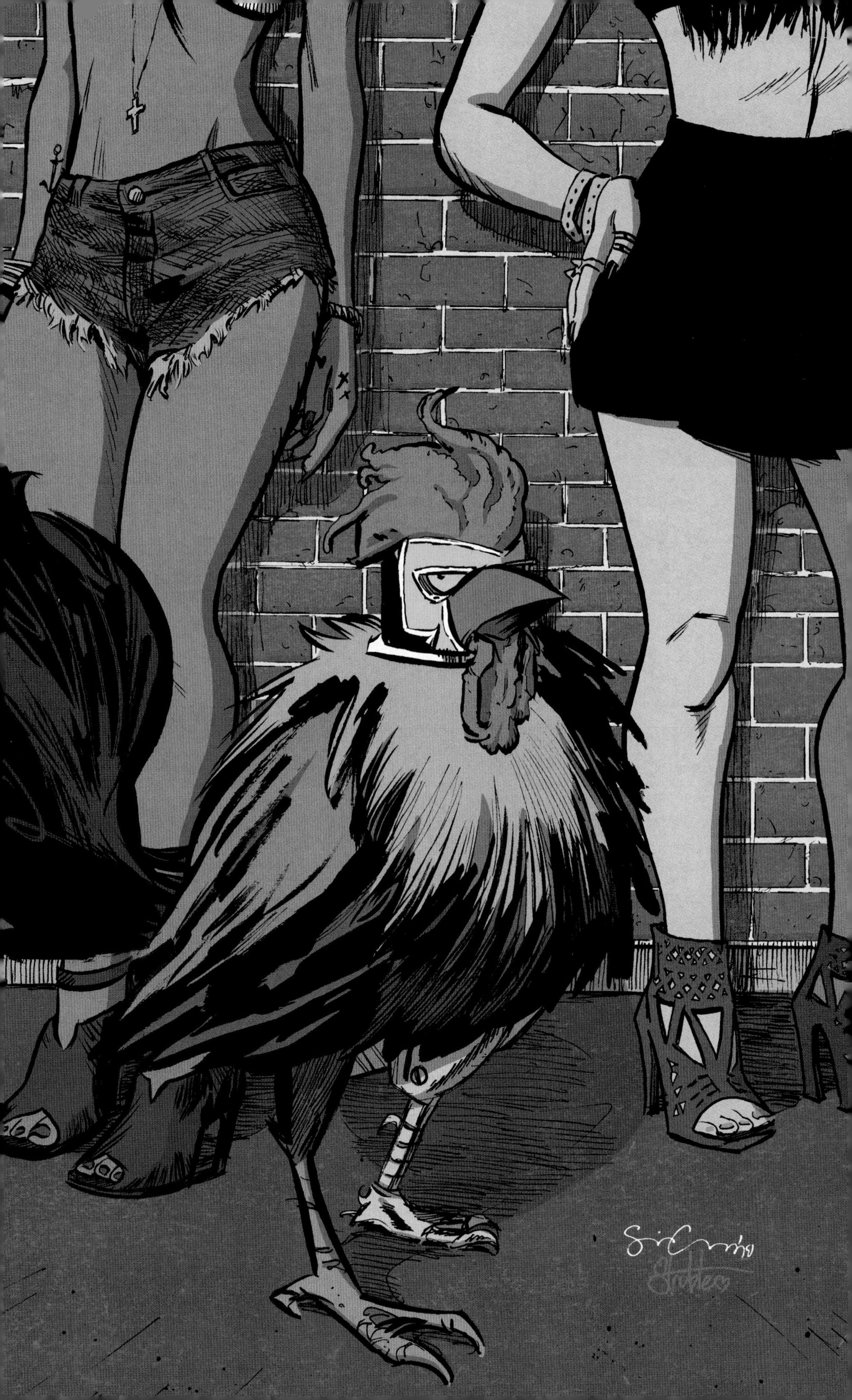

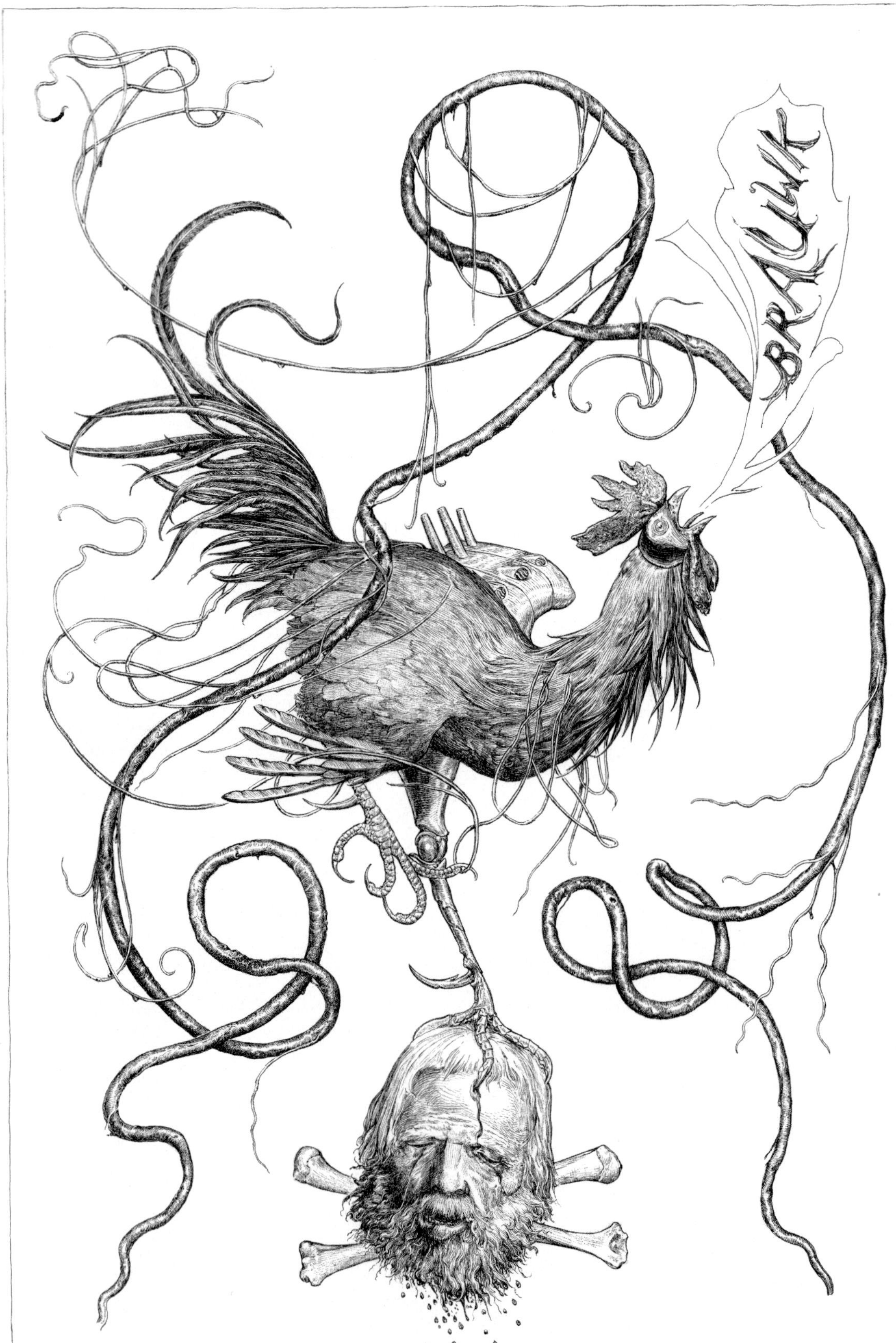
BRAWK
JEREMY A. BASTIAN

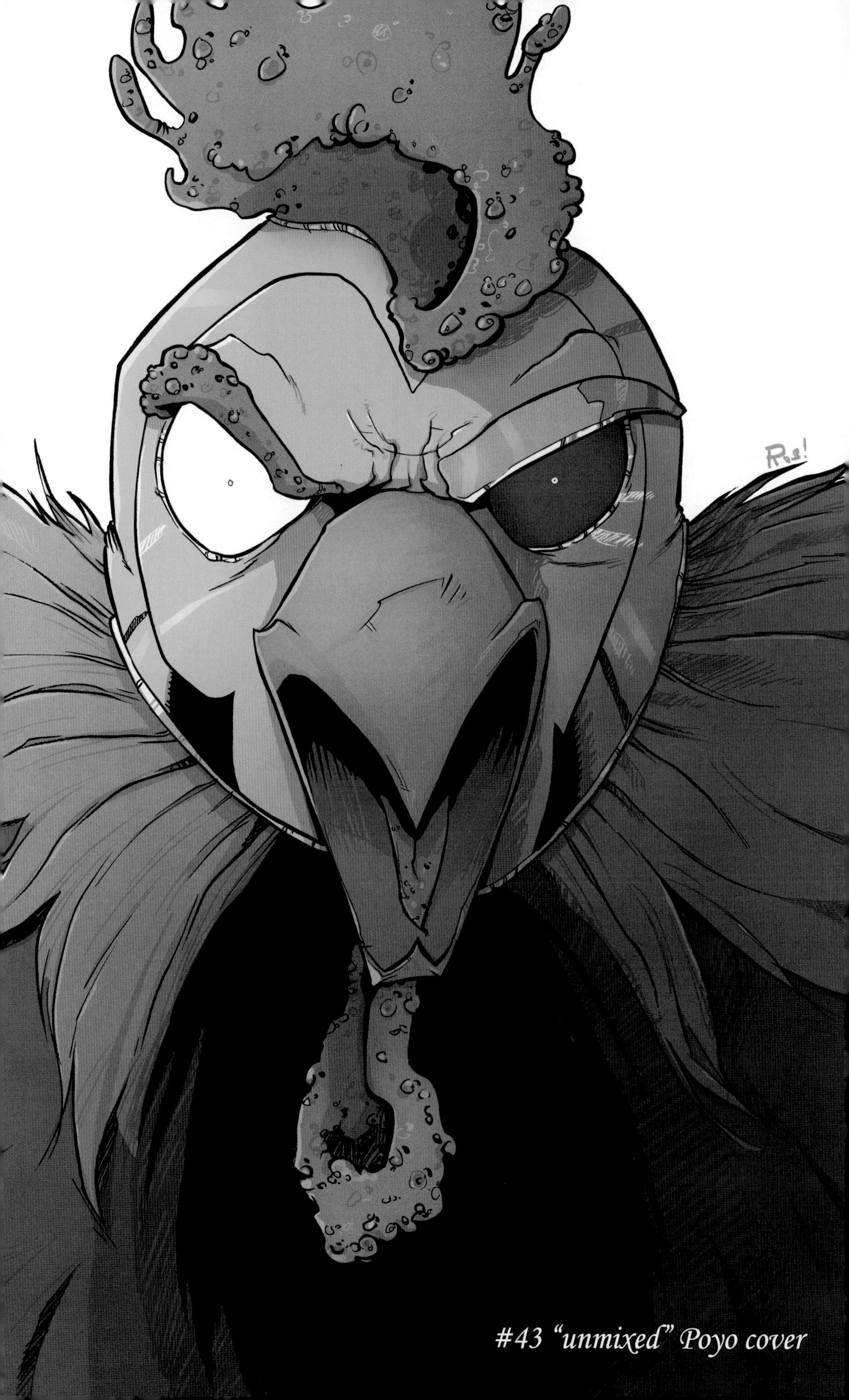

#43 "unmixed" Poyo cover

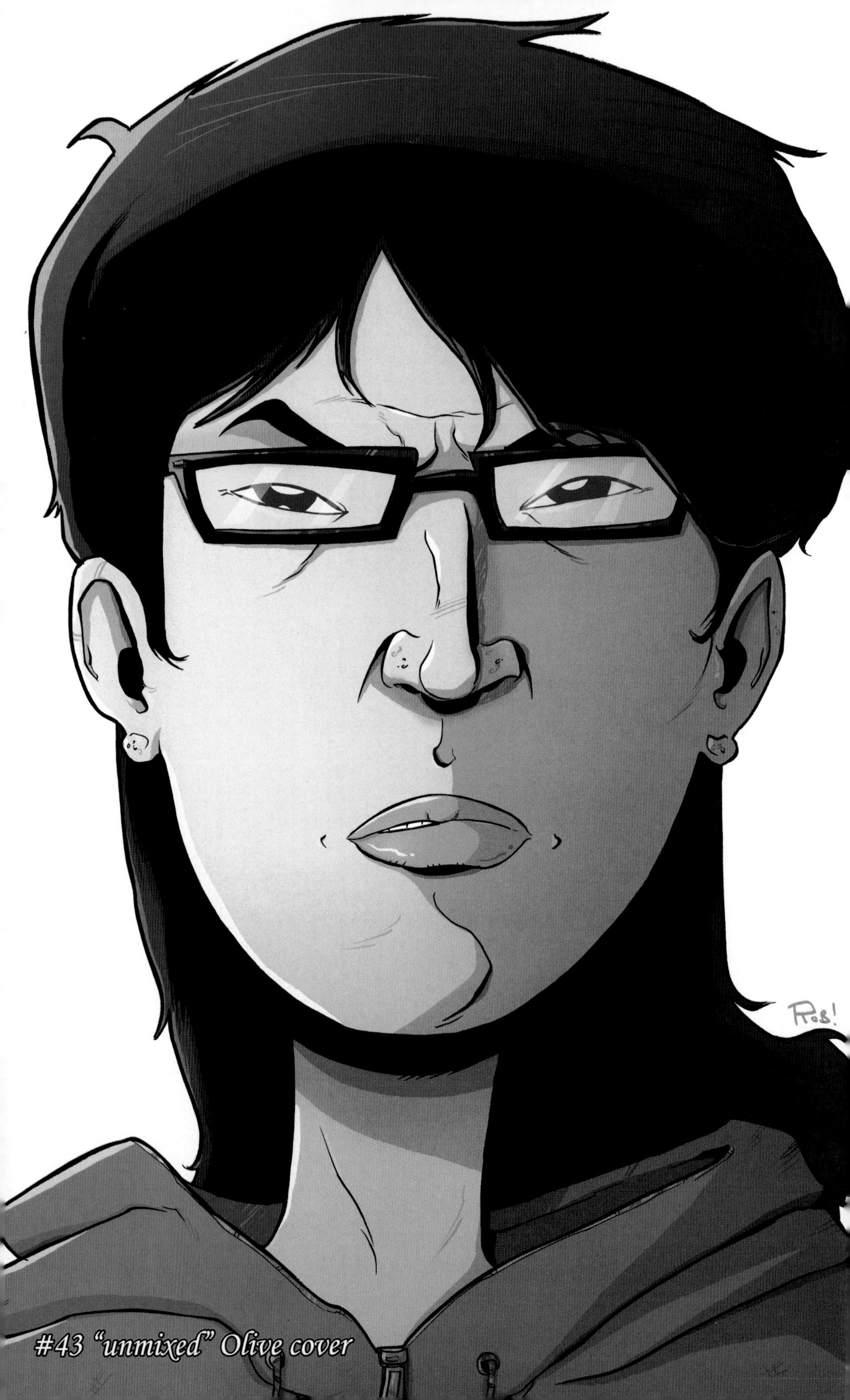
Rob!

#43 “unmixed” Olive cover

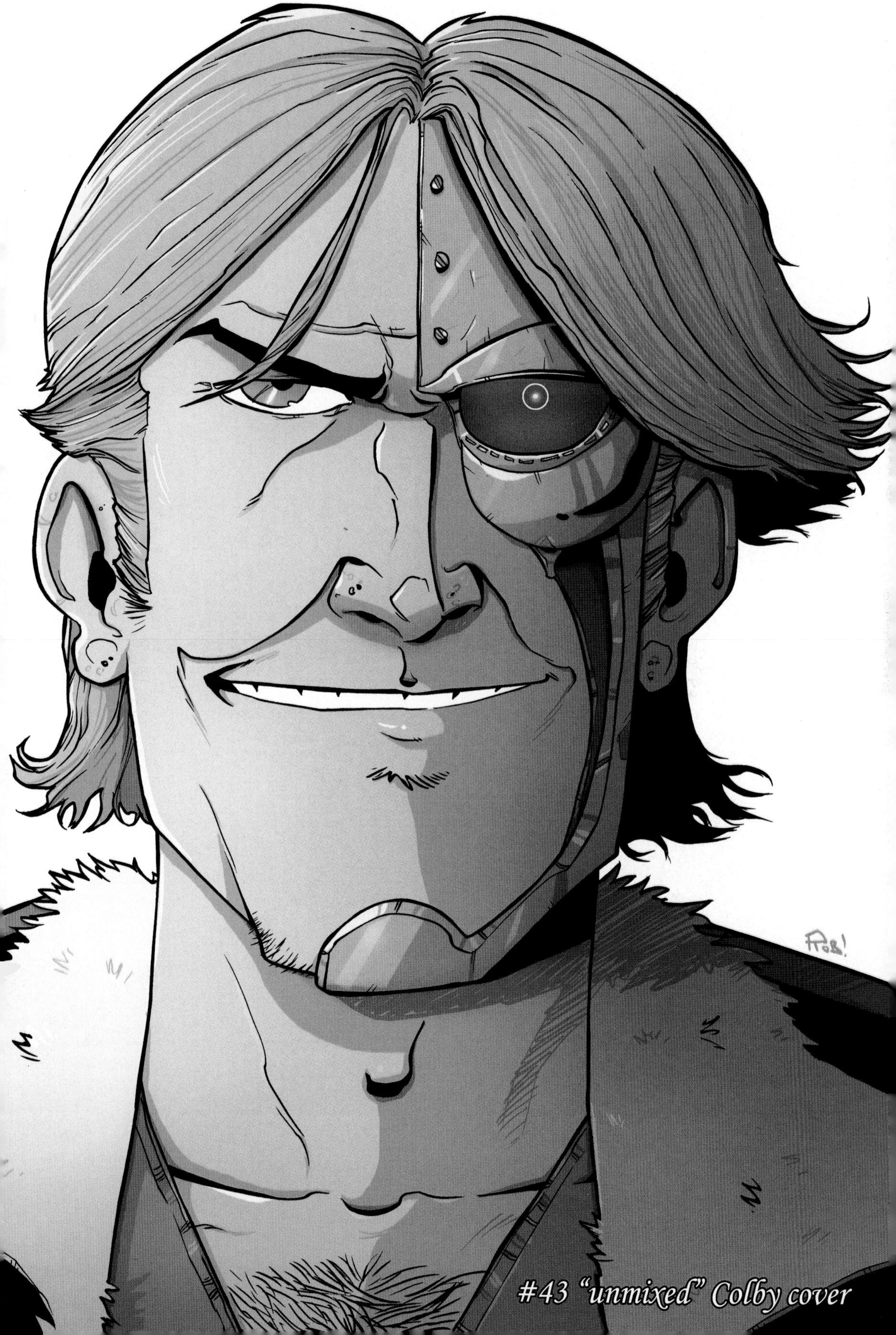

#43 "unmixed" Colby cover

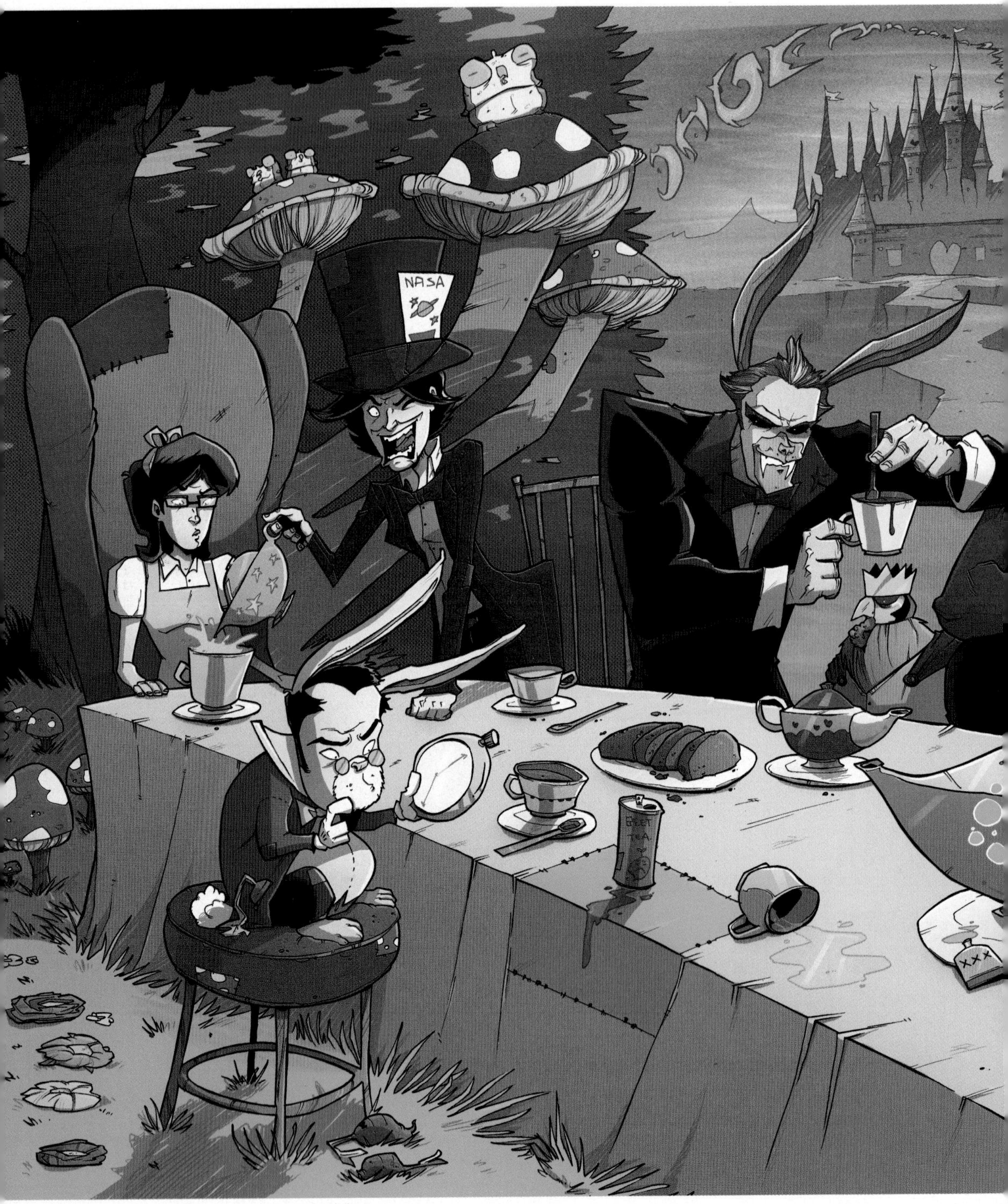
NASA
BEET TEA.
XXX

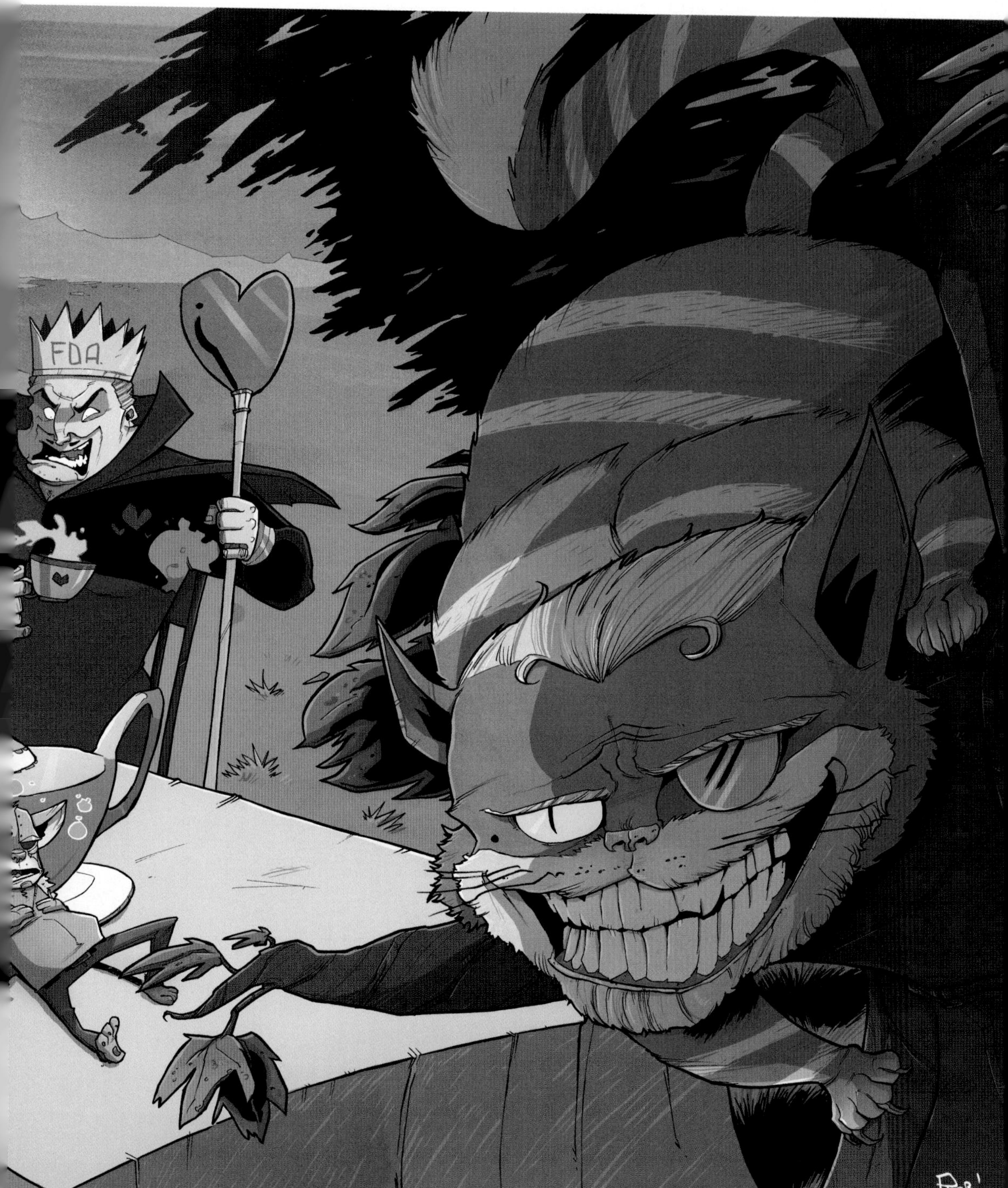
FDA.
ROB!

CHEW Wonderland Commission.